MURDER TRIAL . . .
OR JUST PLAIN MURDER

Rudin continued as if reading from a script. "And has counsel advised you that if you waive your right to a hearing, the State of Texas will transport you to Dallas for trial on murder charges, and that once you waive your right to this hearing there is no avenue available for you to retract this waiver?"

"Yes, sir."

There was a tightness in Sharon's throat. . . . Sharon wondered if . . . God, if . . .

"Given this information, Miss Cowan," the judge said, "is it your desire to waive the hearing . . . ?" Sharon made up her mind. *Okay, you want a circus? We'll give you a three-ringer with a trapeze act.*

Darla opened her mouth to answer.

Sharon squeezed the actress's arm. Darla paused and turned to her. Sharon leaned over and whispered, "Say 'no,' Darla."

Darla's lips parted in shock.

"I'll have to explain later," Sharon said softly. "Repeat after me. 'Your honor, I do not waive this right, and request a hearing of the matter forthwith.' "

Rudin gaped in obvious surprise. "Does the court understand that you're *not* waiving your right to a hearing, Miss Cowan?"

"That's correct, Your Honor."

THE BEST DEFENSE

THE BEST DEFENSE

DEFENSE

Sarah Gregory

A SIGNET BOOK

SIGNET
Published by the Penguin Group
Penguin Putnam Inc., 375 Hudson Street,
New York, New York 10014, U.S.A.
Penguin Books Ltd, 27 Wrights Lane,
London W8 5TZ, England
Penguin Books Australia Ltd, Ringwood,
Victoria, Australia
Penguin Books Canada Ltd, 10 Alcorn Avenue,
Toronto, Ontario, Canada M4V 3B2
Penguin Books (N.Z.) Ltd, 182–190 Wairau Road,
Auckland 10, New Zealand

Penguin Books Ltd, Registered Offices:
Harmondsworth, Middlesex, England

First published by Signet, an imprint of Dutton NAL,
a member of Penguin Putnam Inc.

First Printing, January, 1999
10 9 8 7 6 5 4 3 2 1

For Dominick

The Guy Behind It All

"In the end it was her talent which brought success and all that went with it—the unending scrutiny of the public with which she could never deal, the enormous wealth with which she could buy anything she wanted, and with which she could pay any obligation save for the brutal debt to her fame."

—Public Radio commentary
on the tragic life and death
of Marilyn Monroe

1
***

On the morning that *Minions of Justice: The Streets* climbed to number two in the Neilsens, Sharon Hays called Rob's agent out in L.A. She identified herself. There was a pregnant pause.

Finally he said, "I got no Hays. Look, hon, send me a resumé. Curtis Nussbaum can always use someone willing to exhibit some skin."

Sharon held the receiver away. She looked at the ceiling. She jammed the receiver against her ear and said, "Rob Stanley fathered my daughter, Mr. Nussbaum, when we lived together in New York."

"Hmm. Yeah, okay, you want to shake us down, Curtis Nussbaum's got a shakedown lawyer as well. Let me give you his number."

"Sharon Hays, sir. H-A-Y-S. I met you last in a TV studio in Dallas when Rob was touring."

There were five seconds of silence, during which the sound of rattling paper came over the line. Then the agent said, "Sure. Sure, the girl in Texas. How's the little princess?" He inhaled and then blew out, likely puffing on a cigar.

"Going on fourteen," Sharon said. "She's now a *big* princess."

"Old Rob-oh's setting the woods on fire, isn't he? You catch Tuesday's episode? Poignant."

"He's not setting the postal service on fire, sending his child support." In the corner of Sharon's office, her boxed impatiens drooped. Later today she'd set them out on the sidewalk so that the flowers could catch some sun.

"Damn. You didn't get your check this month?"

"Or last month, or the month before. Look, I—"

"My secretary must be dropping the ball," Nussbaum said.

"—didn't want anything from Rob to begin with. Melanie and I did just fine for nearly twelve years on our own. Sending the support was your idea, when he started to make a name for himself. Improve his public image."

"I'll have to jump her about it."

Sharon snapped a pencil in two. "Yes, maybe you should . . . *have a word* with her. I wouldn't be calling now, but we just made a trip to the orthodontist. You have any idea what braces cost?"

There was more rustling on the line. "Dallas, didn't I just . . . ? Hey, that's where Planet Hollywood's having a grand opening this week, isn't it?"

"In the West End," Sharon said. "The entire treatment is almost five—"

"Bet you and the little princess—"

"—thousand dollars."

"—would like a couple of ringsides. That'll be the ticket of the week in your town."

"I beg your pardon?"

"Schwarzenegger . . . Willis . . . Chuck Norris . . . see all those people up close. Be something for the child to remember."

"I thought I'd hold off beginning the treatments until this summer. That way she could get used to the shock of wearing them by the time school starts next—"

"Willis's agent owes Nussbaum, you know? Probably I could swing four seats. She could take a friend. You got a significant other, you could—"

"I don't think we're on the same wavelength," Sharon said. "Besides, my boss is on a trip. That restaurant opening is in the middle of the afternoon. I might have court appearances, anything."

"This is a once in a lifetime, hon. I'll take care of it."

"Look, if you'll just tell me Rob doesn't want to pay me any more, we'll get by. But expecting it and not getting it . . ."

"I'll put in a call right now."

"The only call I want you to put in is to Rob, to see about my money."

"Get you right up next to the floor, where they'll all be walking through. Willis might be bringing Demi."

Sharon shifted the phone from one ear to the other. "Dammit, I need my money."

"I'll jump my secretary about it. You guys have a nice time. Hey, and let us hear how you're getting along."

The tickets arrived via Federal Express on a Friday in October, the morning of the grand opening for Dallas's Planet Hollywood. Sharon slit the envelope and stared at its contents. Four lonely pieces of pasteboard. She shook the empty package, upside down. No check. She called Sheila Winston.

"We may as well go," Sheila said. "Trish and Melanie would get a kick out of it. Plus it will get me out of something."

"God, Melanie's mouth," Sharon said.

"There's nothing wrong with her mouth, Sharon. She doesn't have perfect white pearlies, but neither do ninety percent of the rest of the population."

"It's not even a day's pay for him." Sharon thumbed through her calendar. Only one hearing, at eleven o'clock in the 375th, to plead out a burglar named Tired Darnell. A court appointment—the county would get around to paying her fee sometime after Christmas. Tired Darnell would be tired. He always was. She said halfheartedly, "We'd have to take the kids out of school."

"I can handle that," Sheila said. "I'll stop by and get them as soon as I take care of two patients this morning. I'd do about anything to get out of this panel I'm supposed to be on."

"What panel is that?"

"I put my foot in my mouth by accepting to begin with. A Black Coalition meeting, on being black and professional in America. Would be okay, except that the other two people on the panel are Muslims. I'd rather just be professional, thanks."

"They consider you an inspiration," Sharon said. "How many other psychiatrists . . . ?"

"Then why don't you join a discussion panel on being *white* and professional if you think it's so neat? You and a couple of Ku Klux Klan lawyers."

Sharon sighed. Her barriers dissolving . . . "There won't be anybody to stay in the office," Sharon said.

"Oh? Where's Herr Guru Russell Black, king of the trial lawyers?"

"Took his daughter to Europe. First vacation he's had in fifteen years or so, I can't begrudge him." Sharon picked up the tickets and shuffled them top to bottom, one at a time.

"Planet Hollywood, Sharon. Arnold the Gorgeous might notice us."

"He's got a wife."

"So we'll dream."

Sharon leaned back in her swivel chair and watched the transom over her door. "What time can you meet me with the kids?"

"I'll have to run them by the house to change. Say, three o'clock?"

"That'll do," Sharon said. "I don't think the stars arrive until four. I've got a hearing that should be over by noon. Guess I can set the answering machine and let the office take care of itself."

"You'll be glad you did," Sheila said.

"I hope you're right," Sharon said.

Tired Darnell said, "Guilty, sir." He sounded like Froggy the Gremlin. He wore a jumpsuit with COUNTY JAIL stenciled across the back in large black letters. His shoulders slumped. His stomach pooched out. Tired's given name was Francis. The nickname came from a botched warehouse burglary, wherein a seventy-year-old night watchman had caught and tackled him a half block from the scene.

Judge Arnold Shiver had sparse snow white hair, a scowl like the Terrible Oz, and had been on the bench, Sharon believed, since before the time of Christ. He said, "Son, are you pleadin' guilty because you *are* guilty, and for no other reason?"

Tired swiveled his head to look at Sharon. She gave him a nod. Actually, Tired had agreed to cop out because of the three-year plea-bargain deal which at the moment rested in Sharon's shoulder bag. The prosecutor—Harold Benning by name, who was second banana to the main ADA in Shiver's courtroom—peered around the defendant and looked at Sharon as well. This was Tired Darnell's third felony and, counting misdemeanors, his fifth guilty plea, so he didn't need for Sharon to tell him that Shiver's question was strictly for the record. "Yes, sir," Tired said.

"All right, then, son, I'm sentencin' you to . . ." Shiver rattled pages in his file and peered at his copy of the plea-bargain agreement. "I'm sentencin' you to . . ." He scowled at Benning. "Mr. Benning, is the district attorney agreein' to this?"

Benning looked uncertain. Sharon's deal was with Benning's boss, who today had fallen victim to an overheated radiator, and Benning was doing stand-in duty.

Sharon chipped in, "I have the signed plea bargain with me, Your Honor, if you'd like to see it." She wore a navy blue business dress with a waist-length jacket. Her dark hair was short, fluffed into bangs in front. "Mr. Tadley, Mr. Benning's superior, signed on behalf of the state. My client has executed the agreement as well."

This brought a snicker from the judge, who turned his scowl on the defendant. "I'll just bet ol' Tired agreed to it. Didn't you?"

Tired appeared exhausted but nervous. "Sure did, Judge."

"Since this is your third or fourth time in fronta

me, I ain't surprised. You ain't no dummy, Tired. You'd be a fool *not* to take this deal." Shiver dropped the plea bargain into his file and closed the folder. "This defendant needs a little more time to think on his sins. I'm givin' him *five* years."

Well, here we go, Sharon thought. Of all the judges in the county, only Arnold Shiver questioned plea bargains between the defense and prosecution. The practice kept his calendar clogged like a backed-up sewer, but Shiver generally ran unopposed in elections and didn't seem to give a damn. Sharon took a half step forward. "If the court please, let the record reflect that as a matter of law, my client is entitled to withdraw his guilty plea if he receives anything other than the bargained-for sentence."

"I been doin' this a few years, young lady," Shiver said, "an' I'm pretty familiar with the law. An' I'm sentencin' this man to five years' confinement in the Texas Department o' Justice."

Oh, up yours, Sharon thought. She stood up straight. "Then, Your Honor, my client hereby withdraws his guilty plea."

Tired looked confused, as did ADA Harold Benning.

Shiver pointed a finger. "Oh, no, he don't. He's done pled guilty. Five years. Take him away, bailiff." The uniformed deputy got up from his seat in the jury box and came around the railing.

Sharon couldn't believe her ears. An appellate court would overturn this nonsense in a heartbeat, and Shiver knew it. Sharon said, "In that case, Your Honor, we're giving verbal notice of appeal."

"You do that, Miss Hays," Shiver said pugnaciously.

"I will, Your Honor," Sharon said sweetly.

"I sure am tired," Tired Darnell said exhaustedly. "Listen, Judge, you mind if I sit down?"

As the end result of her day in court, Sharon sat at a table in Planet Hollywood at four in the afternoon with her nose in a book. She felt like the original party poop, all but ignoring Sheila and the girls as she took notes on a legal pad. She wore reading glasses with tiny lenses. The book was a red-jacketed paperback edition of *Vernon's Annotated Texas Code of Criminal Procedure*. Hardhead Shiver was the first judge in her eight years as a lawyer who'd violated a plea-bargain agreement she'd entered into, and Sharon had to bone up on the procedure for getting Tired's sentence overturned. She had to move quickly; if she didn't have her papers ready for filing at the Court of Appeals by Monday morning, Shiver would have Tired transferred to the penitentiary on the first thing smokin'.

Throughout Planet Hollywood, the good-time crowd—guys in slacks and sports shirts, women in everything from stylish jean outfits to skimpy bits of nothing—stamped their feet, whistled, and called for the matinee idols to appear. Wooden grandstands were set up outside to handle the overflow, and so crowded was the restaurant that any kind of service was out of the question. Just inside the entry were long tables lined with hors d'oeuvres, and Melanie and Trish had loaded down a couple of plates with fried mushrooms and chicken wings. At the far end of the room was a temporary stage, and on the stage a combo was playing. Ten feet away on Sharon's left sat the motorcycle from *The Terminator*. She pictured Judge Arnold Shiver, complete with black leather outfit and black sunglasses, astride the damned cycle and curled her lip.

Sheila tugged on Sharon's arm. "They say Bruce is coming in first. Be still my heart." Sheila wore a pair of hugging black pants along with a pink bolero shirt with puffed sleeves.

"Mmmm," Sharon said. "Thought you didn't believe in crossing the color barrier."

"Bruce hasn't asked me yet." Sheila was nonstop movement, crossing and uncrossing her legs, twisting around in her seat, pretty dark eyes dancing as she looked around. Sharon lowered her head, and made a note that Judge Shiver had failed to warn Tired

Darnell in advance that the court might not accept the
plea bargain. A bona fide point on appeal.

Melanie said, "Bruce Willis is coming, Mom? Bruce
Willis?" She and Trish Winston bubbled and giggled
and craned their necks toward the entry. Both were
mature-looking thirteen-year-olds. Trish had inherited
Sheila's button nose and smooth chocolate-colored
complexion. Melanie's thoughtful expressions and high
IQ came from Rob's side of the family—*damn* him,
Sharon thought—but she also came equipped with
Sharon's long and elegant dancer's legs. Sheila had let
the girls get away with wearing outfits which were a
bit racy for Sharon's tastes—Melanie wore snug jeans
and a loose blue sweater, while Trish had on a pantsuit
which Sharon suspected was her mom's—but then
again it's Planet Hollywood, Sharon thought, so what
the hell. Still, she kept a sharp eye on the girls and
an even sharper eye on the older men at nearby tables.
Sheila did the same.

"Bruce *Willis*, Mom?" Melanie said again.

"So they tell me," Sharon said, and went back to
her note taking.

As if on Melanie's cue, a woman near the entry
shouted, "It's *them*." A male p.a. announcer boomed
out, "Bruce Willis, ladies and gentlemen, accompanied
by his wife, the lovely . . . *Dem*-mi . . . *Moore*." The
place was suddenly a madhouse, a din of applause
accompanied by shrill whistles. The restaurant people
had cleared out the center of the room, forming an
aisle, and into the throng paraded the star-studded
couple themselves. Trish and Melanie jumped up,
blocking Sharon's view, and Sheila leaped to her feet
as well. Sharon stood and rose on the balls of her feet.

Oh, to be a star, Sharon thought. All during her
stint as a starving off-Broadway actress, in fact, Sharon
had had just such a fantasy; she'd laid awake nights
picturing herself showing up at the Oscars or some
such thing, alighting from a limo, smiling into a spotlight while adoring fans screamed her name. The only
person screaming her name in those days had been

the landlord when the rent came due, but the fantasy had kept her going. Demi Moore had the moves down to a T; she was one of the hottest stars going at the moment and looked the part. Into Planet Hollywood she strolled, the world her oyster, chic in denim pants and vest straight from Rodeo Drive. She smiled in acknowledgment left and right as the applause reached a crescendo, then moved in confident modeling-runway strides toward the stage. Sharon clapped until her palms stung.

On the heels of the Demi show, Bruce Willis's appearance was a bit of a letdown. Not that his parade down the walkway wasn't grand. Willis was casual Bruce, the guy straight from *Die Hard.* He wore jeans and cycler boots, a white tee and vest, and dark sunglasses, but there was a slouch to his bearing, and Sharon thought he looked sort of bored. Bored and . . . Sharon had a sudden flashback to Tired Darnell at his sentencing as Willis slumped onto the stage near the microphone. Willis said something, but the crowd noise drowned him out and the acoustics were terrible, and Sharon couldn't understand a word. Whatever he'd said must have been pretty good, because the customers stomped their feet and clapped even louder than before. Willis and Moore took a little bow, then retired to a stage-side table which was roped off from the rest of the audience. The throng barely had time to catch its breath before the p.a. announcer came on once more and Schwarzenegger himself appeared.

This is too, too much, Sharon thought. She decided to let Sheila and the girls enjoy old Arnold on their own, sank back into her chair, picked up her pen, and put on her reading glasses. Tired Darnell, you're ruining my day, she thought. She noted a Texas Court of Appeals case wherein a man's guilty plea had stood up because his time in the pen hadn't been specified in his bargaining agreement, which didn't apply to Tired Darnell. She lost her train of thought as Schwarzenegger's thick Austrian accent boomed over the mike, inviting everyone to try the steamed clams. The cheering died down as Arnold took his seat alongside Demi and Bruce. Sharon shook her head in admiration and went back to her research.

Now the MC's amplified voice echoed through the restaurant: "A real surprise treat now, folks. Direct from his box-office smash, *Spring of the Comanche* . . . America's heartthrob . . . *Da*-vid . . . *Spencer*."

Sheila jumped up and down like a berserk adolescent, and Trish and Melanie squealed loudly enough to fracture eardrums a block away. Sheila yelled, "Omigod, omigod," and Sharon hoped that none of Sheila's psychiatry patients were in attendance. She chuckled to herself as she turned over a page in the *Code of Criminal Procedure*. David Spencer was a surprise celebrity, all right. Along with Brad Pitt, Spencer was responsible for a nationwide increase in vibrator sales, but the gorgeous young star missed the mark where Sharon Hays was concerned. Not that he wasn't beautiful and all that, it was just . . . Sharon attributed her lack of interest to having reached her thirties. An older man, maybe someone like Dustin Hoffman, was more her cup of tea. At any rate, she kept her seat, plugging right along with her legal research.

"And accompanying David today," the P.A. announcer boomed, "is the current light of his life . . . the vivacious . . . *Dar*-la . . . *Cow*-an."

As the mob whooped it up, Sharon laid down her pen. Well, I'll be double damned, she thought. She took off her glasses, stood, and stretched her neck to see over the crowd.

Her gaze fell first on David Spencer just as he grinned at an overweight woman near the aisle. The lady squealed, shut her eyes tightly, and clasped her hands, and Sharon wondered if she was about to witness a fatal stroke. Spencer turned his attention to someone else in the crowd, and Sharon had to admit that the boy was absolutely gorgeous. He had wavy brown hair and a perfect sunlamp tan, and light glinted from teeth like snow white curbstones. Spen-

cer's teeth reminded Sharon of a picture in the orthodontist's office. She looked across the table at
Melanie, and imagined the orthodontist filing a lien
on her home. Damn Rob anyway, Sharon thought.
Just as she began to get angry all over again, thinking
of Rob, David Spencer stopped to blow someone a
kiss and Darla Cowan strutted into view. Sharon's features softened in . . . envy, yes, but there was a surge
of pity as well.

Darla had weathered the years quite well, thanks.
Her waist was trim, her hips curvy and full, her thighs
firm as if she'd just stepped off the Stairmaster. Her
honey blond hair was fluffed around her face in curls,
falling to her shoulders just so. A herd of cosmetolo-
gists had likely contributed to the makeup job. The
result was more than perfect; in fact, the lipstick outline added a petulant curve to Darla's mouth which
Sharon didn't recall. No one would ever guess that
Darla had ten years on her lover boy, she looked that
good. Large, firm breasts tented the front of Darla's
clinging gold lamé . . . *lounging pajamas,* Sharon
thought, that's the only way to describe the outfit. As
Darla smiled left and right, Sharon noted women
around the restaurant shooting catty glances and talking to each other from the side of their mouth. They're
wondering if it's a silicone job, Sharon thought. Well,
it isn't, girls; they're real, they're perfect, and they
used to turn me pea green with envy.

Sheila bent closer to Sharon and said, "You catch
her *Playboy* layout last month? Airbrushing, right?"

Sharon answered matter-of-factly, "Didn't have to
be, the shape she's in. And since when do you read
Playboy?"

"A patient left a copy."

"Well, hang onto it," Sharon said. "I'd like to have
a peep." She laughed along with Sheila, then sensed
someone watching her and returned her attention to
the aisle. Darla had spotted her.

Darla's smile dissolved, replaced by recognition,
surprise, and consternation, all in the space of a couple

of seconds. Then the artificial smile reappeared. She grabbed Spencer's elbow and whispered something to him. Spencer looked toward Sharon, but not directly at her, and gave a brief so-what shrug. Then he returned to the job of shooting fetching glances in all directions as he moved on toward the stage. Darla left Spencer's side and made a beeline in Sharon's direction.

"Sharon. *Sha*-ron." Darla was barely audible over the hubbub from nearby tables.

Sheila gaped at Sharon, as did Trish, and Melanie regarded her mother as if she'd just grown a second head. "Just an old friend," Sharon said offhandedly. Then Darla squeezed in between two men in slacks and sports coats, moved up beside Sharon, and kissed first one cheek and then the other.

More customers crowded around for a better look, forming a circle with Sharon and Darla at the center. Sharon gave apologetic looks in all directions as Darla continued to fawn.

"I've got *so* much to tell you," Darla said, her tone childlike, the same begging whine which Sharon would recognize anywhere.

Sharon grabbed Sheila's hand. "Darla Cowan, this is my best friend, Sheila Winston, and—"

"Will you have dinner with me?" Darla didn't so much as acknowledge that anyone else was in the restaurant. Almost fifteen years fled in the wink of an eye as she looked at Sharon with the same wistful expression she'd used back in Brooklyn Heights when she'd say, sometimes as late as three in the morning, "Want to go for doughnuts? We can rehearse lines together. I've got *so* much to tell you, Sharon."

"Dinner?" Sharon said hesitantly. "Looks like you're pretty committed to me."

A woman nearby said to her male companion, "Who's the brunette? What was *she* in?"

Sharon's cheeks were suddenly warm. She said, "Look, Darla, I . . ."

"You have to, Sharon." Darla's look was pleading.

Once upon a time Darla had interrupted Sharon and Rob in the throes of passion. She'd walked right in sometime after midnight and demanded that Sharon have a heart-to-heart with her right then and there. You never knew about Darla, what she was going to do. "I don't know," Sharon tried, "I've got my daughter with me, and I'm working on a case."

"You *have* to, Sharon." As if they'd last seen each other yesterday instead of thirteen years ago at La-Guardia, when Sharon had boarded a flight for Texas with Melanie in her arms. Darla was pushy, demanding, and in spite of it all a damned good actress. And above everything else, especially during the last months of Sharon's unmarried pregnancy, Darla had once been a loyal friend.

"You *have* to, Sharon," Darla said again.

Sharon gave a little shrug. "Sure, if you want." You'd just have to know this lady, folks, she thought. If she refused, Darla was likely to cause one helluva scene.

Darla backed away. "You won't forget? Second limo outside. Wait for me. We'll go somewhere quiet. You *have* to, Sharon."

Sharon nodded, and hoped that her reluctance didn't show. Then Darla was gone, the plastic smile back in place, tripping down the aisle in pursuit of David Spencer. The couple climbed onstage to loud applause and a few shrill wolf whistles.

Melanie said, "How do you know her, Mom?"

And a man behind Sharon said jokingly, "Can I have your autograph, ma'am?"

And Sheila said, "How do you do, Madame Celebrity?"

Sharon was embarrassed. She sat down quickly and picked up her legal pad. "Just an old friend," she said, almost to herself, then grabbed her pen and took notes like mad.

2

‟**S**ure, she's insecure," Sharon said. "But aren't we all?" She inhaled coolish air. It was five-thirty and getting dark; in another week daylight saving time would kick in. Planet Hollywood had shut down after its two-hour grand opening, leaving the crowd to wander around and gape at the row of waiting limos. The celebs were still inside, the beautiful people partying apart from the rank and file.

"She didn't look insecure in *Fatal Instinct*," Sheila said, "wrapping her legs around that guy. I was afraid my date was going to jump me right then and there. Sexiest thing I've ever seen on the screen." The women stood inside the ropes separating the crowd from the limos. A few minutes after the restaurant had shut its doors, a uniformed chauffeur had come out and called Sharon's name. Sheila had been surprised. Sharon hadn't been; in spite of her faults, Darla Cowan had always been true to her word.

Over near the grandstand Melanie and Trish flirted with two boys who looked to be around twenty years old. Not a step closer, young man, Sharon thought. Sheila looked toward the girls as well, and a worried frown appeared.

"You'd never believe it now," Sharon said, "but Darla used to wear baggy clothes to hide her figure. The first time, gee, about six months after I met her. A bunch of us went out to one of the directors' place, on Long Island. He had a pool. It was the first time I ever saw her in anything less than tent size, and when she came out in that bikini you could hear jaws popping all over the place. We were determined to make it on talent in those days. Made a pact against nudity. Were we ever full of it, huh?"

"If you believe her reviews, her talent is all in those gazooms."

"She's a good actress, Sheila."

"Does well on the heavy breathing."

"I'm telling you, she can act. I did *Midsummer Night's Dream* with her once, in a theater down in SoHo. She stole the show."

"With her clothes on?"

"Darla would have committed hari-kari before she would have done that *Playboy* thing back then. She nearly rode her morals out of the business, and starved to death until that *Fatal Instinct* role. They can say what they want, but I've never had a truer friend. Including you, and that's saying a mouthful. When I was pregnant, she came by every day. The last view I had of New York, Melanie in my arms as I entered the sky walk, Darla at the gate waving to me."

Sheila leaned on the fender of the lead limousine. There were four of the jazzy autos parallel to the curb, three white Lincolns and a long gray Cadillac, each one equipped with blackened windows.

"Darla does Shakespeare," Sheila said. "Might make a good title for her next film."

"Her acting is no joke. Don't think those sex scenes don't require some ability."

Sheila arched an eyebrow.

"As in talent, dopey," Sharon said. "Plus four thousand miles of nerve. You can say what you want, but Darla knows where stardom lies."

Sheila was all at once composed and serious. "However she may have changed, it will be more rather than less."

Sharon studied her friend. Sheila was in her psychiatrist's mode, intelligent features relaxed in thought. Finally Sharon said, "More rather than less of what?"

"It's the celebrity syndrome. It would change you, it would change me, it would change freaking Mother

Teresa, for God's sake. These people expect to be idolized. She won't be the same old buddyroo, that you can count on."

"Maybe. I'm only going to dinner with her."

"If she . . ." Sheila trailed off, her gaze now back to the grandstand.

Sharon turned her head. One of the boys, a tall blonde with a surfer's tan, had his hand on Melanie's shoulder in what was a great deal more than a platonic gesture. Sharon felt a surge of panic. She stood away from the limo and moved over to the rope. "Melanie. Melanie, come here a minute."

Melanie looked disdainfully skyward, then disengaged herself and came over with more than a little sass in her walk. The thirteen-year-old seemed a bit puffy of late. Water retention. Melanie's periods were likely to begin soon, and Sharon had stocked up on the tampons in anticipation of the great event. Melanie's adolescence was going to be as much fun as a root canal.

"We were *talking,* Mom," Melanie said, folding her arms.

Oh, terrific, the respectful years. "Who are those boys?" Sharon said. Sheila edged up nearer to listen in. Over by the grandstand the young guys continued to engage Trish in animated conversation. Trish grinned and wriggled like a puppy. "Who are those boys?" Sheila parroted.

"Mom already asked me that. They're these guys we met. See you later." Melanie turned on her heel and flounced away.

"You stop right there, young lady." Sharon had had it up to here, and the sharpness in her tone turned heads among the crowd. Melanie halted in mid-flounce. Her mouth curved in a pout. Sharon said, "We want to know who they are, and what you'all are talking about. How old are they, anyway?"

"Sixteen."

"In a pig's freaking eye. How old are those boys?" Melanie put fists on hips. "Oh, give me a break."

"I'll give you a break," Sharon said. "How would you like for Mrs. Winston to take you home, right now?"

"We aren't doing anything."

Sharon did a toe tap. "I'll be the judge of that. Who are they, Melanie? Right this minute."

"If you *must* know . . ."

"Damn right I must," Sharon said.

"Their names are William and John. They're not *groping* us or anything. They're impressed that you know Darla Cowan."

Sharon and Sheila exchanged a look. "How do they know that's who I'm waiting for?" Sharon said.

"Are you ever out of it, Mom. Everybody around here heard that chauffeur talking to you."

Sharon breathed a bit easier. What Melanie said was true enough; when Sharon had ducked under the rope with Sheila in tow, a murmur had rippled through the crowd. The boys were now keeping their distance, speaking softly and politely to Trish. Sharon said to Sheila, "Guess it's okay, huh?"

Sheila gave a quick—but uncomfortable—nod. "Seems to be. We're probably too mother-hennish, old girl."

"Okay, Melanie," Sharon said, "have it your way. But we'll be watching you. Don't get out of our sight, are you listening to me?"

Sharon stood uncomfortably by with Sheila while the beautiful people exited the restaurant and drove away, Bruce Willis giving a thumbs-up sign before climbing in the limo after his glamorous wife, Schwarzenegger lugging a toy machine gun, emitting a booming laugh as he sprayed imaginary bullets through the crowd. Chuck Norris made his exit in a buckskin jacket, taking a stance as if ready to deliver a karate blow. The crowd whistled, clapped, and *oh*-ed and *ah*-ed. The caravan loaded up and disappeared around the corner, headed down Elm Street toward Stemmons Expressway, leaving one lone Caddy stretch standing at the curb. Sharon stood first on one foot and then the other. Still no Darla, still no David Spencer.

From within the restaurant a hoarse male voice yelled, "God *damn* you."

Sharon and Sheila exchanged a look of alarm. A murmur rippled through the crowd of two hundred or so.

Darla Cowan hustled out, high heels clicking. She said over her shoulder, "Get your own damned limo." She hurried down the steps.

David Spencer followed at a run. He grabbed Darla's arm and yanked her backward. "You'll go when I tell you, bitch."

A quick flash illuminated the warring couple. Sharon glanced into the mob as a man lowered a camera.

"Let me go, you bastard." Darla twisted and struggled.

Spencer hauled her toward the restaurant entry. "Beat the shit out of you." His voice was thick and his words were slurred.

Oh, Christ, Sharon thought. Spencer wasn't a big man but was pretty muscular; a woman alone was no match for him, no way. Sharon took a long stride toward Darla. Sheila pulled on her arm. "Keep out of it. Something like that is dangerous. You don't know what you might be getting into."

Melanie yelled from beyond the ropes, "Stay away from them, Mom." The concern in Melanie's voice touched a nerve. Usually she only wants to get rid of me these days, Sharon thought.

Darla freed one hand and slapped Spencer's face. A red mark appeared on his cheek, but he didn't let go of her.

Sharon acted on impulse. She broke free from Sheila's grasp and moved forward, marched past Darla, put both hands in the middle of David Spencer's chest, and shoved as hard as she could. "You leave her alone." Sharon felt dread and instinctively tensed, expecting the matinee idol to haul off and belt her as well. Instead, Spencer stumbled drunkenly backward. He made one weak effort to right himself, then over he went, tumbling headlong onto the sidewalk. His head struck the bottom restaurant step with a sound like a bat hitting a soft melon. Blood ran from a gash on his head. He put his hands over his face, rolled over, and began to moan.

Oh, my God, Sharon thought, I've killed the guy. The crowd had surged against the ropes, and Sharon looked helplessly around at the sea of faces. She locked gazes with a slender, rugged-looking man who wore a fringed buckskin jacket and wide-brimmed hat, Crocodile Dundee style. He spread his hands in a shrug and smiled at her. Sharon looked back down as David Spencer wiggled wormlike away from the step and grabbed for her ankle. She took a step back and covered her mouth with her hand.

Darla broke free and sprinted for the limo, sobbing out of control. Another camera flashed. She crossed the sidewalk, threw open the door, and looked frantically around. "Get in, Sharon," Darla yelled. Her voice quavered. "Please hurry. Oh, my *God* . . ."

Spencer took another futile swipe at Sharon's foot. She hesitated. Sheila called out, "Go, kid. The guy's not that hurt, and he had it coming."

Sharon went over and squeezed Sheila's arm. "Just get the girls home, okay?" Sharon said. Then she hurried over to the limo and half fell inside on plush upholstery. She smelled new leather.

Darla climbed in and slammed the door. "Anywhere, just . . . take us anywhere away from here." She covered her face, her shoulders heaving.

The driver watched over the seat back with his mouth agape. He nodded, pulled the bill of his cap down over his eyes, put the limo in gear, and accelerated away from the restaurant. He slowed in traffic to duly note the time of day in his logbook, scribbling rapidly while keeping one eye on the road.

As the driver notated his log, Sharon had a final glimpse of David Spencer through tinted glass as the actor rolled onto his side, lay his cheek on his folded hands, and closed his eyes. His blood dripped on the sidewalk. Two black-and-white DPD vehicles pulled to the curb in front of the restaurant. Four policemen jumped out and sprinted toward the fallen actor. Darla's sobs filled the interior of the limo. The driver speeded up, and as Sharon sank back on plush leather cushions, the scene in front of Planet Hollywood vanished behind the side of a building. Sharon's breathing was rapid and her hands were trembling.

As four of Dallas's finest arrived on the scene, responding to a 911 call from within the restaurant, one of the cops activated the video camera mounted on his dashboard. The camera whirred into action; in the tape the display figures in the upper right-hand corner would clearly read 6:14 P.M. With the video recording their every move, the four officers then vaulted from their cars, dashed over the curb, and into the public eye. They slowed to a walk and approached the fallen actor, who had now begun to snore.

One cop said, grasping Spencer's chin and turning the actor's head for a better look, "Ain't this sumbitch in the movies?"

A second patrolman put his hands on his knees and bent from the waist. "Fuck, I know who he is. *Born on the Fourth of July*. Guy lost his legs in the war."

(The official report of the incident would read: "Officers identified the distressed party as film actor David Spencer." In the handwritten rough draft, however, the actor's name was given as "Tom Cruise," with Cruise's name scratched through and Spencer's name substituted prior to the typist's delivery of the final version. Cruise's publicists would issue a lengthy denial of his presence at the disturbance, widely reported in the "People" insert in thousands of newspapers around the country, and would use the opportunity to mention in print the name of the movie which Cruise had been shooting in San Francisco at the time the policemen leaped over the Dallas curb.)

The lead policeman was a veteran named Whiteside, who was known among his peers as having a Rambo complex, and who considered himself a take-charge kind of guy. He said, "Well, don't just stand there with your fingers up your asses. Do somethin' to help the motherfucker."

(The audio portion of the squad car videotape would become strangely distorted at that point, and Whiteside's words would be lost in a roar of static. The printed report of the incident would state thusly: "Officers identified themselves and offered their assistance.")

A portly man wearing a Dallas Cowboys sideline jacket and a Texas Rangers batting helmet, carrying a Dallas Stars hockey puck—possibly a sports enthusiast, investigators in search of witnesses would later determine—ducked underneath the ropes and approached the officers, staggering slightly and waving a bottle of beer. "I seen the whole thing," he said loudly. "He 'as gonna beat the shit outta this woman, an' this chick lowered the boom on his ass." He pointed at the actor stretched out on the pavement.

Spencer was now awake and was having difficulty. Blood oozed from the laceration on the side of his head. He tried to rise, but couldn't get his feet under him and fell back down. A comely young lady in the crowd called out, "He's hurt. Oh, my God, he's *injured.*" The policemen rushed to the actor's side to offer assistance.

One officer grabbed Spencer's elbow and tried to help him up, but the heartthrob yanked his arm away. "Getcha fuckin' hands offa me," Spencer said. Officers noted that his speech was slurred and that there was a distinct odor of alcohol fumes.

"Just take it easy, pal," Whiteside said. "We'll get an ambulance." He sprinted toward the squad cars to put in a call.

"Don't need a goddamn ambulance," Spencer mumbled. "Need my fuckin' agent." The cut on his head was nasty, nearly a half inch wide and almost to the bone.

"We'll get you stitched up," one of the policemen said.

"Fuck you will." Spencer tried once more to rise. As he did, he fumbled in his breast pocket and pulled out a cellophane bag. His legs gave way and he fell, dropping the baggie on the ground. The bag contained an off-white crystalline powder. Spencer flopped onto his back and began to snore.

The three cops hovering over the actor looked at each other. Not being members of the Los Angeles police force, they weren't accustomed to dealing with celebrities and weren't sure how to proceed. The bag of powder lay in plain sight, and therefore they didn't need a search warrant to make an arrest. Their beating victim had just become a cocaine suspect, and the policemen weren't of a mood to pursue a pissant possession beef on a Friday night when they had plenty of other fish to fry. One of the cops placed his foot over the baggie to hide it from view.

The man in the Dallas Cowboys sideline jacket stood nearby. His mouth hung open. He turned to the crowd and waved his hockey puck. "God *day*-um. He's been *tootin'*."

A ripple went through the mob, which now had swelled to five hundred or more. A woman near the ropes yelled, "Any place, any time, darlin', I'll toot some with you." She pulled up her sweater to reveal her naked breasts.

David Spencer continued to moan, and extended his hand toward the officer's boot. "Gimme that. Got a straw in my pocket."

The policemen sighed in unison. Now there were witnesses. Regretfully, one of the officers read Spencer his rights. The actor continued to grope for the baggie. A second cop pushed Spencer's hand away, picked up the dope, and held the baggie gingerly by one corner.

The sports fan, his eyes wide, now announced, "God *day*-um. They're fixin' to bust his ass."

Which brought a rumble of discontent from the crowd, and caused the woman with the bared bosoms to shout, "I'll make your bail, darlin'. Don't you fret none, you hear?"

The policeman paused in the middle of Spencer's Miranda warning as the actor rolled onto his side, rested his cheek on his hands, and snored even louder. A ribbon of drying blood extended from the cut on his head down the side of his face. Officer Whiteside returned from the squad car and, unaware of the cocaine discovery, said to Spencer, "Ambulance is on its way. Try to hang on." Spencer made a noise as if giving the raspberry to an umpire.

The policeman showed the baggie and shook his head. Then one officer grabbed Spencer's ankles, another his arms, and with the third cop running interference, they toted Spencer toward the squad cars. Whiteside's shoulders slumped in disappointment as he trudged along behind the other officers.

After dumping the actor into the rear seat of a squad car, the policemen manned their vehicles and left the scene. As they moved at a snail's pace out of the West End, a cup flew from the crowd and bumped soggily against the lead car's windshield. Crushed ice and bourbon mixed with Coke ran down the window, poured from the auto's side, and puddled in the street as the cops drove away.

The visit to Parkland Hospital's emergency room (where the nurse who sutured Spencer's wound, along with five hospital employees, stood in line and asked for autographs; and where Spencer, now pumped full of hospital Demerol in addition to the cocaine and whiskey he'd administered on his own, responded to his fans by saying, "Fuck no. I want my agent") took up more than three hours. By the time the motorcade arrived at Main Police Headquarters' underground garage to book the actor for possession, it was nearing ten p.m. Spencer, now semi-coherent, sat in the rear of a black-and-white with his head swathed in bandages. He wasn't handcuffed, and nastily refused the policemen's offers of assistance as he stumbled toward the jail.

Two men wearing suits and toting briefcases waited at the booking desk. They identified themselves as lawyers with Malone and Ricks, a Dallas white-collar firm. Apparently David Spencer's agent, through a Los Angeles attorney, had requested the local mouthpieces to come down and post bail. The police finger-printed and photographed the defendant, then took him upstairs to an all-night magistrate. The magistrate noted the actor's celebrity status and released him on his recognizance, after instructing Spencer to keep his attorneys aware of his whereabouts at all times. Spencer responded groggily that he'd think about it, causing the magistrate to revoke his bail, and finally gained his freedom through the intercession of one of the local attorneys. At 11:45 Spencer signed out on the police log and made his exit.

The lawyers then drove the actor to the Mansion on Turtle Creek. Spencer's luggage, along with Darla Cowan's, had already arrived from California and stood waiting in the presidential suite. With Spencer walking unsteadily between his attorneys, the trio entered the hotel lobby and obtained a key from the registration desk. The lawyers accompanied Spencer up on the elevator and bade him good night at the door to his room. They would later recall that he was coherent, and that the actor seemed to have calmed down.

3

"You being a lawyer makes me jealous," Darla Cowan said.

Sharon had a bite of Caesar salad. "I can't imagine anybody in the country who'd rather be me than you."

"I'm somebody in the country, and most of the time I'd rather be you." Darla spooned mushroom soup from a bowl.

The lighting inside the 8.0 Restaurant was cozy and dim, the *clippety-clop* of hooves on Fort Worth's downtown pavement pleasant to the ears. Sharon looked up as the carriage passed the restaurant, the horse straining, the driver hunched over the reins, a couple in the passenger seat holding hands. The thirty-mile trip on Interstate 30 had been Sharon's idea; the women couldn't have had dinner anywhere in Dallas without the celebrity watchers bugging the devil out of them. It was Darla's brainstorm to ditch the limo, driver and all, for a rental car at Love Field, and the idea wasn't a bad one. After all, who'd look for a movie star to arrive in a Geo? To complete the incognito bit, Darla had dug a pair of slacks and a simple beige sweater from her overnight bag and had changed in an Exxon station's rest room. During the drive over she'd tried on sunglasses, and the two had agreed that at night she'd be less conspicuous without the damned things.

In comparison to the madhouse of Big D, downtown Fort Worth was as laid back as Bug Tussle. Men in boots and jeans and women in casual western wear roamed the sidewalks at a leisurely pace, as if they had no place to go and were in no particular hurry to get there. Whereas Dallas literally broke its neck being modern and upscale, Fort Worth had restored itself to the old-days look. Gaslights lined the curbs. 8.0's headwaiter had recognized Darla the moment she'd stepped through the entry, but a twenty across his palm had bought his silence. The women sat at a corner table. Occasionally one of the other diners would shoot hey-who-is-that? glances in their direction, but otherwise they had their privacy. Sharon suspected that the headwaiter would place a call, and that gossip columnists in both the *Dallas Morning News* and *Fort Worth Star-Telegram* would report a celebrity sighting in the old Eight-Oh.

"Face it, you're living the American dream," Sharon said. "The things we used to fantasize about, you've got them." Sharon kept her tone upbeat, her dialogue complimentary; she'd learned years ago that feeding Darla's ego was a round-the-clock job. Five minutes after the limo had pulled away from Planet Hollywood, Darla had dried her tears and hadn't mentioned the incident with David Spencer since. Which was all right with Sharon—she let Darla set the conversation's pace and merely followed leads. Prying wasn't necessary; sooner or later Darla would tell more about Spencer than Sharon wanted to know.

"Arguing in front of a jury is as much of a dream as being an actress," Darla said.

"It might be unless you're doing it. Lawyering is grunt work."

"So's acting." Darla lowered her lashes, watched her lap, then looked up and said, "I see Rob some."

Sharon had known it was coming, and had mentally prepared herself. She'd made it a practice never to bad-mouth Melanie's father to anyone. She said merely, "Oh? How's he doing?"

"You know how he's doing. He's becoming America's sex symbol. Rob's got talent, you know."

Sharon didn't necessarily agree with that—she'd spent enough hours going over Rob's lines with him in the old days, and had secretly thought that his character interpretation left a lot to be desired—but she had to admit that he had a certain charisma in his role as a tough-soft police detective. She also thought, however, that once *Minions of Justice: The Streets* had run its course—as all weekly television shows must do eventually—that Rob would go the way of Eric Estrada, David Soul, and countless others whose star status became history once their series was cancelled. She didn't think Rob had the range required to make it on the big screen, but to say so now would sound like a dose of Bitter Old Flame. So she said to Darla, "A lot of people have the talent. Rob got the break as well."

Darla showed a smile. "I was in on his break."

Sharon had been stirring her salad around in preparation for spearing another bite, but now laid her fork aside. "Oh?"

"I was filming *Fatal Instinct*," Darla said, "and Rob showed up one day at a casting call. The desk clerk part, the one where I vamp the guy in order to get into a room where I stab a couple of people. He didn't get the part, but he and I talked. The next day I tried to get my agent to represent him, but *Fatal Instinct* wasn't in release yet and I didn't have the stroke to get Aaron's ear." She laughed. "Aaron Levy's still crying in his beer over that one."

"That's your agent?"

Darla nodded. "Then later on, after David Spencer and I sort of . . . got together, I talked David into introducing Rob to his agent. David did have the proper stroke, of course, and the rest is history. Curtis Nussbaum has never stopped thanking me."

Sharon's jaws clenched. "Curtis Nussbaum is David Spencer's agent?"

"He has one of the better stables. Why, do you know him?"

One of the better stables, Sharon thought, and the absolutely freaking champion stall when it came to dispensing child support. "I've met him," she said.

"Talked to him on the phone, about . . . Rob's relationship to his daughter."

"Curt Nussbaum does everything on behalf of his clients," Darla said. "Pays their bills . . . screens their scripts . . . He's even talked to me about doing a picture with David, and optioned a novel with that in mind. Commissioned a screenwriter—God, no telling how much Curt is out of pocket, but I sort of suspect he's trying to steal me from Aaron Levy. Missing out on Rob and then losing me to Curtis Nussbaum, I'm afraid that might do poor Aaron in."

Sharon pictured David Spencer and Darla in steamy roles opposite each other and, considering the donnybrook she'd witnessed outside Planet Hollywood, almost laughed out loud. She said, "I've seen every one of your pictures." She was trying to change the subject without being obvious, but she didn't feel as if she'd put the transition over very well. She didn't want to butt in where Darla and David Spencer were concerned, and Rob and his freaking agent were subjects she'd just as soon avoid.

"Oh? Which film stands out in your mind?" Darla seemed on the defensive. In the old days her career had been her favorite subject, which was the case with every writer or actor Sharon had ever met. Darla waited for an answer.

"Oh . . . the big ones you've made," Sharon said.

"And which ones are those?"

"Wasn't *Fatal Instinct* the number one box office in . . . ?

"1994. Two years ago. What other roles do you remember?"

"Gee, Darla, what is this? *Role* roles, I've seen a lot of them. As talented an actress as you are . . ."

"Lay off, will you? You don't have to patronize me. I do a bitchin' fuck scene, which is all anyone knows about me. It's put a lot of money in my bank account, but that's all it's done. A large percentage of my fan mail comes from perverts. How would you like to open my letters every day? I'm shacked up with a boy who's got the body of a god and the intelligence of a weed eater, not to mention the liquor-holding capacity of a thimble." Darla looked past Sharon, and seemed ready to burst into tears.

"Lighten up, will you? You're one of the most famous people in America."

"So was Linda Lovelace. Ever since I got my first so-called starring role I've wanted to contact you, drop you a line or something. You know why I haven't? Because I'm ashamed to. Ditto with my folks. I haven't talked to my mother in three years."

The venom in Darla's tone was shocking. Back in New York she used to call her mom in Indianapolis every other night. Sharon toyed with her salad and didn't say anything. Listening to this discourse was painful, but Darla had sympathized with Sharon while she made auditions carrying Melanie in her womb. My turn, Sharon thought.

"You know when the happiest time was for me?" Darla said.

"It couldn't have been when we were all starving to death. You can keep those—"

"Oh, yes, it was," Darla said urgently. "We were all broke and we were all friends, and what we said to each other meant something. Not like now, for God's sake, when nobody wants to so much as split a hot dog with you unless they've got an angle. David and I shared a table with Rob and some bimbo just a couple of weeks ago out in Westwood, and that's what he and I were talking about. Rob said his days with you were the best he ever spent. Mine, too. You'll never guess how much I miss you."

Sharon chewed Romaine lettuce brushed with cheese curds and Caesar dressing, and hoped the dimness of the restaurant hid the blush in her cheeks. One thing about Darla, her compliments came straight from the heart, no holds barred. One of the most unpredictable people Sharon had ever met, but one of the most likable as well. As for Rob and the happy days in the Big Apple . . . well, Sharon took *that* pill along with several grains of salt. Darla would tell her that Rob had said something nice even if in truth he'd called her the bitch of the century. "I miss you, too, kid," Sharon said, and meant it. "Look, if you're not happy with the guy, why don't you split?"

"Oh, I will. Eventually. You have to do it right in Hollywood. Just ask my agent. Move in while the spotlight's on you, move out when it's big news, whatever gets your name in the paper. If you have a slugfest in public the press crucifies you, but then everybody flocks to your next film. Lovely world."

Sharon thoughtfully bit her lower lip. "That fight outside Planet Hollywood looked like the real thing to me."

"Oh, it was. And don't think I won't hear more about it." Darla laid her spoon aside.

"I think Mr. Spencer got the worst of it," Sharon said.

"Thanks to you." Darla's lip quivered. "There's another reason I can't leave David right now. I'm afraid."

"You could be in danger. There are laws about that sort of thing, if you want protection."

Darla quickly regained her composure. "You don't call the police unless you want more publicity. The cops have been known to leak a few things in our neck of the woods."

Sharon felt a burst of anger. "Has he hurt you?"

"Not permanently."

"Darla, you listen. If you're in an abusive relationship, you get out of it. And right now. I wish I'd brought Sheila along."

"Your black friend?"

Sharon nodded. "She's a psychiatrist. About half her practice are battered wives, girlfriends . . ."

Darla gave a harsh, bitter laugh, loud enough that a man at the next table turned his head. "I don't know that I'm battered," said Darla. "He's only really beat the shit out of me a couple of times."

"Get away from him, then. I'm serious."

"So am I." Darla studied her lap, the voluptuous cinema queen now looking sad and vulnerable. "You'd be surprised what some of us put up with for image's sake." She pushed her soup aside and picked at her salad. "You know how long it's been since I had a really good time with anyone? When I first got to California, a few times. Guys I worked with on day jobs. One I met with this temp service, and darn if I didn't feel there was really something there. Then along comes *Fatal Instinct*. All during shooting I didn't say a word to him about my role, and he didn't ask. I suppose he thought it was just another bit part. Opening night for the film I went with him, and guess what. It wasn't a week until he wanted to tie me to a chair and whip me. No way could I convince him that wasn't really what I wanted. I finally slapped him silly and walked out.

"I met David at an AIDS fund-raiser shortly after that," Darla said. "He's ten years younger and full of hormones, okay? Set me in orbit sexually, that I'll admit, but then we moved in together. Half the time he's gone or I'm gone, shooting a film or something, or maybe just seeking solitude while we search for our true identities. That kind of crap, you know? And when we're together, half of that time he's so zonked on whiskey or drugs or both that he doesn't know what's going on. When he sobers up he feels bad, so he beats me up. Then later he apologizes. Jesus, practically on his knees, and that's almost as bad as the beating." Darla shrugged. "So that's life among the beautiful people. But I take it. For a certain amount of time, you have to."

"No, you don't," Sharon said. "Not one more second."

"Oh, I'm going back to the hotel in a huff and snatch up my things. Tonight I'll flee to California in tears. That will make the tabloids. We'll be on-again, off-again for a month, just to keep up the publicity, then it's going to be splitsville. David will pretend to care that I'm gone, but he really won't give a damn.

For someone with his drawing power, punching bags are a dime a dozen.''

"What hotel?"

"The Mansion."

"I should go with you. You never know what might happen."

"He won't hit me tonight," Darla said. "He was worked up enough to knock me silly back at Planet Hollywood, but by the time I get you home and then drive to the hotel, he'll be in a stupor. I'll just pack my gear and I'm out of there."

Sharon turned her fork prongs down on her plate. Another carriage went past the window, *clippety-clop*. She said, "Can I ask you something personal?"

"Sure. We never had to get permission to ask each other anything we wanted, you know that."

"Well, there's a lot of water under the bridge."

"Not with us. So ask."

"Well . . . if you never had any feeling for the guy to begin with . . ."

"Why did I move in with him?"

Sharon studied her, the same, so-familiar face she'd known before, but now a face she'd seen on billboards as well. "Something like that," she finally said.

A soft smile touched Darla's lips. "Remember what they used to tell us in acting class, when we'd think our characters weren't doing things the way they would in real life?"

Sharon chuckled, remembering. " 'That may be life, but this is a play'?"

"Yes. They say the same thing in Hollywood. 'That may be life, but this is the films.' We get tied up in these roles we play. One month you might be a whore, the next month a nun. If you play-act that you're falling in love, sometimes you think you are. Then you try it for real, and life kicks in."

Sharon folded her hands in her lap. "I think that might've been true with Rob and me."

"Maybe," Darla said. "And if it was, then you know what I'm talking about. Feelings for David Spencer?

Sure, I convinced myself I had some, the same way I convince myself I'm getting horny playing some of those scenes I do. But it isn't real life, Sharon. It's the movies, kid, what can I say? So don't ever feel envious of me. People like you, people with lives, you're the ones who have got it made."

4

Darla leaned back until her face was in shadow, the glow from Sharon's porch light illuminating her hands on the steering wheel. "What a neat little house," Darla said.

"I'll grant you it's little." Sharon reached for the door handle. "But anything beats a cold-water flat in Brooklyn Heights."

"Come on, it wasn't that bad. We had hot water."

"As long as nobody else in the building showered at the same time we did. So tell me about the castle where you live now."

Darla sighed. "Where I'm camping out is what you mean. I don't feel as if I live anywhere."

"I'll bet it's nice, though." Sharon looked up the driveway to where her dented Volvo sat nose-on to the garage, with Sheila's Buick wagon parked behind the Volvo. The living room lights were on, and Sheila and the girls would be watching TV as they waited up for her. She said to Darla, "Is it on the beach?"

"Sure, just like . . . well, just like in the movies, what can I say? We're on a cliff, fifty feet up. There's a sliding door leading from the bedroom onto a balcony, and at night you can sit outside and listen to the surf pounding. Whitecaps on the ocean at night are something to see, like ghosts on black water. They make this restful swishing noise, and keep me company while David's sleeping one off. If I concentrate really hard on the ocean sounds I can't even hear him snoring. Salt breeze on your cheeks and all that. Best that money can buy."

How can she sound so bitter, Sharon thought, that lifestyle? "Guess you take walks on the beach," she said.

A parallelogram of brightness shined on Darla's mouth and nose. "Yeah, all the time. It's the only way I'm ever really alone, nothing but me and the seagulls. I can close my eyes and imagine I'm just about anywhere, no security guards, nothing. Which is a rarity for me these days. This is the first time I've been anywhere without a shadow since I don't know when. Feels sort of strange with no one bird-dogging me."

"Come on, it can't be that bad. What people wouldn't give."

Darla's mouth puckered. "Can't it? The people who haven't tried it just don't know. You can believe this or not, but I'd give up every nickel, all the glamour, if I could just live in a little house like you've got and be myself. I can't be myself, Sharon. I'm not even certain that myself exists anymore. Ever since I compromised everything I'd preached for so long, just for one great big fuck scene. My whole life is a fuck scene now, you want to trade places? I'll warn you beforehand, there's no backing out." She sniffled and looked at the dashboard clock. "Oh, hell, I'm whining again. If I'm going to adios David and catch the red-eye, I've got to step on it."

Sharon looked down, hesitating. "I wish you'd let me go to the hotel with you. I'd feel as if you were safer."

"From David? No way he's going to be a problem, it's after nine o'clock. He's in a stupor by now, believe me." Darla squeezed Sharon's arm. "Now that I've got you located," Darla said, "you mind if I call you once in a while? Just to talk."

"Of course not."

"Thanks. I'm a little short of friends right now, someone I know isn't after something. You may keep me from jumping out the window some night. And, hey, if I drive you crazy taking you up on your offer, I apologize in advance." She tightened her grip, the pressure on Sharon's arm desperate. "And thanks just for being my friend. To know how much that means, you'd just have to be in my shoes."

Sharon stood on the curb and watched the Geo's taillights bounce through an intersection, brighten as Darla hit the brakes, then disappear from view as the Geo rounded the corner. If the neighbors had any idea who's driving that little car, Sharon thought, they'd all be outside in their bathrobes. She softly sang the opening bars to "Take Back Your Mink" as she lugged her briefcase and shoulder bag up the sidewalk. Once upon a time she'd gone with Darla to the umpteenth Broadway revival of *Guys and Dolls,* after standing in line for an hour at half-price tickets—the sign suspended over the joining of Broadway, Seventh Avenue and 47th Street read, TKTS, with half the letters missing from the word—across from the theater. Darla had been short of money and had bummed a dollar to make up the difference. After the show they'd walked up into the Fifties and split a piece of Lindy's cheesecake, two penniless young women on a lark, having a ball. Sharon had loved New York and often missed it. She continued to sing, and even added a few saucy bumps and grinds to her walk as she climbed onto her porch and inserted the key into the lock. The air was clear, the nighttime temperature down in the forties. She shivered slightly as she opened the door.

Commander mugged her in the entry hall. The German shepherd reared up on his hindquarters to lick her face, whining as if he hadn't seen her in years. Sharon giggled as she said, "Down. *Down,* dammit, you're going to mess up my . . ." She turned toward the den. Sheila and the teenagers huddled in the alcove.

Sheila glanced sideways, out the front window. "Is she with you?"

Melanie breathed, "*Is* she, Mom?"

Trish stared bug-eyed. Sheila was in the same hugging pants and puff-sleeved blouse she'd worn to

Planet Hollywood. The girls had changed into jeans and tees.

Sharon grinned. "Is who with me?"

"Come on." Melanie brushed past her mother, half ran to the front door, and peered out through the peephole. She turned back. "Where is she, Mom?"

Sharon rubbed Commander's snout. "She had to go."

Sheila and the teenagers sagged in unison.

"She'll be calling me. Maybe we can visit her." Sharon moved into the den with the others following. Commander panted along, nuzzling Sharon's leg.

Melanie's voice was an octave higher than normal. "The paper says she'll be here several days."

Sharon sank down on the couch, dumped her belongings on the cushion, and scratched Commander behind the ears. "Afraid she's changed her plans."

Melanie's features screwed up in a frown. "Aw, Mom . . ."

"Couldn't be helped. She has commitments." Sharon felt Commander's hindquarters, near the hip joint. The lump in the shepherd's flesh seemed larger than in the past, and Sharon wondered if the vet should have a look. Touching the imbedded bullet sent tremors racing up her spine, and brought back images of the man who'd shot Commander two years ago. Later that same night Sharon had killed the guy. She patted the dog and leaned back on the sofa.

Trish poked Sheila from behind. "Are you going to ask her?"

Sharon frowned. "Ask me what?"

"Okay, I'm guilty," Sheila said. "I've invited us'ns to spend the night with you. Even rented *Dumb and Dumber* for the kids to watch in the bedroom. Got a movie for us old ladies, too."

"Of course it's okay," Sharon said. "And what are we watching?"

Sheila cleared her throat, moved across the room to the VCR, and held up a Blockbuster Video case. Rather sheepishly she exhibited the title. *Fatal Instinct.*

Sharon expelled a sigh of exasperation. "Sheila . . ."

Both girls regarded Sharon as if she were the Wicked Witch of the West. "You always get to watch the good stuff," Melanie grumbled.

Sharon rolled her eyes. She folded her arms. "Okay, girls, into the bedroom. You'll love Jim Carrey, trust me. If I catch either of you peeking at what's showing in the living room, there's going to be the devil to pay. Namely me."

Sharon slung one arm over the back of the sofa, her lips parted in envy. Shown on the home entertainment center screen, Darla Cowan's bare buns were ridges of muscle. God, as if a hypodermic needle wouldn't penetrate. The camera followed as Darla crept toward a naked couple writhing in a king-size bed, a butcher knife held loosely by her thigh. As Darla neared the bed and raised the knife, Sharon wondered whether her head-to-toe tan was from nude sunbathing, or if they'd applied some body makeup. Sharon said to Sheila, "I don't know about this."

Sheila poked a mound of vanilla ice cream into her mouth and licked the spoon. "If it bothers you, stop watching. I'm just getting into it."

Sharon had a sip of apple juice. That Sheila could pig out on ice cream—or chicken fried steak, pasta, just about anything, for that matter—and never seem to gain an ounce made Sharon want to regurgitate. Sharon had weakened earlier in the week and had consumed an old-fashioned chocolate malt at lunch. The following morning she'd gained a pound. A half hour ago she'd shed her courtroom suit and put on cutoffs along with an old Texas Longhorns sweatshirt. She said to Sheila, "How can she?"

"You're not with the program, sister. Come on, if it didn't bother Darla Cowan to film that scene, why should we worry about watching it?"

Sharon blinked and looked away as Darla executed the couple in the bed, the camera panning to the ceiling as blood spattered the walls in gory gobs. "Oh, it bothered her," Sharon said. "At least it did at first. By now she may play those scenes without thinking twice about it."

Sheila twirled her spoon around inside the carton of Häagen-Dazs vanilla Swiss almond. Commander lay nearby, his gaze riveted on the ice cream, his tongue lolling to one side in a begging attitude. Sheila had a bite and snickered.

"What's so funny?" Sharon said.

"Just you."

"Why me?"

"You come unglued over those scenes your ex lover boy plays on that television series, and his stuff is under the blankets or through a shower curtain where you can't see anything. But Darla Cowan's practically doing it on-screen, and you're defending her."

"I think anything sexual on network television is out of place," Sharon said, "regardless of whether it's Rob or anyone else."

Sheila pointed at the TV. "And that *isn't* out of place? It's whatever's out of place that seems to make the world go 'round."

Sharon thought that one over. Damn Sheila and her points anyway. Finally Sharon said, "Consenting adults can watch anything they want."

"So I'm consenting. Let me watch already."

"You think I'm overreacting to Rob's show because he's Melanie's father?"

Sheila jammed her spoon into the ice cream and left the handle sticking up. "That's putting it mildly."

"So okay, I'm partial to Darla," Sharon said. "She was the first person I met in New York. First day of acting classes. A long time before Rob and me."

"Which means that you won't criticize a friend. That's what I like about you. I'll confide in you my plans to be a hooker."

"Darla's a helluva lot more than a friend. We were both twenty-one when we moved to New York. Both scared to death. We got our first parts on the very same day. Even after Rob and I got together, Darla moved into the same building with us just to be near me. Rob resented it some."

"What's to resent?" Sheila said. "Considering that absolutely goddess body, I'm surprised he didn't hit on her."

"Oh, he did. And pulled back more than one bloody nub for his efforts. She didn't tell me until after Rob and I had split the blankets. Darla's the kind who would never horn in on a friend's relationship, and with that school of piranhas swimming around the showbiz circuit, I'll tell you that's a rarity.

"The first night I spent away from Rob," Sharon said, "I was at her place. All through my pregnancy she'd call me every day, come by if she possibly could. And when Melanie was born, that was a tough delivery, Sheil. I don't want to ever go through something like that alone. I woke up in the hospital and there she was, sitting by the end of the bed. First thing she did was kiss both of my cheeks, God love her." Sharon lowered her gaze, kneading her hands. "I hope she hasn't gotten herself in trouble."

Sheila looked up, attentive. "With that actor piece of dung?"

Sharon managed a smile. "You don't even know him."

"I know the type. She needs to get away from that guy."

"That's where she's headed," Sharon said. "To get her things and hook 'em back to L.A. Says with the publicity, she'll break it off gradually. On again, off again for a while, and then splitsville."

"Baloney. She has to end it right here, right now. The more she sees of him, the better chance she'll get seriously hurt. The psychology of abuse is my ballyard, and that's what she should do."

Sharon licked her lips and had a sip of apple juice. She set down her glass. "That's the way she'd do it in real life, Sheil. But Darla's in the movies. It's this expression they've got, you know?"

5

Marian Cortez, the graveyard-shift desk clerk at the Mansion on Turtle Creek, was well groomed, articulate, and versed in the art of being snooty. She was tall and slender, spoke with a faint Hispanic accent, and watched over her station with the sharpest of eyes.

For a personality of Darla Cowan's stature to hurry into the lobby alone at that time of night, minus bodyguards, hoopla, and drumroll, surprised Cortez greatly, but she was far too cool for public displays and quickly hid her surprise. She warmly greeted the actress, handed the presidential suite card key over the counter, and snappily clicked her clicker. Uniformed bellhops came from two directions as if their pants were on fire. One of the bellmen reached for the overnight case which dangled from Cowan's fingers.

"No, thanks," Darla said firmly. "I won't be needing these guys, and I won't be staying long." Then she turned on her heel and marched beneath a crystal chandelier on her way to the elevators. She passed a gentleman in a tux and a woman with blued hair wearing an evening dress, both of whom did double-takes and stared after Cowan as if they'd just seen the queen.

Cortez nervously shuffled papers as the actress paraded through the lobby. It was a rigid Mansion policy that no one—but *no one,* and most certainly not an international sex symbol—was to flit unattended through the hotel without an offer of assistance. Cortez's predecessor, in fact, had lost her job for letting George Carlin carry his own suitcase from the desk to the elevator.

Keeping the rules in mind, and recalling that the key to survival in the celebrity-pampering business lay in covering one's ass, Cortez flew into action. She had a quick and pointed conference with the bellhops. All agreed that Darla Cowan had turned down their offer to help tote her belongings, and further agreed that documentation was imperative in case management should climb their backsides. For assurances' sake, they signed their names to a written description of the incident which Cortez penned on hotel stationery, squinting at the ornate lobby clock to record the time of Darla's arrival as she did. It was 12:07 A.M., seven minutes after midnight, in the wee small hours of Saturday morning.

Darla Cowan's reappearance in the lobby came sometime between twelve-thirty and one A.M., and under the circumstances it wasn't surprising that not a single witness could pinpoint the time. She stumbled as she came off the elevator, pulling a suitcase on wheels and carrying the same overnight case that she'd taken upstairs. Tears ran down her face, streaking her makeup. Her hair was in wild disarray. One side of her sweater was ripped, exposing a creamy shoulder and half of one breast. There was an ugly red mark, rapidly turning purple, on her left cheek, and her lip was swollen. She dragged her luggage halfway to the exit, where a bellman intercepted her. He offered assistance and, trained to be delicate in such matters, pretended not to notice that Darla looked beat to hell.

"Just leave me alone," Darla screamed hysterically, causing all heads within earshot to turn in her direction. There were only four people in the lobby: two bellhops, an elderly man who sat on a couch reading a newspaper, and Marian Cortez, who'd closed out the register at half past midnight and was counting the evening's receipts. Darla tugged the suitcase toward the exit, sobbing, pausing long enough to say to the bellman, "Call me a taxi, will you?" The bellman complied, sprinting over to the concierge desk to use the phone. Marian Cortez made a precise record of the bellman's offer of assistance,

winking at him across the lobby as he dialed for a cab, but somehow failed to note the time.

Darla hauled her belongings out onto the porch to wait, and weathered the stares of passersby and honks of recognition from cruising autos for about fifteen minutes until her taxi arrived. The doorman would remember that as he held the cab's door open for her, Darla trembled and cried out of control. Her rented Geo Prism was to remain in the hotel drive for several days.

The cab driver was a half Mexican-American, half Cherokee Indian named Stand-in-the-Water Dominguez, who did his best to console Darla on the ride to DFW Airport. His efforts were to no avail. She continued to sob as the cabbie deposited her at the American terminal, where she paid the fare and included a generous tip. The driver waited until Darla's luggage was loaded onto a cart, then watched as Darla followed the skycap into the terminal.

It was to be a matter of record that Darla Cowan bought a one-way ticket on AA Flight 3062 bound for Los Angeles, and that her suitcase and overnight bag made it safely into the airliner's luggage compartment. There was only one other first-class passenger on board the 707, a businessman from Atlanta whose ticket included a Dallas stopover. Darla sat as far as possible from the man and ignored his attempts at getting friendly.

Apparently she'd regained her composure by the time she landed at LAX because—the media in Los Angeles being on a twenty-four-hour celebrity watch—a photographer from the *Times,* at the airport to pick up his cousin, snapped her picture as she boarded a limousine. In the photo which appeared in the following day's arts section, her hair was perfectly fixed. She'd changed into a fresh blouse, and she displayed her most dazzling, knock-'em-dead smile. The shadows and the angle of the picture hid her bruises, and her swollen lip lent a pouty effect to her grin.

6

When David Spencer was a no-show for the Saturday morning taping of *Good Morning, Texas* on Channel 8, the Dallas ABC affiliate, the Mansion's switchboard lit up like Mission Control. First the station called, then the ABC coordinator from New York, and finally Curtis Nussbaum, Spencer's agent from out in L.A. "Look, sweetheart," he told the desk clerk, "I got no time to dally. You go upstairs and raise that boy from his hangover, and tell him Nussbaum's on the line. You don't want heat from your boss, you get a move on."

The Mansion's daytime desk clerk was named Anna Dorn, a willowy, thirty-fivish woman who was every bit as snooty as Marian Cortez on the graveyard shift. She listened nervously. Threats to go over one's head were sticky wickets, because she never knew how much stroke the threatener might have. She put Nussbaum on hold while she called her supervisor at home to learn that, yes, Curtis Nussbaum was David Spencer's agent, and that, yes, Curtis Nussbaum had mucho clout with the Mansion's corporate offices. Dorn then clicked back on to tell Nussbaum that she'd take his number and have Spencer return the call. Nussbaum responded that if he didn't hear from the actor in twenty minutes, there'd be hell to pay.

Dorn then rang up housekeeping and told one of the cleaning people to check David Spencer's room. "No, missy," the Hispanic maid told her, "bustin' in on somebody got a Do Not Disturb sign on they door ain't in my job description. Never know what the guy's

got goin', all them womens pantin' for his underwear."
There was a click and the line went dead.

Dorn fretted, then decided to take matters into her
own hands. She ran a blank card key through the mag-
netized slot, creating a spare for the presidential suite,
had her assistant relieve her at the desk, and went up
on the elevator.

The presidential suite was half a hallway removed
from its neighboring rooms, and overlooked the patio
and rose garden. Anna Dorn timidly knocked, then
waited five full minutes before she knocked a bit
louder, but still got no response. She then slid the card
key through the slot, listened to the tumblers hum,
opened the door, and went inside.

The room was in darkness, the thick drapes drawn
over the windows. Dorn reached inside the bathroom
and flicked on the light, casting dim illumination over
the canopied four-poster king-size, the French provin-
cial rose-patterned sofa and chairs. She squinted at the
bed; there was indeed a human form huddled beneath
the covers.

The situation was weird; Anna Dorn was about to
walk into a darkened hotel suite to awaken Hollywood's sexiest male star. She wondered what thousands of women would give to be in her place. Her
spit dried and her knees trembled. She firmed her resolve and walked slowly ahead. Halfway through the
foyer her foot slipped. She took another step and
slipped again.

Dorn fished in the waist pocket of her uniform for
a tiny flashlight and clicked the switch, and shined the
light around her on brown Mexican tile. She stood in
a pool of red liquid, which looked for all the world
like blood.

Dallas homicide detective Stan Green thought that
day duty was a piece of cake after three months on
the graveyard shift. Jesus, on the night shift he'd seen
women raped and stabbed, convenience store clerks
with half their heads blown away, and one Jamaican

drug dealer with his ears cut off and a crack pipe shoved up his rectum. Daylight duty generally consisted of investigative work: interviewing witnesses, reading lab reports, cleaning up details after the night crews had viewed all the corpses in person. Not only was the day shift safer, investigation required a lot of time away from the office, tracking leads, which gave a man plenty of opportunity to catch up on his fucking off. Fucking off, in fact, was what Green liked best about his job.

When the shift lieutenant ordered him to proceed to the Mansion on Turtle Creek, Green thought that someone must be joking. Though he'd lived in Dallas all of his life, he had never so much as set foot inside the Mansion lobby. He'd heard that a man could get soaked twenty bucks for a bowl of soup in the place, Jesus, *eight dollars* for a whiskey neat, water back, which a homicide cop could mooch for free in one of the Ross Avenue Mexican joints, seven nights a week. A stiff at the Mansion has to be a put-on, Green thought, someone from the night shift calling from home to pull the lieutenant's leg. David Spencer? Sure, and Marlon fucking Brando, too. Green's partner had gone to lunch in their assigned vehicle, so Green fired up an unmarked Ford Taurus from the motor pool and headed for the Mansion alone.

He arrived in the parking lot at a few minutes after noon in sixty-degree weather, with a strong fall breeze stripping red and yellow leaves from branches all along Turtle Creek Boulevard. The leaves rose and fell in the wind like flushed birds. A gray CSU truck sat off to one side, and Green decided that if this was a joke, there were a lot of people in on it. He parked and walked toward the hotel entry, tilted against the wind, his pants molded around his legs, his tie standing out like a flag at the Ballpark in Arlington.

Ten minutes later, Green followed the hotel manager down the corridor outside the presidential suite. The manager was around forty, the hand-wringing type, and Green responded to the man's questions with a series of noncommittal grunts. Could the media be kept out of this? How the hell would Green know? Could the police keep from alarming the other guests? Green supposed they could, as long as questioning the shit out of them didn't scare anybody. The manager frowned as he ushered the detective into the suite. Green crossed the threshold, stepped over a pool of blood, and looked around.

The lab techs had it in gear, dusting for prints, vacuuming, dumping the contents of the cleaner bags into plastic evidence containers. A wiry Oriental was down on his haunches, soaking up blood with a cotton swab. The soaked cotton he carefully placed in a Ziploc baggie, then folded the baggie into an envelope for transmission to the DNA people. There's plenty of blood, Green thought, Jesus, red smears on the walls and across the mirrors, puddles in the foyer, pools soaked into the carpets. The assistant M.E. in charge was named Tupelow, a gray-haired man with a bald spot at his crown, wearing a knee-length white coat. Tupelow stood near the bed, looking down at a corpse face up on the mattress. A plastic sheet covered the body from the neck down. Green went up and tapped the AME on the shoulder.

Tupelow looked around. Shaggy eyebrows moved closer together as he peered beyond the detective toward the exit. "What, you're flying solo?" Tupelow said.

"Partner's grabbing a bite." Green looked at the body. "I saw his latest."

"And his lastest. I don't know, my teenage daughter thinks this one might rise like Jesus."

The famous face was slack in death. There was a small entry wound in David Spencer's temple, with blood and brain matter smeared on the pillow. Green looked around the room. "Lot of blood, huh?"

Tupelow shook his head, at the same time drawing a thermometer from his breast pocket. He wore surgical gloves. "Evidently the bullet was insurance. Stab wounds all over the chest and abdomen, penetrated both the heart and lungs. No need to shoot this guy to put his lights out. Gimme a hand rolling him over, will you?" He yanked the sheet and grinned at the corpse. "Excuse me, Mr. Matinee Idol Super Cockhound, sir," the M.E. said, "but I gotta take your temperature. Your tongue don't look in good shape, so I'm gonna shove this up your butt. You mind? Won't hurt a bit, okay?"

7

Sharon Hays whooped it up as her law school alma mater played Oklahoma in the Cotton Bowl. She bounced around on the sofa, stuffing popcorn, giving the hook 'em horns sign over and over as the Longhorns drove steadily forward. Sheila Winston sat in a recliner reading a novel. On the tube, an orange tight end snared one over his shoulder, held on as a defensive back practically cut him in half, and rolled to a stop at the Sooner four-yard line. Sharon growled in bloodlust. Sheila yawned and turned a page.

"Go, Horns," Sharon yelled. "Stuff it down their throats."

"Could you lower the volume?" Sheila said. "You're going to wake up the dusk-till-dawn crowd."

The women had turned in at one in the morning, leaving Trish and Melanie still going strong. Sharon got up around seven o'clock and went in to fix coffee. She'd gone to the VCR and hit the Rewind button, but the *Fatal Instinct* tape had been missing from its slot. Sharon had repossessed the erotic murder flick from the sleeping teenagers, mentally kicking herself for her failure to lock up the videocassette to begin with. Now it was after two in the afternoon, and she'd yet to hear a peep out of the girls. Commander was curled up in the corner of the living room, snoring away, and Sharon wondered if multiple showings of Darla Cowan in the nude had done the shepherd in.

The Texas team broke the huddle and trotted up to the line; Sharon sat intensely forward as the quarterback barked the signals. Eight years removed from her

U of Texas days, tremors still raced up her backbone whenever the Longhorn band played "The Eyes of Texas." The sight of the orange and white team racing onto the field, fists pumping, drove her into a frenzy.

"Rock 'em. Go." Sharon tensed in anticipation as the center snapped the ball. Visible in the corner of her eye, Sheila put down her book and stuck her fingers in her ears. Well, pooh, Sharon thought, what does a Yalie know?

The quarterback rolled to his right behind a wall of blockers, and streaked for the corner of the end zone. Sharon leaped from the couch, yelling. They're going to score, she thought, sweet hallelujah and Daryl Royal, they're going to . . .

The screen went blank. A male announcer cut in, saying, "We interrupt this program for a CNN News bulletin."

The wind whooshed out of Sharon's sails in a gust. Her body sagged. "What are they . . . ?" She turned in bewilderment. "Sheila, did you see . . ."

Sheila picked up her book. "Probably just some insignificant Middle East crisis. Nothing as important as the Big Orange, right?"

"Big Orange is a drink." Sharon took a step toward the television. "They interrupted right in the middle of . . ."

Sheila testily rustled pages. "Oh, for God's sake. You're only talking a minute or two. Relax." She glanced past Sharon toward the set, started to look away, then stared wide-eyed at the screen. "Sharon," she said softly.

Sharon turned her attention back to the TV. At first the scene didn't register, the wide steps, the ornate white pillars, paramedics rolling a gurney to a waiting ambulance. There was a shrouded body strapped to the gurney. The scene changed instantly to a long-distance shot, the same porch and pillars with stately elms and sycamores towering on all sides. Sharon sank down on the sofa. As she watched, an athletic-looking man in a cheap suit walked toward the ambulance, moving in an arrogant slouch, his arms swinging. God, Sharon thought, Stan Green. "It's the Mansion," she murmured. She grabbed the remote and boosted the volume a couple of notches. Sheila laid her book aside and straightened the recliner to its upright position.

The announcer droned, "The body has been positively identified as that of David Spencer. The actor was in Texas for a Planet Hollywood opening. Authorities have declined comment as to the cause of death.

"Spencer, star of the recent hit *Spring of the Comanche,* was traveling in the company of his girlfriend, actress Darla Cowan. There's no word at present of the actress's condition or whereabouts. More on the national news at five. For now, back to your network programming."

The scene changed again, accompanied by a surge of crowd noise, as the Texas Longhorns celebrated a touchdown in the end zone. Players jumped up and down, hugging each other, patting rumps and slapping helmets. The point-after unit streamed onto the field.

"Damn," Sharon said, grabbing the remote. "God *damn* them, interrupting with this silly football." She pointed the remote and grabbed the *TV Guide* from the end table. "What's the twenty-four-hour news channel, Sheil?"

The story was on every network and cable station. Sharon spent the rest of the afternoon flipping channels while Sheila watched with her book open across her lap. When the girls bounced in around three o'clock, clamoring for food, their mothers responded in unison by hissing, "Shh!" Trish and Melanie buttoned their lips and sat on the floor, silent for the only time in recent memory. Commander, his bladder filled to the bursting point, got up around four o'clock to scratch and whine at the back door. Trish let the shepherd out and returned at once to her viewing station.

The networks played one-up, scrambling for ratings, airing anything which even hinted at news of the killing, the result being total confusion as to what had actually occurred. The first reports hinted that both David Spencer and Darla Cowan were dead, with a later revelation that Darla had been only wounded. Then the reporters rescinded *that* incorrect bit of information and replaced it with another untruth, that Darla was missing. This error produced a heated telephone call to the network from Darla's agent, Aaron Levy, who stated that the actress was at home in L.A. The talking heads then did another about-face, reporting that Darla hadn't been in Texas at all. A witness—a man in a Dallas Cowboys sideline jacket and Texas Rangers batting helmet, carrying a Dallas Stars hockey puck—shot down *that* theory by swearing he'd seen Darla in the flesh outside Planet Hollywood, and that Spencer " 'as gonna beat the . . . he 'as gonna rough her up 'fore this chick come around an' lowered the boom on his . . ." At which point the interview terminated with the sports enthusiast gaping helplessly at the camera.

This is ridiculous, Sharon thought. She dropped the remote on the sofa, left Sheila and the girls riveted to the television reports, and stalked into her bedroom. Enough of this. Sharon was going to get the story straight from the horse's mouth.

She found her purse on the dresser and rummaged inside for Darla's number, the private line at the house in Malibu or Pacific Palisades or wherever it was that the fantasy couple lived. Sharon sat on the edge of the bed to punch in the number. After three rings a click sounded. With tape static in the background, David Spencer said, "You've reached 555-3030. Leave a message after the tone." There were two more clicks, followed by a beep.

Sharon licked her lips. This was really weird, listening to a dead man's voice from a half continent away. She nearly hung up, then realized that with the hoopla brewing on television, Darla wouldn't have answered even if she'd been at home. Sharon inhaled a breath, then said softly, "It's Sharon Hays, Darla. I've been watching the news, and I'm worried to death about you. Call me, huh?" She dictated her own number, then replaced the receiver in its cradle and drummed her fingers.

Melanie called out from the living room, "It's you, Mom."

Sharon watched the phone. She raised her voice. "I'm in the bedroom waiting for a call back, Melanie. What's me?"

"On television. It's you."

And Sheila added, "And me, too, Sharon. Better have a look."

Sharon left the bedroom and stood in the corridor leading to the den. Visible over the top of Sheila's head, the TV picture showed yesterday's scene in front of Planet Hollywood. The voice-over announced that this footage was "exclusive to Channel 5." There were crystal-clear pictures of Darla wrestling with David Spencer near the restaurant entry, of Sharon as she pushed the actor down and his head slammed onto the step, of Sharon gaping dumbly at the man in the Crocodile Dundee outfit as Spencer writhed on the ground and, finally, of Darla and Sharon as they fled the scene.

The announcer said, "The woman shoving David Spencer and then entering the car with Darla Cowan is local criminal attorney Sharon Hays, who, sources say, is a longtime friend of Miss Cowan's dating back to the time when both were stage actresses in New York City. Miss Hays's former lover is *Minions of Justice* star Rob Stanley—"

Oh, God, Sharon thought, please don't say it.

"—who is the father of Hays's child."

Sharon's heart skipped a beat as she looked at Melanie. Her relationship with Rob had been pretty much general knowledge since Rob had hit the big time and spouted off to the media that he had a daughter in Dallas, but, *God*. Kicking that dead horse on a newscast, that was . . .

Melanie turned to her mother, as did Trish. Melanie said, "He's talking about me, isn't he?"

Sharon lowered her lashes and absorbed a sharp look from Sheila. "Yes, sweetheart, he is," Sharon said.

"It's okay, Mom," Melanie said. "It's cool." She turned back to the screen.

But it wasn't cool, and Sharon damn well knew it. That Melanie was born out of wedlock, and that everyone in creation knew it, that would *never* be cool, never in a million—

The bedroom telephone rang.

Sharon went in to take the call with her heart sinking into her stomach. Melanie had known the story of her birth since she'd been old enough to understand anything, and accepted the situation for what it was, but that didn't make public broadcasts on the subject any easier to take. Damn the mighty media all to hell.

The phone rang a second time. Sharon reached the bed, picked up the receiver, and said, "Darla?"

It wasn't Darla. A man said in a cracking basso, "Sharon?"

Sharon didn't recognize the voice, and at once assumed a businesslike tone. "Yes? This is Sharon Hays." Could be a prospective client, anything.

"It's Stan, Sharon."

"Green?" Sharon felt a surge of irritation; just talking to her one-time lover churned her emotions into an uproar.

"Yep," he said. "Just old Stan the Man."

"Yeah, right."

"Darla Cowan is a friend of yours?"

Sharon gritted her teeth. "I guess you'd say that."

"Well, listen, you been watching television?"

"Yes." Sharon's tone was cool and impersonal.

"We're up to our fannies in alligators on this one, Shar."

"Sharon, Stan. Sharon Hays."

"Yeah, sure. We've known each other, right?" Green laughed.

Sharon moved the receiver from one ear to the other. "What do you want?"

"Hey, I know it's Saturday and all."

"That it is."

"But, well, you know, the mail must go through."

"Sure. Rain, sleet, and snow."

There were four beats of silence, accompanied by crackling static. Green said, "The thing is, we need to talk to you."

"Who's 'we?' "

"Me. Milt Breyer. Kathleen, couple of other people."

Oh, great, Sharon thought. Mr. Ex-Lover-Mistake-of-My-Life Green, and Mr. Sexual-Harassment-Grab-Your-Boob-for-You Breyer, along with Ms.-Lay-Your-Superior of the D.A.'s staff Kathleen Fraterno. What a lovely weekend this has turned out to be. "What about?" Sharon said.

"Just a couple of things, about you and the actress. Look, we could come by, won't take long."

Sharon forced herself to think rationally. No matter her personal feelings, Green had a point; in any murder investigation timing was a very big deal. "I'll talk to you," Sharon said. "But I'd as soon none of this went on in my home."

8

Sharon watched the television monitor until Darla Cowan's limo pulled away from Planet Hollywood. So there we go again, she thought. She listened to a series of metallic clicks as the technician reset the VCR and the screen went blank. She propped one knee against the edge of the conference table. "I don't remember anything other than what I've told you. And I've already seen that tape, earlier today on my TV at home." The shot of her shoving David Spencer had been a whole lot clearer than Sharon would have liked. The camera had lingered forever on her dumbstruck pose as she'd gaped into the crowd, her gaze resting on a man in a buckskin jacket and wide-brimmed hat. The poor guy had stared back at her, of course, and the TV picture made them look like old friends instead of ships passing in the night. The man's hands-up shrug had seemed a gesture of communication, but Sharon now decided that the guy had been saying to himself, What's with this crazy female? She pictured him now as he explained to his wife or friends that he'd been an innocent bystander, and that he'd never seen the insane Hays woman before in his life. She turned her attention to the group around the conference table.

Across from Sharon sat an FBI agent named Leamon, a pipe smoker who burned a sweet-smelling tobacco. He was thin-faced and wore the standard government I-don't-believe-a-word-you're-saying expression. He held the pipe by its bowl, waving the stem around. "And you're certain Miss Cowan made no threats to Mr. Spencer?"

"Darla was only trying to get away," Sharon said. "I took my eyes off her for a few seconds while I was shoving the guy, but I don't think Darla was shooting Spencer the bird over my shoulder or anything. Believe me, she was too frightened to be making threats."

"We?" Leamon remained deadpan. "You said, 'We watched her every movement.' "

"Right. Sheila Winston and I. Sheila's a psychiatrist, listed in the phone book if you want to talk to her."

Milton Breyer cut in. "You should add that Sheila Winston is your close friend, shouldn't you?"

Sharon set her jaw. "I don't know why I should add that, Milton. Sheila wouldn't lie to protect her own mother, and you know it."

She was the center of attention inside the FBI's grill-'em-and-drill-'em room. The Dallas fibbies officed in a refurbished warehouse building overlooking the West End district. Seven stories below, the Saturday night crowd milled around outside Dick's Last Resort, the Gator Café, and Planet Hollywood. It was gathering dusk; the streetlights cast greenish sodium glows through the conference-room windows. Huddled around the ten-seat table were Milton Breyer and Kathleen Fraterno from the Dallas County D.A.'s staff, homicide detective Stan Green, and a herd of federal people. Leamon, the man with the pipe—droll little mouth drawn up in a bow, a right jolly old elf and all that, Sharon thought—was doing most of the talking. The guy on his left, with close-cropped kinky hair, was the special agent in charge of the region, and the chubby-cheeked woman seated beside the AIC had flown in this afternoon from Washington. Big Potatoes with a capital P. Sharon now had a feel for what was going on; the FBI, sensing the publicity, had horned in on the local investigation, all of which was S.O.P. when one dealt with the feds. Sharon was so angry she was practically quivering. What Stan

Green had said was a fact-finding session had already turned into an evidence-gathering ordeal, with the emphasis clearly on Darla Cowan. It didn't surprise her that Darla was a suspect, given the circumstances, but that the investigation team had already ruled out all other possibilities was a bit of a shock.

Leamon wore glasses in wire frames and had a mole on his cheek. His occasional eye twitch said that he didn't like having his superiors looking over his shoulder. With the big dogs in the room Leamon was pretty much sticking to the manual, and for that Sharon was glad. Unsupervised, the FBI could be an unbelievable pain in the ass. Leamon said, "And what about Miss Cowan's attitude?"

"I'm not sure what you're asking," Sharon said.

"Did she seem to harbor resentment toward Mr. Spencer?"

"You'd have to ask her. Look, the guy was abusive, and there would be something wrong with her if she wasn't resentful of that. But that's my own observation, nothing Darla told me."

"Seems odd that you ladies would spend the evening together and the subject wouldn't come up." Leamon looked at the AIC, then at the lady from Washington.

Sharon twisted in her chair and crossed one denim-clad leg over the other. "Oh, it came up, mainly in the context of Darla's plan to leave the guy. I never specifically asked her if she resented David Spencer, and I don't recall her saying one way or the other. If you want my opinion, you're barking up the wrong tree listing Darla as a suspect."

Leamon said, "She was totally passive in the relationship?"

"Those are your words, Agent. But Darla was never an aggressive person when I knew her well, and I didn't see that her personality had changed much during the brief time we spent together. It's been thirteen years since we were really close."

"Let's talk about last night. The two of you went to dinner—"

"In Fort Worth, yes."

"—and then Miss Cowan drove you home around eleven. That's your story?"

"Right as rain," Sharon said.

"And until this evening you weren't even aware of the incident at the Mansion?"

"Of the killing?"

Leamon nodded. The pipe bobbed up and down. The sign which had greeted Sharon outside the office stated that this was a no-smoking facility. If Leamon's bosses didn't object, Sharon wasn't about to.

"Early this afternoon, actually," Sharon said, "when the bulletin cut in on the football game. We watched the news reports most of the day. When I saw myself on television and then received the phone call from Mr. Green, I agreed to meet with the Dallas County people."

"So you came in voluntarily," Leamon said.

The agent's tone sent Sharon into orbit. She detested Stan Green and Milton Breyer—not necessarily in that order—and had a coolish relationship with Kathleen Fraterno, but at least she could be up-front with the locals. The feds burned her fanny no end with their openly suspicious attitudes. These people wouldn't believe Christ on the cross, Sharon thought, so why am I wasting my time? She showed Leamon her most impersonal smile. "Come in voluntarily before what, Agent? Before you surrounded my home and rolled out the bazookas?"

Leamon clenched his pipe lightly between his teeth. "Before we came to you."

"This may surprise you," Sharon said, "but everybody in the world isn't hiding something. I learned of the killing. After I received the phone call, I felt that I had useful information. I have law enforcement training and know that the sooner such information is presented, the better. I expected to give this information to Detective Green. Frankly, if I'd known I'd end

up in a summit meeting on Saturday night, I might've
waited until Monday."

"Good that you came in when you did," Leamon
said.

Sharon testily drummed her fingers. "You mean, it
makes me less of a suspect?"

Leamon didn't bat an eye. He had a receding hair-
line and a narrow forehead. Reels turned inside a tape
recorder next to his elbow. "I've got to say, you don't
seem particularly frightened. Killer running around
and all."

Oh, for God's sake, Sharon thought. She blinked.
"How does one go about sounding frightened, Agent?
Go, *eek*? I live with my thirteen-year-old daughter, no
man around the house, but I haven't seen anything
which places us in danger. But, *eek,* if it makes me
more convincing."

The feds watched her. Just what they want, Sharon
thought, someone flying off the handle, and she was
damned if she'd give them one more ounce of satisfaction. She fought for composure.

Leamon looked questioningly around at his cohorts.

The lady from Washington spoke up. "Just what did
you discuss over dinner with Miss Cowan?"

"Old times. Acting classes. A few plays in which we
appeared." Sharon measured her words, careful to tell
the truth but at the same time revealing as little as
possible. She'd stopped communicating voluntarily
with federal people shortly after leaving the District
Attorney's staff, when the Equal Opportunity folks
had pressured her to file sexual-harassment charges
against Milton Breyer. She'd made the mistake of responding to a couple of OEO requests, then had spent
the better part of a year in getting rid of the freaking pests.

"I don't know as we'd agree," Leamon said, "that
she isn't a viable suspect. She was on the scene at the
proper time, and there is ample evidence of conflict
between Miss Cowan and the victim. As a matter of
record, we're not investigating a murder here. That's

their"—he indicated Breyer, Kathleen Fraterno, and Stan Green—"function. We don't interfere in local affairs if we can help it."

Yeah, Sharon thought. And tomorrow pigs will fly. "Okay, I'll bite," she said. "Exactly why are the feds involved?"

The lady from Washington spoke up in a husky voice reminiscent of Faye Dunaway. "Miss Hays, I'm Mariah Davis. Let me outline our role for you. We're attached to the violent-crimes unit. Our interest is, has someone crossed interstate boundaries to avoid prosecution or to aid in commission of a crime?" Mariah Davis was a large woman, wearing an oversized dress with padded shoulders.

Sharon nodded. "You folks move quickly, Ms. Davis." She had it now, picturing FBI Washington tuning in on the newscasts and then dispatching Mariah Davis to discover if there was anything afoot to allow the fibbies to cash in on the publicity. Likely the feds would throw their weight around for a few days, making certain that the newspapers were aware that the FBI was on the case, and then retreat into the sunset. In the meantime, Breyer, Green, and Fraterno wouldn't be able to do anything productive with the fibbies in their faces, with the result that the investigation was fucked beyond repair. Sharon watched Mariah Davis with feigned interest. "If anyone crossed state lines to commit a murder, it wasn't Darla Cowan."

"What makes you so certain?" Davis said. "Our experience is with these artistic types, actors and whatnot, they're pretty tightly wound." She poured herself a glass of water. Sharon noted that Ms. Davis's tone of voice had reflected a low opinion of actors in general, which was pretty much the view from Pompey's head. Brad Pitt? Julia Roberts? Oh, the envy. Sharon Hays (or anyone else, for that matter, whose view of showbiz came mainly from a subway train)? Wasted lives. Sharon would love to have a dollar for every time someone had asked her during her New York stint, When are you going to stop this nonsense and do something productive? Gets in your blood, ladies and gents, Sharon thought, and the itch is with you for life. She was certain that if she hadn't become pregnant with Melanie, she'd be riding subways to auditions and existing on bologna sandwiches to this very day. Mariah Davis had a sip of water and went on.

"Miss Cowan's face was swollen as if she'd been in a fight when she left the hotel. Her clothes were torn, and witnesses tell us she was very distraught. If you have information that might dispel our suspicions, Miss Hays, we'd like to hear it."

Sharon opened, then closed her mouth. She wanted to help Darla all she could, but had to admit that Davis had a point. A thought came to her, and she said, "You have the murder weapons? The television report says Spencer was both shot and stabbed. Show me Darla's prints on a gun or knife, and I might feel differently."

Mariah Davis and the other feds exchanged a look which told Sharon she'd struck a nerve. They had no gun, no knife as yet, so score one for Darla's defense. An almost venomous glance from Davis in Milton Breyer's direction told Sharon even more; in mouthing off to the press, old Milt had told more about the crime than the feds would like to have out over the wires. Only the killer could know that Spencer was shot and stabbed, and keeping that a secret from the public should have been priority number one at this point, but thanks to Milt it was all general knowledge. Sharon said, "Sheila would say that Darla wasn't in a frame of mind to kill the guy."

Davis seemed confused. "Sheila?"

"My friend who's a psychiatrist. I've used her as an expert witness in the past. Look, Darla was leaving the guy and spoke very rationally about it. He'd attacked her before, so even if he roughed her up at the hotel she wouldn't come unglued. She'd just make as fast an exit as possible."

Sharon paused. Everyone in the room stared at her.

She leaned back. "I don't have a psychiatry license, folks. Sheila gave a lecture on this topic a couple of months ago. I take pretty good notes, if I'm interested in a subject. The point is, before you haul off and cast accusations, at the very least you should get a doctor's opinion of Darla's state of mind."

Davis glanced around the room, exchanged a couple of looks, then returned her attention to Sharon. "Things will develop on this, of course, and don't think we haven't considered the possibility that someone other than Darla Cowan is the perpetrator. If we're going to eliminate her as a suspect, we do need to talk to her."

Sharon paused. These people could think what they wanted, but she was heaping no coals on the fire without a lot of thought. She said merely, "Darla shouldn't be hard to find. I don't think she's left the country."

"Come on, Sharon." This from Milt Breyer, leaning forward and butting in. "The guy's dead. Cowan leaves the hotel at a gallop and hot-foots it back to California. What are we supposed to think?"

Sharon shrugged and smiled. "You're not supposed to think. You're supposed to deal in hard facts and evidence. Which, apparently, you don't have much of."

Breyer opened his mouth to speak, but Mariah Davis quickly cut in. "It's too early to be identifying suspects, or even to classify this as a murder. Could be self-defense, but without talking to the principal player we can't make such a determination."

Sharon leaned back and scratched her forehead. "The news reports say she landed last night at LAX. Had her picture taken getting into a limo. Doesn't sound as if she's incognito, does it?"

Davis extended a palm-up hand across the table. "Mr. Green, Miss Hayes has made a point. Do you have a comment?"

Green folded his arms and canted sideways in his chair, in a lounging attitude. "We tried to contact her. The only phone number we get is her agent's. Guy named Aaron Levy, tells us he'll talk to Cowan and get back to us. When, he don't say. We don't have time to wait on these people."

Sharon crossed her forearms on the table and scootched up in her chair. "You'all won't like this. But that's part of an agent's job."

"And it's part of our job," Green said, "to determine who offed this bozo and why. Hey, Shar, we're not trying to hardass anybody, but whatever it takes to talk to this woman, we got to do it."

Sharon's eyebrow arched, but otherwise her expression didn't change. "I can't comment on David Spencer from any relevant point of view, because anything I could say would only be what I've heard. Other than yesterday at Planet Hollywood I've never seen him in person, and I've never spoken to the man other than to tell him to leave Darla alone when I pushed him down. I can't speak officially for Darla, since I'm not her attorney. But I do know her fairly well. Darla's a bit of a kook, but I doubt she could kill anyone, and she does believe in mother and flag and all that. I'm sure that as soon as she receives assurances that she's not some sort of murder suspect, she'd be happy to tell you anything you want to know."

"That's one reason we wanted to talk to you, Miss Hays," Agent Leamon said. "Without a lot of legal rigmarole and so we wouldn't have to deal through this agent, do you think you could arrange a meeting for us?"

A corner of Sharon's mouth bunched in thought. Then she said, "I'm afraid you'd find that dealing through me might be tougher than dealing through Darla's agent. I've asked twice whether you consider Darla a suspect, and I'm not getting an answer. Do you, or don't you?"

Green and Breyer looked at each other. Fraterno regarded her folded hands. The federal people showed noncommittal looks. Finally Fraterno said, "Suspect, witness, what's the difference?"

Sharon had a surge of anger. "Oh, beans, Kathleen.

There's a big difference and you know it. Aside from the fact that you're being ridiculous by even hinting that Darla could be involved, unless you're just wanting the publicity."

"Are we?" Breyer suddenly asked.

Sharon showed Breyer a sharp look. "Are you what, Milton?"

"Being ridiculous. We have a dead guy in a hotel room occupied by two people. She's now gone. Publicity's got nothing to do with it. You don't have to be a celebrity to come under suspicion in these circumstances. Joe Shmoe would get the same scrutiny."

Sharon angrily drummed her fingers on her armrest. "Not the *same* scrutiny, Milton, Joe Shmoe would get the benefit of the doubt until you came up with some concrete evidence." She stood. "This meeting is over, ladies and gents."

Leamon raised a hand. "We have more questions."

"Oh, no, you don't." Sharon stepped toward the exit.

"You're a witness as well, Miss Hays," Leamon said. "You went to dinner with the woman."

Sharon paused at the door. She turned back. "That I may be, so why don't you call me Monday and ask for an appointment? I can't tell Darla what to do, but believe me, I'm going to suggest that she not say a word to you without her lawyer present." She opened the door, stepped out into the hall, then came back in. "And I may hire an attorney myself. Anyone talking to you people without one has got a hole in their head."

Sharon got home, stalked past Sheila and the girls as they sat glued to CNN, went into the bedroom, and snatched up the phone. She called Darla's number once more, and once again listened to David Spencer's recording. After the beep Sharon said, "Darla, it's Sharon again. Message number two, and you may now disregard message number one. I'm a bit more than worried about you at this point. Whatever you do, kid, don't discuss all this crap that's on television with anyone before you talk to me, okay?"

9

Sharon spent Sunday afternoon forcing Darla Cowan, CNN news reports transforming her thirteen-year-old affair with Rob into a national event, and all other such matters out of her mind as she drove to the law library at SMU. There she went grimly to work in preparing briefs and other documents in support of her motion to have Tired Darnell's sentence overturned. She stayed until the library closed at midnight, and it was all she could do to drag herself home and into bed.

On Monday morning, armed to the teeth with legal weaponry, she drove directly to the Crowley Courts Building west of downtown. She presented her motion to Judge Arnold Shiver when his court convened at nine a.m., before he'd had a chance to go over his morning calendar. If she followed the normal procedure, sitting timidly in the spectators section until Shiver asked what matters needed to be heard in addition to those already scheduled, then the old goat would leave her cooling her heels until hell froze over. "An urgent matter, Your Honor," she said as she slapped her papers down. "Won't take but a second."

Shiver perched his spectacles on his nose and read the title, which identified the document as a request for reconsideration in the case of Francis Ben Darnell. "Accordin' to the news reports, you should have more on your mind than this nonsense, Miss Hays." Shiver took off his glasses and folded the earpieces. "I got a full calendar."

Sharon looked over her shoulder, where two or

three lawyers lounged in the gallery, reading sports sections or talking to their clients. Full calendar my off hind foot, Sharon thought. "I'm sure you do, Judge," she said. "But due to the time frame on my client's transfer to the penitentiary, I feel this takes precedence."

Shiver's chin thrust out in a pugnacious attitude. "I determine precedence in this courtroom, young lady."

Sharon chewed her lower lip. She looked at the court reporter, who had yet to turn on her shorthand machine. "Your Honor," Sharon said, "may I go on the record here?"

"No, you may not," Shiver snapped. "This boy's got five years, an' five years is what he's gonna do."

Sharon wondered why she was spending so much time on a court appointment. Something about sense of duty to her client. She pictured Tired Darnell and almost lost her resolve. Good Lord, Tired could sleep in the pen as well as on the street. She squared her posture. "I request a ruling on my motion, Your Honor."

"Yeah, okay, bein' as how you're determined." Shiver flipped to the last page in the motion without reading a word, and scribbled his signature on the order which Sharon had prepared. "Motion denied, Miss Hays. Now, I got other matters." He pushed the motion over in Sharon's direction.

Sharon took the bull by the horns. She dug in her satchel and produced another stack of papers. "In that case, Your Honor, please accept our notice of appeal. Also our request for stay of execution on my client's sentence until the appeal's heard. We're asking that he remain in the county jail pending a ruling by the appellate court, Your Honor." She stifled a yawn. It had been her turn to carpool, so she'd been up at six and delivered Trish and Melanie to school around seven.

Shiver continued to bluster, but uncertainty crept into his look. "I've denied your motion to resentence him. Now, you're makin' a motion to keep him outta the penitentiary until you appeal my other rulin'?"

"That's the nuts and bolts, Your Honor."

"I'm denyin' that motion, too, Miss Hays."

"Fine, Judge." Sharon dug into her satchel and piled more paper onto the stack, which was now so high that Shiver was having difficulty seeing over the mess. "Then I also have our notice of appeal on *that* ruling," Sharon said, "which I'll hand-carry to the appeals court down the street."

Shiver seemed on the verge of apoplexy. "Appeal whatever you want to. Just get this mess out of my courtroom." He lifted the stack, and for an instant Sharon thought he was going to hurl the papers at her. She flinched.

A youngish female voice on Sharon's left said, "Miss Hays?"

Shiver looked toward the sound as Sharon turned her head. Standing near the court reporter's station was Shiver's secretary, a slick-chick type in her twenties named Paula, who Sharon had always thought was as flighty as they came. There were rumors floating about concerning the judge's relationship with Paula. Though Sharon thought the rumors far-fetched, there was nothing she'd put past the old reprobate. She said impersonally, "Hi, Paula."

Paula vacantly batted her eyelashes. "There's a call holding for you back in chambers."

Sharon was puzzled. She couldn't recall telling anyone where she'd be this morning. "For me?" she said.

"I think it's some nut," Paula said.

Sharon had a sudden chill, remembering Bradford Brie, since he'd stalked her a couple of years ago. "A man?" she asked.

"No, it's a chick," Paula said.

"A woman? Does she sound unbalanced?"

"Oh, she *sounds* okay, but . . ." Paula gave a sudden nasal laugh. "She claims she's Darla Cowan, Miss Hays. I go, yeah, right. If you want me to, I'll hang up on her."

Sharon turned quickly to the judge. "Can I take it in your office, Your Honor?" She hurried toward the judge's private courtroom entry as Shiver's complexion turned beet red. He glared helplessly at the stack of papers. "Thanks, Judge," Sharon said, batting her eyelashes in a perfect imitation of Shiver's secretary. "I just knew you wouldn't mind."

Sharon went in through Judge Shiver's reception area, past Paula's desk, which was cluttered with nail files and bottles of polish remover, and entered the jurist's chambers. Shiver's office had navy blue velvet drapes, opened partway, and dark wood paneling. On the wall were his undergraduate and law degrees—SMU, God, class of ought something or other, Sharon thought—surrounding a painting of a cattle drive. The office was done in dark colors while the painting featured bursts of orange and red, and Sharon thought the combination was just god-awful. She sat down in a plush high-backed leather swivel chair, pressed the flashing button, and picked up the receiver. "Darla? Is it really you?"

"Thank God." Yes, it was Darla, her panicked tone showing a hint of relief.

"You got my messages, then."

"I didn't kill anyone, Sharon."

Sharon thoughtfully rubbed her chin, the lawyer inside her coming out. "I didn't ask you who did what, and really you shouldn't be telling me or anyone else what you did or didn't do." The *Dallas Morning News* lay on the judge's desk, folded over, and Sharon hadn't had time this morning to read the paper. She unfolded the *News* and scanned the headlines as she said, "You'll have a herd of lawyers advising you about this, but let me put in my two cents' worth. Ignore the hints you hear on the news, because that's all speculation. If the talking heads intimate that you did it, that increases their viewing audience. The truth is, all anyone knows right now is that David Spencer's dead and you're in California. Until you have official notification that you're not a suspect, I wouldn't be discussing it, period. I know the parties investigating the case on this end, very well, and I wouldn't trust any of them as far as I can throw the lot of them at once. Your problem at this point is in looking out for number one." There was a small headline reading DID COWAN GIVE IN TO FATAL INSTINCT? underneath the lead story about the murder. God, as if Milton Breyer had choreographed the freaking thing. Sharon testily rattled the pages.

"I didn't do anything, Sharon. When I left David, he was alive enough to take one final swing at me. I flew to L.A. and came straight home. I've had the phone turned off ever since I saw the first reports on television."

"The Dallas cops have been in contact with your agent. Maybe you should get in touch with him."

"I already have, five minutes ago. You know agents, Sharon. What Aaron has for me is deals. People wanting to talk to me, tabloids offering money. David beat me up the other night as a farewell present. I didn't think he'd be sober enough, but I was wrong. After I left you, I did just what I told you I would. Went to the hotel to pack, and David—"

"Darla. Please. Do not. It's hard not to, I know, but the FBI's already called me in, and I'm in the middle of it. If I wind up being a witness, they can force me under oath to outline everything you tell me. If what you tell me differs one iota from any future statement you make, they'll barbecue you for it. For now, speak only to your lawyer about what happened. No one else."

"You're scaring me to death." Darla's voice broke.

Sharon was halfway through with the "Fatal Instinct" article. The story was pure poppycock, speculation from some phony psychologist about whether playing a homicidal temptress in a movie could have messed with Darla's mind. Sharon said, "Cruel as it sounds, I'm trying to scare you."

There was a pause, Darla's measured breathing

slowing down. "My agent gave me the name of the Dallas policeman who talked to him. A Mr. . . . *Breyer?*"

"Milton Breyer isn't a cop. He's a prosecutor. What goes for the police goes double for him. Don't talk to him without your attorney."

"Surely if I just answer their questions truthfully—"

"Darla." Sharon fiddled with Judge Shiver's ink pen set. "If I had a dollar for every client who thought it was all right to talk to the police, prosecutors, whatever, and then had it broken off in them, I could retire. If someone's guilty, they should never talk to the police, and that goes double for people who are pure as the driven. Opposed to what they might tell you, those people are not your friends. They deal in convictions, and they're not anyone's friends. Let your attorney handle it."

More silence, for a count of five. "Sharon?"

"Yes?" Sharon sat forward, now reading about Milt Breyer's press conference, held on Sunday afternoon on the front steps of the Crowley Building. Milton had said that no one was officially accused, then had spent the better part of a half hour explaining why Darla had likely committed the crime. Milt's theory was oddly similar to that of the phony psychologist, that playing the part in *Fatal Instinct* may have sent Darla over the edge. Evidence the vicious stab wounds, Breyer had reasoned. Sharon curled her lip.

"Will you be my lawyer?" Darla asked.

Sharon hesitated in surprise. "Come on, Darla, you should already have a herd of attorneys."

"I do, for contracts, but no one who knows zip about murder cases. Chet Verdon handles my studio dealings, but he wants to call in someone criminal. He gave me a list, and I never heard of any of these people."

Sharon suppressed a chuckle. "I'll bet that none of them ever heard of me, either." Chet Verdon would be a muckety-muck partner in a California entertainment firm, and the criminal lawyers he had in mind would be Hollywood Harry types who wouldn't be adverse to splitting their fees with the entertainment lawyers. Darla suggesting that she employ Sharon only-a-woman Hays in Dallas middle-of-nowhere Texas would leave the L.A. attorneys scratching their heads.

"You have to, Sharon," Darla said.

"There are about four thousand reasons why I can't. To begin with, I'm out of my element. You're going to have national media running over you, and you need someone accustomed to dealing with that. For the second f'rinstance, the fact that I went to dinner with you Friday night automatically makes me a witness, to corroborate your story, and no one can be a lawyer and a witness to boot."

There was a sharp intake of breath over the line. "Why would I need a witness? I thought you said . . ."

"That no one's accused you, right," Sharon said. "But you never know. Regardless of who did what, whether you're officially accused, you're going to have to testify at some point as to your activities on Friday night. When that happens, you should have legal counsel every step of the way until the Dallas D.A. gets your story as it actually happened."

"Gets my story?" Darla sounded puzzled. "I thought you said I shouldn't be talking to them."

"Shouldn't be talking to them alone. With your attorney present, that's a different story. If you give these cops and prosecutors the total cold shoulder, they'll hound you to your grave, and will go right on leaking to the papers that you might be the homicidal maniac of the year. With your lawyer there, the legal eagle can weed out fishing expeditions and make them stick to the issues. Any question it's not in your best interest to answer, the lawyer can intercede. Trust me. You have the advantage that you can cause the meeting to happen on your turf. Make them fly to L.A., Darla. It'll put them in an inferior position from the get-go." Sharon pictured Milton Breyer, with Stan Green's able assistance, seated across from an international sex symbol with palm trees outside the window and starlets walking the sidewalks, both Breyer and Green trying to think up a nifty string of questions. Might take those two bozos awhile.

"Couldn't you do that?" Darla said.

Sharon's brow knitted. "Do what?"

"Talk to the police with me?"

Sharon felt a surge of exasperation. Sure, she was concerned about Darla, but God, dealing with Darla Cowan was sometimes more difficult than coping with Melanie's adolescent tantrums. How many different ways were there to explain all this? "What did I just say?" Sharon asked.

"That you couldn't be my lawyer. But, just while I tell my story to the police? How could that hurt?"

Sharon covered the mouthpiece and uttered a resigned sigh. Judge Shiver's cattle-drive painting showed one cowboy waving a coiled lariat. She said to Darla, "Technically it wouldn't hurt anything, but it's just not a good idea. I could advise you during the questioning, but the second they said they wanted to talk to me as a witness, I'd have to resign. The same attorney should do the whole enchilada, represent you during the questioning and on from there."

"Good," Darla said. "Then you'll do it."

Sharon folded the newspaper and tossed it aside. "No, I won't. We're not communicating or something."

"You *have* to, Sharon."

"I'm not even licensed in California. At the very least I'd have to get co-counsel."

"That could be Chet Verdon."

Sure, Sharon thought, old Chet would just love it. "Get an attorney out there," she said.

"I'd want to pay you." Darla paused. "Get you a plane ticket. Pay your expenses. Money's one thing there's no problem with."

Sharon had a sudden picture of the orthodontist leering as he exhibited Melanie's X rays, then quickly dismissed the image from her mind. "You've got a lot more to worry about than money. I can't, Darla, and that's that."

Darla began to sob. Sharon rolled her eyes. God love Darla, but when she went into her pleading mode, she was damn near unbearable.

Darla said, "Couldn't you just, maybe, be with me when I talk to this criminal attorney? To be sure whatever he's telling me is right? I don't trust all these people, Sharon."

Sharon's exasperation dissolved into pity. The vultures would be huddled around, all right, looking for bones on which to feast. Sharon wondered about her own stability, turning down representation of a movie star in order to do battle for Tired Darnell. She weakened a bit. "It would have to be arm's length if I was your lawyer, Darla. As a friend, I'm at your beck and call and always will be. There will be no money changing hands, period. If you want me to hold your hand while you talk to this lawyer, I'm yours, babe. I wouldn't be much of a friend if I wasn't."

"When can you come?" Darla said anxiously.

Sharon dug in her shoulder bag and opened her checkbook. Her pitiful balance would last until the end of the month if she cut a few corners. "I'll level with you," she said. "I can't afford the trip. If you want to spring for a ticket, I can be on the next thing smokin'. I don't have anything scheduled for trial for two weeks, and there are things I could put off."

"Just tell me where to send the money," Darla said, and after a pause added, "Would you like to bring your little girl? Her father does live out here, you know."

Sharon was suddenly overcome with gratitude. Darla could be insufferable, but not one person in a million would think of Melanie at a time like this. "Melanie will love you for it. Plus, hey, I've got a few financial matters to discuss with old Rob-oh myself. Such as a certain orthodontist's quote which resembles the national debt." Sharon thought for a moment. "I hate to come across like one of the homeless, but my current financial situation borders on the desperate. It will be awfully expensive for you."

Darla sighed. "Chet Verdon's demanded a twenty-five-thousand-dollar retainer just to help me pick out a lawyer. What's a couple of airline tickets more? You could stay at the Malibu place with me."

Sharon thought about the details, what clothing she'd need for the trip. Her standard lawyerly attire, of course. Couple of loud prints for lounging around Studio City or wherever. What the hell, maybe a pair of sunglasses with "L.A. Eyewear" etched into the lens. She opened Judge Shiver's middle drawer and found a pen, averting her gaze from the *Penthouse* magazine which the old goat had stashed and weighted down with a spare gavel. "Give me your phone number. It's written down at home, but I don't have it handy," Sharon said.

Darla dictated the number as Sharon wrote it down. "It's settled, then," Darla said.

"Darla, this matter is so far from settled you wouldn't believe. I'll check the airline schedules and call you back with the flight number, time and whatnot, and you can phone in with a credit card number and leave the tickets at the counter. Unofficially I can nose around over at the D.A.'s office and determine when Milt Breyer can get a crew together to come out and interview you. Knowing him, he'll drop everything and haul ass for the airport." Sharon mentally snapped her fingers. "One more thing. How did you know to call me in court?"

"Some guy at your office."

"No one's at my office. You should have gotten a machine."

"I talked to a Russ something. He put me on hold while he called the courthouse to run you down. How else could I find you? I don't have ESP."

Sharon was stunned. Russell Black wasn't due to return for two weeks. "Or a direct line to Paris," she said. "I'll call you when I have the flight number. I have to hustle back to the office. If it wasn't Russ you talked with, then we have a ghost clanking around."

Sharon reentered the courtroom as Judge Shiver, scratching his head, finished reading over the stack of motions and appeals regarding Tired Darnell. She stood before the bench. "Sorry for the delay, Judge. I've had something come up."

Shiver's mouth twisted in resignation. "So have I. A calendar fulla' cases, and you wanting to bring the wheels of justice grindin' to a halt over this one second-rate burglary case."

Sharon sniffed through her nose. "My client's constitutional rights aren't second-rate to him, Your Honor."

Shiver pinched his chin. "How far you willin' to pursue this, Miss Hays?"

"All the way. I'd be lax in my duty if I didn't."

"And all you're wantin' is for me to reduce Tired's sentence to three years?" Shiver's look said he was giving up, just as he'd have to do eventually when the appeals were heard. Sharon had him and he knew it.

Normally she would have left well enough alone, but Shiver's obstinance had kept her up until the wee hours. She said, "For starters that's all, Your Honor. That's all in accordance with his plea bargain. We're only asking for what he agreed to."

Shiver regarded Sharon with the look of a man watching a lazily circling bee, one with its stinger out. He said, "For starters? You mean there's more?"

Sharon produced another legal paper from her satchel. "There is, Your Honor. We're asking the court to consider now our application for bail." She laid the motion before the judge, then pulled out more papers and held them in her hand. These were her appeal notices in case Shiver denied bail. The waver in Shiver's gaze said he understood very well that if he turned her down, she was going over his head.

"Miss Hays, askin' for bail on a man I've just sentenced to the penitentiary is a little bit far out, even for you. In anybody's court." He squinted. "What's the basis for your motion for bail?"

"That he's already done his time," Sharon said. "Look, Judge, Tired's been in the county six months. With allotted good time and parole eligibility requirements, he's already eligible for release."

"Tired would know that," Shiver said, "as much time as he's done in his sparklin' career."

Sharon ignored the dig. "If they take him to Huntsville, they'll parole him from the walls in two or three days anyhow, Judge. If I can have him released on bail, we can apply directly for parole while he's on the street and save the taxpayer the expense of housing him for unnecessary time."

"An' save Tired's butt from the hard bench on the prison bus," Shiver said.

"That, too, Your Honor." Sharon blinked. "Could I have the court's consideration?" She glanced down at the appellate papers.

Shiver expelled a long sigh. He snatched up a pen and scribbled his signature. "Bail petition granted, Miss Hays. Now will you get outta my courtroom."

Sharon stuffed the appellate papers away. "Thank you, Your Honor."

Shiver eyed the stack of motions before him." Get the hell outta here, Miss Hays," the jurist said.

Sharon stepped across the street to Fuzzy Breedlove's bail bond office, and gave Fuzzy the bail papers along with a check for the bond fee for Tired Darnell. Normally she would have accompanied the bondsman to the jail and waited for her client's release, but she had other things to do. She left the bondsman and drove to the office.

She parked her Volvo in the converted service station-parking garage across from the back of the George Allen Courts Building, and hurried across the street. Her high heels clicked snappily on pavement, her pleated skirt swirled around her calves, and her satchel bumped her hip with every step. The zocko fall weather had held up; the temperature was in the middle sixties, and the sky was robin's egg blue. She skipped two steps up from street level and went through a glass-paneled door. There was a sign on the glass: RUSSELL BLACK, ATTORNEY in large letters, with SHARON J. HAYS, ASSOCIATE in smaller characters underneath. She zipped through a reception area containing a secretarial desk but no receptionist, and squinted at the crack underneath Russ's door. His light was on. She threw open the door without knocking and stood in the entryway. Black was at his desk with his feet propped up, reading a magazine.

"You cut your trip short," Sharon said. "You promised me you'd stay a month and relax."

Black frowned at her. He had a craggy, lined face, with leathery creases around his eyes, and Sharon thought her boss and mentor looked like the sheriff of Last Ditch Gulch. He had the courtroom voice of a tree-stump evangelist and gave jurors the impression that he was their fishing buddy.

"So unless you've got a good excuse for being here," she said, "don't unpack your bags."

"Don't know as how I need any excuse," Black said. "My associate might need one, gettin' involved in a mess like this." He showed her the cover of *Time*. David Spencer was front and center in a buckskin-jacketed pose from *Spring of the Comanche,* with the caption DEATH OF AN IDOL above and to the right. Darla's photo was in an insert positioned beside Spencer, a still from *Fatal Instinct* wherein she wore a low-cut tank top. It could only be worse, Sharon thought, if they'd showed her with a knife raised over her head.

Sharon sank down in one of Russ's visitors chairs. "I don't think the headline's very original." She swallowed. "Don't tell me I'm mentioned in the story."

"Nope," Black said. "The killin' only happened Friday night, an' I suspect the magazine folks were up till all hours gettin' this out. All that's in the story is early stuff. The information that my assistant was mixed up in it, that came on French TV. I'm gettin' out of the shower, an' there you are on the tube. I had to get one o' the bellhops to interpret what they were sayin'.'"

Sharon scrunched her shoulders together. "The scenes in front of Planet Hollywood?"

Black nodded.

"Oh, that," Sharon said nonchalantly. She'd been so wrapped up that the worldwide impact of this whole mess hadn't struck home. "Look, Russ," she said, "it's not that big of a deal. Nothing to make you cancel all your plans."

Black took his feet down and folded his arms. "Somebody's gotta do some practicin' of law around here, young lady."

"That's what I'm here for. I told you before you left I'd take care of things." Sharon felt a touch of resentment.

"Just how you plan to do that?" Black reached inside his desk and produced a stack of call slips. He thumbed through the pink pieces of paper. "*Dallas Mornin' News.* This is from Andy Wade, I guess it's okay to talk to him. But these other people . . . *New York Times.* Los Angeles, both papers. *Boston Globe.* Hell, even the *National Enquirer.* I thought all they reported was women claimin' that Martians fathered their kids."

Sharon couldn't help laughing. "Used to be like that, but I think they've cleaned up their act some."

"These," Black said, waving the call slips, "are only for starters. I cleaned all the messages off the machine two hours ago, and already the tape's full again. Clients can't even get through."

As if on cue, the phone buzzed in the reception area. Sharon reflexively started to rise. Black raised a hand. "The machine, Sharon, that's what it's for. I made that mistake already, takin' a call. It was that actress. She get you in the courtroom?"

Sharon nodded. Russ had spoken to one of the most famous people in the world and wasn't batting an eye. "That actress" would be about as far as he'd go; they all looked like Ned in the first to Russell Black.

"So what I got," Black said, "is my associate involved in the biggest crime around here since the Kennedy assassination, an' she wants to know how come I can't loll around overseas." He showed a sharp look. "You know you can't represent anybody in that case, dontcha? From what I'm seein', you'll be a witness."

"This sounds like a recording," Sharon said, "of a conversation I just had with Darla Cowan."

"What'd she say?"

"She wanted me to represent her in something. I told her I couldn't." Sharon folded her hands. "That's not quite true. I am going to help her select a lawyer, but that's a freebie. She's an old friend, and she's awfully confused."

Black opened the magazine. "I thought I read she'd gone back to Los Angeles."

Sharon had put her foot squarely into her mouth. She watched her lap as she said, "She has."

"Well, then, how are you goin' to . . . ?"

Sharon looked at him.

Black sank back in his chair. "You're goin' to L.A."

She nodded sheepishly.

"An' I'm supposed to be runnin' around the Riviera with nobody here coverin' home plate."

"I won't be neglecting the office," Sharon said. "We've got nothing set for trial for two weeks. Go back to Europe, Russ. You and Ginny need the quality time."

Black's mouth twisted. He spun his chair around and looked out the window, across Jackson Street toward the Allen Building. On the wall were his framed law degree—U of Houston, Class of '69—along with two photos of himself, one shot on horseback and another with him behind a steaming pot at the Terlingua Chili Cook-off. Sharon watched the back of Russ's head for a moment, then said, "It's something else, isn't it?"

"Hmm?" Black's tone was vacant and detached.

"You didn't come racing home just because you saw

me on television. Did you." Sharon made a statement out of a question.

Black turned back around. His eyes looked very tired. "My daughter's grown up an' left me, Sharon."

Sharon expelled a breath. Tender moments for Russell Black were few and far between. "Bummer of a trip?" she said.

"I wanted to show her things. What I wanted to show her she didn' want to see, an' what she wanted to see I didn' want to take her to. I was an old man travelin' in the company of a young woman. I want my little girl back. This young woman scares me."

Sharon watched him. A similar experience was in store for her, with Melanie, and not too many years down the line. Hate it though she might, the time was coming. She said, "As for old, you're barely fifty. As for little girls, they must disappear someday just like little boys. Ginny's going to be twenty-one soon, and next year she'll be a college graduate. I doubt she's still interested in Bugs Bunny, but that's something all us parents will have to get used to."

"Paris," Black said, "all she wanted to see was the nightlife. I got about as much business in a disco as I do drivin' a racecar. We had a trip. We planned it to last too long. Believe me, she's as glad it's over as I am. Practicin' law in Dallas, Texas, is what I've done for a quarter century. It's what I like doin'. European vacations are for guys I don't even know."

Holy smoke, Sharon thought, he feels left out. Russell Black, the king of the courtroom, is miffed because his assistant, me, has gotten herself involved in something and hasn't asked his advice. She felt a twinge of guilt. "I've got to level, boss," she said, "I've come within a whisker of contacting you, but I didn't want to interrupt your fun. I may be in over my head here."

Black's interest picked up. He raised one shaggy eyebrow. "Well, tell me about it, girl," he said. "Like I been sayin' to my daughter. It's what I'm here for, to help you youngsters."

* * *

Sharon told the story from moment one, when Darla had first spotted her at Planet Hollywood, up to Darla's call to the courtroom an hour ago. Black listened, scratching his chin, going to the Mr. Coffee for a steaming cupful, sipping as he listened. Sharon thought that Russ's memory was one of the wonders of the world; the man never took notes but had total recall.

When she'd finished he said, "You know they're gonna arrest her."

Sharon nodded. "Would appear so, if they can dig up probable cause to identify her as a suspect."

"They got probable cause up to here without liftin' a finger. She got into a fight with him in public. Witnesses saw her leavin' the scene o' the crime, and didn' see anyone else comin' or goin'. They can pick her up on that alone."

"They can pinpoint her arrival at the hotel, too. What they can't establish right now is the exact time of death. Within a couple of hours give or take, but it will be up to Darla's defense to show he could have died after Darla was already gone."

"You're not talkin' a trial yet. You're talkin' only probable cause to arrest this woman. They'll have to extradite her, but that's only a matter of showin' they got a valid warrant. Somebody needs to prepare this lady that she's goin' to jail."

"It's not up to me to do that," Sharon said. "That's for her lawyer. Milt Breyer being the prosecutor will help the defense, Russ. Whatever Milt knows, the newspaper knows. There are times I'm surprised he doesn't furnish reporters copies of his opening and closing arguments in advance." She chewed her lower lip. "I've already been to an interview. Milt Breyer, Kathleen Fraterno, Stan Green, and the FBI."

Black scowled, scratching above his eyebrow. "The feds have somethin' legitimate, or just snoopin' around?"

"More the latter, I think. They're in the prosecution's way, which is a plus for the defense. I doubt we'll see much more of the fibbies now that their presence is in the headlines."

"And that they're monitorin' the case, which they'll do from Washington by readin' the newspaper. Yeah, okay, that much I understand." Black picked up his cup and blew on the hot liquid. "I wouldn't let the actress talk to Milt Breyer. Not yet." He sipped.

"She'll have a lawyer present."

"Not even that way. I'd feel better if the lawyer was you, but not some person we know nothin' about. No way."

"Look, I can't advise her. All I'm supposed to do is help her select a California attorney. Hold her hand. It's as far as I can get ethically involved."

"There's ethics and there's right, and a lot of the time it's two different things. Nine lawyers outta ten are gonna see dollar signs, which will interfere with what they know to be proper legal counselin'. The best advice she can get right now is to keep her mouth shut. She can tell them what she wants to once they clear her, but the best way for a lawyer to build up a fee is to have her talk her bloomers off. Like I say, two different things."

All of which Sharon knew to be on target, and she suspected that things in fast-track California were even worse than she was accustomed to in Texas. "I don't think Darla wears bloomers, Russ," she said. "That was Fanny Brice."

"Well, whatever. You can represent her when she talks to Milt Breyer without gettin' in any conflicts, an' I think you ought to."

"I've already told her I couldn't. I can't do an about-face and hire myself, now, can I? What I've agreed to do is test the water with Milt Breyer, find out when the Dallas people can go to California to talk to her."

"Now, that," Black said, his expression dead serious, "is somethin' you *shouldn'* be doin'."

Sharon was puzzled. "That's not performing any legal function. I'm just coordinating travel schedules."

"From the actress's standpoint, yeah. Your whole thrust is, she's only a witness, an' until the D.A. agrees that's her only function, they don't hear a word from her. I'm talkin' about your position in this thing. You're a witness, too, and if you go over there tryin' to make travel plans, they'll put you on the hot seat. You should keep away from the D.A. for the same reason Darla Cowan's s'posed to. Should never have talked to the feds, for that matter."

"That's a little silly, Russ. No way could I be a suspect."

Black's scowl was suddenly more intense. "When you're dealin' with Milt Breyer, anything's possible."

Sharon's puzzlement vanished as a flashbulb exploded in her head. You're not fooling me, Mr. Black, Sharon thought. She pictured Black mother-henning his daughter around eastern Europe, trying to dictate her comings and goings, and imagined that had been quite a battle. Ginny Black was a headstrong young woman. Well, so was Sharon Hays. But she did recognize concern, and that Russell Black viewed her about as much as family as he did his only child. His legal arguments were weak as watered-down whiskey, but Russ was sending a message that he wanted to be involved. Time for a little diplomacy, Sharon thought. She reached into the past, to her stage career, and put on her best round-eyed look, the little-girl-lost-in-the-woods approach. "Well, maybe I should have a lawyer of my own," she said.

Black's expression softened. "At the very least, if you're goin' ahead with this thing."

"I hate to ask, boss," Sharon said, "but do you think you could call the D.A. for me?"

Black made a show of looking at his calendar, which Sharon happened to know was blank because he was scheduled to be away. "Reckon I could," Black said. "Don't seem to have anything else goin' on."

"Great." Sharon's mind was moving a mile a minute now, planning her trip, what she was going to tell Darla, thinking of things which, as a lawyer, she needed to know in advance. Such as what she might run into in California, the laws being somewhat different out there. She started to rise, then remembered Black's feelings and sat back down. "Something else I'd like to run by you, Russ."

"Shoot," Black said. "I'll help ya if I can."

"They've got a section of the SMU law library for statutes of foreign states. I'm thinking, maybe I should scan the California code. See what might be different out there. I've never handled an extradition, and I think I should know the procedure from A to Z."

"Good idea," Black said. "I never said you weren't sharp as a tack when it comes to gettin' prepared."

Though she kept her help-me expression, she smiled an inward smile as broad as a Cheshire cat's. Russ hated research with a passion and always had. "What I was wondering," Sharon said, "could you come with me? You might come up with something in the California code that I'd miss, boss."

Black pretended to think that one over, then dismissed her with a wave of his hand. "I trust your judgment, Sharon. I'll letcha go that one alone."

Sharon stood. On her way to the library she could call the airlines, check the schedules. "Well, after I'm finished, I'll call you and let you know what I find." She smiled. "I'm glad you're back, boss. I don't know how I could manage without you."

10

Sharon entered the law library at SMU, climbed the stairs to the second level, and signed in at the desk. Then she veered to her right in the cavernous research section and went to the stacks containing statutes for the state of California. In moments she trudged to a reading table carrying three doorstop-sized volumes, dumped her load on the table, jammed her Walkman's earphones into her ears, set the dial on Country 96.3, sat down, and went to work.

She briefly scanned the California Criminal Codes. As she studied she silently lip-synced Tammy Wynette, who was belting out "Stand by Your Man" over the airwaves. She didn't find any surprises in the laws themselves; what Texas designated as capital murder was murder with special circumstances in California, though either offense subjected the perp to the death penalty. Sharon thumbed to the index and looked up the questioning of witnesses. As long as Darla wasn't under indictment, she'd be treated as a witness, and any questioning by Texas people would be subject to California law if Milton Breyer flew to L.A. On his home turf Milt could push witnesses around just about any way he wanted to. In La-La Land, however, Sharon suspected that intimidation tactics weren't going to fly.

A smile touched her lips as she read over the law. Milt was going to be more of a fish out of water in California than she'd thought. Not only did Darla have a right to counsel during questioning—a right governed by the U.S. Constitution and therefore applica-

ble in every state—in California she could have the
interrogation conducted in open court in front of a
judge. Ergo, if Milt balked at having a court reporter
take down his questions and Darla's answers, then the
whole group could simply march into the courtroom.
She yanked a legal pad from her satchel and made a
note to question whatever lawyer Darla retained as to
his knowledge of the California witness statutes. Some
hoity-toity L.A. attorney would get his nose bent out
of shape over an upstart woman from Texas putting
him through the meat grinder. Well, that's tough,
Sharon thought. Darla had asked her to aid in the
selection of a lawyer, and that's what Sharon Jenifer
Hays was going to do.

A hand moved into Sharon's line of vision and
touched her on the arm. She looked around. It was
the student worker from the sign-in desk, a Phi-Delt-
looking youngster wearing a Polo shirt. Sharon un-
plugged her earphones and smiled expectantly.

"Miss Hays?" The student's whisper was anxious.
"Are you Sharon Hays?"

Sharon was a regular at the university library, and
had long since gotten used to being recognized. She
said, "Yes, I'm Sharon."

"There's a phone call for you at the desk." He beckoned and walked toward the entry.

Sharon frowned as she laid her earphones down,
got up, and followed the student to the sign-in desk.
The telephone receiver lay off its hook, on the desk
beside a seven-inch TV where the student worker had
been watching *Days of Our Lives*. The student sat
down and looked at the screen. Sharon picked up the
phone and said, "Hello?"

"Better get undercover in a hurry, girl." It was Russell Black, his tone showing disgust.

Sharon leaned one hip against the desk. "What's
wrong?"

"It's that so-and-so Milton Breyer."

Black would have called Breyer a sonofabitch or an
asshole if he'd been speaking to one of his male cro-

nies, but when women were around he watched his language. Sharon suppressed an affectionate grin. "What's Milt done now?" she said.

"I called him to set up a meetin' in California. He says he can fly out tomorrow. That's the good part."

"It's the good part if he doesn't mind cooling his heels in a hotel for a night or two. It's going to take me awhile to get with Darla and let her hire a lawyer. What's the bad part?"

"Two bad parts. They've found a car, in the hotel valet lot. Milton's told the press that you rented it on your credit card."

"Yes, at Love Field. Darla and I wanted to ditch the limo so we could travel on the q.t. I've got receipts, and I think I can establish she took me home before she went to the hotel."

"Which helps you, but not Darla Cowan. Breyer's held a press conference," Black said, "tellin' that she's the prime suspect. Usual prosecutorial baloney, that they've got all this evidence that they don't want to go public with."

"Which means they've got zip for evidence, but are beating the bushes for some," Sharon said. She felt a bit cold as pity for Darla surged through her. She clenched her jaws. There would be plenty of time for hand holding later, but for the moment she had to think legal. "Have they issued a warrant for her?" she said.

"Hadn' had time, but that's next. Expect Breyer to do it in secret and carry the warrant to California with him. Then when the actress shows up expectin' to go through questionin', Milt will have her arrested with the cameras grindin'."

Which would be SOP for Milton Breyer, Sharon thought. She said vacantly, "I suppose I'd better forget the witness statutes and bone up on extradition procedure," she said. She sighed. "You told me there were two bad things, boss. What's the other one?"

"Milt's been givin' all kinds of interviews."

"So what's new? If the newspapers don't call Milton once a week, he starts calling them."

"He's told them all that you're Darla Cowan's lawyer," Black said.

Sharon looked at the floor, then up at the ceiling. "You're joking."

"It's all over the television, the networks," Black said. "CBS ran pictures of you getting in her limo in the West End, then showed your college yearbook photo. The phone's ringing every fifteen seconds, people wanting to interview you."

Sharon drummed her fingers as anger welled within her. "I told that moron I wasn't Darla's lawyer when I saw him at the FBI office the other night. Several times."

"Evidently you wadn' clear enough. We're not set up to deal with all these phone calls, Sharon."

"Don't I know it?" Sharon turned her back to the sign-in desk, ducked her head, and lowered her voice. "I can't take this, boss. I'm leaving town."

"Can't say as I blame ya. Every fifteen minutes I run the message tape back to erase everthing, an' then fifteen minutes later it's full again. I'm goin' to be scarce around here myself."

"Go back to Paris. That or fishing or something. I'm headed for sunny Southern." Sharon hung up. She softly closed her eyes and thought. She called Sheila.

"Have you seen the news?" Sheila said.

"I don't want to see the news. Take Melanie up the street and pack her things, Sheila."

"Pack what?"

"Enough clothes for four or five days in California. I'll need for you to take me to the airport, if it's okay."

Sheila snickered. "Are you out of your mind?"

"More than likely," Sharon said. "Darla wants me to help her with something."

"You're all over the television. Profiles of Darla Cowan's lawyer. Former Broadway star. Ex lover of Rob Stanley. ABC just announced they'll interview

Rob on *Prime Time Live* to get the real skinny on you."

Sharon sagged. She was suddenly weak in the knees. "God, they didn't say I was a *star* . . ."

"They wouldn't exaggerate, would they?" Sheila said. "Represent biggo clients, become biggo news yourself. Ask Robert Shapiro."

"I'm not Darla's lawyer. That false information comes from Milton Breyer's office. Is Melanie there?"

"Sure, I picked them both up from school. Which brings up a point. She'd have to miss school to go on—"

"Her grades are pretty up to snuff, and she hasn't been sick any. So she'll have some makeup work. It might keep her out of my hair for a couple of nights when we get back. Just help her pack, okay? I want to look up a couple of more things in the law, extradition procedure, and then I'll be on home."

There was a pause, and Sharon pictured Sheila standing there holding the phone, rolling her eyes. Finally Sheila said, "When is this trip supposed to occur?"

"Tonight."

"Sharon . . ."

"I've got to get out of here before these newspeople drive Russ completely crazy. I don't think I'm going to have another moment's peace until I can get this over with. I'm going to call Darla, have the tickets left for us at DFW, and I'll see you in, oh, a half hour."

"Sharon, this is insane."

Sharon backed away from the desk and peered around the corner, at the table where her satchel and Walkman sat along with the California law books. Extradition statutes would be in the federal code, way down at the other end of the library. "I suppose I am a little crazy, Sheila. Just help Melanie pack, okay? For the rest of our lives I'll be indebted to you."

Darla wasn't in, but had erased Spencer's message from the answering machine and substituted one of her own. Her soft voice was much more pleasant than David Spencer's, which had sounded as if whoever was calling was being a pest. Sharon waited for the beep, gave Darla's machine her flight number and the information as to where to call to arrange for the tickets, then paused and thought, carefully selecting her words. Finally she said, "You'll have heard by now that Mr. Breyer is spouting off to the press that you're now his main suspect. He isn't joking, Darla, and he's just off balance enough to be dangerous. Beginning right now, love, right this second. Don't say a word about this matter to anyone other than me, and whatever lawyer we end up choosing for you. Pay attention, Darla. To discuss this with anyone is suicide."

11

Sharon rode to DFW Airport scrunched down low on the passenger side of Sheila's Pontiac station wagon, wearing big sunglasses and a scarf tied around her head to complete her disguise. She felt dumb, dumb, dumb, but feeling stupid was better than having the media on her trail. They'd tracked her down at the house, the doorbell *bong-bong*-ing as Sharon was in the midst of packing her things. She had peeked through the drapes and thought she was having a stroke. There'd been two mobile news units parked outside and three harried-looking guys on the lawn toting minicams. Sharon had crept to the front door and put her eye to the peephole. Two coiffed on-the-spot reporters punched the doorbell button relentlessly. Sheila had then slipped on Sharon's housecoat and answered the bell, and Sharon listened from the kitchen as Sheila told the reporters in her best piping Aunt Jemima soprano, "Miz Hays, she ain't heah. I's jus' cleanin' house fo' de lady."

Then, once she'd packed and changed, she had exited through the back door and climbed the fence as Commander raised a ruckus and did his best to follow her over. She'd waited at the end of the alley as Sheila made the block, then made a mad dash for the station wagon with her head down. She hoped that in the confusion she'd left the shepherd plenty of provisions. If a washtub of Kibbles 'n' Bits and a rain barrel full of water wouldn't tide Commander over for two or three days, however, Sharon didn't know what else to do.

Trish and Melanie were in back, bouncing off the windows, jabbering nonstop with luggage piled high on all sides, the idea of missing school for a West Coast trip putting Melanie in orbit. Sharon pictured the ordeal of getting the sky-high adolescent into bed, even after the rigors of a three-hour flight, and decided that the task would be more than Job could bear. Separate rooms, Sharon thought. The only answer will be separate rooms. Darla had insisted that the visitors stay in the Malibu beach house. Sharon pictured pounding surf below, and Melanie plunging to her death on the rocks after trying a tightrope routine on the balcony rail. The station wagon's headlamps illuminated a sign which said that the south entry to DFW was a half mile ahead. Sheila slowed and moved into the right-hand lane.

Sharon straightened, threw her arm over the seat back, and turned around to face the teenagers. "Tell you what, Melanie. While I'm taking care of business tomorrow, maybe Darla can arrange for you to take the Universal Studio tour. See the shark from *Jaws,* all that stuff."

Trish brightened, but Melanie sat back thoughtfully. Now what chain have I pulled? Sharon thought. The single mother bit was really a pain at times. She said, "What is it, Melanie?"

Melanie rested her chin on her lightly clenched fist. "A studio tour would be fine, Mom," she said. "But if I can, I think I'd like to visit my dad."

Oh, my sweet Jesus, Sharon thought. It seemed that nothing would stop Rob's ugly head from rearing for the rest of her life, and now she was headed straight for his lair in La-La Land. Slow-walkin' Rob, Sharon thought, remembering an old rock 'n' roll number from the sixties. Slow-talkin', slow-payin' Rob. The s.o.b. had visited Dallas, for Christ's sake, and he'd been too busy with self-promo to spend any time with his daughter even then. Sharon could imagine what it would be like on Rob's home turf. "We'll see," Sharon said.

"Maybe we could visit his house," Melanie said.

Sheila stirred behind the wheel. Nice subject, Sharon thought. She said, "I don't know, Melanie. I'm sure he has rehearsals. They shoot part of the show in New York City; he may not be in town."

"Well, could we call him and ask?" Melanie said.

Sharon turned around to face the front, folding her arms as Sheila steered onto the ramp leading to the airport entry. Of all the freaking times for this to come up, Sharon thought. Any encouragement now would set Melanie up for the hardest of falls if Rob was to duck seeing her. Sharon sighed and watched the road. "We'll see, Melanie," she finally said.

Sharon sat alone in an isolated portion of the passenger boarding area, shades in place, the scarf disguising her hair. She thought she looked like Mata Hari. Sheila and the girls were two rows of chairs away, their backs turned, watching TV on a giant screen which faced the check-in station. Visible through the picture window overlooking the runways, a 747 rolled up to the gate. The walkway extended and clamped onto the airliner's side. Jet engines whined to a standstill.

There were a dozen or so passengers waiting to board the red-eye, sleepy businessmen mostly, collars undone, and a teenage boy and girl who were holding hands. The television was tuned to CNN, and the picture showed Stan Green bossing a group of medics as they toted David Spencer's shrouded corpse to an ambulance in front of the Mansion. During the ten minutes she'd been watching, there'd been what seemed like forty thousand clips of David Spencer in *Spring of the Comanche* plus a like number of shots of Darla in *Fatal Instinct*. The *Fatal Instinct* footage included the bloody bedroom slashing, with black rectangles superimposed over Darla's bare fanny and breasts. There had been multiple showings of the scene in front of Planet Hollywood, of course, with Sharon and Sheila in the background as Spencer grabbed Darla and yanked her toward the restaurant entry. Then there was Milton Breyer, an extra layer of Grecian Formula on his hair as he faced a bank of microphones and laid his case out to the media. And finally—ta-*taa*, Sharon thought—there was her law school picture complete with cap and gown. The photo made her want to barf, her eyes round and innocent in a sort of ain't-life-a-ball expression. Sharon testily jiggled her foot and looked away.

When she returned her attention to the television, she at first thought that the David Spencer murder segment was over. The TV picture showed a play in progress. There were two actresses center stage, and they were obviously in dramatic conflict. The dress was early 1900s, and in the background was scenery depicting a train station. Bit-part actors stood on a platform, waving good-bye as if the Atchison, Topeka, and Santa Fe had just left town. Sharon thought it nice that off-Broadway was at last getting some recognition. Then she narrowed her eyes and leaned intently forward. God, she thought, there's something familiar here. Now, where on earth did CNN get *this* freaking footage?

She remembered the play, all right, *Avengers and Lovers.* No way could she forget the production, and she recalled in detail all three performances before the theatrical supply company had showed up to repossess the scenery and costumes. The theater had been in Hell's Kitchen, a lovely walk for Sharon and Darla from the subway station at 50th and Eighth Avenue past muggers, rapists, and cross-dressing whores. There'd been no dressing rooms, and they'd had to put on their costumes in full view of alcoholic stage hands. The playwright's uncle had been the producer, and had spent a lot of time organizing parties to include himself, an unsuspecting actress or two, and one of the producer's bankroll men. Sharon and Darla had fallen once for the come-on, then politely excused themselves when the producer's buddy had trotted out porno films.

Sharon grinned in spite of herself as she mouthed the line along with her image on television: "You are noting but a trollop, Winfred Dismore. You will never be woman enough for Jeffrey. Never." She wondered if this was the performance when Darla had broken into giggles in the middle of Sharon's dialogue. Yep, there she goes, Sharon thought as Darla's shoulders began to heave for the viewing pleasure of the CNN audience. She can't help it, ladies and gents, Sharon thought, this performance was the night after the producer lured us over for the porno party, and Jeffrey happened to be the dirty old bankroll man's name. Sharon recalled that the playwright had been running around with a camcorder during the performance, and now she suspected that the insipid little worm had sold this footage to the media for a bundle. She briefly considered looking up the playwright in the Manhattan phone book, calling him and demanding that he cut her in on the proceeds, which were likely more than *Avengers and Lovers'* entire take at the box office. Sharon's grin faded instantly as an image of Rob flashed on the screen.

It was a shot which Sharon had seen over and over, Rob dressed in his tough detective's suit from *Minions of Justice,* a public-service ad telling teenagers to stay free of drugs. God, Sharon thought, the news hounds are kicking that dead horse again. Her gaze shifted quickly to Melanie, and the slump in her daughter's posture told Sharon all she needed to know. The TV announcer was telling the world that this bozo of a star had knocked up Sharon Hays long ago in New York City. And that Melanie Hays was Rob Stanley's bastard child.

Sharon lowered her head and reached under her sunglasses to wipe a tear away. He'll see you on this trip, Melanie, Sharon thought, that I promise you. If the s.o.b. is in town, I absolutely guarantee that he will.

The 747 banked over the ocean and did a one-eighty to head back to the east, then floated in over twinkling lights as far as the eye could see, and finally laid stripes of rubber on LAX's tar-veined runway. The landing jarred Sharon into wakefulness. She looked around in confusion for a second, and actually reached for her bedside alarm to turn the buzzer off. No clock radio there. No bedcovers, either, no Commander scratching at the door. She worried about the shepherd for a moment, picturing him whining morosely in anticipation of his masters' return, and finally gazed out the window as the brightly lit terminal drew closer and closer. The airliner rolled smoothly on, and in the distance freeway flashers blinked. City of Dreams, Sharon thought. Stars that never were, parking cars, pumping gas, and practicing freaking law. Melanie was in the aisle seat, and peered excitedly around her mother for a glimpse of California.

"Only eleven here," Sharon said, her voice crackly with sleep. "The nightcrawlers are barely awake in Los Angeles. Jet lag will make a zombie out of me."

The first-class flight attendant, a woman in her forties with honey blond hair, passed down the aisle flipping open overhead luggage compartments. Melanie told Sharon that if her father was in town, she was certain he'd take her on a tour of the studio. "I just know he will, Mom," Melanie said. Sharon didn't answer, just reached out and touched her daughter's cheek. Then she pinched her own chin between a thumb and forefinger, and watched the runway roll briskly under the wing.

They deplaned in the lead, with business-class passengers straggling along behind, Sharon and Melanie pulling their rolling carry-ons. During the flight Sharon had thought, to hell with it, and had shed her disguise. It's the real me, folks, wilted hair, no makeup, the entire freaking horror show. If anyone recognized her fifteen hundred miles from home, it would be a shock to her.

Melanie was nonstop movement, forging excitedly ahead, acting as if the check-in desk in L.A.—which was identical to the one in front of the gate at DFW—was the neatest thing she'd ever seen. Sharon trudged wearily along, wondering if the thirteen-year-old would sleep a wink during the entire trip. Sharon watched her with a wry cant to her mouth, then stopped a few feet past the check-in desk and looked around.

She didn't know what she was looking for. It was a given that Darla wouldn't leave her wandering around LAX like Little Match Girl, but she was just as certain that a world-famous personality—particularly one involved in the Media Blitz of the Week—wouldn't be standing at the gate waving a hanky. She felt a twinge of uncertainty as fellow passengers shook hands with greeters or hugged their wives or husbands, and she was within an inch of heading for the bank of phones at the head of the escalator when a hand touched her arm. A pleasant male voice with a British accent said, "Miss Hays? Sharon Hays?"

Sharon turned.

The man didn't go with the voice at all. He was a couple of inches over six feet with thick graying hair, had the shoulders of a hockey goalie and the weather-beaten features of a mountain climber. He was dressed in a dark suit, and his manner was as respectful as his tone. "Lyndon Gray, Miss Hays. I'm driving for Miss Cowan this evening. And this is Mr. Yadaka. He works with me."

Sharon shook hands with Gray, and offered her hand to Yadaka as well. The second man was Oriental and was shorter than Sharon's five-nine by a couple of inches. He was very slim with athletic movements, and Sharon suspected that this guy could handle himself. This pair could call themselves drivers, assistants, or whatever, but Sharon immediately pegged them as a couple of well-trained bodyguards. Yadaka's grip was light and fleeting. Sharon said, "How do you do?" The Oriental smiled and bowed.

Gray surveyed the gate area, missing nothing, his

gaze taking in every nook and cranny. "Your traveling companion?" he asked.

"Sure." Sharon raised her voice and called out to Melanie, who was reading a lighted ad for the Century Plaza Hotel. "Melanie. Over here." Sharon frantically waved. Melanie approached, warily regarding the Englishman.

"Mr. Yadaka will get your bags, miss," Gray said.

Sharon and Melanie handed over their ticket folders with claim checks stapled inside. Yadaka accepted the folders and mounted the escalator, taking steps two at a time on the way down. As Sharon watched, the Oriental hit the lower level at a jog and took off in the direction of the baggage claim.

"Good," Gray said. "Come along, please." He stood aside while Melanie climbed aboard the moving staircase, waited for Sharon to get on, and then brought up the rear one step above her.

As the escalator rolled downward, Sharon said over her shoulder, "Darla's not with you?"

"Miss Cowan is waiting in the car." Gray looked apologetically upward. "Afraid there's a bit of a problem."

"Oh?" Sharon turned partway around.

"Seems the newsies got wind. We gave them the slip on the way in, but I suspect you're in for some jostling when we leave the terminal. Mr. Yadaka and I can handle them if you'd like. You need merely walk straight ahead, eyes front. If you'd prefer to answer a few questions, feel free. A warning is in order. If you do answer a single question, they'll keep firing away until their muskets are empty."

Sharon's posture sagged. "Poor Darla. They won't leave her alone, huh?"

"As a rule, no. But celebrity sightings in Los Angeles are nothing new to newspapermen, and the media has ample background on Miss Cowan to use without ever speaking to her. I think you'll find it's you they're interested in."

"Oh, come on," Sharon said. "I'm not even part of the story here."

Gray's tone was tinged with sympathy. "Yesterday you weren't. Tomorrow you may not be again. But the media has zeroed in on you, Miss Hays, as evidenced by the pictures of you over and over on the telly. You being a former actress, in addition to the Rob Stanley clips, all that has whetted media appetites considerably. Miss Cowan has advised that you're not officially her attorney, but that's the way you've been introduced to the world. The first reporter to come up with an interview will consider it a career boost. They will devil you to death if you let them. People in Miss Cowan's position are used to the attention. You'd best become accustomed to it as well, at least on your journey through movieland." He smiled impersonally and professionally. "It's what I do, Miss Hays. Take my advice, it's a zoo out here."

During her starving actress days Sharon had envisioned just this scenario, rapid-fire questions coming from either side as she moved down a human corridor made up of reporters, minicams grinding, and bodyguards protecting her flanks. In her fantasy she was entering the Palladium on Oscar night, wearing a strapless and backless number she'd picked up on Rodeo Drive for five thousand bucks or so, and the newspeople were dying to know what she thought of her chances of taking the Best Actress award. She'd even imagined her own zippy response, something like, Oh no, not me, Kathleen's work in *Body Heat* was simply stunning, didn't you think? Actually, of course, she'd be hoping that Kathleen had a wreck on the way to the ceremony. As she'd run the gamut of reporters, she'd been giddy with ecstasy.

The reality was a bit of a letdown. The press was about as she'd imagined, young men and women in everything from suits and ties to jeans and T-shirts, waving steno pads and ballpoints in her face as the TV folks brandished microphones and cameramen pointed lenses in her direction. Sharon was far from ecstatic, however; she was exhausted and felt stupid as well. She walked at a fast clip in chilly night air, chin down, her gaze riveted on Melanie's carry-on as it rolled along ahead of her.

Yadaka and Gray must once have been Secret Service agents. The Brit and the Oriental moved along in half crouches and seemed to look everywhere at once, their gazes wary and watchful. The jostling became fierce as they passed the taxi stand; Gray shoved a skinny male reporter aside and then gently bumped Sharon in recoil. He uttered a crisp British "Excuse me, miss," before resuming his stalking posture, but Sharon had leaned hard enough against the guy to feel his shoulder rig. Driver, my foot, Sharon thought. He answers to Double-oh-something-or-other, and pinches Moneypenny's bottom on his way in to visit with M.

Melanie was in princess mode, ogling the reporters and giggling coquettishly, and any hope Sharon had harbored of the teenager sleeping a wink tonight went flying out the window. Twenty steps away, a shiny black Lincoln stretch waited at the curb.

A woman called out on Sharon's left, "What years were you on Broadway, Miss Hays?"

To which Sharon wanted to answer, It wasn't *on* Broadway, it was off, and it was sometime during the Jurassic era, but kept her head down and kept on trucking.

A man with a hoarse voice said loudly from the right, "Have you formed a plan for defending Darla Cowan as yet?"

Which caused Sharon to pause in mid-stride, wanting to say, I'm not defending anybody, bozo. Besides, Darla hasn't been charged, don't you read your own paper? Damn Milton Breyer and his public innuendoes all to hell. She ignored the question, but made a mental note that the next time she bumped into Breyer, the pompous ass was in for a tongue-lashing.

Yadaka jumped nimbly ahead, opened the limo

door, and hustled Melanie into the passenger compartment. Sharon glanced over her shoulder. The skycap whom Yadaka had recruited pulled his cart dutifully along, and Sharon thought the poor man looked scared to death. She turned back to the front, pushed down on her carry-on handle with a solid *click,* then scooped up the weightless piece of luggage and entered the limo as Yadaka smiled and bowed. The limo's passenger section had seats facing each other, and Sharon plopped down so that she looked out the rear window. Yadaka slammed the door, shutting out the noise just as a reporter screamed, "Miss Cowan? Any comment?" The limo's wraparound stereo played "Tara's Theme." Sharon blinked in shock as the trunk lid popped up and cut off her view. There was a series of thuds as the skycap tossed luggage into the trunk.

Melanie was seated directly across from Sharon, eyes shining as she peered out the window with her mouth agape. The overhead interior light came on as Gray climbed in behind the wheel, illuminating Darla Cowan as she leaned against the door behind the driver. Darla's hair and makeup were perfect. She looked at Sharon and grinned.

"You have some kind of following, lady," Darla said. "Excuse me for asking, but are you a movie star?"

Melanie was speechless at first, being in the company of a famous actress, but about fifteen minutes into the drive she began to pester Darla in a manner which would have driven Sharon up the wall. Melanie wanted to know what it was like to be in a movie. Sharon very nearly intervened, telling her that Miss Cowan was too tired for all this, but before Sharon could open her mouth Darla had launched into a full-blown discourse. Sharon sank back, every bit as mesmerized as her daughter.

Darla began with the first script reading, continued on through auditions, rehearsals, and shooting schedules, and even gave her impression of the first time she had seen her own image on the screen. Melanie was just getting started; now she wanted to know what Sean Penn was really like, and damned if Darla didn't know a few stories about Penn as well. There was the tiniest vibe in Darla's voice, a tremor in the dialogue which Sharon caught that no one else was likely to. She hadn't spent the better part of a year in Darla's constant company without latching on to the actress's changing moods. Darla was wound up like a two-bit alarm clock, a fact which made her patience with Melanie even more remarkable. Darla Cowan, kook, egomaniac, confused personality, taking time out from the murder of the year to converse with a starstruck kid. Sharon blinked in awe.

It was Sharon's first ever trip to Los Angeles, and she listened to Darla with one ear while watching the scenery out the window. A road sign told her that they were headed north on Highway One, which at this point was also called Lincoln Boulevard. Another sign on the left pointed toward Marina del Rey. Alongside the highway stood the most humongous miniature golf course that Sharon had ever seen, complete with a castle and a waterfall. Up ahead were still more reflecting signs, these pointing toward the Santa Monica Freeway. Sharon was so caught up in surveying the landscape that Melanie's questions became background noise—until she all at once asked, "Miss Cowan, do you know my dad?"

Sharon snapped her head around.

There was pin-drop silence, broken only by the music from the stereo. Sharon inhaled and held her breath. In the dimness, Darla looked her a question. Sharon gulped, shrugged, and nodded her head. She crossed both her fingers and her toes.

"Why, yes," Darla said, caution in her tone. "Known him since before you were born, in fact."

"From New York, when my mom lived there?"

Sharon pictured Darla auditioning for the part of "Old Woman Storyteller" in a Mother Goose production. The image was a stretch, but Darla made the role plausible by never batting an eye. She fixed Melanie with a confidential smile. Sharon resumed her peering out the window, but had one ear cocked in a listening attitude.

"You don't remember this," Darla said, "but except for your mother and the doctors and nurses, I was the first person to see you after you were born. You drooled all over my blouse, young lady."

Melanie wriggled in fascination. "Even before my dad saw me?"

Uh-oh, Sharon thought, not good. Not only had Rob never visited the hospital, Sharon had sworn Darla to secrecy that she was pregnant at all, and if Rob *had* shown up he likely would have brought his current sweetie along. None of which Melanie knew; ever since Rob had come back into their lives, Sharon had allowed her daughter to live with the fantasy that Rob had been All-American Dad, and that it was only the rigors of his career which had kept him away for, oh, eleven years or so. As if Rob were freaking Ulysses or something.

Darla said, simply and quietly, "Right. Even before your dad."

Melanie sat proudly upright. "While we're in California, my dad may take us on a tour of the studio."

Sharon's jaws clenched. Darla watched her, but Sharon looked at her lap. Me and my big mouth, Sharon thought. With his current status regarding child support, it's unlikely we'll be able to get Rob on the phone.

Darla's mouth set in determination as she returned her attention to Melanie and patted the teenager's hand. "Right. I run into him occasionally, and he's dying to see you. And as for the studio tour, you can bet your boots that he's going to take you. Sometime tomorrow I'll give him a call."

They drove by places with names straight from Aaron Spelling television shows, Pacific Palisades, Topanga Canyon, Sunset Boulevard, Malibu Canyon

Drive. On the driver's side of the car were majestic cliffs, below which the night black Pacific Ocean rolled and swelled. Melanie *oh*-ed and *ah*-ed at every bend in the road. Sharon and Darla exchanged buddy-buddy glances, and Darla grinned in satisfaction. Sharon looked over her shoulder. Gray and Yadaka sat in front like wooden sentinels.

They left the highway a mile or so past Malibu Canyon Road and took to the cliffs, up a narrow gravel road with barely enough room for two autos to pass abreast, twisting and turning as the headlights reflected from boulders the size of modest homes. Gray finally steered the limo between two giant slabs of granite and entered a clearing bathed in moonlight. The ground was flat and covered with twisting broadleaf vines. The plateau extended ahead for a hundred yards or so, and ended abruptly in a dropoff. Visible over the precipice were snow white rocks and crashing waves. Directly ahead was a driveway leading to a high iron gate. The gate was centered in a ten-foot brick wall which extended on either side to the dropoff. Visible through the gate was a monstrous house, its front bright as day in a floodlight's beam. Tall white pillars fronted the porch, and the entry door was dark wood with a brass knocker in the shape of eagle's wings. In the driveway between the gate and the house sat a sports car which Sharon believed to be a Jag. She sucked in a breath and murmured, "God."

The limo rolled smoothly forward, crunching gravel. A panel truck sat before the gate, both front doors swinging open as the limo approached. A man toting a minicam emerged from behind the wheel as a woman alighted from the passenger seat. As the limo stopped before the gate, Sharon read the sign on the side of the truck. KERA TV. Yadaka pointed a remote, and the gate swung wide. The reporter tapped on the window by Sharon's ear, and the cameraman pointed his lens. Sharon ignored both the woman and the minicam as Gray steered the limo through the gate and parked behind the Jag. As the bodyguards opened the trunk to remove the luggage, and as the women and the teenager got out of the limo and walked up on the porch, the on-the-spot news lady stood at the gate and fired a question through the bars. Any comment on the murders? Christ, Sharon thought, if anyone in this group had a comment, sweetie, you'd have gotten it by now. Try Milton Breyer, he'll give you the scoop of the century. Darla used a key to open the door, and then led the way inside. Sharon followed Melanie into the biggest entry hall she'd ever seen. Darla went over and peered outside. "Any comment, Miss Cowan?" the newswoman yelled. Darla slammed the huge front door, cutting the outside world off from their view.

The ocean made a never ending hissing sound, a constant *sssssst!* as if it had secrets to tell. Sharon watched the breakers roll in, white gashes on a field of black, appearing in the distance out of nothingness, dissolving into foam as the waves hit the rocks fifty feet below. The air was free of smog this far from the city, and a three-quarter moon showed above the edge of a cliff. The strip of beach was even whiter than the breakers. She was certain she'd never seen anything so gorgeous in her life, not even when she and Darla had played a local theater gig at Cape Cod. She sipped Cutty, made a face, and clinked the ice around. "I could die happy here," Sharon said.

Darla reclined on a chaise longue near the balcony railing, classic legs stretched out below a thigh-length kimono. Her ankles were crossed. "I thought I was going to, several times."

Sharon raised her rock glass to her lips. "Die happy here?"

"Just die."

"You need to shake out of it. You've got a lot of decades left to live."

Darla lifted her own drink, Tanqueray with tonic and a twist of lime. "I'm sad for David, even though there were times I could have done it myself." She managed a halfhearted chuckle. "That I'm a suspect in something like that is pretty silly, isn't it?"

Sharon continued to watch the ocean, and felt a tug of despair. She debated leveling with Darla about her situation, telling the actress that arrest was likely imminent, then decided against it. She said, changing the subject, "Melanie will beat those video games of yours to death. Forget her sleeping tonight."

Darla sat up and hugged her knees. "She's darling. I wish I had kids."

"You need to know them when they're small and cuddly, and then hang on to the memory through the lovely teens," Sharon said. She got up from her director's chair, walked up to the balcony, and peered down on the rocks. "It's not near as cool out here as I thought it would be. The forecast said what on the beaches, in the forties?"

"Television weathermen never include Malibu in their prognostics." Darla gestured to the south, waving her glass. "There's a point down there shielding the wind. We'll average ten degrees warmer here than the beaches south of L.A. Something about the currents, they tell me."

Sharon had changed into bedclothes, which for her consisted of a tee, size XXL, and panties. The T-shirt was orange, with black lettering on the front saying, "I'm a Virgin." On the back was a smaller parenthetical caption, "This is a very old shirt." She'd bought the garment in Deep Ellum and had thought it hilarious, but had never gotten up the nerve to wear it anyplace outside her bedroom. She peered down at pounding surf and at waves breaking up on the beach, and felt a bit dizzy.

Darla left the chaise and stood beside Sharon at the rail. She rolled her glass across her forehead. "God, Sharon. I just want all of this to go away."

One corner of Sharon's mouth tugged to the side. She tried a dose of reality. "Get used to it. For you it won't ever be over, as long as you're a public figure. People will remember." She walked back over and sat in the director's chair, and had a sip of scotch. "Do something to take your mind off it. Read a few scripts, plan your next movie. I suspect you can name your price, as long as you don't wait until the iron is cold."

"*Hah.*" Darla went back to the chaise, curled up her legs, and sat on her ankles. "I've got seven or eight scripts downstairs my agent sent. Top directors, hotshot writers, all of them. In every plot I'm fucking somebody. A cop in one, the president in another. Half the guys are married, but my character's not supposed to care about that. There's even one where I'm a murderous lunatic again." She stared off into space for a moment. "You know what I did? When they were casting *Little Women,* I offered to work for scale if they'd just give me a part. The casting director told my agent"—she tucked her chin and deepened her voice—" 'We got no fuck-me roles. Call you back when I get one, okay?' I swear, Sharon, I'd rather be selling Playskool blocks."

The reference brought a smile to Sharon's lips. Once she and Darla, out of work and down to their last slice of bologna, had accepted a gig during Christmas season at F.A.O. Schwarz. There they'd dressed up as alphabet blocks and jiggled kiddies on their knees, and one of the little darlings had poured glue in Darla's hair. They'd cursed their agent for weeks. They had, however, laughed all the way home. They'd found something funny in every situation in those days, which had had a lot to do with seeing them through the lean times. Sharon sighed and looked out to sea. "What's tomorrow's schedule?" she said.

"We're due in Chet Verdon's office at ten. It's downtown."

"Verdon being your contracts attorney?"

"Right. Beginning at one, we're supposed to talk to a string of criminal lawyers." Darla seemed thoughtful. "I should tell you, Chet didn't like the idea of my bringing you along."

"I suspect that's putting it mildly. Look, Darla, if you want me to bow out of the picture—"

"No way." Darla showed her classic profile, her gaze to the west. "I told you on the phone, I don't trust these people. I don't even trust Chet all that much. I had to put my foot down. Told him, without you by my side I'm speaking to no one."

Sharon was flattered, but a bit awestruck as well. "If the meetings aren't till one, isn't ten a bit early for us to show up?"

"There'll be the two-hour lunch before. People in L.A. make careers out of lunch, just like in New York. Saves me some on my fees, believe it or not. Chet's theory is, if he's seen with me and I'm his client, it'll drum up more business for him." She laughed. "That's not something he told me. It's just that every time we're in a restaurant, all of a sudden I'm introduced to all these people I never heard of. Chet represents me for three hundred dollars an hour. For common people he charges *four* hundred."

Sharon wondered how much business she could drum up by lunching with her illustrious client Tired Darnell. Now, that would really impress the crowd at Sfuzzi's or wherever. A coolish ocean breeze wafted across her legs, raising a few goose bumps. "Power lunch, check," she said. "That'll be from eleven till one. What do we do for the first hour, plan strategy?"

Darla seemed hesitant. "Well, first there's the press conference. That's at ten-fifteen."

Sharon's eyes widened in the moonlight. "There's the what?"

Darla finished her drink and set the glass aside. "I told Chet you wouldn't approve. That's when we first got into it over my bringing you at all."

"You shouldn't be talking to the press, Darla. That's true in Texas *and* in California. It's true in freaking *Afganistan,* for God's sake."

"Chet thinks you're being paranoid. That the idea I'm any kind of suspect is ridiculous."

"Milton Breyer is ridiculous. *Criminal law* is ridiculous, but that doesn't change anything."

"Chet says, what I need to do is get things out in the open. Let the public know I'm not hiding something."

Sharon couldn't believe her ears. "A *lawyer* told you that?"

Darla shrugged. "UCLA. Class of '73, unless his sheepskin is a phony."

Sharon set her glass down and folded her arms. "I think perhaps I should stay here at the house tomorrow and catch up on my ocean watching."

There was a sudden edge in Darla's tone. "You promised you'd go with me."

"I'm afraid I'll spoil your meeting."

"Without you there is no meeting. I've made that clear to Chet."

Sharon pretended to sneeze, to give herself just a second to think. Just as quickly as Darla had charmed the pants off Melanie, she'd now lapsed into her bitchy mode. One of the most impossible, totally unpredictable . . . no, check that, *the* most impossible . . .

"You *have* to, Sharon," Darla said.

Sharon lost it. "Let me tell you something. I don't have to do a goddamned thing."

Darla's mouth went slack in shock.

Sharon testily flipped her bangs. "I'll tell you something about evidence. There was a dead man found in the hotel room where you were registered, Darla, and there are about four thousand witnesses who can place you on the scene within the right time frame. The dead man just happened to be this guy you've been living with, and you and that gentleman just happened to have a screaming fight in front of four thousand more witnesses about six hours before the murder. Oh, yes, you also left your rental car at the hotel and fled the scene in a taxi, before which you came screaming into the lobby with your clothes torn half off. Those circumstances alone are enough for Dallas County to issue a probable-cause warrant for your arrest, if they haven't already. If you talk to the media, they're going to question you about all of this. Your choices will be to refuse to answer, in which case you'll look guilty as hell, or to give a lengthy denial, every detail of which the district attorney can pin you down to at a later date. No press conferences, Darla, and that's *so* important . . ."

"Dammit, Sharon, I can explain. I walked out on David and gave him the keys to that car as I was leaving. Told him if he was through beating me up, here was his transportation to the airport. Told him the rental contract was in the glove compartment."

Sharon expelled air through her nose. "You left him alive?"

Darla gave an emphatic nod. "Damned straight."

"Okay," Sharon said, "now I'll cross-examine. You left him alive in front of who as a witness?"

Darla turned her back. "We were alone in the room. You know that."

"Yeah, right." Sharon walked around so that she and Darla were eye to eye. "And what happened next, Miss Cowan? Was David Spencer then so grief-stricken over your departure that he ran around the room stabbing himself and then shot himself in the head? And if he did, who put him in bed and tucked the covers up under his chinny-chin-chin, and who took the gun and knife away?"

Darla closed her eyes and hugged herself. "Someone. Someone besides me."

Sharon felt a twinge of conscience. "Look, I told you on the phone, you shouldn't discuss anything without your lawyer present, and this is an example of why. You're going to be asked all kinds of questions, and you need to think your responses over very carefully. You certainly shouldn't be giving any answers to the media."

"Chet will be sitting right there when I lay it out to the reporters. So will you. Come on, Sharon, the idea that anyone suspects me, that's silly."

"You'll think silly," Sharon said, "once Milton Breyer is finished with you. Look, I'm not commenting on what Dallas County will or won't do; that will come out in the wash. But talking to the police without an understanding, especially where you're so near to the crime, that's akin to suicide, and that goes double for talking to the newspapers. If Milton has no plans to indict you, that's all well and good. But the newspapers are going to twist your words around to fit whatever slant they're putting on the story, and telling them anything can't possibly help you. And if what they say in print paints Dallas County in any sort of bad light, then granting an interview will prompt Milt Breyer to charge you out of spite. And I don't care if your Mr. Verdon wrote the California Legal Statutes, if he's advising you to talk to the media, he's advising you wrong."

Darla's mouth quivered. Sharon had seen the expression before, and it meant that Darla was about to burst into tears. Which she always did at the most inconvenient times imaginable. Darla laid her palm alongside her face. "I just don't know who to believe."

"Try me," Sharon said. "I don't have a profit motive."

Darla sniffled. "Will you please go with me? Explain all this to Chet?"

"He's a lawyer, so he understands every smidgen of it. He sure doesn't need me to lay it out. The problem is, he sounds like one of these publicity hounds."

Darla began to shake, the preliminary to an out-and-out bawling session. "Please go, Sharon. Whatever you tell me, I'll do."

Sharon got up, went over to the rail, and peered down at the sea. The scenery somehow didn't seem as breathtaking as before. She had no business cutting in between Darla and her paid counsel, and was certain now that any meeting with Verdon would be a nasty scene. She was also Darla's friend, of course. She tossed off the rest of her scotch. "It's almost two where I come from," Sharon said. "Let's sleep on it, Darla, okay?"

12

Sharon spent the night in a dead man's bed, and had a bad dream. In the dream she stood at one end of a tunnel. Darla ran toward her, naked and panting from exertion, nameless beasts in pursuit, their forelegs sprouting hands with clawlike fingers. The fingers snatched at Darla's breasts and buttocks and twisted in her hair. The monsters snarled like wolves. They had no faces, only slitted yellow eyes. Her legs pumping for all she was worth, Darla neared the end of the tunnel, where Sharon waited with open arms.

Sharon hugged Darla in a protective embrace, then shoved her back and stood between her and the monsters. The beast-things were on them at once, and Sharon lifted her hands as a shield. One monster's teeth sank into her forearm, tearing away skin, muscle, and a chunk of bone. Sharon was drenched in blood. Her body was wet from head to toe.

She awoke with a chill and sat bolt upright. The sheets beneath her were soaked, and she'd kicked the covers into wilted pretzels of cloth. Morning daylight filtered in from the balcony. The bed lamp was on, and she switched it off. The clock showed a few minutes after seven. She stretched and yawned, stood up on padded carpet, and walked outside. Her T-shirt was wet with perspiration and rode up to expose her panties. The cool air made her shiver. She yanked down the T-shirt's hem and covered herself to her knees.

The sun's rays over the roof lent a yellowish tint to the rocks and painted the ocean crystal blue. The breakers were whiter than they'd appeared in night-time. A string of buoys floated in the distance, rocking and bobbing. Nearer the shore, seagulls dove and struck and cawed. Sharon filled her lungs with the sweetest air imaginable and went back inside.

She bathed in a sunken Jacuzzi tub the size of her room back in Dallas, and turned on the jets for a while. A ledge was lined with every fragrant soap, shampoo, or body oil known to woman. Sharon selected lilac. She finished her bath, toweled herself to a healthy pink, blow-dried her hair, and went downstairs in a terry-cloth robe.

Darla had conducted the cook's tour the night before, and the house had two kitchens. One was the standard bard's variety, complete with island stove, and the other was a nook behind the bar which opened into both the den and the game room. The larger kitchen was deserted, so she passed through and walked toward the den. A sizzling noise reached her ears, and the odor of smoky maple bacon frying wafted into her nostrils. Visible inside the kitchenette, Lyndon Gray waved a spatula in greeting. He wore a cook's hat and had an apron tied around his waist. "Morning, miss," he called out. "And you'll have your eggs . . . ?"

Sharon normally ate only a piece of toast for breakfast, but the salt air had made her ravenous. "Over easy," she said. "Do you have orange juice?"

Gray's arm dipped out of sight as he used the spatula to flip something over on the stove. "Frozen or squeezed?"

She blinked. "Squeezed. What if I'd said, Benedict with Hollandaise?"

He looked up mildly. "Is that what you want?"

Her chin tilted. "No, just . . . over easy, please."

"My pleasure, miss." Gray raised his voice and looked through the window into the den. "Your pancakes will be ready in a moment, Miss Hays. Maple syrup or strawberry jam?" He grinned at Sharon. "The other Miss Hays, Miss Hays."

Melanie answered, from somewhere around the corner, "The jam, Jeeves, the jam. Wow, you're spoiling me."

Gray smiled, picked up tongs, and expertly turned a slice of bacon. Sharon rounded the corner and entered the den.

Melanie was seated on a chintz sofa half the length of a football field. She was dead center on the cushions with a television remote in her lap. A sixty-inch television screen practically covered one wall of the den, and Joan Lunden's image seemed seven feet tall. On the wall adjacent to the television was a case with plastic doors, its shelves lined with videotapes. *Spring of the Comanche*, four copies, five copies of *Termination*, a thriller in which David Spencer had appeared with Harrison Ford. Every tape in the case was one of Spencer's movies. Sharon quickly scanned the titles. Nothing featuring Darla, unless it was one of the unlabeled cartridges near the bottom. She said to Melanie, "Sleep good?"

Melanie gave a sideways smirk. "Are you kidding? Slept none, Mom. I was awake at three a.m., and I've been sitting here fooling with this thing since four o'clock."

Sharon sat on the end of the sofa and watched *Good Morning, America*. "You could get whiplash, like sitting on the front row in a movie theater."

"You ain't seen nothing yet."

Sharon's tone sharpened. "Haven't seen anything, Melanie. Haven't seen anything."

"Oh, be cool, Mom." Melanie thumbed the remote, and as if by magic a program schedule appeared, superimposed over Joan Lunden's image. The schedule was identical to the one in *TV Guide*, with times of day heading a row of columns in which various programs appeared. The top row was shaded. Melanie clicked something on the remote, and the shaded area moved down a row. She clicked some more, and the shaded area jumped downward until it covered a Three Stooges title. Melanie pressed a button. Joan

Lunden vanished in a flash, and Sharon chuckled as Larry hit Curly in the face with a pie. Melanie said, "Satellite dish. Two hundred stations. Twenty or thirty movie channels. If I lived here, I'd watch TV all day, every day, and with Jeeves in there on duty I'd weigh a million pounds."

"His name is Mr. Gray," Sharon said. Her gaze roamed to the doorway through which she'd just entered the room. "At least you'll have something to keep you occupied while I'm downtown with Miss Cowan."

"Plenty occupied. I'm going on a tour of Hollywood."

Sharon's forehead tightened. "Oh? With whom?"

Melanie brought the schedule back up on the screen and moved the shaded area down. "Don't worry, Mom. Just be cool."

Sharon snatched the remote away and laid it on the coffee table. "I *am* cool. Let me tell you something, young lady."

Melanie turned with a retort on her lips, then caught something in her mother's look which caused her to close her mouth.

"You are thirteen years old," Sharon said. "You've got several more years to put up with me, and put up you must. Now. What tour is this, and with whom?"

"Just something Jeeves said." Melanie scooted down on the sofa.

Gray walked in from the kitchen carrying a plate of fluffy pancakes. "Do you wish to eat at the table, Miss Hays, that's Miss *Melanie* Hays, or do you want service on the porch?" He stopped, took in the scene, and said to Sharon, "I've arranged entertainment for the young lady. I hope you don't mind."

Sharon stood. "Sure, if it's safe."

"Oh, it is right enough, ma'am. One of our operatives will take her to Universal Studios and on a tour of Hollywood homes. It's quite the thing for visitors."

Sharon frowned. "Your operatives?"

Gray nodded. "From our security agency. Mrs. Welton. She's retired from the L.A. Police. Is a grand-mother and quite taken with children."

Sharon looked at Melanie, who was watching with a hopeful expression. She said to Gray, "Well, sure. The woman will be with her constantly?"

"Every step of the way, miss," Gray said.

Sharon smiled at her daughter. "Of course, then." She stepped around the sofa. "I was wondering, all those videotapes. There are none of Darla's movies?"

Gray looked toward the stand-up case. His forehead wrinkled. "Mr. Spencer was taken with his image on the screen. Miss Cowan wasn't taken with hers, so they compromised by watching him."

"Not even those blanks . . . ?"

Gray seemed puzzled, then his gaze rested on the unlabeled cartridges near the bottom of the case. "Oh, no, miss. That's a project of mine."

Sharon looked at him.

"I've recorded every news report I can since Mr. Spencer's death." Gray pointed at a VCR on a low table in the corner. The red light glowed, indicating that the machine was on. "I'm taping CNN even as we speak. Just anticipating, miss, that Miss Cowan's defense team should review them if the worst happens for her."

Sharon was impressed. "Marvelous idea, Mr. Gray. You've got quite a bit of law enforcement training, don't you?"

"Some." Gray stepped toward the kitchen. "Your eggs will be ready soon."

Sharon grinned as a thought came to her. "How do you take your martinis, Mr. Gray?"

Gray paused in the doorway, then showed a smile of his own. "Stirred, Miss Hays. That shaking bit, that bruises the gin." He disappeared into the alcove.

Sharon followed and stood behind the Englishman as he expertly flipped sizzling eggs with a spatula. "Has Darla already eaten?" Sharon asked.

Gray's features creased in worry. "I fancy she's in

a bit of a foul mood. She didn't respond when I rang her up."

Sharon glanced at the clock on the mantel. "If we're to be downtown by ten, she'd better get a move on."

Gray looked perturbed. "Miss Cowan's wants are changeable, I've discovered." He had the look of a man speaking from experience.

So *that's* the deal, Sharon thought. She chewed her lip. She'd given Darla a pretty good verbal thrashing last night. As retribution Darla had gotten up this morning and decided to be difficult. In her off-Broadway days she'd driven more than one director bananas, and Sharon could imagine what she was like now that she was a major star. For just how long the actress might pout was anybody's guess; Darla's highs and lows were far enough apart to be on the manic-depressive side. Once in New York, after a director had given her a dressing-down, Darla had refused to come out of her room for two or three days. Sharon had considered herself a better than passable actress, in the eighty percentile range, but Darla's talent had been ten zillion cuts above. The really great ones, a writer had once told Sharon, are ninety percent schizo. Of all the times, Sharon thought. Of all the freaking times.

She strode briskly through the den as Gray paused in the kitchen door. "I'll have a word with Miss Cowan, Mr. Gray," Sharon said.

Gray seemed relieved. "I was hoping you would. Sometimes a woman's touch . . ."

As Sharon left the room, she threw the Englishman a confident wink. "Better hold the eggs, okay?" she said. "You just keep providing the muscle, Mr. Gray, and leave the celebrity pampering up to me. I've got a teenage daughter I've been practicing on."

Sharon climbed the stairs and hustled down the hall-way with terry cloth swirling around her calves. She felt as if she'd checked into the inn at Bonkersville. Thirteen years removed from showbiz, she'd forgotten the problems involved in dealing with High-Strung

Artist Syndrome. Once long ago she'd lured Darla onstage for Act II by promising to do her nails. She reached the door to Darla's bedroom and knocked softly.

"Go away." The door muffled Darla's voice.

"It's Sharon, sweetie. Mind if I come in?"

"Sharon who? I used to have a friend named Sharon."

Sharon scratched her chin. She knocked again, more firmly this time. "Open up, Darla. We need to visit."

"Visit about what? You've made your feelings clear."

Sharon puffed out her lower lip and blew upward through her bangs, and rested clenched fists on her waist. "Well, let me make them clearer. I'm worried to death about you."

"Hah!"

"Darla, if you don't get ready and come with me to your attorney's office, Texas may very well issue a warrant and haul you back to Dallas in handcuffs." And likely will anyway, Sharon thought, though telling Darla now would only create more problems.

"Let them, then."

Sharon rolled her eyes.

"Besides, you told me you weren't going," Darla said.

Sharon sighed in exasperation. "I said no such thing."

"Did, too."

"I said we'd sleep on it."

"I'm not any publicity hound, Sharon. I didn't ask for this."

It was an effort, but Sharon softened her voice into a sympathetic purr. "No one said that you did. You're a victim of circumstance if ever there was one."

"Damn right. Not that anyone cares."

Sharon gently jiggled the door handle. "Come on, let me in."

"No. Go away."

Sharon actually took a step in the direction of the

stairs. To hell with Darla, let her learn about the justice system the hard way. Then she had a flashback, Darla in a hospital room thirteen years ago, holding Melanie in her arms. She'd looked as if she was afraid of hurting the baby, and had looked upon Melanie with an adoration akin to worship. Sharon sidled up to the door and gently knocked. She tried her last resort. "Can't we talk things over?" she cooed. "Come on, I'll do your nails."

There was silence, followed by the sound of approaching footsteps. The latch clicked. The footsteps retreated.

Sharon pushed the door halfway open. Darla was seated at a vanity wearing a shortie nightgown. She'd set Pearl Drops polish and a bottle of remover in front of her. Her hair was disheveled. Even without makeup Darla Cowan was one of the most stunning women Sharon had ever laid eyes on.

Sharon walked over and leaned a hip against the vanity. "You're having one helluva time of it, aren't you?"

Darla extended a hand, fingers spread. "I'm not promising I'll go."

Sharon reached for the polish remover. "I think you should. You must. If I wasn't your friend, I wouldn't be telling you that."

Darla's lower lip trembled. "Will you look out for me with those lawyers?"

Sharon briskly shook the bottle. The liquid gurgled and glugged. She uncapped the bottle, soaked a cotton ball with polish remover, and used her free hand to grip Darla's forefinger lightly. "Of course I will."

Darla testily crossed her legs. "You *have to,* Sharon," she said.

Mrs. Welton turned out to be totally no sweat, as far as Melanie's safety was concerned. She was British like Lyndon Gray, a trim woman who could have been fifty, and five minutes after she arrived at the house she and Melanie were thick as thieves. As Mrs. Welton opened her purse to exhibit pictures of her grand-daughter, the butt of a pistol protruded above the compact box of Kleenex and package of Beechnut gum stowed inside. Sometime during her visit Mrs. Welton winked at Sharon and said conspiratorially, "She'll be fine with me, ma'am." Sharon quit worrying on the spot.

Later she stood beside the limo along with Gray and Yadaka, and watched the Jag stop inside the gate with Mrs. Welton behind the wheel. Melanie sat in the passenger seat, giggling. She was coordinated in red from head to toe, and wore big, round sunglasses perched atop her head. Visible through the Jag's rear window, Mrs. Welton fiddled with something on the dashboard. The electronic gate hummed open. The Jag rolled smoothly out and turned down the mountain road toward the freeway as the gate swung closed.

Sharon turned conversationally to Yadaka. "What do you guys do when you're not playing nursemaid?" She'd yet to hear the Oriental utter a word, and half-way expected him to say he went home, left his shoes outside, and sat cross-legged on the floor while enjoying a nice warm sake.

Instead Yadaka folded his arms. "There's a couple of dance joints out in the Valley," he said in an accentless tenor. "After a day of guarding *this* lady, I gotta let my hair down."

Sharon closed her mouth. She was dressed in a summerweight gray courtroom suit and medium black heels, and had a red filmy scarf around her throat to add a splash of color. She turned to Gray. "You go along with him?" she said.

The Englishman had replaced his chef's outfit with a black suit, complete with bulge under his arm. "I'm past all that, Miss Hays, and I've got children at home. I leave the partying up to Benny."

Sharon's eyebrow arched. "Benny?"

"That's me," Yadaka said.

"Besides," Gray said, "I'm afraid Miss Cowan

keeps me busy enough that I'm too exhausted for evening frivolity."

"That I can imagine," Sharon said.

The Englishman looked toward the house. "Speaking of whom," he said.

Sharon peered toward the mansion as well. Darla came out on the porch wearing a navy suit which showed a tasteful amount of knee, and matching spikes. Her hair was up, blond tresses swirled around in a little curl over one ear. She held out her hand, fingers spread, examining her nail polish. I was a little rusty, Sharon thought, but considering the circumstances it ain't a bad job. Darla closed the door and clicked rapidly down the steps, smiling. Kim Novak, Sharon thought, the spitting image. *Vertigo* was one of her favorites, and she wondered if anyone in Hollywood had considered a remake. Darla could play the part standing on her head. Sharon watched a seagull drift lazily over the precipice, then swoop toward the ocean like a dive bomber. "God, this is gorgeous," she said. "Back home we spend most of our time at the courthouse with trash lining the streets and drunks all over the sidewalks. Talk about a change."

Gray chuckled as he climbed into the driver's seat. "We're going to downtown L.A., Miss Hays," he said. "I expect you might find yourself in familiar surroundings there."

Darla's mood had changed again. In the less than twelve hours that Sharon had been in California, Darla had gone from patient storyteller (with Melanie last night in the limo) to petulant neurotic (this morning in her room), and now showed panicky fear. On the drive into L.A., she sat with her spine straight as a ramrod, taking a death grip on the door handle at every bend in the freeway. Her lips were set in a worried line. Sharon would have liked to say something, anything, to snap Darla out of her frightened state, but decided to let well enough alone. Darla had been through a ton in the past three days. If Sharon had been in Darla's place, she might go on the run.

Gray had pegged the downtown section of Los Angeles pretty well. As they left the elevated Hollywood Freeway and took the ramp to ground level, Southern California—or at least its image—the ocean, the beaches, wooded San Gabriel peaks, and avenues loaded with movie stars—ceased to exist, and Downtown Bigcity, Anytown U.S.A., popped into view. They drove among towering skyscrapers, with drug emporiums and clothing stores occupying glass-front locations along the sidewalks. The streets were jammed with autos. Taxis dodged in and out, changing lanes, and buses chugged and coughed exhaust fumes. On the sidewalks were hustling businesspeople toting briefcases, and a like number of homeless men. Sharon had never set foot in Los Angeles in her life, but when they passed an area of ground-floor lawyers' offices and signs advertising bail bondsmen, she scanned the horizon in search of the L.A. Criminal Courts Building. And sure enough, she spotted the place, an ornate, wide structure with pillars in front, surrounded by parks with benches for pigeon feeding and graft exchange. Catwalks led from the criminal courts to a massive adjacent structure, and Sharon knew without being told that she was looking at the jail.

Gray steered the limo into a multistory garage a mile south of the courts, and parked on the sixth level between a Chevy Blazer and a cement post. Visible across fifty feet of slanted concrete floor, men and women streamed to and from a bank of elevators. Gray snappily held Sharon's door open while Yadaka played usher on Darla's side. Sharon started to climb out, then paused. Darla hadn't moved. She stared helplessly at Sharon, as if frozen in her seat.

Sharon leaned over close to the actress. "Look," Sharon said, "it won't be as bad as you think. Anytime you think you're going to faint, feel free to lean on me. It's what I came here for." She gave Darla's hand an affectionate pat and scooted toward the door.

Gray and Yadaka did their job without a lot of fanfare, stopping one elevator by using the emergency button, then courteously but forcefully herding passengers into a separate car so that the Darla Cowan entourage could ride up alone. Sharon waited with Darla off to one side. The meeting with Darla's paid civil attorney now at hand, Sharon had some last-minute planning to do.

Diplomacy had never been her strong suit, as several Dallas County judges and prosecutors would attest, but she was far from her turf here and on the ragged edge of legality. She couldn't afford to get off on the wrong foot with Mr. Verdon for several reasons. Though she'd been adamant in telling Darla that she couldn't act as her attorney, Milton Breyer's popping off to the media had placed her in a shaky position. She didn't have a California license and didn't plan to make appearances in L.A. courts; outside the courtroom, however, there was a large gray area as to what was and wasn't practicing law. She'd agreed to give Darla her advice as to retaining a lawyer. So okay, when did friendly advice become legal advice? She wasn't taking any money for her services, but the fact that Darla wasn't paying her didn't necessarily mean she wasn't functioning as a lawyer. This Chet Verdon person was already in a snit over Darla's bringing Sharon along, and if she crossed him, Verdon could give her a lot of grief with the Bar Association. Sharon decided that the most prudent course was to walk on eggs.

She bent her head and said to Darla, "I think Mr. Verdon and I should visit alone."

Darla looked up fearfully, her gaze flicking to Gray and Yadaka as they herded passengers onto the adjacent elevator. "Without me?" Darla said.

"Just for a few minutes. I want to make sure he

doesn't think I'm trying to horn in on his legal practice."

"I've already told him you had the final word."

Just super, Sharon thought. Verdon might already have a restraining order prepared, to serve on this smartass Texas female. "I want to be on good terms with this guy," Sharon said, "and need to tell him in private exactly where I'm coming from."

Darla's mouth curved petulantly. "Well, what am I going to do while you accomplish this?"

Sharon paused. Dealing with Darla was a lot like dealing with Melanie. *What can I play with while you're trying some nasty old murder case, Mom?* With Melanie the answer was to purchase more video games. Sharon wondered if Darla would be interested in a quick round of Sonic the Hedgehog, or possibly some comic books to read as she sat in the waiting room. Sharon had an idea. "Why don't you get a hold of Rob?" she asked.

Darla frowned. "Rob Stanley?"

"Sure. It was so right on the way you handled Melanie last night, I thought we could talk to Rob about showing his daughter around. You remember, you promised you'd call him?"

Darla examined her nails. She stepped determinedly into the elevator with Sharon on her heels and Gray and Yadaka bringing up the rear. "Damn right I did," Darla said. "No way is he going to get away with ignoring his own child. No way." She reached over and patted Sharon on the shoulder. "I'll be glad to handle it for you, Sharon. Just think. What would you do without me?"

Sharon built a strong dislike for Chet Verdon at her first glimpse of the guy. As they exited the elevator on the skyscraper's twenty-third floor, the corridor was jammed with media people. Yadaka led the way over foam-padded carpet in a replay of last night's airport scene, reporters firing questions and minicams humming. Sharon was stunned. She'd known that Verdon

had arranged a press conference, but she'd expected
something more orderly. It's a zoo out here, Gray had
told her. Definitely a freak show, Sharon thought, the
people watching the animals and vice versa.

They approached a set of clear glass partitions, with
gilt letters spelling out VERDON & RUMINEK, P.C., AT-
TORNEYS AND COUNSELORS AT LAW. Beyond the partitions was a huge semicircular reception desk, and
behind the desk sat an I'm-gorgeous starlet type who
was pressing buttons and routing calls. As Sharon followed Yadaka down the hall, a man hurried through
the reception area and out into the corridor.

Hollywood Harry to a T, Sharon thought. The guy
was an inch or two over six feet tall, with thick razored
hair graying just so around his temples, and he sported
a golf course tan. He wore a pale gray silk suit and
matching tie, showing a full six inches of snow white
cuff at either wrist. His cuff links were silver with inset
diamonds. His teeth were perfect, obviously capped,
and his muscular neck and broad shoulders indicated
that he spent a lot of time in the weight room. Sharon's hackles stirred in reflex.

"Darla, love," the man said, elbowing past the Oriental, practically running Sharon over as she scram-
bled to get out of his way, taking Darla's hands and
giving her a peck, first on one cheek and then the
other. "So glad you could. So glad you could." He
backpedaled now, sending Sharon up against the wall
among the reporters as he hauled Darla back toward
his office. Darla moved docilely along, eyes wide. "Hi,
Chet," she timidly said. Gray and Yadaka exchanged
a look as they followed. Sharon blew upward through
her bangs as she trudged along behind.

Verdon paused in his office entry and turned to the
media. "Give us a second, guys," he said. "Hey, appreciate your cooperation. I'll let you know when it's
all right to come in."

Darla pulled away and steered Sharon forward by
the elbow. "Chet, this is Sharon Hays, my friend from
Dallas. She's a lawyer, too."

Verdon's mouth curved in a humorless smile. He extended his hand. "Yes, I know. Nice to meet you, Cheryl."

Sharon forced a smile of her own. Verdon's skin was smooth and dry. "Sharon," she said.

"Sharon," he repeated disinterestedly, then raised a hand to the reporters. "Be just a minute. We'll let you know." He led Darla into the reception area, letting the door swing closed in Sharon's face. She pushed through with her shoulder with Gray and Yadaka on her heels. The Englishman and the Oriental sat on a plush leather sofa and picked up magazines.

"Let's go back," Verdon said, extending his arm toward the interior of the office. "We should go over a few things."

Darla seemed hesitant, obviously scared to death of this guy. Major star or whatever, Darla was basically a timid person. L.A. would be crawling with people who knew how to take advantage of people's fear, which was how stars became puppets and the puppeteers bought houses in the South of France. Darla needed someone to stand up for her when Verdon decided to push her around. She showed Sharon a help-me look. Sharon imperceptibly nodded her head.

"First I have to make a call," Darla said, then added emphasis to her tone before saying, "In private."

Verdon's look at Darla was patronizing. "Couldn't it wait? We have all these people." He gestured toward the media folk, who had their noses pressed to the glass from out in the hall.

"Well, I'm not . . ." Darla looked fearfully in Sharon's direction.

Well, so much for staying out of Verdon's way, Sharon thought. She stepped forward. "It's my fault. A favor Darla's doing for me, and I'm afraid we're on a deadline."

"Oh?" Verdon looked at Darla.

"We are, Chet," Darla said timidly. "If you could just . . ."

Verdon had the look of a man who'd just been

dancing with his prospective lay for the evening, only to have a rival cut in. "Down the hall, Darla," he said with no enthusiasm. "You know where it is, the little anteroom down there." Then, as Darla hustled down the corridor like someone with a stay of execution, Verdon called after her, "Make it quick, can you? We've really got a lot to . . ." He turned a glare on Sharon.

She smiled sweetly. "While she's doing that, maybe we could visit."

"Right," he said. "Maybe we could." He held the door for her. "After you, Cheryl."

Sharon started down the carpeted hallway. "Sharon," she said.

Sharon wondered if Russell Black's entire suite of offices was as large as Verdon's private lair. Verdon had room for a wet bar on which sat liters of Cutty, Jack Daniel's, and Tanqueray, and on whose sink rested a syrup gun with buttons marked COKE, SPRITE, SODA, and QUININE. In one corner sat an Exercycle. Visible through a picture window was the elevated portion of the Hollywood Freeway with San Gabriel peaks towering on the horizon. A leather sofa and matching armchairs were set up around a glass-topped coffee table. On the table was a Mr. Coffee with its pot full of dark brown liquid, and an expresso machine. Beside the sofa was a cabinet holding bags of Starbuck's, marked EXPRESSO, MOCHA, and COCOA, and a can of Redi-Whip. Verdon's handball court-sized desk sat before a second picture window. His visitors chairs were velour, and in one of them sat a man. The man had pinched features and a hooked nose, and wore a yellow blazer. He was on the phone, the cord stretched out across Verdon's desk.

The man was saying, "Well, get 'em, we got no time to waste on this. Tell them this isn't an auction yet, emphasis on the 'yet,' because of our prior good relations and all that bullshit, and that we'll give them until four o'clock, which we wouldn't do for just anybody. I am tired of fucking with these people." He hung up and turned to Verdon. "Bastards are being ridiculous." He then looked Sharon over with piercing black eyes. "Who's this?" he said.

"Sharon, is it?" Verdon said tonelessly. Sharon nodded. Verdon turned to the stranger, "Sharon Hays, Darla's friend from Dallas. Meet Aaron Levy." He acted as if she should have heard of the guy.

She hadn't. She nodded in greeting. "Mr. Levy."

"Yeah, sit over here." Levy moved to one of the chairs at the coffee table. Sharon sat at one end of the couch, folding her arms in puzzlement as Verdon perched on the front edge of another of the chairs. Levy watched Sharon over the top of the coffee maker and expresso machine. "Coffee or something?"

"No, thanks," Sharon said, turning to Verdon. "I just wanted to explain to you, I have no legal status in this."

"I checked the California Bar Register," Verdon said. "You spell your name with an *e* between the *y* and the *s*?"

Sharon hooked one arm over the back of her chair. "I'm not licensed to practice law here."

"Oh? A word to the wise, then. California is tough on outsiders doing business."

Sharon blinked. "I'm not doing business, Mr. Verdon. Darla's a personal friend of mine and asked for my advice."

"That's the point. You need to be admitted for that."

"Not legal advice," Sharon said. "Personal advice."

Verdon examined his manicure. "Sounds like a pretty fine line to me. I'd have to check with—"

"Chet." Levy spoke up, tossing a bag of mocha from hand to hand. "Stop being a hardass. Thing we're trying to understand here, Sharon, exactly what you're angling for."

Sharon folded her hands in her lap. "And you are . . . ?"

"Oh. Excuse me. I represent Darla."

"I'm sorry, but I thought Mr. Verdon was Darla's lawyer."

"I'm her agent," Levy said. "Chet and I work together on a few things. He's the lawyer for several of my people."

Which explains where Verdon gets his entertainment referrals, Sharon thought. "I see." She turned to Verdon. "I'm well aware of the Bar Association rules, sir. That's why I told Darla I couldn't be her lawyer in California without co-counsel. Actually, my licensing requirement is only one of the reasons. Another is, Darla and I are so close I'd lose my objectivity. I don't suppose that applies to agents."

Levy pulled out a folded sheet of paper. "I'm close to all my clients, Sharon." He unfolded the page. "So Darla wants you, as far as I'm concerned you're in." He studied a row of figures. "Problem is, we don't have as much of a pie here as people think."

Sharon bit the inside of her lower lip. "I beg your pardon?"

Verdon sat forward and touched his fingertips together. "I can attest that Aaron's right. Used to be you could depend on the book people for a little taste. That market's pretty well dried up, but everyone's still thinking O.J. O.J. was a deal unto itself."

"Not that this couldn't be a second O.J.," Levy said, "with the right parameters. You have to wait and see."

"Right," Verdon said. "But as for now, considering the bird in the hand, I've got two book people calling, but they're not offering. Both of them say if they're not first on the shelf, there may not even be a book, plus there's not enough advance to split. I'm having some New York contacts get a feel for the advance they're getting, but it's likely they're telling the truth. In this day and age book money's not generally a consideration."

Sharon scooted her rump forward and crossed her legs. "Oh?"

"And the TV movie interest," Levy cut in, "is at

this point minimal. If they bust somebody and damned soon, we might have something, but it's got to be quick enough so's they could shoot and be ready for the air during sweeps. And a television deal, we could have still another finger in the pie."

Sharon had been nervous when first she'd come in, but now was calm and collected. "Whose finger is that?"

"Poor dead David had his own agent, Curtis Nussbaum."

"Yes, I know," Sharon said.

"Oh?" Levy's eyes widened. "You know Nuss the Cuss?"

"I've met him. Talked to him on the phone. He represents another actor I know, Rob Stanley."

Levy snapped his fingers. "That's right, you're . . ."

Sharon looked away.

"No sweat, I'm not into getting personal," Levy said, "but in a TV movie we got Nussbaum to deal with. Hey, I'm not a hundred percent certain the guy would be technically entitled. I mean, who's going to pay a dead person, right? But this is a small community out here. I don't cut him in, I can have future problems."

"I see," Sharon said.

"A good part is, don't worry about any TV movie people shafting us. They're doing that a lot, claiming a story's public domain and going ahead without paying for no rights from anybody, but they know better than to fuck with Aaron C. Levy in such a manner. Am I right, Chet, or am I right?"

"You are right, Aaron," Verdon said. "Slap a TRO on their ass before they can get a camera crew together."

"But movie or no," Levy said, "that's the question we won't have an answer to until the police get off their asses and do something. Meantime, as of right now, today, we have a couple of tabloid offers, period. One TV tabloid and one print. Don't amount to a lot. This newspaper interview Darla's doing today could turn up something, but that remains to be seen." Levy produced a steno pad and ballpoint, turned over a page, and prepared to write. "So with all that as a reference point, Sharon, what did you have in mind?"

Sharon eye-measured the distance between her chair and the exit. "Have in mind in relation to what, Mr. Levy?"

Levy winked broadly. "So you won't have to dazzle us with footwork, hey. We know you people down in Texas are hip to what's what. The pie is about what we told you. You don't want to commit without talking to your people, I understand. So how's about I give you a ballpark, so's you and whoever will have something to toss around."

Sharon gestured toward the door. "That's what those media people are all about, to try to interest someone in a movie deal?"

"The more in the papers the better," Verdon said. "Plus, Darla Cowan's not just anybody. Reporters eat from her hand."

"Well, they might," Sharon said. "I just don't think it's in Darla's best interests to be feeding them at this point."

"I forgot another guy," Levy said. "This other lawyer."

"The one we're supposed to choose this afternoon," Sharon said, "who's going to represent her on criminal charges?"

"Right." Levy looked at Verdon. "Don't expect this person to agree to a flat rate, Chet, not when we've got the other potentials here. The other lawyer's share has to go into the pot. If we don't have to spend it, hey."

"It's certainly a consideration," Verdon said. "Darla will be here soon. We should talk some pretty quick turkey."

Sharon brushed her skirt. "I'll tell you, Chet," she said, "I don't want anything."

Verdon and Levy exchanged a look. Levy sat forward. "If you've got something going on your own, we can live with that. With Darla in your corner, you hold quite a few cards. Not all by a long shot, but quite a few. So, what, your idea is to make *us* an offer?"

Sharon let her gaze drift out the window, resting on tree-covered peaks in the distance under a bluish, smoggy haze. "Gentlemen, I'm not trying to hold any cards. I agreed to help my friend, and that's what I intend to do. And helping her—"

"Perhaps we could concentrate on some kind of 'if, if, and' proposal," Levy said.

"—seems at cross purposes with what I see here."

"For example," Levy said, "something I like to play around with, if things remain status quo we're talking a figure, if the tabloids up the ante something more, if we have the tabs *and* a TV production you can do even better. You'll have to roll the dice with us, but, hey, this is Hollywood, right?"

"Darla's going to ask me what to do," Sharon said.

"She seems adamant about that, Aaron." Verdon fiddled with one of his cuff links. Light glinted from a diamond, reflecting in Sharon's eye.

Sharon let her hand dangle from the end of the sofa armrest. "I know nothing about this deal or that deal. I'm not looking for profit here. If Dallas County, Texas, gives Darla a clean bill of health, meaning total immunity in connection with the murder, you can do whatever you want to. Until then, though, she shouldn't be holding any press conferences."

Verdon coughed into his cupped hand. "She needs to speak out."

"No, she doesn't," Sharon said. "What she needs is to keep a low profile. Anything she says to the media can be used against her."

"What's this?" Levy spoke to Verdon while extending a hand in Sharon's direction. "She talking legal here?"

Verdon gave a hands-up shrug. "Seems that way."

"Don't double-talk us, Miss Hays," Levy said. "You want more points, be up-front about it."

Sharon rolled her eyes. "Oh, for Christ's sake."

Levy put pen to paper. "Let me do some figuring." He paused, then looked slowly in the direction of the exit. "Just putting some figures together, sweetheart."

Sharon turned. Darla stood just inside the door. Her brows were raised in curiosity. She gave Sharon a thumbs-up sign. "I set it up," she said.

Sharon's eyebrows moved closer together. "With Rob?"

Darla nodded. "What about in here? Everything copasetic?"

Sharon, Levy, and Verdon all looked at each other. Sharon stood. "Afraid not."

"Wait." Levy picked up his ballpoint. "You're not satisfied? We happen to be in the satisfaction business."

"I've seen enough," Sharon said. She turned to Darla. "I'm not interfering, Darla. Do what you want."

Darla showed her petulant face. "That's not our arrangement, and you know it."

Sharon sadly shook her head. "Our arrangement is, I'm to tell you what I think. What I think is, you should leave here and start over."

"Now, hold on." Levy stood up. "I took her when she was nothing. Beat the bushes for that girl."

"Oh, for God's sake," Sharon said. "I don't mean, change agents, Darla. You're a better judge of that than I am. I just think you need to get with a lawyer who's only interested in protecting you in this criminal matter. Not feathering everybody's nest with deals that don't have anything to do with it."

"That could be you, couldn't it?" Darla looked hopeful.

Verdon stood up, angrily pointing a finger. "She's not licensed here. Don't think I'd stand still for it."

Sharon gave Verdon a look that could melt cobalt. She took Darla by the arm. "Come on. I can't practice in California without local co-counsel, so I suppose we'll take the bull by the horns."

Verdon followed them into the reception area, Darla keeping a step ahead so as not to have to face the guy. Sharon steered Darla toward the exit. A hallway full of reporters waited beyond the glass. Verdon said, "You haven't heard the last of this, *Cheryl*."

Sharon paused near the door as Gray and Yadaka came to their feet, dropping their magazines. Gray had been reading *Time* while Yadaka looked over this month's issue of *GQ*. "Mr. Yadaka," Sharon said, "could you clear us a path through those people, please?" The Oriental nodded, and pushed through the entry into the corridor.

Gray started to follow Yadaka out. Sharon stopped the Englishman with a hand on his arm. She pointed toward Verdon, who glowered alongside the switchboard operator's station. "Please stay between me and that guy, Mr. Gray," Sharon said. "And if he takes a step in my direction, feel free to lower the boom."

They drove toward the Hollywood Freeway, and stopped for a light near the Criminal Courts. Sharon peered ahead, toward a row of street-level windows and bail-bond signs. She said, "Turn left at the next corner." Gray looked inquisitively in the rearview.

Darla had stayed mute since leaving the attorney's office but now said, "You've never been here before."

"Trust me," Sharon said. She leaned forward. "I haven't gone crazy, Mr. Gray. Left, please, next intersection."

Yadaka gave a curious look over his shoulder. Gray complied, waiting for the light to change, moving into the center lane with his blinker flashing, steering the limo onto a narrow street lined with storefront offices. On the sidewalks were slouchy men with tattoos, a couple of women in loud, tight pants, and a homeless guy seated on the curb with his toes poking out of his shoes. A billboard in front of one building read, JIMMY YAT'S BAIL BONDS over a cartoon logo of a man parachuting out of a barred window. Next door to the bond office was a sign reading, PRESTON TRIGG, LAWYER, with the Spanish word *Abogado* spelled out underneath. Sharon directed Gray to pull to the curb. As the limo idled in front of the seedy-looking storefront, Sharon said to Darla, "Come on. I don't think anybody's going to recognize you. But keep your head down, okay?" She reached over Darla to open the door, and followed the actress onto the sidewalk.

Sharon's watch read one-thirty, Dallas time, which made it half past eleven in Los Angeles, so either Preston Trigg's secretary had taken an early lunch or Trigg didn't have a secretary at all. As she stood alongside Darla in Trigg's reception area, the phone buzzed constantly. The desk where the secretary-receptionist should have been sitting was made of worm-eaten pine. Scratches crisscrossed the top and front, and on its otherwise bare surface were a catalog-sized L.A. telephone directory and one plain black phone. The phone had three lines. One button was lit, and the others flashed repeatedly as the calls came in. The phone was hooked up to an answering machine. Sharon smiled through the storefront window and waggled her fingers at Yadaka and Gray sitting in the limo.

Darla was obviously bewildered. "What are we doing here?"

"Taking the bull by the horns," Sharon said. "Finding a lawyer who can represent your best interests in the state of California."

Darla's gaze fell dubiously on a bookcase containing a gavel marked MOOT COURT, CAL-IRVINE, 1992, a junked auto battery atop a pile of shop cloths, a book entitled, *Rapid Settlements in Personal Injury,* and a couple of paperback western novels. One was entitled *Cherokee Squaw,* and its cover pictured a big-hipped, buckskin-clad woman whose breasts were about to fall out in the open, her mouth curved sensuously as a muscular cowpoke pinned her against the wall of a saloon. "Do you know this attorney, Sharon?" Darla said.

"Know the type. Trust me." Sharon gave a smile of confidence.

"What type is he?"

"Shh!" Sharon put a finger to her lips as the answering machine spouted its recorded message and clicked in anticipation.

The voice on the speaker was hoarse. "Yeah, Pres, this is Jimmy Yat next door. Guess you know your asshole of a client skipped. You guaranteed this guy, which means I'm expecting you to pony up fifteen hundred bucks over here, pronto. Call me by four, or it's your ass." There was a series of electronic beeps as the machine reset itself.

Sharon murmured, "Perfect."

Darla blinked helplessly.

"Come on." Sharon skirted the desk and led the way to a partially open door at the rear. She peeked inside.

The guy had his back turned, his feet propped on his credenza as he talked on the phone. He wore cowboy boots along with a green western-cut suit. His reddish-brown hair was long in back, below his collar, and as he spoke into the mouthpiece he waved a cheroot around, thumping ashes on the floor. Sharon closed her nasal passages as smoke wafted up her nostrils. From her side-angle view she could see a smooth young-man's cheek and one edge of a mustache.

The man was saying, "The deal is solid as a rock. No back-outs, no doubt. You just stand up there and take the two years, hey, you'll be on the street before you know it. But we need to talk. You owe me five hundred dollars, Jethro. What's the chance of . . . ?"

As the man listened over the line, Sharon gave Darla a come-on wave. The two women crept in and sat across from the attorney, wrinkling their noses as he continued to wave the cigar.

"Well, that's real unfortunate," he said finally. "But I've had a few setbacks myself. You see, the thing is, Jethro . . . no, wait a minute, let me talk. The thing is, the five hundred dollars stands between you getting the two years and you getting something like, oh, fifteen or more. You get my drift?" He listened some more, turning partway around and exposing his profile. He had a brown birthmark on his left cheek, and his mustache needed trimming. "You don't think? This judge and me are pretty tight. You want to try me, feel free, but I'd recommend you get my money down here. Oh, yeah? You do that, Jethro." He hung up, drummed his fingers, and spun around.

Sharon said, "Hi. Can you use a client?"

His gaze fell first on Sharon, then on Darla Cowan. He gaped at Darla as if seeing a ghost.

"Are you Preston Trigg?" Sharon said.

He continued to stare at Darla. She shifted nervously.

"Yoo-hoo," Sharon said. "Over here."

"No way. You can't be," the man said. "I've got it, there's a look-alike contest. Yeah, I'm Pres. What can I do you for?" He chuckled at his own joke.

"I'm Sharon Hays, from Texas. And she's the real thing," Sharon said. Darla sat confidently erect, a pleased smile on her face.

Trigg balanced his cheroot on an ashtray. "You pulling my leg?"

"Not really, Mr. Trigg. Miss Cowan needs a lawyer to represent her in California, in connection with possible Texas criminal charges. If you're interested, we'd like to talk."

Trigg tilted his chair and intertwined his fingers behind his head. "Sure, and tomorrow Clinton's going to call wanting me for this Whitewater deal. Listen, I don't know what you girls are part of. Her makeup's damned good. But I got things to do."

"You do have a California law license, don't you?" Sharon said.

A look near panic spread over his face. "What, you've been talking to the Bar Association?"

"No. Should we have been?"

Trigg waved a hand as if brushing a fly away, and pointed at a plaque on the wall. "My license is right there, current. Complaints, yeah, I got 'em. Mostly from stiffs, like the guy I was just talking to."

"Good," Sharon said. "At present all we're looking at is a meeting with the Dallas D.A.'s reps. There are no charges against Darla, though that could change very quickly. Here's what you'll have to do. Arrange for a court reporter and get us a meeting room in the Criminal Courts Building tomorrow after lunch. Also, you'd have a motion prepared so that if they give Miss Cowan a lot of hassle, we can walk into a courtroom and have her answer their questions in front of a judge." She tilted her chin. "You are familiar with the court procedure I'm talking about, aren't you?"

Trigg had an uncertain look.

"I was afraid of that," Sharon said. "When I found the provision in the California statutes, I suspected that it wasn't done very often. No sweat. I have chapter and verse, and I'll show you how to prepare the motion if you'd like."

"Okay, super," Trigg said. "I'm just supposed to start running around doing all this. Yeah, right."

Darla looked back and forth between Sharon and Lawyer Trigg like a woman watching a tennis match.

" 'Yeah, right,' is right," Sharon said. "What's going to be your fee, Mr. Trigg?"

He looked at the ceiling and laughed out loud. "If we're going to play Let's Pretend, why not? Hundred grand." He spread his hands.

Sharon shook her head. "That's too much. How about ten?"

Trigg's jaw dropped. "Grand?"

"I wouldn't expect you to do it for ten *dollars,* Mr. Trigg."

His eyes narrowed. "You serious about this?"

"As cancer." Sharon pointed at Darla. "She's Darla Cowan, sir, your eyes aren't playing tricks. I'm Sharon Hays, a Dallas attorney who can't officially represent Miss Cowan in California. For reasons I won't get into, her regular L.A. lawyer won't be helping us. So, would you like to pick up some easy money?"

Trigg now rubbed his mustache. "How would I get paid?"

Sharon looked to her right. "Darla?"

Darla reached inside her handbag and produced a checkbook.

"I'll need some ID," Trigg said. "Driver's license or . . ."

"Done," Sharon said. "You're familiar with the case we're talking? The David Spencer murder."

"Who isn't? Listen, this is for real?"

"Total reality," Sharon said.

Trigg leaned over and studied Darla's face. "You look like her, all right." He tilted back. "Okay, why me?"

Sharon smiled sweetly. "I liked your sign. Thanks to the innuendoes all over the newspapers, Darla's the main suspect, but at this point there's nothing official. But the Dallas D.A.'s have popped off so much to the media that I'm not about to let her answer any questions without a grant of immunity. Which they won't agree to, which will terminate the meeting. Darla's not guilty, Mr. Trigg. The real killer is running around somewhere between here and Texas."

Trigg pursed his lips. He picked up his cheroot and puffed, but the cigar had gone out. He used a butane lighter to apply flame to the butt. "How mucha my time is this going to take?"

Sharon's chin tilted. "Ten thousand dollars' worth. I suspect we'll be here a few hours. Why, do you have an appointment?"

"Well, no. But you're talking about doing these motions, I got no assistant or nothing. No typist. No lawbooks, either."

"I'd think that was a drawback in the practice of law, Mr. Trigg. Does L.A. County maintain a library?"

Trigg seemed thoughtful. "Yeah, they got one someplace."

Sharon couldn't believe the guy. "Don't you know where it is?"

"I can call somebody. I can find out."

"Good," Sharon said. "That's the first order of business, to find the library. They'll have word processors you can rent by the hour, and I can hunt and peck." She stood. "You might want to take some notes, Mr. Trigg. In the future, knowing the way to the law library could prove useful to you."

13

"Riskin' one's law license is no laughin' matter, Sharon," Russell Black said. "I already heard from the Bar Association."

Sharon shifted the pay phone receiver from one ear to the other. "The California bar? How did they . . . ?"

"This is the Texas bar, but they're callin' as a result of a complaint from a California attorney. You know a . . . ? Just a minute, I got the name written down." There was a rattling sound over the line as Black put down the phone.

Sharon stood before a bank of phones located on a wall between the men's and women's rest rooms. She stepped back and peered into the restaurant. The room was a kaleidoscope of color; walls, ceilings, and floors were done in shrieking mural themes, showing red and yellow tropical fish, bright green vines, and water which was an impossible shade of blue. Even the waiters and waitresses were decked out like tropical fish, energetic young men and women in vests and ties which were red, yellow, pink, or green, hustling to and from the kitchen toting trays laden with grilled Atlantic salmon, spotted prawns, or Chinese duck with ginger mango relish. Sharon assumed that the food was terrific, but thought the decorum just godawful. Here and there were glistening saltwater aquariums containing live swordfish, eels, and wiggly octupii. As the maître d' had hustled Sharon and Darla to a choice window table, Jack Nicholson had accosted Darla and kissed her hand. Darla had said offhandedly, "Hey, Jack, how's it going?" and then continued through the restaurant as Sharon practically tripped over her feet, gaping at the famous actor over her shoulder. Darla now sat alone at a table for four. There was a martini in front of her, and a Tanqueray and tonic in front of Sharon's empty chair. Darla caught Sharon's eye and smiled a question. Sharon held up a finger and then moved in closer to the bank of phones. There was a *clunk* over the line as, fifteen hundred miles away, Russell Black picked up the receiver.

"You know a Chet Verdon?" Black said.

"Just became acquainted with him."

"He's the one complainin'. Says you're tryin' to practice law out there without a license."

"That's b.s., old boss," Sharon said. "He was trying to throw his client to the media wolves, and I got in his way. I'll handle the bar association, Russ. Trust me, we're okay on that."

"Just keep your skirts clean. What time is it out there?"

"Nearly seven, I think. Our appointment's at seven on the nose, but it's with my old friend Rob. Unless he's changed, we'll be cooling our heels for a while."

"It's nine here," Black said. "Which is precious close to bedtime. Where are you? Sounds like a barroom."

"It's a restaurant," Sharon said, raising her voice as two women giggled their way into the ladies'. "Granita, in Malibu."

"They got Tex-Mex food in California now?"

Sharon laughed. "I don't think it's a Spanish word. I think it's the name of a drink. Wolfgang Puck owns the place."

"Yeah? I thought he was dead."

Sharon frowned. "Wolfgang Puck?"

"Yeah. He hadn' been in a Dracula movie in thirty years."

Just talking to Russ made troubles evaporate. Sharon grinned broadly. "That's Bela Lugosi, boss."

Her smile faded. "You have any word on whether Milt plans to have Darla arrested out here?"

"The D.A.'s staff is mum. I interpret it to mean that they're goin' to. You should get ready. Any meetin' with Milt Breyer, he's liable to have some arrestin' officers along."

"Along with forty million television cameras." Sharon backed up and looked once more at Darla, sipping her drink. "We spent several hours at the law library this afternoon," Sharon said, "along with this California attorney Darla's hired. I spent some time researching the extradition statutes. If Milton springs a warrant on us, I'm ready for him."

Black grumpily cleared his throat. "Fightin' extradition would be a waste of time."

"I agree. The law is, in order to extradite her, all they've got to show is that a valid warrant exists in another state. The only way to stop extradition is to attack the validity of the warrant on its face, and then they've got to show their probable cause. I researched it more for Darla's benefit than ours, Russ. If and when they arrest her, she's going to panic, and it's going to take some persuasion to get her to sign the extradition waiver. I'll have to convince her that her quickest route out of jail is to waive extradition, and that once they get her to Texas we can try to arrange bail for her." Sharon's mouth puckered in worry. "They've got more evidence than just, Darla was on the scene, Russ. Otherwise they wouldn't dare charge her. Not even Milton Breyer is that stupid. We're really going to have to get it in gear."

"How come you keep sayin', 'we'?"

Sharon watched the ceiling. Gee, this was going to take some diplomacy. "If Dallas County indicts Darla, we're going to represent her. You and I." She held her breath, waiting for the tirade.

There were five seconds of silence. "I knew it," Black said. "You're fixin' to get our business in a wringer. Thought you said she had a lawyer out there."

"What she has is a front. A guy you wouldn't believe. Darla's a babe in the woods, and all these wolves are more interested in book and movie deals than they are in defending her. She's my friend, Russ, and I'm not about to desert her."

"You bein' the lady's friend is the whole problem, Sharon. Plus the fact that you're a potential witness. You can't be her lawyer."

Sharon collected her thoughts. "You can," she finally said.

"*Me*? First I got my assistant treadin' on the edge of legality; now she wants me to join in the act. I suppose now you're goin' to say, you're my second chair."

"Yep. Think, Russ. I might have to testify that Darla and I went to dinner. That's all. I've got no other conflict. Darla can't get better help than Russell Black, and that's a fact." Sharon mentally crossed her fingers. Russ normally didn't take to buttering up, but he had a soft spot where Sharon was concerned.

There was a rustling noise over the line as Black fiddled. He cleared his throat. "We'd have to make it clear that you're not the lead attorney from the get-go."

Relieved air whooshed out of Sharon's lungs. "That's the spirit, boss. I knew you'd—"

"I ain't sayin' I will, and I ain't sayin' I won't. I'm sayin' I'll sleep on it. Which it's time for me to do. If Milt Breyer has the actress arrested out there, you get on the honk to me. Listen, Sharon, I got the name of the place where Milt an' Stan Green are stayin' if you—"

"I'm a step ahead of you. I've already left word for them at the Beverly Hills Hotel. We're set up for one o'clock downtown at the Criminal Courts Building."

"How'd you know where to leave a message?"

"Let's just say I know Milt and how he'd operate on the county's expense account," Sharon said. "Wow, I'd hate to have to pay the tab at the Polo Lounge.

Look, boss, I need to go. I've sort of left Darla hanging."

There were five seconds of silence. "Sharon?" Black said.

"I'm here."

"This bar association business can be serious."

"She's got a California attorney, I already told you. I'm just in an advisory capacity. There'll be a brief hearing where she waives extradition, during which I'm only her out-of-town counsel. Once they get her to Texas, you can take over from there."

"I haven't said I'd—"

"Thanks, boss, you're the best in the world. You take care, now."

She hung up and hurried through the restaurant to the table where Darla was toying with her martini. The actress ignored the stares from nearby patrons, and Sharon now understood why celebrity became the ultimate pain. They'd spent the afternoon with attorney Preston Trigg, then had arrived at the Malibu Colony Mall a couple of hours early for their dinner date with Rob. With time to kill, the women had decided to window-shop, and the mere sight of Darla Cowan peering at dresses and skimpy underwear in the Victoria's Secret display had caused clerks and passersby to behave like raving lunatics. Victoria's Secret employees had rubbernecked themselves into a lather, and one deranged woman had approached with a drooling baby and asked Darla to kiss the child. Sharon thought it a credit to Darla that she had the nerve to appear in public at all.

Sharon sat down at the table. Her fanny had barely touched the springy velour seat when a waitress appeared as if by magic. She was a coed-looking brunette with her hair in tight curls, and wore black, slim pants along with an orange vest, white shirt, and chartreuse bowtie. "Need a few more minutes, Miss Cowan?" she said. "Or are you ready to order?"

Sharon buried her nose in the menu, sipping her gin and tonic as she looked over dishes such as "Grilled

Atlantic Salmon, presented on a luscious bed of roasted Chino corn salsa," or "Alaskan Spotted Prawns resting amid saffron riscotto and crispy ginger," all entries priced from twenty to thirty bucks. She wanted to ask what came with the main dishes, then noted separate prices for veggies (God, five bucks for a squash and zucchini combo, Sharon thought), blinked, and swallowed hard. Darla was footing the bill, but criminy. Sharon pretended to be torn between a couple of items while waiting for Darla to order. Whatever Darla had, Sharon would order the next cheapest thing.

Darla tossed the menu aside. "What's the pizza?"

The waitress recited from memory. "Specially roasted chicken with an olive sauce, prepared in our wood-burning oven."

Sharon flipped her menu over. Pizza? She didn't see any . . .

"You have the potato gazette?" Darla asked.

"With smoked salmon, Miss Cowan. Excellent season for Alaskan salmon this year. Long spawning season."

"All right," Darla said, "I'll have that along with the chicken soup." Her forehead wrinkled. "No egg noodles in the soup, right?"

"Certainly not. Angel hair pasta, is that all right?"

Darla nodded and sipped her martini.

The waitress turned her smile on Sharon. "And you, please?"

Sharon stared at the menu in desperation, like a horseplayer with minutes until post time. She said, "I don't find any soup."

Darla took the menu from Sharon's hands. "You won't," Darla said. "Order the soup. You'll like it, and picking something not on the menu makes you automatically one of the in-crowd."

Sharon looked at the waitress and shrugged helplessly. "I'll have what she's having," she said.

"Oh, and we're expecting someone," Darla said. "Rob Stanley. I don't know if he'll enter from the

front or the kitchen, but watch for him, will you?"
She examined her martini, which was half gone, and
looked at Sharon's near-empty glass as well. "And
bring us two more of these, all right?" Darla said.

The waitress nodded, smiled, and walked away.

"One of the only places in the world I'm in my
element," Darla said after the waitress had left. "And
to tell the truth, I can make better soup at home.
Ordering something not on the menu at Granita, it's
what we're supposed to do along with all the other
phony . . ." She looked toward the entry. "Rob will
be late."

"You think I don't know? I lived with him,
remember?"

"No, Sharon, I think he'll be *extra* late."

Sharon watched an octopus wave its tentacles in an
aquarium across the way. Good old Rob was a topic
she'd as soon avoid. She said to Darla, "Because
I'm here?"

"Yes."

There was a sudden tightness in Sharon's chest.
"I'm not crazy about seeing him, either. Other than
the one time in Dallas, and that for about five minutes,
Rob and I haven't had a conversation since I moved
out of the place in Brooklyn Heights. Melanie just
turned thirteen, so add nine months to that . . . Don't
think I want any of his precious time for me, Darla.
But he's going to see Melanie, that's the least he can
do. If it lowers his star-studded standards to greet me
in public, that's just tough. All he's got to do is give
his daughter some of his time, not that he can ever
give her as much as he owes. But if he'll just make
some sort of effort where his child is concerned, I'll
be just as satisfied if he pretends he doesn't know me."

Darla's expression was soft and sad. "I think you've
got the roles reversed."

"My role or Rob's role?"

"Both. Rob doesn't look down on you."

Sharon scratched her nail across the tablecloth. "I

don't know. He is a big star and all. Runs in a different echelon now."

"I'm a pretty big star myself. What echelon do you see me in? If I wasn't lucky enough to have you here, I'd be sitting by myself. Rob doesn't want to see you because he's scared to death to be with someone who doesn't worship him."

"I don't think I could buy that," Sharon said. "He might be afraid because he hasn't been paying his child support, but that would be the only reason."

"No, it isn't. He's not worthy of your time, and he knows it. Just like I know that I'm not." Darla managed a small chuckle. "It's ironic. You're tying yourself in knots thinking Rob's gotten too big for you, when in reality he's sunk miles beneath what he was when you knew him. Right now he's getting up his nerve, fighting the terror of facing you. Instead of being antsy, you should feel sorry for him."

Sharon had some of her drink and bit down on the lime. Bitter juice flowed across her tongue. She pictured Melanie on the plane, her body wriggling like a contortionist's, her eyes dancing at the thought of seeing her all-American dad in the flesh. "Just so long as he comes, Darla," Sharon said. "Just so long as he comes."

Darla was right. Rob *was* even later than usual, an hour on the nose, to be exact, and by the time he arrived Sharon had worked up half a snootful. More than half, actually, and if it hadn't been for the delicious chicken noodle soup resting in her belly to dispel some of the alcohol, Sharon might've been wearing a lamp shade on her head. Her normal limit on gin and tonic was two drinks. The one set before her at the moment was either number four or five.

Darla was saying, "Way down in Tribeca, wasn't it?" Her martini glass was half full, and was Darla's third or fourth. She didn't seem giddy in the slightest, and Sharon thought that Darla's capacity had increased considerably. Once in a club over in Jersey, Darla had gotten sick on a couple of beers.

Sharon giggled into her napkin. "No, the one in Tribeca that did an el foldo was called *Aunts and Other Enemies*. This was the thing in Hell's Kitchen. You remember, you broke out laughing in the middle of my most important line. 'You are nothing but a trollop'—"

" 'Winfred Dismore,' " Darla finished. Her eyes grew big and round. "God, that dreadful producer . . ."

"Porno Pete, right," Sharon said. A man across the room was watching her. She briefly met his gaze. He smiled in greeting and lifted his glass in a toast. Sharon looked quickly away. All through the restaurant people were staring at Darla, nudging each other and talking in whispers. A half hour earlier Jack Nicholson had left, and heads had snapped around at every table he passed.

"And that's the clip they showed on TV?" Darla looked incredulous.

"Threw me as well," Sharon said. "There weren't any networks covering that turkey when we were doing it. I seem to remember that tweaky little writer with a video camera." She sipped her drink and pinched her numb forehead. Loss of feeling in the cranial area was a sign that she was getting into her cups.

"God, yes," Darla said. "He tried to shoot me while I was dressing."

"I thought about calling him up," Sharon said. "I suspect he sold that footage for . . ." She trailed off. Darla's gaze had shifted toward the back of the room. Sharon turned. Unobtrusively, Rob had come in.

Or not so unobtrusively, actually, more like a man who pretends to sneak around, all the while knowing that his feigned stealth will draw more attention than normal behavior. Rob milked the scene for all it was worth, entering from the kitchen, stiffening in mock surprise as rubbernecking diners stared at him, then giving a few you've-caught-me nods of acknowledgment. He slowly scanned the room—he knows god-damn well where we're sitting, Sharon thought, five'll get you ten that Darla's already told him we'll be at her usual table—until he finally zeroed in on Sharon. He looked her over. Then his lips formed sort of a James Dean, I'm-cool-but-casual expression. He raised a hand, made a pistol with his thumb and forefinger, and shot her with an imaginary bullet.

Excuse me while I barf on the table, Sharon thought. Anger fueled with gin and tonic welled up as she cringed in embarrassment. A hundred heads turned as one, searching for the object of Rob's attention. What do I do now, Sharon thought, yank off my panties and heave them into the crowd? Men and women stared mutely at her, their jaws working as they chewed on salmon or Chinese duck. A lady on Sharon's right said in a stage whisper, "Is she an actress?" then paused as if listening, and then said, "That's not who she is. That old gal would be sixty by now. Does resemble her, though." Sharon lifted her own glass in Rob's direction, smirking hatefully as she did. Darla gave her an odd look. Sharon wondered briefly if she should now toss the drink over her shoulder, smash the glass on the fireplace.

A thick-bodied, balding man followed Rob in, dogging the actor's tracks, an older-model version of Ya-daka and Gray. Your bodyguard won't save you, Rob, Sharon thought. If you don't do something for your daughter while she's in town, it'll take a hundred bodyguards just to protect you from me. Rob strolled toward her like Redford on a Streisand alert. The way *we* were was a little bit different from Bob and Barbra, Sharon thought, heat which didn't work half the time and shower nozzles which sprayed tepid, rusty water. The rust would disappear from the stream about the time the water went from lukewarm to ice cold, giving one a choice between freezing to death and bathing in flakes of oxidized iron. She had a slug of gin and tonic, reflecting on how Rob's appearance had changed.

His dental work was the most noticeable difference. Once upon a time Rob had had a gap between his front teeth, but now he showed a dazzling row of snow white porcelain. There were subtler changes as well, a broadening of the shoulders, a deepening of the chest, likely a result of daily sessions with a personal trainer. His thick brown hair was layered into a just-so tousled effect, the same as it appeared in the TV show. Sharon had liked the sort of confused-but-intelligent aura he'd portrayed in the old days. At least he looked human back then, she thought. The man now gliding toward her might as well have been a toy action figure. Rob wore faded jeans with holes worn at the knees, a blue knit shirt, a denim jacket with the collar turned up, and a gleaming wristwatch which had to be a Piaget. His feet were in white athletic socks and moccasins. He was tan as a tamale and hadn't shaved, the Don Johnson look, proof that Rob had arrived, and also proof that he was a big enough star to go around dressed like a slob. A perk, Sharon thought, reserved for television idols and eight-year-olds.

He stopped before her and extended his hands. "Muffin. Hey, how long has it . . . ?"

Sharon threw Darla a panicked glance. No help there; Darla acted as if Rob's appearance and demeanor were right in line. Sharon decided that if she didn't do something in a hurry, Rob might turn to molded plastic. She stood. Rob grasped her hands, then near-missed each of her cheeks with kisses. She wouldn't have been able to smell liquor on his breath in her current state, but there was an odor of peppermint which could have been a cover-up. Sharon sat down. Rob flopped into a chair adjacent to hers as his bodyguard hunkered at a nearby table. Sharon, Darla, and Rob looked at each other. The restaurant crowd went back to their dinners, exchanging surreptitious glances and chatting among themselves.

"Two years," Sharon said. "Before that, eleven."

"Hmm?" Rob pinched his chin. "What's two years?"

"You asked how long it had been. That's two years since you've spoken to me, eleven before that when I moved out of our apartment in Brooklyn Heights. You've never had anything to do with your child since the day she was born, other than pat her on the head when you were in Dallas on a publicity tour. Eleven years of that was my fault because I didn't want Melanie to see you. Since you thrust yourself into our lives because your agent thought it would make good public relations, the past two years that you've ignored her I'll chalk up to your indifference. Time frames clear to you now?" She smiled.

Rob didn't seem to understand, or wasn't insulted if he did. He raised a hand, palm out, and grinned across the table. "Darl. How've you been?" His expression sobered. "Sorry about David. He was the tops, what can I say?"

Darla's expression remained deadpan. "He'd appreciate the thought." Sharon wondered if Darla was mentally comparing Rob's entrance to her own. God love Darla, but Jesus Christ, there's hardly room for hers and Rob's egos on the same planet.

"Yeah, well . . ." Rob folded his hands. "Read any good scripts?"

Darla sipped her martini. "Not lately."

"Tough to find," Rob said. "Tough to find." He turned to Sharon. "So, you're a lawyer now."

Which I have been for a number of years, as you very well know, Sharon thought. She said, "Right, an attorney. Melanie watches your program every time I'll let her."

Rob frowned in thought. "You mean, sometimes she can't?" He seemed disappointed.

"I do some editing."

"Really? What would that be?"

One corner of Sharon's mouth bunched. "The nudity."

"Aw, that." Rob waved a hand as if batting mosquitoes. "Hell, you can't really see anything. Besides, she's thirteen, isn't she?"

"You sound just like your daughter," Sharon said. "Who came with me on this trip, by the way."

"Oh, yeah?" Rob's brows lifted in surprise.

Sharon wiped frost from her glass and gave a curt nod. "Oh, yeah," she said. "And thirteen isn't old enough for R-rated stuff." She wondered if the booze wasn't tipping her just a bit over the edge, and also wondered what Sheila would think about the last conversational exchange. Likely she'd tell me I'm overreacting, Sharon thought.

The waitress appeared. Rob made a big show of looking the menu over, then said he'd already eaten and ordered scotch neat, water back. His fingertips trembled just a hair, which in the old days had been a dead giveaway that he'd been drinking. He breathed through his nose. Yep, Sharon thought, he's had a few. Their only real donnybrooks had occurred after they'd been hitting the clubs, and Sharon couldn't remember being snockered since she and Rob had split the blankets. Until possibly now. I wonder if someone's trying to clue me in, Sharon thought, that Rob Stanley wasn't the best medicine for me. The waitress hustled away toward the bar. Rob turned to Sharon and hooked an arm over his chair back. "Speaking of the kid . . ." He reached in his pocket.

Sharon blinked. The kid. The freaking *kid*? "Your daughter, you mean?"

"Yeah, well . . ." Rob produced a folded-over slip of paper, which he dropped on the table. "That should square things up."

Sharon picked up the piece of paper and looked at it. It was a check, payable to Sharon J. Hays, in the amount of fifteen thousand dollars, with the notation in the lower left-hand corner: "chld sup, 3 mos." The account was entitled "Robert Stanley Trust." The signature was that of everyone's favorite agent, Curtis Nussbaum. Sharon looked up. "It's a check," she said.

"Money makes the world go 'round, right?" Rob's

tone wasn't the least bit apologetic. "Hey, these agents, you have to watch these people. They forget things."

"Seems they do. You think this makes us even?"

Rob seemed to think that one over. "Three months is all I owe, isn't it?"

"Three months' child support," Sharon said. "That's all?"

"Yeah, right. Hey, if I owe more . . ."

Sharon's buzz was accelerating. She pictured Melanie, flying all the way to California only to learn that a tour of movie land would have to substitute for a real-life visit from her dad. Over my dead body, Sharon thought. "You owe a whole lot more than this, Rob," Sharon said. "A whole, *whole* lot more."

Rob's mouth formed a petulant curve. "Now, wait a minute. My agent has a record, every dime I've—"

"Oh? I thought he forgot things."

"Not anything this important."

The waitress set down three fingers of scotch along with a glass of water, and hurried off once more. Rob knocked off a full inch of whiskey in a swallow, and chased the drink with H-two-oh.

"He keeps my finances up to snuff," Rob said. "Look, Muffin, if you need some money, sure. But don't be doubting our record keeping."

Sharon let the check flutter to the table. "If I need some money. If I need some *money*? Jesus Christ, you think this is about money?" Her tone went up an octave.

Across the table, Darla said quickly, "I see someone over there. You guys excuse me." She got up fast, passing two clusters of tables as she walked up to a man who was having dinner alone and sat down across from him. She said something and smiled. The man's jaw dropped. Darla daintily picked up a menu and began to read.

Rob placed one hand over Sharon's two. "Muffin, you're causing a scene here."

Sharon pushed him away. "You ain't seen nothin' yet."

He rubbed his temples. "Gee, Muffin, I—"

"And don't call me Muffin. Ever again. I always hated that. My name is Sharon. Did I ever tell you that pet names suck?" Anger surged through her, stronger than before. She glugged more gin to help her buzz along, and waved her glass at the waitress. The waitress nodded and took off for the bar. People around them were once again staring. Good, Sharon thought. You want the real skinny on this superhero? Okay, folks, lend me your ears. She glanced contemptuously at the check he'd tossed her like a bone, and stowed it away in her purse.

Rob leaned closer to her. "I think you should calm down."

"Sure. *Sure*, Rob."

He touched her arm. "Doesn't what we used to have, doesn't it still mean something?"

She let her gaze soften for a second. "Of course it does."

He slid his hand under the table and squeezed her thigh. "That's my girl."

"It means we have a child," Sharon said. "What else does it mean?"

His face was inches from hers. He wore a zocko cologne. "You remember making love in Central Park, on that bench with muggers running around?"

She gently closed her eyes. "God, it was cold."

"Before we finished it was warm and wild." His fingers kneaded her thigh, his touch firm, demanding.

Her voice took on a husky quality. "Could you show Melanie around the studio tomorrow? It's all she's talked about the whole trip, getting to see you."

His chin tilted. "I got a shoot."

"How about before the shoot? Or after. It would tickle Melanie to death to watch you perform."

"I'm going to be busy all day." He put his lips close to her ear. "But tonight I'm reserving for you, babe. I've got a place up Highway One. Fifteen minutes."

Her eyes popped open. "Rob," she said. "Take your fucking hand off my leg."

He tilted his head, his expression mild.

"I'm not quivering for your body," Sharon said. "I know that's hard for you to believe. I'll give you a count of two to let go of my leg. Then I'm going to scream. Remember my performance in *Mansion of Terror*? The show was a stinker, but at least I left 'em with their eardrums vibrating."

He jumped back as if he'd touched a hot coal. "What's—?"

"You're going to show Melanie around. You'll be at Darla's beach house at ten a.m., *capiche*?" Sharon accepted a fresh drink from the waitress, picked up the glass, and swigged.

He leaned back and folded his arms, looking irritated. "No can do, Muffin."

She gritted her teeth. "Sharon."

He angrily waved a hand. "Sharon. No can do. I got a business meeting."

"Which you'll postpone."

He pushed back from the table. "We're current on the support. Nice seeing you."

"I'll forget the money if you'll only start giving your child what she deserves."

"That was in another life." He started to rise.

"Which spills over to haunt you in your later years. I know it's tough to swallow, but it does. Sit down, Rob. I want to tell you something." Sharon's gaze moved past him, to the table where Darla now had a shrimp cocktail in front of her, engaging a total stranger in conversation. Wonder if it's on his tab or hers, Sharon thought.

Rob relaxed, leaned up, and crossed his forearms on the table. "Make it fast. I've got a lady waiting."

"Oh? What happened to your panting for me?" Sharon folded her hands. "You won't like this. But, at least for tomorrow, you're going to function as something other than a sperm dispenser, which is all you've been for thirteen years."

"I'm paying my support."

She sighed. "Okay, Rob, a one-time sperm dispenser and a sporadic cash dispenser. Is that better? Tomorrow you're going to be a love dispenser, even though we both know you'll be faking it. You're an actor, though, it's what you do. Have you watched any television this week?"

"Now, don't start in on me," Rob said. "It wasn't me who told the press we had a kid."

"Oh, I know that. It was a creep named Milton Breyer. I just asked you if you'd watched any television."

He looked uncertain. "Well . . . sure I have."

"Seen me giving any interviews?"

Now he was thoughtful. "I wondered about that."

"Unlike you," Sharon said, "I don't make my living by being in the spotlight. I've had to hogtie Darla to keep her away from the press, but it's worked. After she and I meet with the Dallas D.A. in the morning, it might not hurt for her to speak out. If she gives an interview, I might give one as well."

His expression clouded. "About David's murder?"

She shrugged. "Among other things."

He looked away from her. "They'll want to know about us."

Sharon nodded. "You bet they will. What's going to happen when the public learns I moved out because I discovered you were gay?"

He touched his chest with the palm of his hand. "Me? Come on."

Sharon showed her best smile of innocence. "It sent Ellen's ratings through the roof. Wouldn't it do the same for yours?"

"Our personas are different. Hey, I've got a lot of gay friends, but . . ." His eyes widened. "You wouldn't."

"Not for anything in the world," Sharon said, "except my daughter. Gay, Rob. I had to move because I couldn't afford to replace my underwear you were stretching out of shape by wearing it all the time.

How's that going to affect the viewer the next time you go"—she tucked her chin, deepened her voice, and curled her upper lip—" 'Give it up, punk, or I'm bouncing you off the walls.' "

He tried a bluff. "You're living in the past if you think being gay's going to hurt an actor's career."

"Right. Gays have come a long way in the world. But your main viewership is straight guys, sitting around in their undershirts and fantasizing after the kids are in bed. Trust me, Rob. Your sponsors will have a cow."

He studied his hands. "Jesus Christ."

"And the Virgin Mary and all the angels," Sharon said. "You're going to show your little girl around tomorrow, and you're going to treat her like she's the most important thing in the world to you. You'll be faking it, of course, because both of us know that nothing could ever take your own place in your life. I don't even care if you have a few photographers around, 'Rob Stanley's Domestic Life' and whatnot. Melanie would love to have her picture taken with you. But you will do it, Rob, or you may as well get ready for a role in *The Boys in the Band*. Don't worry, though. The gay community makes for small box office, but they're loyal to a T."

His forehead wrinkled. His jaw thrust forward. "This is nothing but blackmail."

"Yeah," Sharon said, grinning. "Isn't it cool, though?" She stood. "You've got a lady waiting, and Darla and I have people at home. My daughter for one, the one who's dumb enough to pine away for you." She took a step away from the table, then paused. "Ten in the morning, Rob. If you're not there, the interview begins around one. We'd love to have you, if you'd care to sit in."

The limo ride from Highway One to the beach house cleared the cobwebs from Sharon's mind, but she wasn't sure that rational thinking was helping matters. The cool night air in Malibu had sobered her completely—and made her think, God, was it really me causing that scene in front of all those people?—but with stone-cold sobriety had come misgivings.

Rob would appear Johnny-on-the-spot in the morning, of that she was certain, but the question she couldn't answer was whether or not she wanted him to. After years of arching her back, rejecting all suggestions that she create any sort of relationship between Melanie and her father, here she was throwing her child at the guy and resorting to blackmail in the process. With Sharon's threat hanging over his head, Rob would play loving dad tomorrow, but what effect could that have on Melanie in the future? Would the teenager now feel that the door was open for her to contact her father at will? If that was the case, Melanie was in for years of heartbreak. Sharon wondered if she'd traded one day of happiness in her little girl's existence for a lifetime of the child's feeling rejected. Two short years ago, Rob was no more real to Melanie than a fairy-tale prince, but now . . . Sharon leaned her head back against the cushions, used the electronic button to lower the window a fraction, and let the wind blow on her face and riffle her hair. A tear ran down from the corner of her eye.

As the limo rolled between the enormous entry boulders and approached the beach home, Sharon's heart came up in her mouth. Before the gate sat two police cars, rooflights flashing, along with two dark-colored four-door sedans. Off to one side were two TV mobile news units. Six vehicles in all, and Sharon didn't have to wonder who'd alerted the media. Three cameramen leaned on the fender of one of the vans, shooting the bull, minicams hung by their sides. Darla stiffened and gasped. Sharon reached over and squeezed the actress's hand. "As of right now, right this second," Sharon said, "don't say a word to anyone except me." Darla sniffled and cradled her forehead in her palm.

Sharon threw open her door and hit the ground at a trot before Gray could bring the limo to a standstill.

She slowed to a walk as she approached the gate, her high heels crunching on gravel. She marched past the two units who stood guard near the patrol cars, walked up to the four men in suits who leaned on the gate, hands in pockets, and said professionally, "Can I help you gentlemen?"

The tallest suit stepped toward her. He was smooth-faced and clean-shaven, a man pretty near Sharon's own age. He snapped open a wallet and produced a picture ID. No badge, Sharon thought with some relief, this isn't a local cop. The man said, "Agent Moretta, miss, FBI. I have a warrant. Is Darla Cowan with you?"

So the fibbies were still in the picture, which made sense. Federal agents could move faster than county cops in securing warrants, under the theory that Darla could have traveled interstate to avoid prosecution. Any federal charges would be quickly dismissed once Darla was in custody, of course, to be replaced by whatever Texas indictments Breyer could come up with. Involuntarily, Sharon's upper lip curled.

"I'm Miss Cowan's attorney, sir," she said. "I can accept service of the warrant." The spinning rooflights cast flashes of red across the ground. She showed the agent her best timid, help-me smile. "Look, is there some way we could put off taking her into custody until morning? I'll take the warrant and have Darla at whatever location you designate by ten a.m. She's not going anywhere, sir. Can't you give her this one little break?"

The agent looked confused for just an instant, then shook his head. "We're not taking anyone into custody, miss. We will need unrestricted access, though." He unfolded a stapled sheath of papers and handed them over.

Sharon frowned and tilted the papers to her right, squinting to read in the flashing glow of the rooflights. Christ, it was a search warrant. Of all the freaking . . . The warrant stated that Darla Cowan's presence at a murder scene in Dallas, Texas, coupled with the fact that she'd fled Texas for California, gave the FBI probable cause to search her residence in Malibu, and bore the signature of a California federal magistrate named Roland T. Mistlebrand. Criminal discovery statutes were broad, Sharon knew, but this was really stretching things. She immediately thought trial, and motions to exclude evidence based on the validity of the search warrant. The magistrate had signed the warrant at 8:47 P.M., California time. The ink was barely dry.

Sharon let the papers dangle beside her hip and expelled a long sigh. "Just have at it, fellas," she said. "My daughter will be asleep upstairs, and don't you dare wake her." She stepped toward the limo, then stopped and turned back to the agent with her eyes flashing fire. "I'm taking inventory, too," she said. "If you break anything, you'll save yourself a lot of trouble by writing a personal check for the damages before you leave, okay?"

Mrs. Welton, the security employee who'd escorted Melanie for the day, waited in the downstairs den watching television. She looked up as Sharon entered with the FBI close on her heels, and watched the proceedings with steady gray eyes. Sharon walked quickly over to the sofa and said, "Has Melanie gone to bed?"

Mrs. Welton kept her gaze on the FBI agents, who waited menacingly just inside the entry. "The child was quite bushed," she said.

"These guys," Sharon said, "are FBI. They have a search warrant for the grounds and premises. I'd like you to take the upstairs, monitoring their activities, while Mr. Yadaka and Mr. Gray cover the ground floor and outside perimeter. Any drawers these people open, make sure they close them when they're through. Any doors they open, same thing. They'll trash the place if you don't watch them." Sharon glared at the four agents, who watched the floor. "Under no circumstances are they to wake my daughter. If they try to go in the room where she's sleeping, bring them to me."

Mrs. Welton stood. Her expression was calm: she'd been through scenes like this one before. "Be glad to, mum," she said, then strode purposefully past the agents and down the hall, passing Gray and Yadaka on the way. The Englishman and the Oriental had taken charge of Darla the second she'd alighted from the limo, and now escorted her in past the federal men. Gray gently led Darla over and sat her down on the sofa.

Darla's expression was numb, and her hands were trembling. She looked up at Sharon and said, "What are these people . . . ?"

"Get a hold of yourself," Sharon said. "They're going to search the house. They have a warrant, and if you refuse to let them, they can have you jailed for contempt."

Darla's features twisted in frustration. "What are they looking for?"

One corner of Sharon's mouth bunched. "I don't know, and I doubt if they do, either. It's a form of legal harassment, but for now there's nothing we can do except let them." She turned to Yadaka and Gray. "Would you guys please escort these gentlemen around? We wouldn't want them to miss anything."

Yadaka showed a wide grin as he and Gray went over and stood with the federal guys. The lead agent looked nettled, but issued instructions. Two agents took off down the hall with Gray on their heels. The head man and the fourth fibbie entered the kitchen and began to open cabinets. Yadaka leaned on the doorjamb and watched them.

Sharon told Darla to stay put, then picked up the phone and punched in Russ Black's number in Dallas. She listened to a series of rings as, visible through the opening into the kitchen, the lead FBI agent took some glasses from the cabinet and set them on the counter. He then peered around inside the cabinet, shrugged, and opened a drawer. Yadaka strolled over and touched the agent on the arm. The two locked gazes. The FBI man gave in, carefully replaced the glasses in the cabinet and gently closed the door. There was a click on the line, and Russ Black said sleepily, "H'lo?"

"Wake up, boss. They're about to come down hard." She tried to sound calm and collected, but there was a catch in her voice.

Black caught Sharon's mood; ordinarily he would have grumped around about the time of night, but his tone was brisk and businesslike. "Have they arrested the actress?"

Sharon looked to the sofa where Darla sat, head down. Sharon turned her back and lowered her voice. "No, but that's next. As we speak, the FBI's tossing Darla's place."

"A federal warrant?"

"To go along with the feds who met with me the other night. They're continuing to stick their noses in."

"At Milton Breyer's request. Anything they find under their warrant they'll turn over to Dallas County."

"That's my thinking," Sharon said. "They're alleging interstate flight to avoid prosecution, but that's weak. Darla wasn't charged with anything when she left Texas."

"Saves them time. An interstate warrant would take weeks, shufflin' around from jurisdiction to jurisdiction, but the feds can serve their warrant anyplace in the country. Any idea what they're lookin' for?"

"None."

"Did you ask the actress?"

"Her name is Darla, boss. You should learn that if you're going to be her lawyer. I think she's as much in the dark as I am. Her story is, David Spencer beat her up in that hotel, she walked out and left him alive." Sharon eyed the bookcase, the row containing the David Spencer movie tapes. She said, "I'm dreading the meeting with Milton Breyer tomorrow. That's where he'll probably pull his arrest warrant. God, poor Darla.''

There was a rustling noise over the phone. Black said, "Nothing we can do about it until she waives extradition and we get back on our home turf. Then we can ask for bail. You going to prepare Miss Cowan for the worst?"

"She's too much in shock. I doubt it would register. Darla would be easier to defend if she confessed to doing it, boss. That way we could argue abuse. But with her insisting she didn't do it . . . Well, we can hardly argue that she's innocent, then start yelling abuse during the penalty phase of the trial."

"Should I call Anthony Gear an' tell him to clear his calendar?"

Sharon paused. Anthony Gear was a former FBI agent, a crack private investigator who'd assisted on the Midge Rathermore case and in Raymond Burnside's release from death row. He was a hard-core racist and Sharon personally couldn't stand the guy, but his work was second to none. She watched through the opening as Yadaka made the federal man close another drawer after he'd finished his search. She said to Black, "Not yet, boss. We'll need some local investigation in Texas at some point, but I'm pretty sure the nuts and bolts of this case are right here in California. I think we have all the investigators we need for now. Couple of Darla's security guards who come across like spies."

"They dependable?"

"You can bet on it. One was British Secret Service."

"We got to think, Sharon. Keep your eyes and ears open, and keep in mind where we're goin' with this. We have a dead man alone in a hotel room. Milton Breyer's got to have a theory of the crime other than that Miss Cowan was on the premises. She didn' stab David Spencer, then haul him over, put him in bed and shoot him all by her lonesome. So whatever theory Breyer has got, how she committed it, we've got to have an alternative theory."

"At the moment I haven't the foggiest idea what ours could be."

"An' won't have until you hear Breyer's story. I think once the actress is under arrest, Milt will outline his case in the papers. Give us one-up on him at any rate."

"That's what I . . ." Sharon trailed off, her lips parting in surprise as the lead FBI man came out of the kitchen. Yadaka followed closely, his face impassive. The federal man carried a pistol suspended from a ballpoint pen stuck through the trigger guard. Darla stared mutely at the gun. Sharon had been around enough cops to recognize a .38 police special when she saw one. She tucked her chin and said into the phone, "I have to go now, boss. I think our federal friends may have found something."

Darla was close to hysterics. "I've never seen that pistol before in my life."

Sharon cradled Darla's head against her shoulder, gently patted the actress's back, and said nothing.

Mrs. Welton watched the FBI's retreat, the unmarked sedans moving leisurely away from the gate with the L.A. police cars following and the mobile news units bringing up the rear. "Well choreographed, Lyndon," Mrs. Welton said. "Wouldn't you agree?"

Gray hulked against one of the snow white pillars. "Would seem so. How much of a search upstairs did they conduct?"

"Very little." Mrs. Welton shifted her weight from one foot to the other. "Went through the motions in one of the bedrooms. Disturbed nothing. The moment they learned of the pistol's discovery, they beat a fast retreat."

Benny Yadaka was seated on the top step with his forearms resting on his thighs. "Carbon copy in the kitchen. They poked around in a couple of cabinets for show, but then the guy goes under the sink and comes up with the gun like he's got radar. They knew exactly where it was all along. Once they get their hands on the piece, the whole search is over in something like ten seconds."

The fivesome was gathered on the porch with the front door open. Cool night air blew on Sharon's cheek. She hugged Darla closer as the actress continued to sob. Sharon said, "Are we talking a plant here?"

Yadaka looked back over his shoulder. "That or a leak."

Mrs. Welton tugged a .45 automatic from her purse, checked the clip, and dropped the gun back into her handbag. "An anonymous tip?"

Gray stood away from the pillar and folded his arms. "Would behoove us to locate the tipster, wot?"

Sharon steered Darla toward the interior of the house. "It would appear so," Sharon said.

14

Sharon sat up with Darla until two in the morning, playing the Calming Influence role, acting as Sympathetic Ear and Cheering Section until the actress dropped off to sleep. The session wasn't easy. When Darla finally dozed in mid-sentence, her words dissolving into a series of gentle snores, Sharon covered her friend with a blanket and trudged away down the hall. Her heart felt as if it weighed a thousand pounds.

She tossed and turned until four a.m. before she finally slept a dreamless slumber. She'd set the alarm for eight, and came to in a stupor with an angry buzzing in her ears. After she'd pressed the button to shut off the noise, she staggered out onto the balcony and looked bleary-eyed out to sea. The air was crystal clear, and white caps rolled in the distance like something she'd seen in a travel agency ad. I hate it, Sharon thought, then stumbled back inside. She somehow managed to slog through her bath without drowning, dried her hair, then stomped in a terry-cloth robe down to the room where Melanie was sleeping. She paused long enough to plaster a smile on her face, then opened the door without knocking.

Melanie was playing Sonic the Hedgehog on the Nintendo 64, a 3-D video game where a little blue rascal danced and spun in a setting so real it blew Sharon's mind. She didn't know beans about computers, but Melanie recited the particulars of the sixty-four-bite illusion as if she'd personally programmed the freaking thing. The hedgehog skittered to and fro, spinning, dodging hazards in his path. Sharon said brightly, "How was the Hollywood tour?"

"Oh, it was cool." Melanie turned. She was in panties and tee and hadn't bathed. The hedgehog slammed into a barrier and tumbled down to earth. "*Mah*-um," Melanie wailed. "You made me foul up."

Sharon leaned against the doorjamb. "Far be it from me to interrupt. I'll just say, you're too tied up to go."

Melanie looked dubious. "Go where?"

"Well, your father was going to come by for you at ten o'clock. But if you'd rather finish your game . . ." She trailed off, grinning, as Melanie disappeared in a flash into the bathroom.

Sharon said to Sheila Winston over the phone, "Rob's due in half an hour."

"Which puts you on pins and needles."

"I must be obvious." Sharon sipped coffee. She was seated in the breakfast nook behind the den. Gray stuck his head around the corner, bacon sizzling in the background, and looked a question. She held up two fingers, then rotated her hand to show that she wanted 'em over easy. Gray nodded cheerfully and went back to his cooking. Sharon said to Sheila, "What's your telltale clue?"

Sheila's voice over long-distance was clear as a bell. "I don't need a clue, I've been through it for too many years. Every time Dean comes for Trish I get butterflies. It's called the single-mom blues, sung once a month throughout the land along with the Tampax jingle. Half of your nifty free weekends, you're worried if your ex is going to take the kid out of state and then shoot you the finger from afar. Then when your child returns, you're panicked that he's somehow alienated her affections from you. Most women spoil their children silly when they get home. A few mothers overreact too far in the opposite direction and begin screaming at the kid. I like to think I'm so well adjusted that I take the middle road, but I probably foul up as much as anyone." She paused, then said, "How's it going out there?"

Sharon peered over her shoulder at the giant TV, debating whether to click on the set. She decided against it; she'd seen enough media coverage of herself over the past couple of days to last a lifetime. The light glowed on the VCR, indicating that Gray was recording more murder reports. "For Darla?" Sharon said. "Not good, though she's not as aware of it as she probably should be."

There was the faintest hint of sympathy in Sheila's voice, like the flick of an eyelash. "They're laying it on thick with the slasher scenes from *Fatal Instinct*. Be a pretty good trick for jurors to separate the reality from the illusion."

"Which is the reason they're showing that stuff. I wouldn't be shocked to learn that Milton Breyer loaned his tape of the movie to the media people."

"It's effective," Sheila said. "Mass perception. I saw an interview with Kevin Spacey the other night. Says he's played so many psychos in the movies that people shy away from him on the street. The guy was only half joking, Sharon."

"And *Fatal Instinct* is the only role Darla's played that people overall relate to. Easy for a jury to picture her butchering the guy. The gun they found here last night kills us as well. It's the murder weapon, that you can count on. Planted . . ."

There were five seconds of silence. Sheila said, "How do you know it's planted?"

"Because Darla told me she'd never seen it before. Look, Sheila, I know this woman. It's not impossible she could lose it if he was beating her up, but if she'd killed the guy, Darla never would have left the scene." Sharon switched ears with the phone. "Good to hear your voice, Sheil."

Sheila laughed.

"What's so funny?" Sharon said.

"You're in your favor-asking mode."

Sharon's tone softened. "How can you tell?"

Static crackled. Sheila didn't say anything.

"If Darla's arrested out here, I'm going to have to stay in L.A. longer than I thought," Sharon said.

"Say no more. Put Melanie on a flight and give me the flight number. Time of arrival would help."

It was Sharon's turn to fall silent. Wind beneath my wings, old Sheila, she thought. Pillow beneath my head.

Sheila said, "If she's charged and maintains her innocence, how *do* you go about defending her?" Her tone was tinged with curiosity.

Sharon expelled air, switching to attorney mode. "You have to create reasonable doubt, of course. The best way to do that is develop an alternate theory of the crime which at least makes as much sense as the prosecution's case."

"Oh? What alternate theory is that?"

Sharon hesitated. Gray set a plate in front of her and retreated to the kitchen. She used her fork to poke a hole in one of the egg yolks, and watched the runny yellow stuff spread across her plate. "Good question, Sheil," she finally said. "If you want my opinion, that's going to be the question of the year."

Sharon's watch read one minute until ten when Rob pulled up to the gate, driving a blue Land Rover. Sharon stood inside the house, looking out. She had already dressed for her meeting, in a gray courtroom suit with a tight skirt and black patent spikes. She thumbed the switch inside the entry hall. The gate swung open, and the Land Rover rolled into the drive. Sharon turned around to give Melanie one final inspection. Her heart came up in her mouth.

Melanie wore a nice gray beltless dress with shoes to match. Sharon had done her hair; it shone with the gleam of an extra hundred brush strokes, and Sharon had added a touch of rouge to Melanie's cheeks. She looked almost grown. What really got to her, however, was Melanie's expression, the nervous twitch in her lower lip and the anxiety in her eyes.

Sharon gave Malanie a hug. "Don't sweat a thing, princess. You look wonderful, and you're going to do fine."

Sharon hung back on the porch as Melanie moved forward and Rob emerged from the Land Rover. Rob looked every bit the star; he wore pressed khaki chinos and an orange oversize polo knit. His Piaget watch gleamed on his wrist, and he had dark sunglasses perched on top of his head. His expression was that of a man headed for the gallows, little bunches at the corners of his mouth and his gaze on his feet. Sharon folded her arms and crossed her ankles. Rob raised his eyes to frown at her. Sharon drummed her fingers on her upper arms, tilted her head, and arched an eyebrow.

Rob's demeanor changed as if by magic. He trotted up to give his daughter a fatherly embrace. "Hey, great to see you," he said. "I've got it arranged for you to sit beside the director during shooting. Think you'll like that?"

Melanie wriggled in delight and threw her arms around her father's neck. "Oh, Dad, I knew you would," she said. Sharon relaxed, and offered Rob a pleasant smile.

With Melanie *ooh*-ing and *ah*-ing in the Land Rover's passenger seat, Sharon stood with Rob beside the driver's door. Sharon said, "Don't be in a hurry to drop her off in the morning. I suspect I might be burning the midnight oil tonight."

"How about seven o'clock?" Rob said.

"That's too early. Make it nine. Melanie won't sleep until she wears herself out, and she'll need her rest." Sharon pinched her chin. "Oh. And no girlfriends, okay? It's only for twenty-four hours; surely you can be celibate that long."

Rob jammed his sunglasses on his nose and testily opened the driver's door. "Just this once, Muffin. Just this once."

"Hey, thanks, Dad," Sharon said. "I just know you're going to show your child the time of her life. I'm counting on it, in fact." She patted Rob on the arm. "You're a real he-man, Rob-oh." Sharon winked. "No wonder all these macho guys around the country look up to you."

Darla wore dark sunglasses and a scarf on her head, Jacqueline Onassis style. Sharon said, "You're a star, not a spy. Besides, no way will you need a disguise."

"It works sometimes in crowds. Shopping in the mall . . ." Darla's suit was coal black with wide lapels. She wore a white starched blouse underneath.

"You're talking about situations where no one's expecting to bump into you. This is different. Those media hounds at the criminal courts will merely go, 'Hey, Joe, that's her wearing the sunglasses.' Then you'll wind up with your picture all over, looking as if you're in hiding. Lose the shades, kid. Put the scarf away." Sharon stood with Darla just inside the front door. Gray and Yadaka waited outside in the limo with the motor running.

Darla removed her glasses and reached for the knot on her scarf. "I'm a little nervous," she said.

Sharon offered what she hoped was a confident wink. "Seems there's an epidemic of that. Relax, but caution is the better part of whatever. Up front, we'll hit Mr. Breyer with immunity for you if you answer his questions. He'll decline, but at least then everyone will be in their respective corners. I may as well get the opposing teams into the proper uniforms."

"I just want it all finished." Darla slid the scarf from her neck and folded it over.

"That's the goal." Sharon looked down, then back up. "This won't be easy, Darla, and I want you to prepare yourself that you could be facing a murder trial."

Darla poked the scarf down into her handbag. Her lashes fluttered uncertainly. Worry fleetingly crossed her face, then dissolved into a smile. "Why, that's silly, Sharon," she said.

15

Sharon thought that Preston Trigg looked a bit choked. "This your first media exposure?" she said. She leaned forward. "Up there to the left, Mr. Gray, please. Just stop underneath the catwalk."

They were cruising past the criminal courts, and the second-story catwalk Sharon was referring to connected the courthouse to the jail. Print and TV reporters were strung out up and down the block, milling around on the sidewalks and courthouse steps. Gray slowed, moved into the center lane, and activated his blinker.

"Hmm?" Trigg said. He was seated by the backseat window, and had exchanged the cowboy outfit he'd worn yesterday for a conservative blue suit and slim striped tie. He'd trimmed his mustache. Sharon sat in the middle, with Darla on her other side.

"The first time you've gotten any ink," Sharon said.

"Oh, no, alla time," Trigg said. "Just a couple of weeks ago I had a guy, Willie Lynch, a whole string of burglaries out in Brentwood. Got my picture in the *Times*, pleading him out."

"Page one?" Sharon said.

"Well, maybe in a later section," Trigg said. "Back of the Metro, actually." He looked through the back window. "Those people are all national, huh?"

"Most of them," Sharon said. "I think even a couple from London, one from Australia. This is good, Mr. Gray." The limo stopped at the curb. Sharon gave Darla a reassuring pat on the arm, then returned her

attention to Preston Trigg. "You know some people
in there, don't you?" She gestured with her head.

Trigg followed her direction, looking toward the
entry to the downtown L.A. County Jail. "In there?"
he said.

"Well, sure. Guards, probation people . . ."

"Oh, yeah, deal with them alla time," Trigg said. "I
thought you meant prisoners. I know some of them,
too."

Sharon gave Darla a broad wink. She said to Trigg,
"Just county employees. Now, here's what we want
you to do."

Preston Trigg came out of the jail, jogging briskly.
His tie flapped in the wind. He came up by the limo
and opened the door on Darla's side. "Got it set up,"
he said, beaming as if he'd just arranged an audience
with the queen.

"Good." Sharon squeezed Darla's upper arm.
"Hustle, kid. Will do us no good if those media
hounds across the way spot you."

Darla smiled bravely, though her lower jaw was
tense, then got out and led Trigg across the sidewalk
with wind whipping her skirt around her calves.
Sharon allowed the actress and lawyer to lead her by
ten steps or so, then snatched up her briefcase, got
out and slammed the door, and hurried into the jail
behind the pair.

Two uniformed deputies led Sharon, Darla, and
Preston Trigg through the catwalk from the jail into
the Criminal Courts Building. Heard behind them,
cheers and wolf whistles sounded from one of the cell
blocks they'd passed along the way. One deputy was
a burly white man, and the other was a slim Hispanic
woman. Both were young, in their twenties, and both
shot surreptitious glances over their shoulders. Sharon's briefcase bumped her outer thigh as she hustled
along. The corridor ahead had a tiled floor, and the
walls were unfinished concrete.

Sharon was saying to Preston Trigg, "One big town, another big town, all the same. Through the hoosegow is the only sure way to go to court without running into the press."

"Don't know why I never thought of it," Trigg said, shaking his head in admiration.

They reached the building proper, entering an area with sprayed-on walls and acoustical ceiling tiles. The deputies led the way into an open elevator; Trigg, Darla, and Sharon stood to the rear. In one back corner of the car was a floor-to-ceiling cage, a contraption used for transporting unruly prisoners. "Guess we're the first willing passengers this buggy's had in a while," Sharon said. Darla stood with her arms folded, looking vacantly ahead.

As the car started upward, the male deputy said softly to the female, "Hope we don't get in a crack over this."

Sharon leaned over and whispered in Darla's ear. The actress nodded. Sharon's weight lurched upward as the elevator halted at its designated floor. The doors rumbled open.

Sharon stepped quickly around Preston Trigg and stood between the two deputies. She smiled, first at the woman and then the man. "We can't tell you how much we appreciate this," Sharon said. "Listen, you guys want autographs? I have pen and paper in here." She thumped her briefcase. "Miss Cowan has time, if it's something you're interested in."

"I agree with you it's ridiculous," Sharon said in a whisper. "You'd just have to know Milton Breyer." She and Preston Trigg hurried down a corridor with Darla several strides in front of them, out of earshot.

"We've got plenty of hardasses with L.A. County," Trigg said. "But no way would even one of those guys have this lady arrested without first giving her a chance to turn herself in."

"Milton will," Sharon said. "Count on it. I'll be surprised if he doesn't have a warrant in his pocket. This questioning session won't go very far because we're going to ask for a grant of immunity before Darla says a word to them. I'm thinking this will be over in five minutes or so. When it's over, look for a couple of arresting officers to appear out of the woodwork. I'd only had a suspicion this would happen before last night, but the FBI finding that gun at the house cinches it."

Trigg nodded toward Darla's back. "Does she know?"

Sharon grimly shook her head. "It was a tough call, but no. I don't see how she could be more upset than she already is, but I didn't tell her. You be available for an extradition hearing? I'm thinking tomorrow."

"I'm yours as long as my fee holds out. Which, hey, ten grand, that could be quite some time." Trigg raised his voice. "Slow up, Miss Cowan. It's right through here." Trigg led the way. They went through a small office with a desk and chairs, and entered a courtroom from behind the judge's bench. The spectators section was empty. Close to the front, a jail trustee operated a vacuum cleaner. He didn't look up.

Trigg pointed to his left. "This judge is on vacation," he said. "We're set up in his conference room."

Sharon nodded. "After you, Pres," she said. Then she hung back, waiting while Trigg ushered Darla through the door. Darla's posture was confident and erect, but she threw Sharon a worried glance over her shoulder. Sharon chewed her lower lip for an instant, blinked back a tear of pity, and carried her briefcase inside.

In the conference room was a long, polished table with seating for ten. At the head of the table sat Milton Breyer, with Stan Green on his right, and Sharon nearly laughed out loud. Breyer's hair was extra dark, the Grecian Formula working overtime, and he wore a light yellow Hollywood Boulevard suit. Sunglasses were folded and poked into the Dallas prosecutor's breast pocket. God, Sharon thought, all he needs is

an open-necked shirt and a medallion on a chain.
Maybe a pinkie ring to complete the outlandish getup.
Stan Green's outfit was even worse than Breyer's. The
detective had on an open-necked shirt—but no medallion dangling below his throat—which was bright
green, its collar folded out over the collar of a pale
blue sports coat. Sunglasses were in his pocket as well,
with one earpiece sticking out and down. Sharon considered asking this duo if she could audition for a part
in their next production, then changed her mind.

A third man was at the table, and this guy seemed
fairly normal. He had dark hair, brows, and eyes, was
dressed in a lightweight navy blue suit, and looked a
bit embarrassed at the company he was keeping. The
stranger regarded Preston Trigg. "Short-time," the
stranger said with a faint Hispanic accent. "What are
you doing here?"

"Representing Darla Cowan." Trigg extended a
palm-up hand in Darla's direction.

"You're kidding me," the stranger said. "Short-time
Trigg on a major case? How did you fall into that?"

Trigg laughed nervously and said to Sharon from
the side of his mouth, "Short-time, that's . . . well, I
handle a lot of plea bargains, you know?"

"I think I could have figured that out eventually,"
Sharon said. "Darla Cowan, meet Mr. Breyer and Mr.
Green from Dallas, and . . ." She looked a question
at the stranger.

He lifted a hand in greeting. "Harold Cuellar, Assistant L.A. County District Attorney. I'm just squiring
these guys around." He started to rise.

"Keep your seat, sir," Sharon said. "I'm Sharon
Hays, no need to be formal." Her gaze fell on a
plumpish woman seated at a small metal table off to
one side, near the Mr. Coffee. A shorthand typewriter
was on the table in front of her. Sharon walked over.
"And I suppose you're the court reporter we asked
for?" The woman smiled, nodded, and handed Sharon
a business card.

"That's the first problem here," Breyer said. "What's the reporter for?"

Sharon blinked. "Why, to record questions and answers. What do court reporters normally do?"

Breyer turned to Cuellar, searching for an ally. "That legal in this state, Harold? We're interviewing a witness here."

Cuellar gave a hands-up shrug. "Not done very often. But it is. She has that right. Your alternative is not to question her."

"Okay," Breyer said, "then here's question two, Miss Hays. Are you the lady's lawyer?" He pointed at Trigg. "Or is this guy?"

Trigg looked as if he was about to speak, then closed his mouth, obviously nervous and more than a little intimidated.

Sharon stepped forward as Darla had a seat at the table and folded her hands. She fixed Breyer with a glare which could melt cobalt. "I'd think you would have asked that question before you popped off to the media," she said. "But now that you've asked, Mr. Trigg's representing Darla in California. I'm representing Miss Cowan's interests in Texas, and in this meeting I'm Mr. Trigg's co-counsel. That clear enough?"

"I'm just establishing rules. Parameters."

"Okay," Sharon said, "so I'm second banana and he's first."

Breyer touched his fingertips together. "Always glad to have you, Miss Hays."

"You may not be in a minute." Sharon looked to her right. "Mr. Trigg?"

He seemed a bit out of breath. "Yes, uh, there's a matter of a few grants we're seeking."

Breyer pyramided his fingers. "Grants?"

"Yes, well . . ." Trigg seemed helpless, out of his element.

Sharon sat forward. "What you may be trying to say, Pres, is that Miss Cowan has nothing to say without a grant of immunity from Dallas County."

"Yeah," Trigg said. "Right. That's what I'm saying."

Breyer waved a hand, as if immunity were a non-issue. "Why would that be necessary? No one's accused this lady of anything. Yet."

Trigg stammered, at a loss for words.

Of all the lawyers in town, Sharon thought, we have to walk into this guy's office. "Not officially accused," she said, "but with what you've been spouting to the press, the public thinks Darla has one foot in the penitentiary. Miss Cowan wants all those innuendoes publicly retracted, so she can get over this and get on with her life. Otherwise, you can learn what she has to say when you call her to the witness stand." Sharon leaned back. "At least that's what I think Mr. Trigg's advice is, to his client."

"Right," Trigg said. "Yeah, right."

A young woman entered the room, walked up behind Cuellar, and tapped him on the shoulder. Cuellar turned. She whispered to him. Cuellar's mouth curved in surprise. He motioned to her. She bent over, and Cuellar spoke softly but urgently into her ear.

Breyer scowled at Sharon across the table. "You mean, as in *written* immunity?"

"That's exactly what Mr. Trigg means, Milt. He wants written immunity for his client and a public retraction of all the nonsense. You no givee, she no talkee."

"Yeah, right," Preston Trigg said.

"We don't give anything in writing," Breyer said.

"You may not in Texas," Sharon said. "Out here you may find it's different."

"Yeah? What's different about it?"

Sharon gestured toward the California defense lawyer. "Man's got a question, Mr. Trigg. Do you have an answer?"

Trigg said, "Huh?"

Sharon let go an exasperated sigh. "As in a motion or something?"

"Yeah, right," Trigg said, reaching into his inside

coat pocket, producing a stapled sheath of papers, and tossing them over in front of Breyer. "A motion," Trigg said. He looked at Sharon for approval. She looked away, rolling her eyes.

Breyer quickly scanned the motion. "She can go in front of a judge?"

Sharon spread her hands. "It's Rome, Milton."

Breyer waved the motion at Cuellar. "Harold, is this . . . ?"

"Just a moment." Cuellar whispered something else to the young woman, who nodded and left the room. Cuellar turned to Breyer. "Is what what?"

"This motion I've been handed. I want to know if it's kosher under you'all's laws out here."

"I don't know what the motion is," Cuellar said, "but I think it's irrelevant."

Now Sharon was every bit as puzzled as Milton Breyer. Breyer said, "Why's that?"

"California, Texas, or on the moon," Cuellar said, "I think when a suspect is formally charged, the suspect becomes entitled to Miranda before any questioning. Our sheriff now has a warrant to serve for Miss Cowan's arrest." As if on cue, two uniformed deputies entered and stood behind Cuellar with their arms folded.

For just an instant it seemed that the room and its occupants were part of a stop-action photo. All faces turned to Darla as she looked up with a puzzled but terrified expression, blinking in disbelief as realization dawned on her. Sharon wondered, Why the phony buildup? They could have pulled their warrant on Darla the moment she'd entered, and apparently had planned to arrest her all along, so why the stall? The still-picture illusion dissolved as the deputies moved forward, dropped their warrant on the table, then stood on either side of Darla and instructed her to rise. As the actress woodenly complied, Sharon snatched up the warrant and scanned its conditions. Oh, sure, she thought. The gun.

Apparently Breyer hadn't been as certain of his

probable cause as it had appeared; the FBI had hauled the pistol from the beach house to a ballistics lab in downtown L.A.—which, interestingly enough, already had samples of the shells and fragments found in David Spencer's hotel room—and had kept the technicians jumping into the wee hours as the lab had done a comparison. The markings on the bullets had matched. No surprise there; Sharon had assumed that she was seeing the murder weapon ever since the federal man had carried the .38 out of the kitchen. With the time required to fax the ballistics info to Dallas, for Breyer's cohorts in Texas to find a judge to sign the warrant, and for the warrant to return to L.A., the papers in Sharon's hands were hot off the griddle. All of which explained why Breyer and his L.A. prosecutor friend had been tooling around with idle conversation. As the deputies cuffed Darla with a rasp of metal, Sharon thought suppression of evidence. There was an affidavit attached to the warrant. Steven Moretta, the lead FBI agent in the beach-house search, had sworn to the affidavit, and his search warrant had borne a federal magistrate's signature. Federal rules regarding probable cause differed widely from state requirements, and there was an outside chance that the gun could be inadmissible in a Texas murder trial even though it could be used against Darla in a federal prosecution. More midnight oil at the law library, Sharon thought.

As the deputy droned her Miranda warning, Darla sobbed and said urgently, "*Sharon . . .*" Her expression of fear was heartbreaking. On Sharon's right, Preston Trigg looked from Sharon to Darla and back again.

Sharon stood. She waited for the deputy to finish, then said, "They're arresting you, babe. For now there's nothing we can do until we try to arrange bail." She looked at the deputy. "Private cell, right?" The deputy nodded. Sharon said to Darla, "They'll keep you separate from the other prisoners, so you won't have to worry about anyone bothering you. Not much

consolation, but some." She said to Breyer, "Arraign-
ment and extradition hearing tomorrow, Milt?" She
tried to keep the contempt out of her tone, but
failed miserably.

Breyer gave a hands-up shrug. "Why wait? We've
arranged for a judge right now. I assume your client's
got the good sense to waive extradition, so why not
get her back to Texas tonight?"

Sharon fiddled, pretending to read over the arrest
warrant while giving herself time to think. Breyer was
as transparent as cellophane; he didn't know his butt
from either end about California statutes, so wanted
to whisk Darla back to Texas, where he could depend
on Kathleen Fraterno to hit the books in his behalf.
But allowing her client the fastest possible route to
Dallas might be to Sharon's advantage as well; bail
for a murder suspect was no cinch even in Texas, but
would be totally out of the question here in L.A. during extradition proceedings. Finally Sharon said, "We
may not have a problem with that."

"Good." Breyer extended a hand toward the exit.
"Shall we?"

Cuellar opened the door and ushered Breyer and
Stan Green out into the corridor. The deputies
grasped Darla's upper arms and led her away. Preston
Trigg remained in his seat, looking helplessly around.
Our California hired gun, Sharon thought. God, the
guy was completely lost. Sharon poked her L.A. co-
counsel on the shoulder. "Come on, Pres. Your public
awaits you." She followed after the deputies, reaching
out impulsively to give Darla a pat on the arm.

Sharon had traveled less than ten steps down the
corridor before her blood was boiling. Reporters and
cameramen lined the entire length of the hallway. A
freaking setup—as the deputies had taken Darla into
custody, Cuellar had sent his female assistant out to
alert the media. Flashes flashed, and newshounds fired
questions from every angle. Darla allowed the depu-

ties to lead her along, keeping her head down and her eyes tightly shut.

The situation inside the courtroom fueled Sharon's anger even more. As she followed Darla and her captors through the rear entry, she sidestepped two reporters armed with pens and notepads. There wasn't a single empty seat, men and women jammed together on the pews like the faithful at a Billy Graham revival. Sharon briefly scanned the audience, recognizing three network media stars—a guy who'd been on three or four different news mags (and who'd obviously had a face-lift or two) along with two women from competing networks who specialized in up-close-and-personal interviews. Sharon glared dagggrs at Milton Breyer, who avoided making eye contact as he talked in whispers to Harold Cuellar. The presence of all these celebrities could only mean that the word had gotten around. Sharon hadn't seen a news report since early morning, but wouldn't be surprised if Darla's arrest had been public knowledge even as Sharon, Darla, and Preston Trigg had entered the criminal courts through the jail. Sharon looked at the jury box. Her jaws clenched.

A television camera was set up above the staggered rows of seats. A red light glowed near the camera's front, and the operator had swiveled the lens to point in Darla's direction. The pasteboard sign attached to the camera read, COURT TV. As Sharon watched, the cameraman thumbed the zoom switch. The deputies had paused just inside the courtroom as if choreographed to do so, and the viewing audience had a close-up shot of Darla Cowan, head down, her hands cuffed behind her. Sharon's looked at the bench.

The judge was a handsome black man around forty, with a thick head of hair and a full, neatly trimmed beard. He was halfway out of his seat, bending over to shake hands with another woman whom Sharon recognized. This jazzed-up black female was a regular on *20/20,* and sometimes spelled the anchor on the weekend evening news.

Preston Trigg gently bumped Sharon from behind. He mumbled, "Excuse me." She turned to him and said, "What's the rundown on this guy?" She jerked her head in the direction of the judge.

Trigg gaped at the jury box camera and acted as if he hadn't heard.

Sharon sighed in exasperation. She yanked Trigg's sleeve so hard that she jerked him off balance. "The judge, Pres. Who is he?"

Trigg came out of his trance. "Uh, Drake Rudin." He resumed his ogling of the jury box and spectator section.

"Okay," Sharon said, "that's his name. He for us or agin us?"

Trigg seemed puzzled.

Sharon said, "Is he prosecution- or defense-oriented? Seems it would be helpful knowledge to someone practicing criminal law around here."

"Yeah, sure. He's on TV a lot."

"Obviously. He's got his own camera crew. Look, Pres, do you know this guy, or don't you?"

Trigg seemed downtrodden. "He presides over some big cases."

Sharon felt resigned. "So you don't know him."

"Talked to him a couple of times. He . . . doesn't handle many plea bargains. Mainly he's a trial judge." Trigg brightened. "His daughter's an actress. Been in a couple of soaps."

"Great, if we wanted an audition." Sharon chewed her lower lip. Judge Drake Rudin gushed over the newswoman like a starstruck fan. Sharon halfway expected him to ask for her autograph. She said thoughtfully, "Likes the limelight, does he?"

Cuellar and Breyer had passed through the gate into the bullpen area and joined the session at the bench. Stan Green slouched into a seat at the prosecution table. The deputies ushered Darla to the defense side and held a chair for her, unlocked her cuffs, and then took seats directly behind her against the rail. Darla moved as if in a trance. Sharon dreaded visiting the actress in jail. Breyer turned around, located Sharon, and beckoned.

Sharon said, "Come on, Pres. We're up."

Trigg looked at her. He swallowed.

Sharon grasped the lawyer's arm. "Come *on,* Pres. And don't worry. If you faint, I'll catch you."

S.O.P. would have been for Preston Trigg to introduce his out-of-state co-counsel to the judge, but Trigg seemed so choked up that Sharon doubted if he'd remember her name. She approached the bench with Trigg bringing up the rear. The judge, Milt Breyer, and Harold Cuellar all turned to her, as did the zippy *20/20* reporter. Sharon wondered if Judge Drake Rudin was going to let the newswoman attend his bench conference. This sure ain't Kansas, Toto, Sharon thought.

Rudin didn't wait for the formalities. He bent forward and extended his hand. "Miss Hays. Glad to meet you in person. We share a common bond."

Sharon pictured the news reports with her and Darla splashed all over the nation's TV screens. She firmly gripped the judge's hand and said demurely, "Glad to know you, Your Honor. And this is . . ." She touched Preston Trigg's elbow. Introducing a California lawyer to a judge in an L.A. courtroom seemed awkward as hell.

Rudin ignored Trigg. He said to Sharon, "My daughter. She's an actress."

Sharon didn't know what to say. She tried, "She's chosen a tough way to make a living. And this is—"

"Miss Hays." The lovely black woman interrupted, stepping forward and grabbing Sharon's hand. "Karen Warren, Miss Hays. *Twenty-Twenty.* Wondering if after this hearing you might have a few moments for us to do an interview."

Christ, Sharon thought, right here in the courtroom. Where she came from, they made the media hawks wait outside in the corridor. She said, "Glad to know you, Karen. Afraid I can't answer that question until we're finished here. Depends on whether my client needs me." She turned her back on the *20/20* reporter and faced the bench. She was going to introduce Preston Trigg come hell or high water. She said, "Your Honor, this is—"

"She's had a million auditions," Judge Rudin said. "Snagged a couple of bit parts. Tough going at first."

Sharon stammered as she looked up at the bench.

"My daughter," Rudin said.

"Oh. She's doing well if she's snagged any parts at all. I auditioned a hundred times before I got my first role. A courier. My one line was, 'Package for Mr. Dunston.' Your Honor, this is Preston Trigg, my co-counsel in L.A."

"Look, I hate to impose on you," Rudin said, "but if you know an agent who could help her . . ."

Sharon couldn't believe it. Right in the middle of a bench conference preceding an extradition hearing, the judge was asking for a talent agent. She watched Milt Breyer from the corner of her eye. Breyer cut his gaze toward the jury box and its television camera. Sharon sensed Darla Cowan behind her, trembling at the defense table. Whatever the result, the best thing Sharon could do for her client was get this looney tunes of a hearing over with.

She drew a shallow breath and plunged ahead. "It's been years since I've had any contacts in the entertainment business or needed an agent, Your Honor. If you'd like, I can ask Miss Cowan." She was trying the gentlest route possible to changing the subject to Darla's extradition, but if she thought that mentioning the defendant would put an end to the nonsense, she was mistaken. Rudin turned a hopeful look on the defense table. God, Sharon thought, this absolutely tears it. She took a step sideways, interjecting herself between the judge and Darla. Sharon said, "Mr. Trigg and I have conferred, Your Honor. We don't think this hearing will take up much of the court's time."

"Meaning you're going to waive extradition?" Milton Breyer said. He looked disappointed.

Sharon grabbed Preston Trigg's coat sleeve and hauled him up beside her. "Ultimately the decision is our client's," Sharon said. "But it's Mr. Trigg's feeling we should waive. Isn't that what you said, Mr. Trigg?"

Preston Trigg opened, then closed his mouth, like a rookie actor with a severe case of stage fright. Finally he choked out, "Yeah, right."

The judge didn't seem to hear. He continued to look wishfully toward Darla. He said, "This agent my daughter's got now doesn't—"

"With that said," Sharon interrupted, "with the court's permission, we'll now confer with our client. Two minutes, Your Honor, then we're ready to proceed." The court reporter's station was in front of and to the right of the bench. Sharon noted that the round Hispanic woman sat with her hands in her lap, and as yet hadn't recorded a word of what was going on. Sharon said, "We are on the record here, aren't we?" The court reporter came out of her trance and poised her fingers over her keyboard.

The judge snapped to as well; placing matters on the record was the best way to get the court's attention in any state. Rudin said sternly, "Two minutes, counsel," as the shorthand machine began its muted clatter. Sharon nodded, then led Preston Trigg back over to the defense table. Halfway there she chanced a look over her shoulder at the bench. Milton Breyer, pale yellow suit and all, continued to pose for *Court TV*. Judge Drake Rudin had assumed a more judicial posture, but still glanced occasionally toward the jury box camera. As if he's freaking *preening,* Sharon thought. She returned her attention to her client. Darla's lips were quivering, and she was on the verge of tears.

The first matter at hand was to keep Darla from breaking down completely. Once she was in her cell for the night she could cry to her heart's content, but for Darla to lose it in public would be a disaster. Sharon sat down beside the actress, withdrew a legal pad and ballpoint from her briefcase, and slapped the pad down on the table with a solid thunk. Darla stiffened, but her terrified expression evaporated. Preston Trigg jumped as if touched by live electric wires.

Sharon leaned close to Darla. "Right here, kid. Right now, the ordeal begins. Let's show 'em the stuff we're made of." She thought she sounded corny, but Darla Cowan was the one person in the world on whom corniness might have a positive effect. Sharon drew a shallow breath and held it.

Darla set her lips and firmed her jaw, in full performer's mode. Whatever the situation, she hadn't missed the TV camera, and now turned her full gaze on the glowing red light in the jury box. "They set it up, didn't they?" she said.

"Right. And what we're trying to do is make their strategy backfire. Don't panic. You're wrongfully accused. You're not afraid. You're not indignant. You have faith in the system. Got it?"

Darla nodded firmly. "I'll do my best. I hope I don't scream."

"If you do, reserve your hysterics for in private." Sharon pushed the notepad forward and handed Darla the pen. "Take notes," Sharon said. "You're going to be in custody at least overnight. This is an extradition proceeding, to return you to Texas to face charges. When the judge asks you, tell him you're waiving a hearing. That way Dallas County will put you on a plane tonight, and tomorrow we can go before a Texas judge and request bail."

Darla looked down, then back up. "Request?"

Sharon wanted to lie but refused to. "It's all we can do, request. As a murder defendant, you're not really entitled. As a public figure, I think I might get a judge to grant you bond. The bail will be high, a million or more, if we get it at all. Going to Texas tonight is your only chance."

Darla met Sharon's gaze. "What are my odds?"

Sharon tugged on her earlobe. "I'd say, at best, fifty-fifty. For now you've got to resign yourself to some time in jail. Take this pad and make a list. I don't have to tell you the gun's a real problem for us, Darla. I want the names of everyone besides you who has access to that beach house. Someone put the pistol in the kitchen, okay?" She squeezed Darla's forearm. "You ready?"

Darla looked down and said softly, "As much as I'll ever be."

"Good." Sharon stood and said to Preston Trigg, "Announce ready, Pres. Let's get this show on the road."

Trigg wet his lips and gaped in the direction of the bench. The judge folded his hands and regarded the defense table with a curious expression. Sharon jabbed Preston Trigg with her elbow. "Announce ready, Pres."

Trigg continued to stare.

Oh, for God's sake, Sharon thought. She raised her voice. "I think Mr. Trigg is ready now, Your Honor."

The judge waited. A pin dropped on the carpet would have sounded like an avalanche. Judge Rudin said, "Is that true, Mr. Trigg?"

Trigg gulped as if he'd swallowed a grapefruit. He tried to speak, but only a croak came out of his mouth. Finally he drew in an enormous breath. "Yeah, right," he finally said.

Habit formed from nine years of practicing law gave Sharon a preconception of what was about to occur in the courtroom. An extradition waiver required only a brief appearance before the bench, a ten-yard march for Sharon and Preston Trigg with their client in tow. During the proceedings there would be very little for the lawyers to do. Mostly they'd stand mute, nodding occasionally to Darla as the judge read her rights, told her she was entitled to a hearing, and then asked if she was voluntarily waiving extradition and surrendering to Dallas County for the cross-country trek to Texas. Darla would then look Sharon a question, and Sharon would nod. Darla would waive formal hearing, the judge would commit her to the custody of Dallas

County, and that would be that. Five minutes at the outside, no more.

So ingrained was the procedure in Sharon's psyche that when Judge Drake Rudin said, "The court calls *State of Texas* v. *Darla Elizabeth Cowan,* a hearing on the matter of extradition," Sharon nudged Darla, tensed her knees, and had risen halfway to her feet when Rudin continued, "Does the state of California have a statement to make?" Deputy L.A. District Attorney Harold Cuellar moved front and center. Sharon relaxed and sat down, puzzled beyond words.

Cuellar stood behind a podium, his features relaxed in a mild expression. "Assistant District Attorney Harold Cuellar for the people of California, Your Honor."

Rudin nodded and folded his hands. "Proceed, Mr. Cuellar."

Sharon blinked in disbelief. As if these two hadn't known each other for a century or so. Sharon wondered if the judge had made a mistake. This was supposed to be a waiver of hearing, a brief chitchat before the bench. No one should be making any open-court statements here, no way. Even Preston Trigg was stunned. He made as if to rise and object. Sharon reached around Darla to place a hand on Trigg's arm. She whispered, "Let's see what this is all about." Trigg leaned back in his chair.

"Actually," Cuellar said, "we have no position in this other than to offer space to our esteemed colleague from Texas. As always, the people of California give the utmost cooperation in these matters, and I'll now yield to Mr. Milton Breyer." He extended a hand toward Breyer, who rose and gave a nod to the bench that was practically a bow.

Well, fuck a duck, Sharon thought. Everyone had already been introduced to each other, in the prehearing bull session in front of the bench. Sharon stared dully at the TV camera; this baloney was posturing for the benefit of the viewing audience, pure and simple. Can't tell the players without a program, folks, and since you're to spend the next few months arguing this case over the breakfast table and around the office water cooler, we'll now give you a quick rundown of who's who. Sharon wondered whether the *Court TV* producer would give a signal, and the judge would make like an NFL referee and call for a commercial break. She gave Darla a reassuring pat on the arm and turned her head to the rear. The gallery spectators sat mesmerized, arms folded. Sharon noted that Karen Warren, the *20/20* reporter, had taken a seat in the front row, but wouldn't be surprised if the beautiful newswoman should suddenly grab a mike, stroll into the bullpen, and begin a play-by-play.

His intro finished, Cuellar marched back to the defense table, sat, and cut his eyes in the direction of the jury box. The judge acknowledged the contingent from Texas. "Greetings, Mr. Breyer. I'm Judge Drake Rudin." Rudin turned his face partway to the camera and enunciated his name slowly and clearly.

In the real world, Breyer should now exchange hellos with the judge and sit down. Instead, his hair a shiny blue-black in color, Grecian Formula working overtime, yellow suit and all, Breyer sauntered around behind the prosecution table, moved up, and stood behind the podium. He smiled. "We don't often come to this gorgeous country, Your Honor. Quite a treat for us."

What a jackass, Sharon thought.

"You've picked a lovely time of year, Counsel," the judge said.

"That we have, Your Honor. That we have."

And the rain in Spain falls mainly on the bullshit, Sharon thought.

Judge Rudin leaned forward. "Are defense counsel present as well?" He looked at the defense table like a director in a *Law & Order* episode. In the jury box, the *Court TV* guy swiveled his camera around.

Sharon didn't know what to do. Preston Trigg took his cue and popped up. "Preston Trigg, Judge, representing Darla Cowan's interests." Trigg was getting with the program in a hurry.

Rudin continued to nod. "Mr. Trigg. And this is . . . ?" He stared at Sharon.

If there had been a way out, Sharon would have jumped at the chance. She was as embarrassed as she'd ever been in her life. Not even last night at the restaurant, when Rob had turned her into a public spectacle, had she felt so freaking stupid. Her knees like jelly, a flush rising into her cheeks, Sharon rose. She said timidly, "Sharon Hays, Your Honor."

Behind her in the gallery, a woman said in a stage whisper, "As if we didn't know."

Sharon wanted to crawl under the table. She was acutely conscious of Darla on her left as the actress tilted her chin upward to watch her. Sharon sat down quickly. The TV camera swiveled toward the bench. It's almost over, Sharon thought. The public had gotten an eyeful. Now all that was left was for Darla to waive a formal hearing, for the television people to fold their tents, and for the entire group to be on their way back to Texas, where the real fight would begin.

"And if the court please," Milton Breyer said, "in laying a foundation for this matter, we have a witness to present."

A witness? Sharon thought. A freaking *witness*? We're waiving extradition; what on earth would they need a witness for? She sat back, curious to see just how far this nonsense would continue.

"Very well, Mr. Breyer," Rudin said. "Call your witness."

Sharon didn't even know what kind of objection she could raise. She sat helplessly in place while Milton Breyer, showboating like mad, turned his profile to the television camera. "Call Detective Stan Green," Breyer said grandly.

Oh, goody, Sharon thought, another character introduced to the public at large. A big, dumb bozo who will now make as big an ass of himself as Milton Breyer. An idea fought its way through her anger and confusion and lodged firmly in her mind. The judge, the L.A. prosecutor, Milton Breyer, and now Stan

Green, all were using this inane format for the maximum in media exposure. Wonder if there's a way to turn these shenanigans around to Darla's advantage, Sharon thought. There had to be. She suspected that if Fraterno was watching this horror show back in Dallas, she was on the verge of apoplexy. As Stan Green rose and approached the witness box in a hired gunslinger's crouch, Sharon pulled a legal pad from her briefcase and began to take notes.

So out of line was the procedure that the court reporter was fooled. The Hispanic lady wasn't prepared to give the oath. She dug frantically around for a Bible, had Green place his hand on the book and swear to tell the truth, the whole truth, and nothing but. Green sauntered into the witness chair, faced the camera, and grinned.

Breyer leaned his elbow on the podium and rested his chin on his lightly clenched fist. "State your name, please."

"Stanley Fred Green." Green uttered the words like a player in a B movie.

"Mmm-hmm. And what is your occupation, sir?" Breyer deepened his voice in an F. Lee Bailey impersonation. And a lousy one at that, Sharon thought.

"I'm a homicide detective."

"In Dallas, Texas?"

"Yes, sir."

"And in connection with your employment, Detective Green, have you had occasion to investigate the death of one David Spencer?"

"I'm the lead detective on the case."

"Meaning that you supervise the collection of evidence—"

"Yes."

"—the examination of the crime scene, the interviewing of possible witnesses—"

"Yes, sir."

"—the removal of the body to the medical examiner's office—"

"Your Honor." Sharon was on her feet, unable to

stand this joke of a proceeding any longer. "Your Honor, if it will save time, we will stipulate that Detective Green is in charge of the investigation. We'd ask, however, that Mr. Breyer make it clear just where this is going. I'd remind the court that we're not at trial here."

Judge Rudin glared at her, all friendliness gone from his posture. "I believe I'm aware of what's going on in my court, miss."

So am I, Sharon thought. You're turning your courtroom into a movie set, trying to sear your own image into the public conscience, you silly . . . She forced herself to calm down. Rudin was, after all, in charge, and showing him up on national TV wasn't to her best interest—or to Darla's, whose interest this was all supposed to be about. Sharon continued in a more subdued voice, "I apologize for any incorrect inference, Your Honor. I would point out, however, that we've already agreed to waive a hearing on extradition. Miss Cowan is perfectly willing to—"

"You are out of order, Miss Hays. Sit down." Rudin flicked his fingers over the sleeve of his robe.

Sharon's teeth clicked in astonishment. She took her seat in a huff. She'd done her best to move the hearing along, and Rudin had treated her like some bit player who'd forgotten her lines. Which in the judge's eyes, she was. *Shut up, dearie, we're shooting a scene here.*

Breyer regarded Sharon with an obvious smirk, then said to Green, "During your investigation, Detective, did you run across any information, evidence, whatever, which caused you to suspect someone of this hideous crime?"

The word "hideous" was entirely out of line, and Sharon nearly objected on general principles. She opened, then closed her mouth.

"I did," Green said.

"And is that person here in the courtroom?"

"She is."

"And could you point this person out to the court?"

Sharon nearly objected again. Stan Green wasn't

personally acquainted with Darla and therefore wasn't qualified to make a positive ID, but what was the use in objecting? Rudin might even sustain, but so what? Anyone in the country who didn't know the accused in this case had been under a rock for the past week or so. As Sharon sighed softly, Preston Trigg leaped to his feet. "Objection," he said loudly.

Sharon laid down her pen and drummed her fingers.

"Grounds?" Rudin asked. He sat forward, taking center stage. If Trigg keeps objecting so that the judge can garner plenty of screen time, Sharon thought, then old Pres might receive a couple of bucks under the table as a reward.

"I'll voir dire the witness, Your Honor," Trigg said forcefully. He turned a hostile glare on the witness box. "Detective Green, have you ever met Darla Cowan, the defendant in this case?" He expansively held out a hand in Darla's direction.

Great, Sharon thought, now the defense lawyer has saved the prosecution the trouble of identifying the suspect. Jesus Christ, Preston Trigg was every bit as caught up in the glamour of being on TV as were Milton Breyer and the rest of the gang. She would have grabbed Trigg's coat sleeve and yanked him down, but that would have been more playacting for the viewing audience.

"Never in person," Green said. "Seen her movies."

"Never in person." Trigg threw a look at the bench, his expression as if he'd struck gold. "Our objection stands, Your Honor."

Rudin assumed a thoughtful look, withdrew an old-timey pocket watch from his robe and wound the stem. Oh, Jesus, Sharon thought, I've seen this one, and so has everyone else. *Anatomy of a Murder,* where the judge allows Jimmy Stewart to get into the issue of Mrs. Manion's panties. The guy playing the role was a real-life judge, Sharon recalled, and the *click-click-click* of the winding pocket watch was amplified for dramatic effect. She suspected that Rudin had a tape of the old sixties flick, and had watched it last night in preparation for his own appearance on the network. Finally Rudin said, "Sustained," and dropped the watch into his pocket. In the jury box, the camera clicked and whirred. Trigg sat down with a satisfied look and glanced at Sharon for approval. Sharon ignored the California lawyer and picked up her pen. She wondered if the people out in viewerland were sufficiently on the edge of their seat as yet for this joke of a performance to draw to a close.

Apparently not. Breyer made a big to-do of rummaging through a pile of notes, as if Trigg's objection had upset his train of thought. He looked up at the witness. "But, without identifying this person, Detective Green, do you have a suspect?"

Green turned partway to the camera. "Yes."

"And who is this person?"

"Darla Cowan."

Big surprise, Sharon thought. She wondered if the television image included some heavy background music.

Breyer now came up with a typewritten sheet of paper. Two or three copies, in fact, one of which he dropped on the defense table and another of which he carried up to set before the judge. Sharon picked up the copy and read. God, the arrest warrant, which Breyer had already served just prior to the deputies taking Darla into custody. Putting the out-of-state warrant into evidence was necessary in an extradition hearing, but the defense had already announced that it was *waiving* the freaking hearing. She was seething, and suspected that the expression on her face said as much.

Judge Rudin read over the warrant and looked up at the defense side. "Any objection?"

Sharon contemptuously allowed her copy to flutter to the table, and didn't say anything. Preston Trigg moved as if to rise. Sharon reached around Darla and poked the California attorney with a stiffened forefinger. Trigg sagged in his chair.

Rudin said in a monotone, "No objection. Admitted, then."

"Thank you, Your Honor," Breyer said grandly, then flopped his final copy of the warrant down in front of the witness box. "Detective Green," Breyer said, "I ask if you will please look over this piece of evidence and tell the court if you can identify it."

Now it was Green's turn to make a major production of the simple act of picking up and reading the warrant. He did so with a studied frown. Finally he said, "It's the probable-cause warrant for Darla Cowan's arrest."

"From a Texas court?"

"Yes."

Breyer strolled halfway to the podium as if deep in thought. "Meaning, Detective, that a judge back in the Lone Star state has gone over your affidavit, and has agreed that there is probable cause to arrest the defendant?"

"That's right," Green said.

"And with this warrant, could you arrest the suspect if she was in Texas?"

"I could."

"Since the suspect is in California, has this warrant gone through the proper channels to have the suspect arrested in this state?"

Green examined the warrant again. "It would appear so."

Which answer was subject to objection, Sharon knew, because Green couldn't possibly know California procedure for serving the warrant, but which objection would be as pointless as all the other freaking objections which came to mind. Sharon stayed mute, and prepared to grab Preston Trigg's collar if he made a move to get up. Trigg remained in his chair. Sharon returned her attention to the front.

Breyer went back to the podium and rustled through his notes, which Sharon would bet her bottom dollar consisted of doodlings and hen scratchings. Without Kathleen Fraterno to back him up, Breyer was helpless. Finally he smiled at the bench. "That's all, Your Honor," he said, and retreated to his seat at the prosecution table. Harold Cuellar whispered something in Breyer's ear. Both prosecutors grinned.

Rudin addressed the defense side. "Cross?"

Before Sharon could speak, Trigg leaped to his feet. "Waive cross, Your Honor." Sharon breathed a sigh of relief that her co-counsel hadn't launched into oratory.

"Very well, the witness is excused," Rudin droned. Then, after Green had climbed down and ambled back to the prosecution table, the judge said, "Is the defense waiving formal extradition?"

We sure are, Sharon thought, which makes the twenty-minute freak show we've just witnessed a waste of time. She smiled. Preston Trigg stood up and said, "That's my understanding, Judge."

"Defendant will rise, then."

Darla looked fearfully at Sharon. Sharon nodded, grasped Darla's elbow, and helped the actress to her feet. At long last, getting it over with.

"Miss Cowan, are you under advice of counsel?" Rudin asked.

There was a tremor in Darla's voice, her words barely audible. "Yes, sir."

Sharon looked at the TV camera, the judge, the prosecution table, and back at the camera again. All this posturing and strutting. A lightbulb flashed inside her head. Her eyes widened.

Rudin continued as if reading from a script. "And has counsel advised you that if you waive your right to a hearing, the state of Texas will transport you to Dallas for trial on murder charges, and that once you waive your right to this hearing, there is no avenue available for you to retract this waiver?"

"Yes, sir."

There was a tightness in Sharon's throat. Even now, with all eyes on the judge and defendant, Breyer was watching the TV camera as if looking for a way to upstage the main performers. Stan Green appeared to be watching the judge, but his jaw was bunched more than normal as he gave the camera a steely-eyed profile shot. Sharon wondered if . . . God, *if* . . .

"And given this information, Miss Cowan," the judge said, "is it your desire to waive the hearing to which you are entitled prior to extradition?"

Sharon made up her mind. *Okay, you want a circus? We'll give you a three-ringer with a trapeze act.*

Darla opened her mouth to answer.

Sharon squeezed the actress's arm. Darla paused and turned to her. Sharon leaned over and whispered, "Say no, Darla."

Darla's lips parted in shock.

"I'll have to explain later," Sharon said softly. "Repeat after me. 'Your Honor, I do not waive this right, and request a hearing on the matter forthwith.' " She wondered if impulse had gotten the best of her. If it had, she was about to be the biggest fool since Darden offered O.J. the bloody gloves.

Darla sighed in frustration, in the same manner she used to in venting displeasure over last-minute script changes. She faced the bench, the thespian within her taking over, and repeated Sharon's words clearly and forcefully. When she'd finished, she cut her gaze in Sharon's direction. Sharon gave an encouraging nod. There was a nervous rustling in the gallery, the hubbub of muted conversation punctuated by the whisper of nylon as women uncrossed and recrossed their legs.

Rudin gaped in obvious surprise. "Does the court understand that you're *not* waiving your right to a hearing, Miss Cowan?"

"That's correct, Your Honor." Darla required no prompting now; her expression even showed faint pleasure, leaving 'em with something to think about, the star of the show relishing her delivery of the spin-around line.

Rudin looked sternly at Preston Trigg. "I thought we'd conferred, Counsel. Did I miss something?"

Trigg threw Sharon a helpless glance. She spoke up. "It's Miss Cowan's decision to make. While I confess

we're a bit eleventh-hour here, I did prompt her.
We're requesting a hearing, Judge." She ignored Milton Breyer's murmur of surprise.

Rudin beckoned. Milton Breyer, Harold Cuellar,
and Preston Trigg rushed the bench as Sharon hung
back and watched them. She was looking for a reac-
tion, and boy, did she ever get one. Breyer was smiling
openly, as were Judge Rudin and Preston Trigg, and
L.A. prosecutor Cuellar seemed pleased as well. Gives
you more opportunity to strut your stuff over the networks, guys, Sharon thought. She motioned for Darla
to have a seat, then came around the defense table
and leisurely approached the bench conference. Her
thoughts were fifteen hundred miles away, and she
mentally winced. She was in for a dressing-down from
Russell Black that would likely turn her ears blue.
You'll just have to hear me out, old boss, she thought.
There's a method to this madness which will require
some explaining. She reached the area before the
judge and stood with her chin tilted up in her best
posture of innocence.

"Miss Hays," Rudin began, "are you sure Miss
Cowan understands what is happening here?"

Before Sharon could answer, Breyer cut in. "I'm
sure she does, Judge. I observed her talking to Miss
Hays just before she made her statement."

Sharon started to speak up, but now it was her co-
counsel who interrupted. "I heard her, too," Preston
Trigg said.

Sharon suppressed a smile. God, they *loved* her performance. She said, "Darla wants to attack the warrant on its face, Your Honor."

Rudin pursed his lips. "She's questioning probable
cause?"

"So the court will be apprised," Sharon said. "The
warrant hinges on the location of the murder weapon
at Miss Cowan's home. Explaining how the gun got
in Darla's kitchen is a trial issue and not debatable in
an extradition hearing. The justification for the search,
however, is. The search came under a federal warrant.

The feds are investigating interstate flight in order to avoid prosecution. It's a matter of record that Darla traveled from Texas to California, and that circumstance alone might give the FBI cause to search, but without some evidence that the gun was in the house to begin with, the state has no right to use the fruits of the FBI's labor." Sharon paused to catch her breath, having said more of a mouthful than she'd intended. "Bottom line, Your Honor. If the federal search warrant's invalid, suppression of the gun is automatic. If the gun is suppressed, then Texas's arrest warrant is invalid on its face and Darla's entitled to go free. Or so we'll argue." She shrugged around at the group in general.

"And your client, totally aware of the circumstance, agrees with this?"

Sharon nodded and lowered her gaze.

Rudin flattened his palms on the bench. The flesh underneath his fingernails was pink, in contrast to his coffee-colored skin. "So it would seem, ladies and gentlemen, that we're dug in for a while. You have evidence to present, Mr. Breyer. How long do you need?"

Breyer's chin bobbed up and down like a fishing cork. "While I hadn't anticipated such a ploy from the defense, we can be ready tomorrow. I have witnesses to fly in, plus members of my staff, but they're on call."

Sharon ignored the "ploy from the defense" barb and smiled at the judge. The "members of my staff" would include Kathleen, of course, which was to be expected. Without expert assistance, Sharon doubted if Milton Breyer could prosecute the running of a stop sign.

"Is tomorrow satisfactory with the defense?"

Sharon said, "They're the ones throwing down the gauntlet, Your Honor. Their time, their place. I think we're limited to the choice of weapons, aren't we?"

"Well put," Rudin said. "I'll clear the decks for ten a.m."

The lawyers all nodded and started to retreat to their corners. Rudin said, "Oh. Just a minute."

The gathering recircled around the bench.

"I allowed that"—Rudin pointed toward the camera in the jury box—"today under the assumption that we were having a hearing waiver. If we're going to have any objections to the presence of television in the courtroom tomorrow, I should hear them now. Mr. Cuellar, we're on your turf here."

The L.A. prosecutor spread his hands. "My field, Judge, but we've got visiting opposing teams. Entirely their call."

Breyer spoke up quickly. "There might be a question at trial, Your Honor. But in an extradition hearing, who cares?"

Sharon looked away. *You* care, you silly ass, she thought.

Rudin folded his hands. "I've yet to hear from the defense. Miss Hays?"

Sharon looked from the judge to Breyer and back again. She had a sudden mental picture of what would occur if she objected to the TV coverage, an imaginary scene where Milton Breyer, Stan Green, and this phony judge surrounded her and punched her lights out. She very nearly giggled out loud. Sharon gave a little shrug. "Fine with us, Judge," she said. "Our client's used to being before the camera. If anyone's to suffer stage fright I think it will be the lawyers. Don't you?"

16

Russell Black asked Sharon if she'd lost her mind.
"Possibly, boss," she said. "But hear me out."

"Extradition's automatic, girl. All you're doin' is givin' Milton Breyer a chance to do more struttin' on television."

"That's the idea."

"We're not in the publicity business. We're in the lawyer business. If I ever taught you anything, I thought it was that."

"Did you catch that judge's act? God."

"Most ludicrous thing I ever seen in a courtroom. What was all that business, puttin' Stan Green on the stand?"

"To introduce the players to the public at large," Sharon said. "All for the camera's benefit. I think the limelight will get in Milt's eye so much, we can turn it around on him."

"Way I see it, you don't have any real grounds for requestin' a hearing."

"You don't have all the facts, boss. Darla's warrant points to the murder weapon, the gun, found at her house on a federal search warrant. I'm going to try and suppress the gun."

"On what grounds?"

"On the grounds that the federal probable cause wouldn't have been sufficient for the state to conduct its own search, so they can't use the fruits of the FBI search in a state prosecution. If I can get a ruling that the Texas warrant is invalid, they'll have to release Darla until they can officially indict her."

There were five seconds of silence. "Never happen,"
Black finally said. "Plus you're wavin' a red flag, re-
vealin' strategy you plan to use at trial. The California
court will allow the extradition an' toss the hot potato
of the gun's admissibility to a Texas judge, and you've
clued in the prosecution on what to be ready for. I've
seen it happen over an' over."

Sharon leaned one shoulder against the corridor
wall as Preston Trigg exited the courtroom, followed
by two minicams and three newswomen who pointed
microphones in his direction. The assembly halted beside a row of benches, and the newswomen cast anticipatory looks at Sharon. She held up a just-a-minute
finger as she said into the phone, "I'm willing to
chance it, boss, in return for what *we're* going to learn.
With admissibility of the gun at issue, Milt Breyer will
trot out his entire case to show his probable cause.
It's the opportunity of the decade, boss. How many
times have you been able to make the state put on all
its evidence in advance? Before it's over, we'll know
everything that Dallas County knows."

"Not in a piddly extradition, Sharon. All they got
to do is show a whit of probable cause. No way will
they fire all their ammo in a proceedin' like that. No
judge worth his salt is goin' to sit there an' listen
to . . ." Black trailed off thoughtfully.

"Right, boss," Sharon said. "No judge worth his
salt. I wouldn't waste my time trying this in a real live
courtroom. But this is a movie set, and what you see
here is as fictional as, oh, *Minions of Justice*. Rob's
show. As long as the reels are turning, this Judge
Rudin will let them put on anything they want to.
Don't you remember all that extemporaneous testimony in O.J.? The Bolivian maid with the inter-
preter"—here Sharon raised her pitch and talked
through her nose—" 'No, *señor*, no, *señor*, no,
señor?' " She resumed her normal tone. "The ex-
policeman hanger-on guy, Shipp? In the real world
none of those people would have ever made it to the
stand, but publicity puts a virus in the system. You

watched today's joke yourself, boss. Didn't you see all the posturing and mugging? And if you're looking for a dog-and-pony operation, you couldn't pick a better candidate to chew up the scenery. Milton Breyer might show up in the morning with the Longhorn marching band."

Black's tone was more subdued, tinged with respect. "Milt's no shrinkin' violet when it comes to the press."

"Which is what I'm counting on. Kathleen Fraterno's going to have a cow, but not even Kathleen's going to be able to slow Milt down. Criminy, he just told the judge he had witnesses to fly in. We'll have a preview of everything the state's got, boss. Just wait."

Now Black gave a deep, hearty chuckle. "An' I don't suppose you'll be objectin' to any of this."

"Little me? I'll be quiet as a mouse. Our California counsel has caught a dose of the public-eye bug, but I'll muzzle him as much as I can." Sharon's tone turned serious. "I mean it about the gun. I think we can probably keep it out at trial."

"Be better for us if she hadn' checked any luggage on the flight from Dallas to L.A. Then they'd have to explain how she carried a .38 through security onto a commercial airliner."

Sharon looked down at her feet. "They've got us there. She checked four pieces. But Darla's never seen the gun before."

"*She* says. Sharon, any defendant—"

"Is subject to lying," Sharon interrupted, "to their lawyer or anyone else. I know her, boss. She's not lying."

"Don't be settin' yourself up for a letdown, believin' in this woman."

Sharon had a pensive moment, leaning against a corridor wall in Los Angeles, California, receiving advice from her boss and mentor from a half continent away. Russell Black seldom missed the target. She watched the knot of newspeople gathered around Preston Trigg. Trigg's mouth worked as he gestured with his hands, Jay Leno style. "I've been wrong be-

fore," Sharon finally said. "But if I can't convince myself, I'll never put anything across to the jury. Darla's
my friend, and I believe in her. I don't know how I'll
get over it if she's lying to me."

Sharon kept pace with Preston Trigg as they
threaded their way through a gaggle of reporters at
the building entry and started down the wide stone
steps. It was nearing five in the afternoon, the sun
sinking behind tall downtown buildings and a chill
creeping into the air. Down below, the Lincoln stretch
waited at the curb. Lyndon Gray, stoic as stone,
leaned a hip against the fender with his arms folded.
Reporters waved notepads and brandished ballpoints,
forming a three-deep human corridor on either side
as the lawyers descended. Questions came from all
directions, on every topic from trial strategy to what
Darla was having for dinner in her cell. Sharon
stepped around a handsome sandy-haired man who
looked familiar, and thought she'd seen him on one
of the networks. Jesus Christ, everyone in L.A. looked
like a star of some kind. The man opened his mouth
as if to say something, then backed away and let her
pass. A newswoman in jeans asked Preston Trigg if
David Spencer had been having an affair behind Darla's back. Trigg stopped in his tracks and started to
answer. Sharon yanked on the California lawyer's
sleeve so hard that he nearly fell headlong, then
stepped on ahead of him. Trigg stumbled and caught
up with her. "What was that for?"

She grimly shook her head. "You're going to have
to cool it with these reporters, Pres. We're representing Darla, not ABC."

Trigg pointed down toward the sidewalk, where Milt
Breyer and Harold Cuellar stood before a bank of
microphones with lights shining in their faces.
"Doesn't stop them from popping off," Trigg said.

"Let them," Sharon said, walking fast. "If they want
to—"

"Miss Hays." The voice was male and slightly effiminate. A hand shot out of the crowd and clamped onto Sharon's arm.

She halted and turned in anger. Some overzealous reporter clawing at her was the very last straw. They wanted a scene? She'd give them a freaking . . .

The hand was connected to a skinny arm, which in turn was encased in a lavender silk sleeve. The flimsy shirt billowed in the wind. The man was pale as a ghost, and Sharon thought of an undertaker who'd accidentally embalmed himself. He held up a photo cut from a magazine. The picture showed a glamorous young model, her hair swept back with one bang drooping seductively over her forehead. Sharon had seen the model somewhere, on a TV commercial perhaps. The man seemed ecstatic. "It's *you,* Miss Hays," he said. "Believe me it is."

Sharon blinked and gaped at the guy. "Excuse me, but that's a model. It isn't me."

"The *hair* is you." He turned the picture so that he could look at it along with her. "Jennifer Aniston," he said. *"Friends."*

Sharon looked at the photo again, recognition dawning. Sure, Jennifer Aniston. "I don't watch sitcoms," Sharon said, and turned to continue down the steps.

The man kept pace, holding a business card in front of her nose. Sharon took the card and read it. Jacque. Hairdresser to the Stars. She said, "That's nice, Mr. Jacque, but I don't—"

"I'll do you for free." Jacque's accent was straight from the Bronx, odd for a Frenchman.

Sharon looked at the picture once more, then back at the hairdresser. "How could you afford to?" she said. "I'd think you were too busy doing the stars."

"You'll be in millions of homes tomorrow. If you'd just mention my name to a reporter or two . . ." Jacque stood up to his full height, which placed his forehead on a level with Sharon's nose. "My normal fee would be . . . just hundreds."

Sharon looked at the picture again, and imagined

herself doing research while having to flip that silly bang out of the way in order to read.

"I have my own limo waiting," Jacque said, "to whisk you away to my studio in Beverly Hills. Only take a couple of hours."

Sharon looked down at the street. Sure enough, there was a second limo down there, this one pink. She sighed. "Appreciate the thought, Mr. Jacque, but I don't have a couple of hours. I have to get ready for this hearing tomorrow." All up and down the steps, reporters stared at her. She turned to her co-counsel. "Come on, Pres, we've got work to do."

Trigg didn't move. He said to Jacque, "Uh, listen. Do you work on guys?"

Jacque's expression softened. He regarded Preston Trigg with one critically arched eyebrow. He put Jennifer Aniston's picture away and produced another magazine photo, this one of Brad Pitt dashing down an alley with Morgan Freeman close on his heels. Pitt's hair was in inch-long quills, with the top front swept forward in a rakish line. Sharon recognized the scene, and had bitten her nails to the quick while watching the gut-wrencher of a movie. *Seven.*

Jacque held the picture as Preston Trigg cradled his elbow in his cupped hand and scratched his chin thoughtfully. Jacque rattled the photo. *"Voilà,"* the hairdresser said.

17

Ted Koppel wanted to know if the defense request for an extradition hearing had shocked the legal experts. Gerry Spence admitted that he hadn't been expecting any such strategy, and openly questioned Sharon Hays's legal smarts. Leslie Abramson disagreed, stating that the move had caught the prosecution off guard.

You tell 'em, Les, Sharon thought. She looked up from her reading and testily rattled the papers in her lap. The scene on the giant TV screen was an over-the-shoulder shot from behind Koppel as he carried on conversations with two television monitors. The monitor on Koppel's right showed Gerry Spence at home in Montana or Wyoming or wherever he lived, resplendent in buckskin behind the desk in his library. Sharon wondered if Spence had any sheep on his ranch, and if he spouted legal theory at cowhands and settlers as he rode the range. Leslie Abramson's pretty blond hair and even features beamed from the other monitor.

Sharon was on the den sofa. Gray, Yadaka, and Mrs. Welton sat in recliners as the quartet watched *Nightline* and Gray taped the show. True to his word, he had recorded anything and everything pertaining to Darla's case which had come over the networks. Two dozen tapes, carefully labeled as to date and content, were now lined up in the upright glass-front case, one shelf below the David Spencer movies.

Sharon held a pile of Xeroxes in her lap, and there was a second six-inch stack of copies on the sofa beside her hip. As Preston Trigg had left the courthouse with Jacque the hairdresser, Sharon had headed for the L.A. County Law Library. She'd nearly worn out two copying machines in duplicating whatever statutes and court decisions she could find pertaining to extradition and suppression of evidence.

The network abruptly switched viewing angles, showing a head-on shot of Koppel at his desk. "We're going to have to cut for a commercial," he said. "When we come back, we'll have just enough time for opposing statements from the prosecution and the defense. Stay with us."

Sharon frowned. Who for the prosecution and who for the defense? In order to get Milt Breyer on the show, the network would merely have to blow in his ear. But who's our spokesman? Sharon thought. God, not Preston Trigg, surely they wouldn't . . .

The lead-in to the commercial consisted of ten seconds of film clip. The first segment was Darla's most famous in cinema, wherein she crept naked toward a couple having intercourse on a king-size bed. She clutched a butcher knife. Superimposed black rectangles hid her breasts and pubic area. The scene switched briefly to a close-up of Darla's face, also from *Fatal Instinct,* her mouth twisted sensuously as she said to her lover, "I'll kill anyone who comes near you." Sharon angrily tossed her ballpoint aside as the commercial began.

Mrs. Welton twisted in her recliner. "The nerve."

Yadaka bent forward and rested his forearms on his thighs. "Doin' a number on 'er."

Which the media certainly was, Sharon knew, and immediately considered ways of shielding potential jurors from those freaking mini-clips. Her first impulse was an injunction, preventing the TV folks from showing fictional carnage featuring Darla, but such a move could call even more attention to the actress's bloodthirsty screen persona. Tomorrow she'd bounce the situation off Russ, see what he had to say. She wrestled with her thoughts through a Nissan commercial, through Michael Jordan ordering a Ballpark Frank, through Troy Aikman asking the concession kid how many Cokes he'd sold while Aikman had gone twenty-four for thirty-six in the passing statistics. She came out of her trance as Ted Koppel reappeared.

Sharon frowned and tilted her head as the over-the-shoulder image came on, because she didn't recognize either of the talking heads who now appeared on Koppel's monitors. There were two men shown, and Sharon wondered if Koppel's guests had somehow wandered into the wrong studio. The guy on the left looked familiar, a handsome mid-forties energetic type, and Sharon was wondering where she'd seen him before as Koppel said, "With us tonight we have Los Angeles County District Attorney Gil Garcetti."

The handsome man nodded, smiled, and answered, "Glad to be here, Ted."

Jesus Christ and all the angels, Sharon thought, what's *that* guy doing on the show? His office isn't even prosecuting the case. Then the answer dawned on her; as long as the hearing was to be held on his turf, Garcetti was exercising the host team's right to comment over the networks.

"And also appearing," Koppel went on, "we're privileged to have Darla Cowan's local L.A. defense counsel, Mr. Preston Trigg. Mr. Trigg, thanks for being with us." The camera zoomed in on the right-hand monitor.

And Sharon thought, *Who*?

The talking head, a smooth-faced man with short hair, answered. "Good to see you, Ted."

Criminy, Sharon thought, it *is* Preston Trigg. Jacque the hairdresser had gone ballistic with the clippers, and Trigg's new do no more resembled Brad Pitt's haircut in *Seven* than Sharon's own hair. The sides of Trigg's head were practically bald, pinkish skin showing through, the hair on top stuck up like porcupine quills. Shaving the mustache hadn't helped; the absence of facial hair called attention to the fact that

Trigg was buck-toothed. God, Sharon thought, he looks like Bucky Beaver.

"First I'll ask Mr. Garcetti," Koppel moderated. "This sudden reversal, the calling for a hearing, has this caught the prosecution unawares, or is it something you feel you can deal with?"

Garcetti assumed a thoughtful pose. "Well, Ted, heh, heh, as you know, we don't have primary responsibility for this case. This is a Texas prosecutor's office arguing in a Los Angeles courtroom, of course, so we're actually not calling the shots here. But I'll say that such delaying tactics never work in the long run. It's just not as big a deal as the defense is letting on."

"Oh?" Koppel seemed to mull things over. "What's your response to that line of reasoning, Mr. Trigg?"

"Well, I'll tell you, Ted," Trigg said, assuming a knowing look, "I believe in playin' 'em close to the vest. So I'm not going to tip my hand here, but if the prosecution wants to think I don't know what I'm doing, that's all the more to my advantage. I'll just say I never do anything without my client's best interest in mind." He looked into the camera and winked.

Sharon's eyes widened in astonishment. She wondered if there was something wrong with her ears. One session with the Hairdresser for the Stars had transformed Preston Trigg, junked auto battery in his reception area and all, into the Bobby Fischer of the courtroom. That's Hollywood for you, Sharon thought—one day the car wash, the next day the moon. She wondered if there were two lawyers in America who knew less about the case than the current guests on *Nightline*. Maybe she should leave the room and come back in. Of all the . . .

"Can we assume from that," Koppel chided, "that we're in for surprises during this hearing?"

Trigg smirked like a football coach in a pregame interview. "All I'll say for now, Ted. All I'll say."

The camera angle switched to the standard head-on shot of Koppel behind his desk. He grinned at the audience, a parting smile which conveyed the message that Preston Trigg, in the host's opinion, was totally full of it. "And with that I'll have to add that it's all *I* can say," Koppel boomed, "because we're out of time. Good night. Thanks for tuning in." Koppel's image faded from view, and more film clips began.

Sharon forced Preston Trigg out of her mind and concentrated on the screen, wanting to memorize as best she could the damaging scenes from Darla's movies aired over the networks. If it came down to an injunction, she needed a list. The closing shots on *Nightline,* however, were pretty tame, and consisted mainly of news clips of Darla and David Spencer taken during their lovebird period. One showed their arrival at the Oscars; another featured the happy couple tossing a volleyball back and forth on the beach. There was the usual footage of Spencer in *Spring of the Comanche,* a steely-eyed horseback pose, followed by a clip which Sharon had never seen before. Comanches wearing war paint watched in the background as Darla gave Spencer an affectionate peck on the cheek. Spencer was in frontier garb, and Darla wore slacks and a pullover. Two guys in nineties dress were on the right-hand fringe of the picture, and both looked familiar. Sharon zeroed in the one in the foreground. Her upper lip curled.

She'd seen the man only once, in a TV studio back in Dallas during Rob Stanley's promo tour, but she'd never forget the face. Curtis Nussbaum in the flesh, Mr. I-can-use-someone-willing-to-exhibit-some-skin, the genius of all geniuses at dodging child support. Rob had found his agent through Darla's intervention and David Spencer's referral. Lucky old Rob, Sharon thought. Nussbaum, in fact, had signed the check which Rob had given her at the restaurant, and which now rested in her handbag. Just before the image dissolved from the screen, Sharon had a glance at the blondish man who stood on Nussbaum's left in the background.

She blinked. She sat bolt upright. She stood. "Mr. Gray?"

The Englishman's chin bobbed. "Yes, Miss Hays."

Sharon's heart raced. "How many VCR's are in this house?"

"Not sure, miss. Everywhere there's a telly. One in the bedroom where you're sleeping, another in Miss Melanie's room . . . the guest room where Miss Cowan's been bunking . . . four or five."

Sharon stood away from the couch. Yadaka looked at her as Mrs. Welton straightened her recliner with a thump. Sharon said, "They all have remotes with freeze-frame buttons?"

"Certainly. Only the latest in equipment here," Gray said.

Sharon walked over to the VCR on which Gray had recorded *Nightline*. She hit the stop switch, the machine clicking to a halt, then depressed the rewind button. The reels whispered and spun. She turned back to Gray. "I'll need some assistance, Mr. Gray. To set something up, do you think you and Mr. Yadaka could do that for me?"

By the time Gray and Yadaka had lugged two table-model TV's and two VCR's from other parts of the house and set them up, Sharon had the image on the big-screen exactly as she wanted it. The remote had required some getting used to, and she'd done a lot of fast-forwarding and backing up, but she finally had Darla and David Spencer frozen in time as she'd kissed his cheek on the set of *Spring of the Comanche*. The warriors sat on horseback in the background, and Curtis Nussbaum and the blondish man stood off to one side.

As Mrs. Welton watched from the sofa, Sharon pulled two videos from the bookcase and checked their labels. She handed one cassette to Yadaka and the other to Gray. The Englishman had placed one small TV and one VCR on top of the big-screen set, and he now clicked in the tape as Sharon stood by with folded arms. This video contained the eleven p.m. news which had aired just prior to *Nightline*. She waited patiently as the Englishman fast-forwarded through the Bosnian Serbs, through clips of Bill Clinton making a speech and Paula Jones giving an interview with her lawyers on either side, until he finally reached the portion of the news featuring the Darla Cowan case.

"Slow down, please," Sharon said.

Gray complied, letting the tape run at normal speed through brief clips of Darla answering the judge's questions, of Sharon stopping the actress in mid-sentence and whispering in her ear. Finally the scene appeared where Sharon and Preston Trigg hustled down the courthouse steps toward the limo. "Slo-mo, Mr. Gray," Sharon said. "Can we do that?"

The Englishman thumbed a switch, and the action slowed to a snail's pace. Sharon watched intently. "Right . . . *there*," she said. Gray hit another button, and the scene froze to a standstill. Sharon blinked in satisfaction. Gray had stopped the imagine just as Sharon had excuse-me'd her way around the handsome blond man, the one whom she was certain she'd seen before. Sharon backed away and turned. "Now yours, Mr. Yadaka, if you would."

The Oriental had positioned his TV set and VCR, one on top of the other, on the floor to one side of the big-screen. Now he squatted on his haunches and rolled the tape. The scenes in this video seemed in the far-distant past—God, Sharon thought, was it only last Friday?—and featured the amateur clips taken in front of Planet Hollywood. There was Darla charging out of the restaurant with Spencer on her heels, the pretty-boy staggering drunkenly as he grabbed her arm and yanked her backward. And then—ta-*taa*, Sharon thought—there was Supersharon to the rescue, her calves flashing like pistons as she charged into the picture and shoved Spencer down in a jumble of arms and legs. Darla hightailed it for the limo as Sharon stood over the fallen actor, her expression vacant as she looked into the crowd for an instant. "Freeze-frame, please," Sharon said softly. Yadaka stopped the action. Sharon said, "Perfect," and then returned her attention to the big screen.

She moved up for a close look of the man standing beside Curtis Nussbaum on the movie set. Then she stood on tiptoes and surveyed the courthouse-steps scene, and squinted to look at the handsome blondish guy she'd sidestepped just before her encounter with Jacque the hairdresser. And finally, using a steadying hand on Yadaka's shoulder for support, she knelt on the floor beside the Oriental. Yadaka's VCR had caught the over-the-shoulder view, freezing Sharon just as she made eye contact with a man in the crowd in front of Dallas's Planet Hollywood. The man wore a fringed buckskin jacket and wide-brimmed hat, Crocodile Dundee style. The day after the murder Sharon had watched this same video in the FBI offices, and had thought at the time that public exposure would embarrass the man in front of friends and family. She narrowed her eyes and looked at his face. Then, just to be certain, she stood for another look at the man on the courthouse steps, and at Curtis Nussbaum's sidekick on the movie set.

Air came out of Sharon's lungs in a sigh of certainty. Absolutely no question. All three pictures. Same freaking guy.

She looked excitedly around at the security trio, and pointed in turn at each of the TV screens. "Is it possible to get stills of those?" Sharon asked. "To carry around with me?"

Gray and Yadaka exchanged shrugs. Gray looked to Mrs. Welton. "Olivia?"

The trim fiftyish woman stood from the couch and appraised the television images with a practiced eye. "Take some pushing up."

Sharon looked helplessly from Gray to Mrs. Welton and back again.

"It's a photographic process, mum," Mrs. Welton said. "You shoot with a low-speed film, pumped through the camera at a higher rate. Eliminates the need for a flash, which would reflect from that glass on the tellies and distort the image. I can do those nicely, I think."

Sharon was excited. "When can I have them?"

Mrs. Welton's forehead tightened in thought. "I've a darkroom. Three different speeds of film. I fancy in the morning early."

Sharon looked around the group in respect. "Gee," she said. "You guys come prepared."

Gray chuckled, pleased with himself. "Part of it, miss. In our line of work you learn all sorts of things."

18

The phone blasted Sharon awake at six-thirty in the morning. She blearily read the time, then struggled across the mattress to pick up the receiver. If this was less than a national emergency, someone was in for a dressing-down. She mumbled hello.

"Morning, Muffin. How's it going?" Rob's tone was sickeningly sweet.

Sharon flopped onto her back. "Do you know what time it is?"

"Not that early. I've already had a session with my trainer."

"If you don't let me go back to sleep," Sharon said, "you are going to have a session with your demon."

Rob's laugh was straight out of Acting 101. "Listen, I was wondering. Mind if I drop the little one off a bit early?"

"Yes, I do," Sharon said, then sat bolt upright as she had a flash of panic. "Is Melanie all right?"

"Oh, great, great. We did the whole nine yards. Ate in the studio cafeteria. I introduced her around."

"How nice of you."

"But listen, I've had this thing come up. An emergency."

"I'll bet."

"I can have her over in a half hour."

"No, you can't. I've got a million things to do today, one of which is to put Melanie on a plane home. I've had four hours' sleep. I can't hack it, Rob, unless you cooperate. Make it around ten."

He was suddenly petulant. "We're having an early shoot."

"Tell them to do the perps' scene first. Where the guys are scared shitless, waiting for you to bounce them off the walls?"

Rob said, "I have someone to see."

Sharon watched the ceiling. "You are getting more limp-wristed by the minute, Rob-oh."

There was static-punctuated silence. Rob said, "Don't start that again, Muffin."

"Sharon. And it's something you started yourself. Thirteen years ago. Hope the brief mind-blowing ecstasy was worth it to you. Not a second before ten, Rob."

"Muffin—"

"*Sharon,* dammit. Maybe after my press conference you could play one of Ellen's off-the-wall homosexual hangers-on. Make a lot of jokes about how some guy's ass happens to look."

Rob blew air into the phone. "What about my breakfast meeting with my agent?"

"Melanie will love to go." Sharon twisted the phone cord around her index finger. "You're breakfasting with Curtis Nussbaum?"

He sighed. "He was my agent last time I checked."

"Sure. You met him through Darla. David Spencer referred you."

"At least you've kept up with my career."

"Not through any breathless daily scanning of the trades. Just something Darla mentioned over dinner." Sharon released the phone cord and touched her hair. "I saw Mr. Nussbaum's picture last night. Listen, Rob. I may ask you to identify someone from a picture for me. Could be a help in Darla's defense."

"What someone is that? I can't afford to be getting involved in Darla's criminal charges, if that's what you're leading up to."

Sharon gritted her teeth. Darla was responsible for Rob's big break, but he couldn't afford to be involved. "That's what friends are for, right?" she said. "You'll

get involved if I ask you to, if it takes a subpoena."
She tightly shut her eyes. When they'd lived together,
Rob had had his faults, but she'd considered him a
sensitive person. Stardom had reduced him to a typical
Hollywood prick, a real me-first kind of guy. "Is Mela-
nie there?" she said.

"Yeah. The kid's been wanting to talk to you."

"You mean *our daughter*? Put her on."

There was a series of rustling noises, after which
Melanie said, "Mom?" Her voice had matured to the
point that Sharon could swear she was talking to
herself.

Sharon said, "Did you have a nice time?"

"I met *Jerry Seinfeld*." Melanie was in ecstasy. "My
dad knows everybody."

"Quite an operator, isn't he?" Sharon stumbled out
of bed and trudged over to the glass doors, carrying
the phone. She looked down on foamy surf and an
expanse of beach. "Did you get to see any TV news,
sweetheart?"

Melanie's tone was all at once sad. "Some. Is Miss
Cowan going to prison?"

"Not if I can help it. You'll know, then, that I'm
going to have to stay in California a few more days.
You've got school, and I'm flying you home today to
stay with Mrs. Winston."

"Do I have to? Can't I be with my father?"

"Now that you've made contact, we can come back
occasionally." Sharon mentally crossed her fingers in
the hope she was telling the truth. She didn't want to
resort to blackmail in order to get Rob to see his
daughter again, but wouldn't hesitate in doing so. "I
have to be in court by ten, Melanie. I won't be here
when your father drops you off, but I'll have your
things ready. Mrs. Welton will take you to the
airport."

Melanie hesitated. She'd be trying to think up arguments in her own behalf, but Sharon had intentionally
made her tone one of finality. Melanie said, "Is that
that?"

Sharon felt a surge of guilt. "It has to be, sweetheart. I'll have you packed, okay?" She paused. "I'll make it up to you. Promise." Then she hung up and drummed her fingers. She didn't know whether to be pleased or horrified over Melanie's ecstasy. Having a relationship with Rob could be good for Melanie, but in the long run it could screw up her life beyond repair. A teenager needed two full-time parents rather than one far-distant dad and one mom who was often too busy for her. Thus far there didn't seem to be any unusual quirks in Melanie's personality over her parental situation, but according to Sheila, problems of childhood became full-blown during the teenage years. As Sharon hustled into the bathroom, she took in air in desperate gulps.

Mrs. Welton had done a corker of a job. Tiny parallel lines ran across the TV screens in the photos, but the stranger's face in all three images was just as clear as it had appeared in the videotapes. Mrs. Welton had made multiple copies. She sat across the table, looking pleased with herself, as Sharon collated the copies into four sets and talked to Sheila Winston on the phone. "American Flight 1156," Sharon said, "lands at DFW at two fifty-four your time. She'll come down with a bout of school-itis in the morning, claiming the trip has drained her energy or something, but don't let her get away with it. She can't afford to miss any more."

"Right-o," Sheila said. She gave a long, exasperated sigh. "No news is good news, Sharon. You may as well have your dose of the bad tidings now. I just got them yesterday afternoon, and it's taken me overnight to get to where I can talk rationally about it."

Sharon leaned back, switched ears with the phone, felt a weakness come over her. "I hope no one's died."

"No, but I nearly did. It's that damned school."

St. Thomas Episcopal again. The trendy private school kept both single mothers drained of funds as the tuition climbed in geometric progression; the

inner-city problems in Dallas public schools gave the
privates a throat lock on all who would have their
children read, write, and not worry about gunfire in
the halls. Sharon said, "How much this time?"

"They didn't raise the rates in mid-year for a
change, thank God, but the new dictum is, all tuition
money paid up-front by the first of December for the
spring term. No exceptions. Ante up or they'll kick
your little darling out on the street. I hadn't budgeted
for it until January, Sharon."

Sharon bit her inner cheek as anger flooded over
her. Private schools had engaged in legalized extortion
for a decade or so, operating under the philosophy
that, hey, you want this good future, this safe environ-
ment, you have to go through us to get it, so ante up,
bud. Private universities were even worse, and it was
Sharon's dream eventually to send Melanie to SMU.
Perhaps she should go into partnerships with Tired
Darnell in the burglary business, make one big score
or something. She said, "Surely they'll make
exceptions."

"Oh, yeah? You know Trudy Munslow, her daughter's in Trish and Melanie's class. This is the third
child she's put through St. Thomas, and Trudy lives
on semi-annual royalties. She got down on her hands
and knees, begging for additional time, and the head-
mistress told her they hoped her child would be happy
busing to public school. I don't know how I'm going
to make it." Sheila's voice broke at the end, and
Sharon had a surge of sympathy. Sheila Winston was
probably the most upbeat person she knew, and if the
school situation was getting *Sheila* down . . .

Sharon said, "I can loan you the money until
January."

"For sure. And where are you planning to get it?"

"Darla's going to pay a hefty fee in the long run.
Plus for the short run, Rob has ante'd up three
months' child support. I'm temporarily flush. You
should strike while the iron is hot." Sharon smiled.

"You could say I'm sort of robbing Rob, to coin a phrase."

Sheila assumed a haughty tone. "I shall not beg."

"With all the times you've taken care of Melanie while I flit about the courtroom, you should have the right to demand. How much do we owe?" Sharon grabbed a pen and turned one of the photos over to doodle on the back.

Sheila dictated the figures, the size of which caused Sharon to take a firm grip on the ballpoint. She didn't speak until her emotions calmed. She laid the pen aside, thought, That freaking bank, and felt anger growing once more as she said, "I think I'd better negotiate Rob's check out here, while I'm in town."

"Bouncy-bouncy?"

"Not likely. Not even Rob would have the nerve for that. No, this is Bloodsucking National I'm thinking about, my bank. A couple of years ago I deposited an out-of-town check which was larger than my balance at the time, so my lovely banker froze the funds for thirty days until the check cleared. Rob-oh's check is about fifteen times my current balance, so this time they might hold the money until the turn of the century. Given experience, I'm going to be a step ahead of them. I'll stop off at Rob's bank out here and have the money wire-transferred to my account in Dallas. Just thinking out loud, Sheil, but you can rest at peace. By the time I'm home, I'll have us the bucks for school."

"I feel rescued," Sheila said.

"I feel like I'm reducing a debt by a small portion," Sharon said. "Don't forget, Sheila, two fifty-four. American's usually late, but they might fool you."

"I'll be there."

"I love you, Sheil," Sharon said, and meant it, then hung up and thumbed through the photos once more. Three sets of prints, the scene in front of Planet Hollywood plus one shot each from the L.A. evening news and *Nightline,* all featuring the handsome blondish man in various poses and states of dress. She looked up and smiled across the table at Mrs. Welton. "You should be proud of these," Sharon said. "They're perfect."

"Not to brag, mum," Mrs. Welton said, "but I've shot more difficult lots of times." She slid one set of the pictures in front of her and lovingly admired her own handiwork. "The telly screens weren't moving. Compared to some, these shots were easy as pie."

Sharon wrote a long I-love-you and rah-rah-school note to Melanie and left it with Mrs. Welton, then squirmed with guilt in the back of the limo on the ride into L.A. She should be there for Melanie in person, dammit. She checked her makeup in her compact mirror, halfway expecting her lipstick to be applied at a forty-five-degree angle and her cheeks to show cartoonish swipes of eyeliner. Despite all the last-minute rushing around, she hadn't done a half-bad job in fixing her face. She straightened her skirt and adjusted the top of her navy courtroom suit, telling herself that her appearance didn't matter that much, that she had work to do. Right, dodo, she thought, with the eyes of the world on you, you're cool as a freaking cucumber. She supposed that in the long run she was every bit as vain as Milton Breyer. She stuffed the compact into her purse with a vengeance.

Rob's branch of the Bank of California showed an address on DeLongpre Avenue in Hollywood, and as Gray steered the limo onto the Vine Boulevard off-ramp, Sharon had a look around. Yesterday had been clear and crisp, but today smog had crept in. The San Gabriel peaks were wispy outlines, and the Capitol Records Building was barely visible through the haze. Sharon dug out Rob's check and read Curtis Nussbaum's signature. The agent signed his name in typical man-in-a-hurry fashion, a C preceding a long horizontal slash, an N before tiny, illegible hen scratchings. She picked up one of Mrs. Welton's photos, the one taken on the movie set, and looked closely at the agent. Nussbaum was bald as an egg with a big, bent nose and cruelly pursed lips. The one time she'd seen him in person, back in Dallas, Nussbaum had worn a permanent smirk. He had the same expression in the photo. Long before now Sharon hadn't particularly liked this guy. As the limo rolled smoothly through Hollywood, her distaste for Curtis Nussbaum grew by leaps and bounds.

The building was glitzy and modern, with eight-foot midget palm trees lining the sidewalk in front. Sharon supposed it was an in place for depositing money, just as there were in restaurants, in shopping areas, and in places for using the bathroom in this fantasy world of a town. She left Yadaka and Gray in the limo and hustled up the sidewalk toward the entry, checking her watch, her handbag swinging by its strap from her forearm. Five after nine; she had to get a move on. As she pushed through the transparent glass door into the lobby, she fumbled with a walletful of ID: driver's license, credit and Social Security cards. She tore a deposit slip from her own checkbook and added the slip to the stack of paper and plastic in her hand. She passed two ATM machines and an information desk, and went directly to the teller windows to wait in line.

She stood in a roped-off area, first on one foot and then the other, while a man cashed a check and a woman deposited what seemed to be, God, a thousand rolls of change. Finally the teller waved her up. Sharon went to the window, laid her ID on the counter, and passed the check in through the opening. "I want to negotiate this, please," she said, "and wire-transfer the money to this"—she handed over her deposit slip—"account."

The teller was a young black woman wearing pink-ish lipstick. She smoothed the check out on the counter. "Rob Stanley," she murmured.

Yep, Sharon thought, *that* Rob Stanley, king of the wild frontier or whatever. "I'm in a bit of a rush," she said in a businesslike manner. "So if you could—"

"Gee, Rob Stanley. I'll have to . . ." The teller

rattled keys on her computer, hit the Enter button, her eyes moving left and right in her head as she read from the monitor screen. She nodded curtly as if agreeing with herself, then shoved the check and deposit slip back over the counter. "You'll need to see Mr. Holtzen," she said.

Sharon already had her pen out, ready to endorse the check. "Look, I'm due in court at ten," she said.

The teller blinked impersonally. "Everyone's in a hurry, lady. This is L.A. And any transactions on this account, you'll need to see Mr. Holtzen." She pointed at a row of glass-fronted offices. "Second door from the right. And not to worry. Mr. Holtzen, he's a very nice guy."

Mr. Holtzen didn't seem like a nice guy at all. He was the consummate banker, complete with white shirt, navy blue tie, and wire-framed, I'm-smart glasses. As Sharon entered his office, Holtzen stood in front of a paper-spewing ink-jet printer. The printer head zipped back and forth, back and forth, with a series of electronic humming noises. The paper inched its way through the platen as the banker eyed Sharon suspiciously. He folded the perforation, ripped the page free, and scanned a row of figures. Then he turned to Sharon like Rumpelstiltskin guarding the gold. "You're the woman with a check on the Rob Stanley account?" he said.

"Yes, Sharon Hays, from Texas." She waited for the banker to offer her a chair. When he didn't, she sat down on her own and crossed her legs. "I know it's an imposition on your time, sir," she said, "but I'm really hustling."

Holtzen was in his forties and exhibited a paunch. He snapped his fingers. "Sharon Hays. I knew you looked familiar. Darla Cowan trial, right?"

"Actually, it's a hearing, but yes. Mr. Holtzen, could you . . . ?"

Holtzen made no move to sit at his desk, holding

the printout at chest level. "Let me see what you've got."

Sharon stood and handed him the check. "A simple wire transfer, sir," she said. "Surely it can't be that much of a problem." She frowned. "As long as Rob has the money in his account. He does, doesn't he?"

Holtzen squinted at the draft, comparing the figures with those on the printout. His glasses slid to the end of his nose. He removed the frames and let them dangle from his fingers by an earpiece. Rob's check might have been the most astonishing thing he'd ever seen.

"Rob Stanley gave me that in person last night," Sharon said. "If you'd like to call him—"

"No, no need to call. You I can identify, from your picture on television. It's this . . ." Holtzen waved the printout around, looking frustrated.

Sharon smiled at him.

Holtzen walked to the door. "Don't move," he said. Then he raised a hand and said, "Wait right here," and hurried off through the lobby. He went behind the teller booths, knocked on a door marked EMPLOY-EES ONLY, spoke to someone through the crack as the door opened, then went through the portal and disappeared from view.

Sharon wondered what in hell was going on. Couldn't be the check. Rob made three times the amount per freaking episode.

Holtzen had left his computer on. The monitor was tilted so that Sharon could see the rows of figures on the screen. She didn't have to wonder where Holtzen had taken the printout; he'd made a beeline for the corporate offices to talk things over with his superior before acting on Sharon's wire-transfer request. She peered through the glass toward the paying and receiving windows. Tellers worked steadily, heads down, cashing checks, rattling keyboards and peering at computer monitors. No one looked in her direction. She fought an inner battle with herself.

Feeling guilty, certain that any second someone would scream at her from the lobby, Sharon went behind the banker's desk. She bent over his chair back and squinted at the computer screen. The account entitled "Robert Jarrett Stanley Trust" showed a current balance of $547,239.76. In the upper left-hand corner was an image of Curtis Nussbaum's signature. God, Sharon thought, there's plenty of money in the account, what could be . . . ?

The instructions at the bottom of the screen said to press the up arrow to view yesterday's transactions. For dates prior to yesterday, one was to press Code plus the date desired, and then hit Return.

Icicles tickling her backbone, Sharon peered once more into the lobby. Still no Holtzen. Men and women in business dress hustled back and forth through the spacious bank and paid her no heed.

She sat down in front of Holtzen's keyboard and hit the up arrow. Yesterday Rob's balance had been a thousand dollars higher than today, with a couple of insignificant checks coming in for payment in the interim. God, Sharon thought, half a million dollars. Looked like a substantial account to her. She pressed the Code key and backed the screen up to the previous Friday. She blinked.

On the day of David Spencer's murder, Rob's balance had been $14.68. She checked to be certain she wasn't missing a comma or a string of zeroes. Nope, fourteen sixty-eight it was. Looks like my account back home, Sharon thought. She tilted the banker's chair and scratched her chin.

She viewed Monday's transactions, then Tuesday's. On Tuesday someone had deposited $600,000 to Rob's account. Which explained why the banker was running around like a chicken with its head cut off. Before he approved the wire transfer he wanted to be certain that the deposit was in certified funds, not in the form of a check which could bounce, thus leaving the Bank of California holding the bag.

My agent does all that, Rob had said. According to Darla, Curtis Nussbaum handled most of his clients' financial affairs. Sharon stared at Nussbaum's signature as it appeared on the screen.

She stood and scanned the area in front of Holtzen's office. No one looked in her direction.

By the time Sharon made up her mind she was already in action, hitting the Print key, typing in the desired pages in response to a monitor prompt, and tightly closing her eyes as she pressed Return. The printer on her left whined into action, the print head zipping back and forth across the page. As the paper inched its way upward, Sharon stood and walked nonchalantly around Holtzen's office. She looked at the ceiling and whistled a tune.

The first page rolled through the platen, then the second; Sharon had called for a total of four sheets. She continued to pace, averting her gaze from the printer as if she didn't know it existed. She looked toward the teller's window.

Holtzen came through the door, circled the cages, and made a beeline in her direction. One end of Rob's check fluttered from his fingertips.

Sharon panicked, and came within a hairsbreadth of ripping the sheets from the printer and stuffing them in the wastebasket. Holtzen watched her intently as he approached. The jig's up for sure, Sharon thought. She tried to think of a legitimate excuse, a reason why she was running a printout of Rob Stanley's checking account. Nothing came to her. A flush of embarrassment crept into her neck as the banker drew nearer and the printer continued to hum.

Holtzen halted in mid-stride, gave Sharon an apologetic smile through the glass, and returned to one of the teller stations. He handed the check over the counter and issued instructions, jerking his head in Sharon's direction as he did.

The printer stopped humming, and the platen came to a standstill.

Sharon spun, ripped the paper from the platen like a wild woman, crumpled the pages together, and shoved the whole mess into her purse. She sat down quickly, dropped her handbag on the floor, and smoothed her skirt as the banker crossed the lobby and entered his office at a fast clip. Sharon offered her best smile of innocence.

Holtzen's attitude was friendlier than before. "I've approved the transaction, Miss Hays. Just go to the third window, and the lady will take care of you." He offered his hand. "So sorry to keep you waiting."

Sharon stood and wrapped her own hand around the banker's. "No problem, Mr. Holtzen," she said. "To tell the truth, I did some serious thinking while you were gone."

19

As the limo rolled toward the Criminal Courts Building, Sharon used the cell phone to call Mrs. Welton at Darla's house. As she spoke, she smoothed the pilfered printout over her lap and looked at the figures once more. It was five after ten; Rob was late as usual and hadn't brought Melanie home. Sharon gave the cell phone number to the Englishwoman and told her to have Rob call pronto, then stuffed the portable phone into her purse along with the printout. She wondered if Rob would return her call, and decided that the odds were about fifty-fifty. By now her old flame would be wishing he'd never heard of her. Well, if the condition of Rob's bank account didn't shock him, their conversation would be a short one. Sharon straightened in her seat as, visible over Lyndon Gray's broad shoulders, the Criminal Courts Building came into view.

A circus, Sharon thought, a three-ringer complete with trapeze artists and a pony show. Reporters and cameramen formed a mob on the building's front steps, and four brightly decorated mobile units were parked across the street. A bearded man had set up a booth near the news trucks and was selling T-shirts. As the limo passed the booth, Sharon squinted toward the huckster as he exhibited his wares to three teenage girls. The shirt bore Darla's image on the front, a silk screen of one of her more deranged-looking poses from *Fatal Instinct*. As Sharon watched, the man switched the tee around for a view of the back, showing David Spencer's likeness.

Gray hit a switch, and the transparent panel hummed open. "Through the jail, mum?" the Englishman said.

"No, I'll be taking the head-on approach today. I'd rather deal with the swarm before court than after." Sharon sighed in resignation. She eyed the steps, looking for the pathway through the mob.

"I think we should escort you up." Gray wheeled to the right and pulled to the curb. A knot of reporters approached.

"Thanks for the offer, but I'll battle on alone. You guys have other things."

Gray looked at her through the panel. His expression was serious. "It's not advisable, Miss Hays. I'd feel more comfortable if you'd allow Benny—"

"I'll be okay." Sharon leaned forward and passed two sets of Mrs. Welton's pictures through the opening. "I've no way of knowing," she said, "if our mystery man will show again. If he does, follow him. I want to know where he lives, what he eats for breakfast, and which side of the bed he sleeps on."

Gray dropped his set of photos on the seat. Yadaka propped a knee against the dash and thumbed through the pictures in his lap, one at a time. "These are pretty good," Yadaka said. "Ought to be easy to spot this guy."

Sharon pushed her door partway open. "Remember, gentlemen. Caution. We don't want to alarm this guy. Criminy, we're grasping at straws. For all we know, he was in Dallas on vacation and decided to stop by Planet Hollywood for a hamburger. Just be careful, okay?"

Yadaka and Gray exchanged a look. Gray turned around and gripped the wheel. "We've done this before," he said. "It's the way we make our living. The gentleman in the picture could be a potential danger at the most, but nothing we haven't confronted before. He's not the current problem. The mob on the steps is a known factor, mum. I won't thrust our services on you. I'll only warn. It would be better if you took one of us along."

Sharon wished she'd taken the Englishman up on his offer before she'd climbed halfway to the courthouse entry. Jesus Christ, did she ever understand now why people like Darla Cowan and David Spencer employed a raft of bodyguards! Each step was a battle, every stride a confrontation. She'd expected the microphones shoved in her face, and dealt with each in turn by keeping her head down and ignoring the mike thruster's questions, but nothing had prepared her for the physical mauling. Reporters and hangers-on grabbed her arms and clutched her sleeves. One woman held out a pad and asked for her autograph, then snarled and called her a bitch as Sharon struggled past without answering. A man did his damnedest to haul her satchel away into the crowd, and one fanatic tore a dime-sized hole in her jacket. Sharon's hair was disheveled, she was out of breath, and her nerves were twisted strands of wire. As a pimply teenager clawed her, she lost it. She screamed, "*Get away from me, you . . .*" And then trailed off as she spotted Preston Trigg at the head of the steps, holding court between two granite pillars.

She never would have recognized her California co-counsel if she hadn't caught his act last night on television. The haircut was even more ridiculous in person than it had appeared on *Nightline*. His smooth-shaven features and glistening scalp made Trigg look like a high school kid playing hookey. On-the-spot interviewers stood in a half circle around him, and two minicams were aimed in his direction. His mouth moved rapidly. He gestured wildly with his hands.

Sharon had an idea. She called out to no one in particular, "There's Darla Cowan's lead counsel. If you want the inside story, talk to him."

One reporter's head snapped around in Trigg's direction. "Talk to who?"

"Preston Trigg," Sharon yelled. "Right up there,

didn't you see him on *Nightline*? He's the horse's mouth, folks." She stifled a giggle. She'd almost said "horse's *ass*" but had caught herself.

A female newsie alternated her gaze between Sharon and the head of the stairs. "Our word is, you're running the show, Miss Hays."

"You've got it all wrong," Sharon said. "California's Mr. Trigg's ball yard, folks, I'm just here to provide assistance. Really. Anything I could tell you I'd have to clear with him anyway, so you might as well . . ."

The media hounds required no further prompting. Upward they surged, leaving Sharon in their wake, bumping each other around as they jockeyed for position near Preston Trigg. In seconds a pathway cleared, and Sharon hurried to the courthouse entry. She skirted the mob and stood a couple of paces to Trigg's rear.

Trigg was saying, ". . . and I'll tell you this much. My client's definitely innocent. As this case unfolds, you'll . . ." He paused as his gaze fell on Sharon. Sheepishly he murmured, "Just trying to hold them at bay."

Sharon smiled. "Nice haircut."

Trigg touched the top of his head. "You really think so?"

"You and Brad Pitt," Sharon said. "You and Brad. Look, Pres, keep these people occupied while I go visit our client. You're doing fine. Buy me ten minutes or so." She started to go inside.

Trigg stopped her. He bent to whisper in her ear, "What should I tell these guys?"

Sharon glanced toward the reporters, then winked at her co-counsel. "Why, just wing it, Pres. Whatever you think will make us sound good on the news. Improvise. With your experience before the camera, it should be a piece of cake for you."

The courtroom level was also a madhouse, but here the reporters and cameramen had plenty to keep them occupied without bugging the lawyers. As Sharon exited the elevator, three different news conferences were in progress. In one group media people fired questions at Barbara Walters as, yards away, Jimmy Smits faced a bank of microphones and, directly behind him, minicams pointed at an L.A. Dodger who had just completed a season where he'd slugged a hundred homers or so. God, *everyone* wanted in on the act. Barbara Walters was telling the mob that she was merely attending the hearing like any other citizen, and as Sharon hurried on down the hall, Jimmy Smits told a second gaggle of reporters that Darla Cowan was a sweet person despite her screen image, and that he couldn't imagine Darla murdering anyone.

Milton Breyer had his entourage from Dallas parked on benches outside the courtroom, and Sharon had a twinge of been-there-done-that as she headed for the double entry doors. God, as if she'd never left home. There was Vernon Tupelow from the Dallas County medical examiner's office seated in between Breyer and Harold Cuellar, Tupelow's bald spot shining over an unruly gray fringe of hair. He was dressed in coroner's whites which, for a change, showed neither grimy cuffs nor bloodstains. Tupelow showed uneven, yellowed teeth in a grin and waggled his fingers. Sharon nodded, walked purposefully past the trio, ignored Stan Green where he sat near the courtroom entry, and stopped to say hello to Kathleen Fraterno. She was reading a paperbound law book. She looked up coldly. The close relationship which Sharon and Kathleen had once shared had long since fallen victim to Kathleen's romance with Milton Breyer.

Sharon said, "How was your flight?"

Fraterno wore her standard form-fitting gray courtroom suit, brunette ringlets falling softly around her shoulders. She said, "I can't believe you're doing this."

Sharon was taken aback. "Doing what?"

"Dragging this out." Fraterno used a dismissive tone.

"*I'm* dragging it out? Come on, you watched that

joke on TV yesterday along with the rest of the world. It wasn't me doing all the posturing."

Fraterno flipped over a page. "It was you with the last-minute theatrics. The sudden change of direction. Who's writing your scripts, Sharon?"

"At least I have grounds. That FBI search is straight from looney tunes, and you know it."

Fraterno looked up once more, her features set. "Even if it is, you picked the wrong theater. This is an extradition proceeding. The place for you to attack the warrant is in pretrial motions. And *you* know *that*."

"Oh, yeah? And what do you think the proper arena is for the coroner's testimony?" Sharon pointed down the hall, where the M.E. sat along with Breyer and the L.A. prosecutor. "It's not me courting the publicity, Kathleen. If you want the case tried properly, talk to your lover boy."

Fraterno opened, then closed her mouth. She snapped her gaze down to her reading. "You go to hell."

Sharon was furious. She pictured a scene in which two women in business suits engaged a slugfest in front of God and *Court TV*. Her instinct told her to walk away, but her anger got the best of her. She snatched the book from Fraterno and looked at the cover. Kathleen had been boning up on the California court procedural codes. Fraterno watched in open contempt. Sharon tossed the book onto the bench. The pages rustled and fluttered.

"You're wasting your time reading that," Sharon said. "It'll be better spent fixing your makeup for your TV appearance. It's Hollywood, Kathleen. If you think anyone's following legal procedure here, you're out in left field."

A somber cloud settled over Sharon's consciousness as she entered the holding cell area. Darla was becoming the forgotten woman in all the hoopla, the lawyers strutting and posing, even the judge mugging for the benefit of the viewing audience. Sharon felt no guilt over leaving Darla alone in jail for the night, using her time in preparation for the legal battle ahead, but she would still have some explaining to do. Darla would be beside herself.

Sharon went up to the desk, signed the entry roster, and waited while the uniformed deputy searched her purse and satchel for contraband. His job finished, the deputy produced a ring of jingling keys and unlocked the door. Sharon stood with her head down, made final adjustments to her clothing, drew a deep breath, and marched professionally in through the entryway.

The holding cell occupied half of a conference-sized room, and Darla was its lone occupant. She sat on a steel bench which was riveted to the wall, her legs crossed, her arms folded, her posture slumped. Sharon had pulled a few strings with the jailers, ordering makeup people for Darla along with a new outfit each day from Neiman-Marcus, and the crew had done their jobs. Darla's hair looked ready for filming. Though her makeup was drop-dead gorgeous, it didn't completely hide the dark circles under her eyes. She wore an expensive but modest blue sheath with the hem a tasteful inch above her knee. She looked up slowly and showed a wounded expression.

Sharon laid her purse on a small table, approached the bars, and slightly spread her feet. "Bad night, huh?"

Darla sniffled. "How could you?"

Sharon lowered her gaze. "Darla, I had to—"

"Desert me? It's a horrible place. People screaming all night. My God, Sharon . . ."

Dealing with Darla was going to be tough under the circumstances, but allowing her to engage in hysterics would be counterproductive. Sharon firmed her mouth. "Nothing I can say will make you feel particularly chipper. But believe I didn't get any sleep, either. My time's better spent on the case than in holding your hand. Jail's tough, and I can't soften the blow, and until we can do something about securing your release, you're going to have to deal with it." She made her tone sterner than necessary. For the time being it was the only way to get her point across; sympathizing with Darla would only create a series of tear-jerker scenes with Sharon Hays in a minor role, as friend and sounding board.

"Chet Verdon would never throw me to the wolves like this." Darla petulantly watched her lap. "Maybe I should call him."

"Yes, why don't you?" Sharon said. "Lawyer Hollywood would spend a lot of time with you, might even get you to pose for pictures in your cell so he could market the negatives to television. You might not like the end result, your murder conviction, but I agree that Mr. Verdon would coddle you." She firmed her mouth. "Come here, Darla. Get up and walk over here."

Woodenly Darla stood. She approached the bars in mincing half steps. From within the cell came the aroma of expensive perfume.

Sharon gripped two of the bars. "Remember what I told you yesterday, about the image you need to project? The jury if we go to trial, the public now, no one's going to see the conditions you're under in jail. All they'll witness is your persona in the courtroom, the way you're dressed and the way you walk, and hangdog looks will make you appear guilty. You hold your chin up, Darla. You're wrongfully accused, and you're mad as hell about it. Got that?"

Darla showed a smirk of self-pity. "I can only try."

"You can do more than that. You're the best actress I've ever seen. Perform like it. I've seen you play comedy scenes with a toothache, and compared to that ordeal, this should be easy as falling off a log."

Darla's expression softened, the same way it had once in New York when a director had dressed her down for not putting enough force behind her lines. Rebuke had always brought out the best in Darla Cowan; she'd always taken pride in her ability to perform under the toughest of circumstances. Sharon's plan seemed to be working. Darla assumed a steadfast look.

"Much better," Sharon said. "Now. Did you think over what we discussed, as to who might have planted the gun? Who had access to the beach house?"

Darla's forehead creased. "David and I, of course. Lyndon Gray, but Mr. Gray wouldn't . . ."

Sharon clutched at a straw. "What about David's agent, Curtis Nussbaum?"

Darla shrugged vacantly. "He could have. That would be between him and David. My agent, Aaron Levy, never had a key, I never saw any reason for him to."

"I want you to look at something." Sharon rummaged for her set of Mrs. Welton's photos, located the picture taken on the *Spring of the Comanche* set, and passed the glossy snapshot in through the bars. "Who is that guy?"

Darla held the photo by one corner and chewed her lower lip. "David. Me. Curt Nussbaum, what . . . ?"

"The guy in the foreground on Nussbaum's right," Sharon said. As she spoke, she examined the photo of the scene in front of Planet Hollywood, picturing the same man in his Crocodile Dundee outfit. The stranger had jutting cheekbones and tightly molded facial skin.

Darla gazed at the picture without recognition. "I remember him being there. I think he's a security guy Curt brought along."

"Security, like Gray and Yadaka?"

"And Mrs. Welton, yes. Everyone even remotely in the public eye requires security in Hollywood, Sharon. It's not one of the more attractive facets of one's existence here, but . . ."

"Have you ever seen Nussbaum's security man since?"

Darla shook her head. "Not that I remember. Probably I was introduced to the guy, but with all the

fighting between David and Curt, I doubt if I caught
his name."

Sharon's chin lifted. "Fighting?"

"Over a part David had agreed to play and then
reneged. Curt had made a special trip to Montana to
talk about that; it's why he was on the set to begin
with. David did that a lot. He'd get fired up over some
role while he was drinking or snorting coke, then he'd
sober up and change his mind." Darla handed the
picture back. "Is the security guy important?"

Sharon spread her fingers and rotated her hand on
her wrist, *comme ci, comme ça.* "We won't know the
answer to that until we locate him. *If* we locate him.
He shows up in two more pictures, one taken yesterday on the courthouse steps and the other in front of
Planet Hollywood during the brouhaha between you
and David."

Darla frowned. "What would he be doing in Dallas?"

"No clue. What was the argument with Nussbaum
all about?"

Darla gripped a bar and leaned her forehead against
her forearm. "Curt optioned a novel, based on David's
commitment to star in the film. It's the one I told you
about earlier, where he wanted me for the love interest.
David's commitment put the deal together with the studio, and when he backed out, the picture fell through.
Curt was furious and said David had cost him a fortune,
but David never gave a damn about things like that. He
accepted every role offered, then crawfished on most.
Tooling people around gave him a charge."

Sharon opened her satchel, found a ballpoint and a
legal pad. "What novel?"

"The title was *Dead On.* A thriller. I never read it.
After David backed out, I never heard of the project again."

"Written by whom?" Sharon steadied her pen, using
her thigh as a backstop for the legal pad.

"An unknown author," Darla said. "I don't know
the details. You should talk with Marissa Cudmore."

Sharon arched an eyebrow.

Darla thoughtfully inclined her head. "She's a studio exec with Mammoth, up in Universal City. Curt Nussbaum pitched the movie to three or four studios, and there was a pretty rousing bidding war. I try not to get into that sort of thing. The saying is, deals are between agents and producers, asshole to asshole, and you're better off staying out of the way."

"Ms. Cudmore just attained a position on my list of things to do." Sharon looked up from her scribbling. "Anything else you remember about the novel or the movie deal?"

Darla's eyes misted. "Most of it is a blank. It was about the time David and I were having our biggest problems. Right after that picture was taken he split, showed up all over Vegas the following week with a string of bimbos. I think he backed out on the picture as much to hurt me as to tweak Curt Nussbaum. David was so evil. God, I wish I'd never heard of him."

"That makes two of us." Sharon stowed her pad and pen away. "But you did hear of him, from a close-up perspective. You can't *unhear* of him, Darla, so we've got to play with the cards they dealt us." She bit her inner cheek. "I've got to go into the courtroom and get set up now. They'll be bringing you in soon." She started to walk away.

"Sharon?" Darla said softly, almost in a whisper. Sharon turned.

"It will be all right, won't it?" Darla's knuckles whitened as her grip tightened on the bars. "Tell me things will be fine."

Sharon sighed. "Which brings us to the lawyer's creed that you're never supposed to represent a friend. Emotional involvement distorts one's neutrality." Sharon pursed her lips as a tear blurred her vision. "Hold your head high, Darla. Always. You'd be surprised what wonders it will work if you show confidence. No teary-eyed looks, okay? I might break down myself if you crater on me."

20

Sharon came into the courtroom from the rear and headed resolutely for the defense side. In the five minutes before the hearing was to begin, she wanted to do some boning up. Proper legal procedure was out the window in this sideshow, that much she understood, but she still had to attack the FBI's search warrant with both barrels. She passed the bench with her chin lowered, her thoughts on the pile of Xeroxed court decisions stowed inside her satchel. With any kind of legitimate ruling, she was certain she could have the gun excluded from evidence, but after the freak show she'd witnessed yesterday she just wasn't sure. She wondered if the judge would pull out three rubber balls and go into a juggling act while he considered everyone's arguments. Or if Milton Breyer might ride a white pony around the courtroom with Kathleen Fraterno, decked out in spangled tights, balanced on his shoulders. She wouldn't be surprised at anything which went on in this joke of a . . .

The judge called out, "Miss Hays? Got a minute?"

Sharon applied the brakes and marched toward the bench. Karen Warren stood before the judge with her face angled expectantly in Sharon's direction. Sharon wondered to what extremes the *20/20* reporter would go in order to scoop the opposition. Checkbook journalism, certainly, but surely she wouldn't sleep with the . . .

As Sharon approached, Karen Warren reached up and patted the judge's hand. Sharon blinked in disbelief. She stopped beside the reporter and forced herself to smile at Judge Rudin. "Morning, Your Honor."

Rudin extended a hand, palm up, in Karen Warren's direction. "You've met Karen, right?"

Sharon acknowledged the reporter's presence with a fleeting nod. "Yes, sir. Yesterday."

Rudin touched his fingertips together. "She was wondering about an interview with you."

Sharon's throat tightened in hesitation. God, was she about to hear the opposite of a gag order? An *ungag* order or something? Not even in this freaking zoo, Sharon thought, no way. She said, "Miss Warren mentioned it yesterday, Your Honor." Visible in the corner of her eye, Karen Warren continued to beam.

Rudin leaned closer and lowered his voice. "Far be it from me to intervene, Miss Hays. Officially at any rate. But have you given any more thought to the matter?"

Sharon couldn't believe her ears. She made up her mind in a hurry. If this phony jurist ordered her to give a press interview, she was marching straight to an appellate judge faster than God could get a weather report. She said evenly and professionally, "I don't make a practice of giving interviews while a case is in progress, Your Honor," then added without thinking, "Courts frown on that sort of thing in my part of the world."

Rudin recoiled as if punched in the solar plexus. His demeanor changed in a flash. He glanced toward Karen Warren, then narrowed his eyes as he zeroed in on Sharon. His look was menacing. "Suit yourself, Counsel," the judge snapped. "But in the future I'd be remembering I was no longer in Texas, if I were you."

Now that she'd alienated the judge, she managed to spoil Darla's courtroom entrance as well. The incident went down as Darla left her jailer escort near the doorway and paraded majestically toward the defense table. Sharon and Preston Trigg stood at arm's length with one vacant chair in between them, and Milton

Breyer and Kathleen Fraterno were in the position of attention on the prosecution side. Harold Cuellar was also at the D.A.'s table, in a chair with his head down, studying the morning edition of the *L.A. Times*. Judge Rudin sat at the bench, his swivel chair angled so that the *Court TV* camera would have a profile view. As the minicam whirred into action, Cuellar quickly folded the paper and stuffed it away. The operator stood in the jury box, hunched over the minicam like a man in the throes of orgasm. The spectator section was wall to wall, men and women jammed on the benches, so tightly packed in that Sharon wondered how they could freaking breathe.

Darla had taken Sharon's holding-cell advice to heart. She walked erect, her expression confident, placing one spike-heeled shoe in front of the other in unbroken rhythm. Preston Trigg backed up to give the actress room to reach her seat. Just as Darla flowed majestically toward her chair, a loud ringing sounded in the courtroom.

Darla froze in mid-stride. The judge's jaw dropped in surprise. Sharon looked quickly around for the source of the noise.

The teeth-jarring *brrr*! peeled forth again, loud and insistent in the pin-drop silence. Throughout the gallery men dug in their pockets and women in their purses, grabbing for cellular phones.

Jesus Christ, Sharon thought, the freaking cell phone. She remembered the message she'd left for Rob at the beach house, and mentally cursed her own stupidity. As the phone rang a third time, Sharon dug the receiver from her purse and fumbled to open the hinged mouthpiece. The phone slipped from her grasp, clattered to the table, and continued to emit its high-pitched buzz. The judge scowled toward the defense table. Visible in the periphery of Sharon's vision, Milton Breyer—the bastard!—showed a goofy smile.

Her face red, Sharon snatched up the phone and clicked the mouthpiece into talking position. The minicam was pointed at her. She turned her back, tucked her chin, and said in a near whisper, "Yes?"

Rob's tone was belligerent. "It's your nickel, Muffin."

Sharon made unintentional eye contact with a woman in the gallery. She looked quickly at the floor, saying, "Look, can I call you back?"

"No, you cannot. You've used enough of my time."

I haven't used one freaking second of your time, you jerk, Sharon thought. Your daughter has. She said, "I'm in court, Rob." She glanced toward the bench. The judge stared daggers in her direction.

"In Darla's trial?" Rob said.

"Hearing. Yes, and we're in the middle of it. I want to talk to you about the check you gave me."

"That's going to have to be enough money to get you by for now. It's all I owe."

"That's not— Never mind. I can't talk now. Be at home tonight, I have to see you."

"Oh, no. You've had your chance."

"I don't mean that way. You be there. You have to be." She disconnected and looked to the bench, turning the power switch on the phone to the off position as she did. "I apologize to the court," she said. "It won't happen again."

Rudin frowned as if deep in thought, then lifted his forefinger. "That's one, Miss Hays. If you don't get the message, ask your California co-counsel. You understand, don't you, Mr. Trigg?"

Preston Trigg half stood, said, "Yes, Your Honor," and sat back down. All through the spectators section, men scratched their heads and women exchanged curious glances.

Rudin folded his hands and addressed the prosecution. "If the contingent from Texas is ready, you may proceed."

Milt Breyer popped up to his feet. "Dallas County calls Vernon Tupelow, Your Honor."

Sharon leaned forward and whispered around Darla, "What's he talking about?"

Preston Trigg bent forward as well and, as Darla looked back and forth between her lawyers, said, "He's calling a witness." As he spoke, the Dallas County M.E. came in the back and walked down the aisle.

"Jesus Christ," Sharon hissed. "I know that much. I'm talking about, with the finger. The 'that's one' business."

"Oh." Trigg glanced at Darla, then looked back at Sharon. "Rudin's notorious for that. Three strikes in his courtroom, then you can look to spend the night in the county for contempt." He closed his mouth, thought, then added, "He generally reserves, one finger, two finger, for lawyers he doesn't like."

"Ridiculous." Sharon was indignant. "I didn't set off the freaking phone on purpose."

Trigg glanced toward the bench as Tupelow came through the gate and approached the clerk for swearing in. He looked at Sharon and said, "Shh!"

" 'Shh!' hell," Sharon said. "I'm not backing down from this guy."

Trigg leaned closer. "You don't understand. Lawyers conversing other than bench conferences and courtroom breaks, that's another pet peeve of his."

Sharon expelled air through her nose. Of all the . . . She looked to the bench. Judge Rudin was watching her.

Rudin smiled and raised two fingers in Sharon's direction, his gaze half on her and half on the television camera. "That's two, Counsel," Rudin said.

Sharon was as furious as she'd ever been in her life. She opened her satchel and sifted viciously through her notes, thumbing aside her copies of the photos she'd given to Yadaka and Gray. She wondered briefly if the security men were having any luck in locating the stranger among the crowd on the street. The way things were going inside the courtroom at the moment, Yadaka and Gray might hold the key to the best chance Darla had. She glanced at her friend and client. Darla's lips were parted in confusion.

Sharon leaned close to Darla and whispered, "You're doing fine, babe. It's me that's screwing up, and that's coming to a screeching halt. You just keep on giving them hell."

Darla lowered her lashes. A tear ran down her face, streaking her makeup, and her knuckles whitened as she wrung her hands.

Working crowds had been Lyndon Gray's specialty in the British Secret Service; he'd once chaperoned Prince Charles and Lady Di on a European tour and, with assistance from Paris *gendarmes,* had apprehended a deranged man as he'd approached the royal couple with sticks of dynamite strapped to his chest. As Gray paced back and forth among the mob in front of the L.A. Criminal Courts Building, he called Benny Yadaka on the cell phone. The Oriental answered on the second ring. "Position?" Gray said.

Crackling static accompanied Yadaka's reply. "Proceeding north on Broadway, chief. Couple of blocks from you. Spotted anything?"

Gray lifted his eyes, looking at the top of the steps, surveying the areas between the granite pillars. The photos Sharon had provided lay in the Englishman's briefcase; he'd memorized the subject's features and would recognize the man anywhere. He said into the phone, "Negative. You?"

"Nothing here," Yadaka said. "Nothing but street bums I can see."

"I feel I've seen this man, Benny." Gray sidestepped a reporter, who shot him a curious glance, and moved nearer the curb.

"Not me. This is L.A., Lyndon, I bump into guys every day who look familiar, but then realize they just resemble somebody else I know."

"This isn't that sort of feeling. I know this man. If I think on it, it will come to me."

"Lemme know if it does," Yadaka said. "I'm signing off now, ring me back in ten."

"Affirmative." Gray disconnected and looked out

across the street, past cruising autos and buses chugging exhaust fumes. Men and women in business dress strolled the sidewalks, going about their business. He turned and watched the courthouse steps once more, wondering if his powers of concentration were slipping with age. Dammit, where had he known the man? If he thought really hard, the answer would have to come.

Benny Yadaka disconnected, stowed his cell phone in his inside breast pocket, and continued down the western sidewalk alongside Broadway. Gray's orders had been to take Broadway north to Arcadia Avenue, cut back to the east, and then head south on Main, finally approaching the criminal courts once again on Temple Street, keeping a lookout for the man in the photos. Yadaka wore a dark brown suit and pale yellow shirt with a pastel tie, and moved with brisk athletic strides while keeping his manner casual, his demeanor almost bored. His lids were at sleepy half-mast. He moved aside as a young Japanese woman passed in the opposite direction. The woman showed a flirtatious smile. Yadaka bid her good day in Japanese. He watched the woman's undulating rear end over his shoulder for a moment, then looked back to the front just as he reached the Arcadia intersection. He quickened his pace and rounded the corner, his gaze darting across the street at a deli, a Chinese takeout place, a barroom with a sign in the shape of a stemmed martini glass. He'd gone three-quarters of a block when, directly in front of him, the man from the photos hustled across Arcadia, going south on Main.

Yadaka fought to maintain his bland expression and mask his surprise. The guy from the pictures wore pale blue coveralls, as if he were a member of a construction crew. His blondish hair gleamed dully, and his tight-stretched facial skin exhibited a tan. He seemed in a hurry, and looked neither right nor left as he jogged across Arcadia, hop-skipped up on the curb, and continued on his way.

Yadaka was careful not to attract attention; the increase in his pace was almost imperceptible as he crossed over Main and fell in step behind the man, ten or fifteen feet to the rear. He kept a constant distance between him and the subject for a quarter of a block, checking right and left, fore and aft, for passersby. This section of Main was practically deserted, freeway traffic rumbling overhead, no one in sight save for a round Hispanic lady ten yards to the rear, looking in a deli window. Yadaka broke into a trot, pulled abreast of the subject, and walked alongside just as the man emerged from beneath the freeway. Yadaka said softly, "Alley up ahead. Turn in there and stop. We need to talk."

The man turned his head to look at the Oriental. His mouth hung open. He didn't answer, continuing along among old one- and two-story brick buildings, low-slung shops with storefront windows.

Yadaka grasped his lapel and lifted his coat to show his shoulder rig. "You think I'm playing with you? Turn in up there like we're buddies, you understand?"

The man's features sagged. He looked fearfully ahead, glanced behind him, then ducked into the alleyway with Yadaka on his heels. The alley was open at both ends, sparse midday traffic flowing by, rows of garbage cans lining brick walls, metal fire escapes overhead at intervals, the air carrying the odor of rotting vegetables and spoiled meat. The man walked ten steps, turned, and looked Yadaka eye to eye. "We don't supposed to be seen together," the man said.

Yadaka lifted his coattail and jammed a hand into his pocket. "*You* aren't supposed to be seen, any place, any time." He groped in his inside breast pocket with his free hand and produced the photos. "What, you like having your picture taken?"

The man looked at the top picture, winced, examined the second photo and closed his eyes. "I can help it there's people with cameras around?"

Yadaka snatched the photos away, thumbed to the shot taken yesterday on the courthouse steps, and shoved that picture in the stranger's face. "What about this? What the fuck are you doing hanging out in front of the courts? Have you gone crazy?"

The man spread his hands, palms up. "I'm protecting my interest here."

Yadaka snorted. "You're buying yourself a collar is what you're doing."

"I got money coming, in case you forgot."

"So? You think this woman Sharon Hays is going to pay you?"

The man straightened in a pugnacious attitude. "Until I see some green, man, I'm staying around."

Yadaka tilted his head and scratched his chin. "You knew it would take awhile. We all did."

"Not this fucking long. Two days, he said. I'm beginning to hurt."

Yadaka reached for his hip pocket. "Maybe I can help you out."

The man extended a hand, palm up. "Be nice if you could."

"Yeah, okay, I . . ." Yadaka glanced up and down the alley, smiled at the guy, then brought up his hand holding a buck knife. He took one step forward and drove the knife up to its hilt in the stranger's chest, below the point of the breastbone, twisting, plunging the blade to the left, toward the heart. The man didn't cry out. His eyes bulged wide. He gasped as if in discomfort, then expelled his final air. Yadaka quickly withdrew the blade and moved aside as the man collapsed to the asphalt, twitched once, and then was still. His head lay in a pool of slickish liquid, motor oil mixed with animal urine.

The entire incident had taken less than a minute. Yadaka stepped over to a garbage can, found a wadded paper towel to wipe the blade, and replaced the knife in his hip pocket. He walked around the body, left the alley, and continued south on Main Street. He'd traveled less than fifty yards when his cell phone buzzed.

Yadaka withdrew the phone from his side pocket

and clicked the mouthpiece into place. "Yeah, Lyndon," he said.

Lyndon Gray's clipped British voice was calm. "Position?"

Yadaka continued to walk, his eyelids at sleepy half-mast. "South on Main, chief. Spotted anything?"

There was a second's hesitation before Gray said, "Negative. You?"

"Me, neither," Yadaka replied. "Nothing but street bums is all I can see."

21

Preston Trigg tried to stretch his fifteen minutes of fame into a lifetime. After listening to her California co-counsel batter Vernon Tupelow for two solid hours, Sharon decided that this was to be the longest extradition hearing in history. The Dallas County medical examiner's direct testimony had established that David Spencer was dead, stabbed umpty-jillion times in the chest and abdomen and then shot through the head with a .38 caliber bullet, all of which was undisputable fact, but Preston Trigg acted as if the M.E. himself was a possible suspect. Milton Breyer's questioning had been tediously long, Sharon thought, complete with maps of the area around the Mansion Hotel and a blown-up layout of the presidential suite, but Preston Tripp had already used up twice as much time as the prosecutor and then some. Sharon's gaze wandered idly to the television camera. She wondered if *Court TV* employed a film editor. If they did, Preston Trigg's big scene would likely wind up on the cutting-room floor.

Trigg's chief cross-examination tool was what Sharon had come to think of as the Poignant Pregnant Pause, PPP for short, which he now employed in earnest, looking at the murder scene layout which Milton Breyer had set up on a tripod during direct. This particular PPP took up a full thirty seconds as Trigg stood with one hand supporting his elbow while he scratched his chin with the other. Finally he picked up a pointer and indicated the bed where the hotel's desk manager had found David Spencer. "The body was here, is that correct?" Trigg said.

Sharon would say this for Vernon Tupelow, the M.E. kept his cool. He employed the standard Professional Witness's ten seconds of hesitation—in order to give the prosecution time to object—before answering. "In that proximity, yes," Tupelow said. "Actually, it was positioned closer to the headboard."

Trigg seemed momentarily confused. The tip of the pointer was touching the foot of the bed. After five more beats of PPP, Trigg indicated an area closer to the top of the chart. "Is that better?" he asked.

"More like it." Tupelow brushed the sleeve of his clean white lab coat.

"I see. But the pools of blood you mentioned earlier, *Doc*-tor"—Trigg moved the pointer to the entry hall, the corridor running just inside the door and alongside the bathroom—"where your lab techs took their swatches. Those were here, weren't they?"

"Yes."

Trigg's chin lifted a fraction, a gesture which said clearly, *aha!* "But if the blood was here and the body was"—he jabbed the pointer at the bed once again—"here, how can you be certain the blood was the victim's?"

"We've run certain tests," Tupelow said, "which would indicate certain things to us. There are other tests for which we don't have the results as yet, having to do with mixtures."

Trigg assumed a suspicious tone. "Mixtures?"

"Yes. As in blood from two different people."

"Oh?" Trigg was incredulous. "Have you established that at the time of death, there was more than one person in the room?"

"We're only surmising, of course. Assuming the victim didn't inflict fourteen stab wounds on his own person and then shoot himself." Tupelow blinked in boredom.

Sharon cringed, and considered resigning from the Dream Team on the spot. If it hadn't have been for

Darla, in fact, she would have. She pictured Russell Black watching this horror show back in Dallas, itching to hurl a paperweight at his TV set. Preston Trigg strolled over to the defense table, poured a glass of water and had a sip, and winked at Sharon before returning to the witness. She looked away, wondering how it would look to the viewing audience if she tackled her co-counsel and then tied him to his chair.

"So to summarize, *Doc*-tor," Trigg said, "the body was in the bed, wasn't it?"

"That's where it was when I came on the scene."

"And the blood was in the foyer?" Trigg rammed his hands into his back pockets and scowled at the camera.

Milton Breyer seized his cue and leaped to his feet. "Objection. Asked and answered."

Judge Rudin proved once again that he could mug for the camera with the best of 'em. He seemed deep in thought before saying, "Sustained."

Trigg favored the jurist with an amused smirk. "Interesting," he said. Then, to the camera, he said, "Interesting," whirled to face the bench and said, "No further questions," and then marched to the table and sat down.

What's so freaking interesting? Sharon thought. After stumbling around half the morning, Trigg had given up just when he was at long last making a point. This was the most ridiculous courtroom exhibition she'd ever witnessed. That *anyone* had ever witnessed, and the fact that Preston Trigg, Milton Breyer, and Judge Rudin all looked pleased with themselves made the whole thing even more unbelievable. Through two solid hours of questioning, Trigg had elicited exactly zero from Vernon Tupelow. No new information, nothing to indicate that the M.E. was somehow in cahoots with the prosecution to frame the defendant, not one single thing beneficial to his client. Zilch. *Nada.* Sharon leaned back and glanced at Kathleen Fraterno. She had a puzzled look, and her cheeks showed tinges of red. Trigg's confused her and Milt's embarrassed her, Sharon thought.

Judge Rudin looked at the prosecution table. "Redirect, Mr. Breyer?"

Sharon thought, Oh, yeah, Milt, do it. Unless Breyer had more questions, Tupelow's appearance on the stand was over and the prosecution would have successfully dodged the bullet courtesy of Preston Trigg. Sharon grabbed her legal pad and went over a couple of notes she'd made. Breyer's ego simply had to get the best of him. No way could he let an opportunity to strut in front of the camera pass him by. If Kathleen Fraterno tried to stop him, Breyer was apt to shove her aside. Come on, Milt, Sharon thought, get up there and . . .

Breyer leaned over to confer with Stan Green, then whispered something in Kathleen Fraterno's ear. She firmly shook her head. Breyer stood and said grandly, "Just a couple of things, Your Honor." Fraterno picked up a pencil and broke it in two.

Sharon experienced a surge of adrenaline.

"In summary, Mr. Tupelow," Breyer said, "did you determine the cause of death?"

Tupelow looked thoughtful. He's trying to remember if he packed his bathing suit, Sharon thought, and would like to spend his remaining time Out West seated under a beach umbrella. Tupelow finally said, "That would be difficult if not impossible. The knife wounds would have eventually been fatal. So would the bullet wound. Either injury would have killed the victim."

"The bullet fragments found in the room," Breyer said, "did come from a .38-caliber weapon, didn't they?"

Sharon could have objected—and had a panicked moment when she feared that Preston Trigg would jump up and do so—because it was the lab techs and not the medical examiner who had collected the shell frags, but Breyer had asked just the question she'd been hoping for. She held her breath as Tupelow said with little certainty, "That they did."

"Thank you," Breyer said, then assumed a knowing look and said, "Thank you," a little more forcefully, and finally turned to the bench and said, "No further questions," and sat down.

Typical Milton Breyer, Sharon thought gleefully, he's once more jabbed his rapier forcefully at empty air. She picked up her notes; pointless as Breyer's redirect had been, the defense now had a chance to correct its own blundering. Which was the direction in which this entire hearing had gone, a blunder here, a blunder there. Judge Rudin looked a bit confused, then asked the defense, "Anything else?"

Preston Trigg turned to Sharon with a questioning look. No way, buster, she thought, your time in the spotlight is over but good. She whispered, "Let me," and was on her feet before Trigg could stop her. "Yes, Your Honor, we have a few things," Sharon said loudly. She addressed the witness. "Mr. Tupelow, you testified that you had the results of at least some of the blood tests, didn't you?"

There was the slightest wavering of Tupelow's gaze, and Sharon wondered if the M.E. knew where she was headed. Too late if he does, Sharon thought, the cat is already out of the bag. Tupelow said, "Yeah. Not all of the results, but some."

Sharon reexamined her notes. "Comparing the samples with samples from the victim?"

"Yes."

"And what were the results of the tests that you do have, sir?"

Tupelow's tone was a bit resigned. "At least some of the blood in the foyer came from the victim."

"Well, wouldn't that indicate," Sharon asked, "that David Spencer was stabbed in the foyer?"

Tupelow shrugged. "It would to me."

Sharon quickened her pace, more excited now. "The crime-scene photos you testified to, didn't those photos show blood and brain matter spattered on the sheets and pillowcases behind the victim's head?"

"There was blood on the bed, yes. Blood all over the room."

"But specifically on the bed, Doctor. Wouldn't that indicate to you that the victim was stabbed in the foyer, then carried over and laid in the bed, where he was shot?"

"I hadn't really speculated on that," Tupelow said.

Sharon's wide-eyed look said incredulously, Well, why haven't you? She asked, "Well, barring that scenario, Doctor, wouldn't the killer have to shoot the victim in the bed, drag him to the foyer and then stab him numerous times, and then haul him back to the bed? A lot of work for our murderer, what?"

Fraterno came to her feet, apparently having had it up to here with waiting for Milton Breyer to do something sensible. "Objection, Your Honor," she said. "The witness has already stated that he hasn't speculated."

Sharon glanced at Kathleen with respect. She hadn't expected Fraterno to take the reins so quickly, and adjusted her thinking along more cautious lines. "All right," Sharon said before the judge could rule on the objection, "I'll withdraw the question. But whichever happened first, the shooting or the stabbing, the victim would have to be moved, wouldn't he?"

Tupelow's mouth twitched. "It would appear so. Unless he moved himself."

Sharon raised her eyebrows and tilted her head. "After he was shot, Doctor? Or after he was stabbed numerous times?"

Tupelow folded his arms and adjusted his position in the chair.

Sharon took a long and pointed look at Darla Cowan, seated with her hands folded and, at the moment, appearing much smaller than she was. She returned her attention to the witness. "Dr. Tupelow, how much did David Spencer weigh?"

Tupelow looked at the prosecution for help, then,

receiving none, spread his hands. "I'd have to examine my report."

"I've already done that, Doctor," Sharon said. "Would it surprise you to learn that your autopsy report listed the victim's weight at one hundred and eighty-seven pounds?"

Tupelow sagged a bit. "I don't guess it would."

"I see." Sharon looked at her notes. "Miss Cowan's last trip to the doctor, she weighed—"

"*Objection!*" Fraterno stood with flared nostrils. "Is counsel for the defense testifying here? If the court *please* . . ."

"Sustained." Rudin lifted a warning finger. "No more of that."

"Yes, Your Honor," Sharon said, but took a final long look at Darla. She then examined her notes, said for effect, "No further . . ." Then, as Tupelow made as if to rise and depart the witness stand, Sharon said, "Oh. One more thing, Doctor."

Tupelow relaxed and offered a stoic blink.

"Under the assumption," Sharon said, "that the stabbing in the foyer occurred first, Doctor, and, as you testified, the knife wounds would have been fatal on their own, can you think of any reason why the killer would then shoot the victim in the head?"

"Objection." Fraterno was on her feet again. "Your Honor, this witness can't possibly know—"

"Is it reasonable," Sharon cut in, "to think that the killer possibly *wanted* those .38 caliber shells to be found near the victim?"

There were five seconds of pin-drop silence.

Fraterno assumed an indignant posture. "Your . . . Honor . . ."

Rudin looked back and forth from Fraterno to Sharon like a spectator at a tennis match.

Sharon broke the silence with a grin. "Withdrawn. I'm out of line, Your Honor. I apologize to the court." She turned her smile on the witness. "Nothing else, Doctor. Thank you." She sat, put her arm around Darla, and gave the actress an affectionate hug.

*   *   *

Tupelow left the stand, looking slightly relieved, as
Breyer rummaged through a pile of paper. Fraterno
having done her best to save his ass, old Milt was
going on the attack once more. Sharon fought to stay
alert. So out-and-out ridiculous was this hearing that
it was difficult to sift out what was relevant to the case
from the fluff for the benefit of the viewing audience.
Darla looked totally confused as Breyer said loudly,
"Call Steven Moretta, Your Honor."

At last, Sharon thought. She opened her briefcase
and dug out her motion to suppress the weapon along
with the stack of Xeroxes she'd made at the library.
Preston Trigg glanced sideways at the stapled sheaf
of paper and showed a questioning look. "It's called
research, Pres," Sharon whispered. Visible in the corner of her eye, Kathleen Fraterno bent sideways and,
from under her chair, removed a box which she set in
front of her at the prosecution table. The box, of
course, held the pistol. Here we go, Sharon thought.
Fraterno looked inside the box, nodded to Breyer,
then closed the lid.

Agent Moretta had overhauled his image since he'd
served the search warrant at the beach house. He'd
traded his Men-in-Black costume for a dove gray business suit, and exhibited a mild but earnest expression
as he raised his hand for swearing in. He ascended to
the stand and, at Breyer's prompting, told the nation
that his full name was Steven Thomas Moretta, that
he'd been with the FBI for fifteen years, and that his
current assignment was to the L.A. branch's sub-office
in Malibu. Moretta answered the questions in a businesslike tenor, with no visible emotion, and acted as
if the TV camera wasn't even there. He knows it's
there, Sharon thought, since the FBI courts the limelight regularly, but he's an old hand at playing to juries
and viewing audiences. Compared to this guy, Milt
Breyer and the judge were like a junior high acting
class in competition against Laurence Olivier.

"And in this capacity, Agent," Breyer went on, "did

you have occasion to travel to . . ." Breyer retreated to the table and looked at his notes, then returned to the podium. "One forty-seven Rocky View Drive in Malibu? That would be this past Tuesday, two evenings ago." Sharon blinked. Now that Darla's address had gone out over the networks, the beach house could expect gawkers from here to hell and gone.

"I did," Moretta said.

"For what purpose?"

"Execution of a search warrant."

First mention of the warrant was all that Sharon had been waiting for. She drew a breath and stood. "Approach?"

Rudin nodded, lifted his hands, and gave a come-hither gesture to both sides. Fraterno went up along with Milton Breyer, while Harold Cuellar remained at the prosecution table. Preston Trigg started to rise. Sharon restrained him with a hand on his shoulder and shook her head. Trigg slumped dejectedly. Sharon gave Darla a smile, then carried her motion and briefs toward the bench. In the ten strides or so before she reached the conference, she had some planning to do.

Accomplishing her purpose was going to require some ham-and-egging on Sharon's part—a role for which she felt eminently more qualified than Milton Breyer—because suppression of the murder weapon simply wasn't going to be enough to bolster Darla's cause. Breyer had already popped off to the media—resulting in a front-page story in the morning *L.A. Times*—that the FBI had found the murder weapon hidden under Darla's kitchen sink, thus injecting a dose of poison into the jury pool, and it was up to Sharon Hays to administer an antidote. In addition to arguing suppression, she had to somehow bring out in front of the camera that Darla had never seen the gun before. She reached the bench, edged her way in between Breyer and Kathleen Fraterno, and said softly to the judge, "We're going to object to any testimony regarding the search warrant, Your Honor, or any reference to evidence found at Miss Cowan's residence." She plopped her motion and brief up in front of Rudin, and passed the state's copy to Kathleen Fraterno. Fraterno looked over the papers in her hand, and her look said she'd been expecting them.

Rudin's gape of surprise—in the direction of the camera, of course—was a bit much to swallow, because Sharon had discussed the suppression question at length in yesterday's bench conference. But gape Rudin did, allowing a full five seconds for the viewing audience to understand that they were seeing a major development in the case. Then the judge leaned back, held the motion at eye level while he scanned the issues, then said in a stage whisper, "An interesting development here."

Interesting, eh? Sharon thought. She wondered if the judge had taken his cue from Preston Trigg. She said evenly, "We have a twofold argument, Judge. One, the search came under a federal warrant, and while we acknowledge that federal discovery is a thousand yards broader than at the state level, it's our position that the feds conducted a scam. That they had no real intent to charge Miss Cowan with a federal crime, that they conducted the search as disguised agents of the state of Texas, and that therefore the search warrant falls under state discovery rules." She was conscious of Agent Moretta's gaze on her from the witness stand. The FBI man showed a hint of amusement. Sharon licked her lips and went on.

"And further," she said, "even if the FBI investigation was a valid attempt to implicate Miss Cowan in a federal offense of some kind, we're going to argue that the warrant is invalid even under *federal* discovery. The warrant on its face is totally groundless, Judge. Agent Moretta, the witness here, has signed an affidavit of probable cause, attesting to facts of which he can't possibly be personally aware. And even if he'd had personal knowledge, the facts themselves do not constitute probable cause to search the defendant's residence. We'll stipulate that Miss Cowan flew interstate on the night of the murder, but so what?

There is nothing in the affidavit which hints of possible evidence to be found at her home, or anything which hints of a purpose for the search." She offered a smile. "Under the same theory Agent Moretta offers in his affidavit, the FBI could ransack *my* home, Your Honor, or yours. We're looking at unreasonable search and seizure, pure and simple."

Rudin had been thumbing madly through the motion and brief as Sharon spoke. He now looked up. "Even if you're right, Miss Hays, I don't think I could rule on a federal question. That would require a trip into federal district court, wouldn't it?"

The judge had just brought up the first proper legal issue that Sharon had heard in this entire procedure. She nodded toward the papers in Rudin's hand. "I researched that point, Your Honor. *DeBruzzo* v. *New York,* a federal warrant for a phone tap with the tapes used in a state bookmaking prosecution. The court can rule on a federal question at the state level. If the court's ruling goes against them, Mr. Breyer and Miss Fraterno have an avenue of appeal directly into federal district court, but . . ." Sharon closed her mouth, aware of her tendency to let her enthusiasm get the best of her. She gestured toward her motion. "It's in there, Judge. The high court's decision speaks for itself." She was conscious of a rustling noise on her right, and looked in that direction.

Kathleen Fraterno had set Sharon's motion and brief aside, and dug into her belongings for a stack of papers of her own. She handed Sharon a copy and stood with the original tucked under her arm. "Just in case," Kathleen murmured.

Sharon blinked in surprise as she read. Fraterno, a step ahead as always, had prepared her own brief on these very issues. Criminy, Sharon thought, she was hauling ass for the library in Dallas yesterday afternoon, the admissibility problem occurring to her even as the California proceeding aired on television. Sharon pictured a bleary-eyed Kathleen Fraterno, marshalling the D.A.'s typists into action even as she called in her reservation for the red-eye into L.A. Sharon glanced sideways at Milton Breyer. What a woman will do for her man, Sharon thought. Kathleen made no move to pass the original of her brief up to the judge. Rudin scratched his forehead.

"How long do you wish to take with this, Miss Hays?" Rudin asked. "It's nearing lunchtime."

A remark of Russell Black's came to Sharon, one he'd made as they searched the Crowley Courts Building in search of a judge to set bond for one of their clients. *Our doors are open to all, rich or poor, black or white, but just don't pester us durin' lunchtime.* "I don't have any witnesses to present, sir," Sharon said, "only argument. But I do plan to put Agent Moretta on voir dire, here and now. Fifteen minutes, max. My motion and brief pretty well speak for themselves. As for the state of Texas's rebuttal, I have no idea. Miss Fraterno's just now handed me her brief on the issue, and I . . ." She threw a slightly puzzled glance in Fraterno's direction. She should have presented her rebuttal brief to the judge at the same time she handed over Sharon's copy, but Fraterno had made no move to do so.

Fraterno stepped quickly forward, front and center. "It's only a partial, anticipatory brief, Your Honor. We had no way of knowing for certain if this issue would come up at all. Before we decide what rebuttal to offer, if any, we have to learn what the defense has to say."

Sharon blinked in irritation. What Fraterno was saying was baloney, of course—so often had Kathleen and Sharon worked together as prosecutors, and opposed each other since Sharon had become a defense lawyer, that their thoughts moved along identical channels, and Kathleen had known damned well what the defense's arguments were going to be—but the strategy was a long way from dumb. If Fraterno committed herself at this point, she'd be stuck with her commitment. Without prestating its intent, however, the state of Texas could sit back and adjust their strategy after hearing what Sharon had to say. Sharon testily rattled the pages in her hand, and then stuffed them away in her satchel. She looked to her right. Fraterno remained eyes front, keeping her gaze riveted on the judge.

Rudin brought out his pocket watch and wound the stem. If he keeps fooling with that thing, Sharon thought, the spring is going to break. She pictured the watch coming apart, gears and springs flying in all directions on national television, and nearly laughed out loud. Rudin said, "The court can live with that. Proceed, Miss Hays. After the defense's presentation we'll break for lunch. Back to your places, ladies and gentlemen."

Both sides returned to their respective corners. Judge Rudin addressed the courtroom at large. "Ladies and gentlemen, the defense is challenging the admissibility of Agent Moretta's testimony, particularly in connection with a pistol found at the residence. The court has agreed to hear argument from Miss Hays, and then will determine whether to admit the gun." He looked at the defense table. "You may proceed now."

Sharon couldn't believe her ears. Rudin had just acted as a sideline commentator for the benefit of the television audience. With a jury in the courtroom, the panel would have to be escorted out before any mention of the murder weapon, but Rudin had ensured that everyone in the country knew that the FBI had found the gun. "Everyone in the country" included all potential jurors, of course, which made official suppression of the murder weapon almost a moot point. Sharon picked up her pen and made a note that if Darla went to trial, she wanted to question each prospective juror as to their knowledge of the murder weapon, pressing so hard with the pen that her knuckles were white. She tossed the pen away and looked to the front. Rudin was glaring at her.

"I said, proceed, Miss Hays," Rudin snapped. "The

court has granted you leeway. Please don't abuse the privilege."

Leeway? Sharon thought. Freaking *leeway*? Arguing the admissibility of a murder weapon had now become *a privilege*? She got up and walked to the podium, breathing through her nose. Right here, right now, she had to put Milton Breyer, Kathleen Fraterno, and this joke of a judge as far out of her mind as possible. Darla's future depended on it. If Sharon let her anger get in the way, she could be throwing her client to the wolves.

Sharon began in a friendly tone. "Agent Moretta, I believe you testified in answer to Mr. Breyer's questions that you had been an FBI agent for fifteen years, is that correct?" She was acutely conscious of the camera, which had swiveled toward the defense table. Keep your chin up, Darla, Sharon thought, the nation is watching you.

Moretta kept his expression mild. "Since 1981. Yes."

"For a little more background, did you join the Bureau directly from college?"

"Georgia State. Yes." Moretta's accent retained the barest hint of the South, tempered by stopoffs at various locations throughout his career. The FBI moved their people a lot, Sharon knew.

"Good. And did your preliminary training include the customary ninety-day indoctrination at the FBI Academy in Quantico, Virginia?"

Moretta's gaze flickered with uncertainty. He wasn't sure where this was going. "It did," he finally said.

"And did your training there include classes in probable cause, dealing specifically with arrest or search and seizure?"

Moretta's expression firmed. He was getting it. "Yes."

"And in your various . . . Strike that. In how many different FBI offices have you worked, Agent Moretta?"

This brought a pause as Moretta frowned his way, mentally, through his career. "Five. Six, if you count a one-year temporary in Puerto Rico."

"Five is quite enough, Agent. It would be fair to say, wouldn't it, that you're not a greenhorn."

Moretta looked at her.

Sharon crossed her forearms on the podium. "That you've been around long enough to be familiar with procedure."

"I suppose you could say that. Other agents have been around longer than I."

"And many for shorter stints?" Sharon was prepared for this guy to dodge and feint, and he wasn't disappointing her.

"Yes, some." Moretta's tone showed the barest hint of resignation.

"Would it be fair to say that at least more than half the agents in the FBI have less service than you?"

"I guess it would."

"Fine," Sharon said. "During your time in service, Agent Moretta, how many warrants have you served?"

"Search warrants?"

Sharon lifted, and then dropped her shoulders. "Search . . . arrest . . . appearance . . ."

"Oh, I couldn't possibly remember all of them," Moretta said.

"Is it more than a hundred?"

Breyer popped up at the prosecution table. "Objection. The witness has stated that—"

"I'll withdraw the question," Sharon said. Breyer sat down. She flipped over a page in her legal pad and pretended to read. "Agent Moretta, you have served warrants before, haven't you?"

"I have."

"Then you are familiar with the difference between a *probable cause* warrant and one issued after an indictment or as the result of a court order, aren't you?"

"I am." Moretta grasped his left hand in his right and squeezed his left-hand fingers together.

"For the record," Sharon said, "please explain the difference." She glanced toward the bench, where Rudin was giving his undivided attention.

Moretta looked at his lap. "Probable cause, that's where we're the ones asking for a warrant."

"We being the FBI?"

"Yes. The other warrants we're merely serving at the request of the court or the grand jury."

"Some other party's origination," Sharon said.

"That's right."

"So when you want to, say, search someone's home, you need a warrant signed by a magistrate to do so."

"That would be a fair assessment," Moretta said.

"When you go to the magistrate, then, the magistrate knows nothing of the circumstances other than what you tell him in your affidavit, is that right?"

"In most cases. Yes."

"And in issuing this warrant, is this magistrate dependent on the truth of what you tell him?"

Moretta put on a show of being puzzled. "I'm not . . ."

"Let me restate the question." Sharon allowed just a tad of sarcasm to creep into her voice. "In asking for a search warrant, you swear out an affidavit, don't you?"

"That's the procedure." Moretta was all at once a bit snappish.

"Telling the circumstances causing you to need the warrant," Sharon went on. "In front of a notary. Right hand raised, left hand on the Bible—"

"Objection." Breyer's voice cracked in indignation. "Your . . . *Honor* . . ."

"That will do, Miss Hays." Rudin frowned at Sharon, then folded his hands.

"I apologize to the court," Sharon said, then returned her attention to the witness. "But wouldn't it be fair to state, Agent Moretta, that if the magistrate has incomplete facts, or possibly the facts contained in the affidavit are false, then the magistrate might sign an improper warrant?"

Breyer popped up so quickly that Sharon wondered
if Kathleen Fraterno had pinched him. Breyer stood
at attention, arms at his sides. "We have to inquire
where this is going. Surely Miss Hays isn't questioning
the integrity of the Bureau here."

I sure am, buster, Sharon thought, as you damned
well know. She said in a businesslike tone, "I'm not
sure that's an objection, Your Honor, since Mr. Breyer
didn't so state, but I'll point out to the court that I
haven't accused anyone of anything. I'm merely placing procedure on the record, and establishing that the
request for the search warrant in this case was origi-
nated by the FBI."

A flood of uncertainty crossed Rudin's features, replaced at once by a politician's smile. "I'll allow it,
Mr. Breyer. But be careful, Miss Hays."

Which is a typical jurist's response, Sharon thought,
when the judge doesn't know what the fuck is going
on. She looked at the witness. "Was this warrant origi-
nated at the FBI's request, Agent Moretta?"

"It was." Moretta's tone was more emphatic than
necessary.

"The FBI's alone?"

Moretta seemed hesitant. He looked toward the
prosecution table.

With the witness off guard, Sharon changed directions in midstream. "More specifically, Agent," Sharon
said, "prior to swearing out the affidavit, were you at
any time in contact with any representative of Dallas
County, Texas?"

Moretta's gaze flickered. "I'm not . . ."

Sharon bore down. "Didn't you find a gun during
your search, Agent Moretta? A thirty-eight-caliber police special?" Since Rudin had already let the nation
in on the fruits of the FBI search with his sidebar
speech, Sharon saw no point in being coy.

"Yes. There was that."

"Mmm-hmm. And didn't you take the gun directly
to the FBI lab in downtown L.A. for comparison with
some bullet fragments? And didn't your lab fax those

results to Dallas County, all causing the arrest warrant for Darla Cowan to be issued?" Sharon pointed at Darla, whose posture remained erect even though she was pale as a ghost. Sharon smiled at the witness. "I've asked you a question, Agent Moretta." Visible in the corner of her eye, Breyer started to come to his feet. Kathleen Fraterno stopped him with a hand on his arm. She looked resigned.

"It . . . seems they did," Moretta admitted.

"Thank you. Didn't the bullet fragments the L.A. lab used for comparison come from Dallas County, Texas?"

Moretta gave a tiny shrug. "They furnished them, yes."

Sharon's eyes flashed fire. "So I'll ask you again, Agent Moretta." She pulled a copy of the search warrant from her notes and waved the copy toward the witness stand. "Before you swore out the affidavit in connection with your search warrant, had you been in contact with any representatives of Dallas County, Texas?"

Moretta paused for a beat of five, waiting for the prosecution to object.

Sharon couldn't resist. She said, "And did they possibly tell you"—she suddenly spoke through her nose in a high, mimicking falsetto—" 'Be sure and get your story straight before you take it to the magistrate, buddy.' "

"Objection." Fraterno took over once more, coming to her feet so quickly that the soles of her shoes nearly left the floor. "Your Honor, this is *so* out of line."

"That it is, Miss Hays," Rudin snapped. "And I'll tell you that your status as a visitor here has already allowed you more latitude than I normally permit. One more time, Counsel, and I'll hold you in contempt."

Sharon pictured herself sharing a cell with Darla in the innards of the jail. She said in a subdued tone, "Yes, sir," then turned to the witness. "Did you talk to Dallas County before you swore to the affidavit, Agent Moretta?"

"I may have."

"You may have or you did? Which is it?"

Moretta's gaze was suddenly riveted on the back of the courtroom. "I did."

"And in taking the warrant in for signature, did you make the magistrate aware that you had done so?"

"I don't recall."

"Oh? Well, if you don't recall that, do you recall if you told the magistrate that Miss Cowan was under investigation on federal charges, or more specifically, interstate flight to avoid prosecution, in violation of federal codes?"

Moretta turned his hands palms up. "I'm sure I must have."

"Because if you hadn't, the magistrate wouldn't have issued the warrant, would he?"

"Objection." Fraterno's voice wasn't nearly as forceful as before. "The witness cannot testify as to what the magistrate would or wouldn't have done."

Rudin brought out his Old Reliable, the watch. "Sustained."

Sharon didn't miss a beat. "Agent Moretta, mustn't one allege violation of the federal code when asking for a federal warrant?"

Moretta's face went suddenly deadpan. "Those are the rules."

"So there will be no question," Sharon said, "I'll refer to the affidavit itself." She flipped through her copy of the search warrant and read off, " 'The subject has crossed state lines in an effort to avoid the jurisdiction of a Texas court.' " She put the warrant away. "Are those your words, Agent Moretta?"

"I suppose they are."

"Thank you. During your search, conducted under this warrant, what did you take from the house other than the pistol?"

Moretta licked his lips, for once at a loss for words.

"Did you find any airline tickets?" Sharon asked. "Or possibly a matchbook from Planet Hollywood's Dallas location?"

Moretta's voice dropped an octave. "No, I didn't."

"In fact, did you take *anything* from Miss Cowan's residence as evidence that she'd been traveling interstate?"

"No." Resolutely, in a monotone.

"Well, did the *pistol* reveal any evidence that Miss Cowan had been flitting about the country? Was it loaded with bullets marked 'Made in Texas,' anything of that nature?"

"No." Moretta was stoic now, accepting his punishment, too old a hand to expect the prosecution to bail him out. Kathleen Fraterno sat mute with her hands folded in her lap. Milton Breyer rubbed his forehead.

Sharon paused and looked down, thinking. Was she through with this guy? Something occurred to her. She lifted her face to regard the witness. "One more question, Agent. Once the lab's comparison of the bullet fragments was complete, you faxed the results to Dallas County, didn't you?"

"Yes, ma'am."

Sharon's forehead wrinkled in a frown of concentration. "And where else did you send a copy of the information?"

Moretta pinched his chin. "I beg your pardon?"

"Sir, your affidavit states that you suspected Miss Cowan of a violation of federal law, but you faxed the results to a *state* authority. Did you also furnish the results to a United States attorney in some jurisdiction?"

"I don't recall that I did," Moretta said softly.

"How about another FBI office, possibly one in Texas?"

"I don't think so."

"You don't think so." Sharon bent over the podium and fixed the federal man with an accusatory glare. "You weren't really conducting a federal investigation at all, Agent Moretta. Were you?" She turned the question into a statement as she shifted her gaze to the bench. "Our objection stands as made, Your Honor. Agent Moretta conducted his search under federal guise when in reality he was acting on behalf of the state of Texas. He had no valid *Texas* warrant, much less a warrant from California, and we submit that any fruits of the search, or any reference whatsoever to the warrant itself, are inadmissible, both in this hearing and at trial, as a matter of law." Sharon nodded for emphasis and resumed her seat. She whispered to Darla, "Let them chew on *that* for a while."

Judge Rudin put his pocket watch away and swiveled his chair to half face the audience, half face the camera. "We're going to break for lunch now, ladies and gentlemen, after which the state of Texas may present any rebuttal to Miss Hays's argument it wishes before I make a ruling. Let's all return at one-thirty, shall we?" He smiled toward the jury box, where the minicam was, and for just an instant Sharon expected the judge to say something like, "This is Dandy Drake Rudin, signing off for now." Or "Peace" perhaps, with his right hand lifted Dave Garroway fashion. Instead, however, Rudin climbed down from the bench and retreated to chambers with his robe swirling about his calves. The cameraman switched off his machine and bent to make some adjustments. Hubbub of conversations drifted through the courtroom. Spectators rose from their seats with a rustle of cloth and a whisper of nylon.

As the deputies moved up to escort Darla back to the holding cell, Sharon said to her, "So you'll understand what's going on. Even if we win in this court, we'll have to argue suppression of the weapon again at trial, and a Texas judge may rule differently from this judge. But if we can get the gun suppressed for extradition purposes, the Texas arrest warrant will be invalid, and they'll have to release you until Texas can move for indictment. Or at least until Texas can get a warrant supported with valid probable cause." She affectionately brushed Darla's collar. "It's all I can do now, babe. I'm fighting like hell for you."

Darla smiled bravely, then inhaled in fear as the deputy tapped her on the shoulder. She stood and walked dejectedly toward the exit, with uniformed men towering over her on either side. Sharon watched the actress go, swallowed a lump from her throat, then stood. Preston Trigg waited for her.

"Are you coming or what?" Trigg said.

Sharon frowned. "Coming where? And with whom?"

Trigg straightened his posture. "Spago. Lady back there's invited us."

Sharon glared out past the spectator section. Just inside the corridor door stood a woman with coiffed hair. She wore a loud yellow outfit and spike heels. She smiled at Sharon and beckoned. "Who's she?" Sharon said.

Trigg handed Sharon a business card which read, CHERRY VICK, LITERARY AGENT. Sharon sighed in exasperation as Trigg said, "She wants to talk about packaging a book deal for us," Trigg said. "Hey, Sharon, I'm not greedy. I propose a fifty-fifty split, because I want you to know going in, I regard you as a one hundred percent equal in this." He showed a patronizing grin.

Sharon watched him. Jesus Christ, she'd created a monster. "You'll have to go it alone, Pres," she finally said. "I've just realized, I've got something else to do." She left the California lawyer standing by the defense table, scratching his head, as she hurried after Darla and her captors. Darla ducked her head as she went through the holding cell entry. "Hey, fellas," Sharon called out. One of the deputies stopped and turned as Sharon rushed up to him. "I think I'll have lunch with my client," she said. "You have any extra chow back there? The way things are going, the holding cell is the safest place for me."

The prisoner's fare consisted of pickle-loaf sandwiches, fragments of dill and pimento mashed into Spam, topped off with a greenish slab of processed cheese, poked in between two stale bread slices, and then flattened into a wax-paper bag along with a mushy chocolate chip cookie. The deputies locked up

Sharon and Darla inside the holding cell and then
went off for cheeseburgers. Sharon sat on a steel
bench on the opposite wall from Darla, with the
barred window on Sharon's right, Darla's left. Sharon
had visited behind-the-courtroom holding tanks many
times in the past, but couldn't remember ever being
locked inside. She said as she chewed, "We should
have tried pickle loaf back when we rode the subway."

Darla hadn't touched her food, which lay, still inside
the bag, on the bench beside her hip. "Harlon Swain,"
she said.

Sharon's forehead tightened. "Who?"

"The writer."

"Good name for a writer. What did he write?"

"*Dead On.* The novel Curtis Nussbaum optioned
for David to play the lead and me to play the love
interest. I thought of his name while you were questioning the FBI agent."

Sharon thoughtfully gazed at the actress. "Darla,
I've had clients tell me, in jail, the time passes faster if
you can focus on other things. Keep your imagination
running full-tilt. There's a guy back home who had
three novels published during a federal prison term.
With your talent, maybe you should think about a
few screenplays. It's good you're dwelling on things
like that."

"I was dwelling on Harlon Swain because you asked
me about the people pictured on the movie set with
David and me. Mr. Nussbaum and that security agent.
And the argument over David backing out on the
Dead On part." Darla's eyes were suddenly moist.
"Can that be important?"

Sharon wanted to lie, but bolstering Darla's hopes
would be only a temporary Band-Aid, far to small to
cover the wound which could come later on. "It could
be, babe," she said. "A lot of things could be, but
we're just grasping so far. What we've got is one guy
who's showed up in three different pictures where
there's no logical explanation for him being there. It
could be nothing. It could be something. Assuming

we're eventually going to wind up in trial over this thing, we need to investigate every possible alternate theory of the crime other than that you did it."

"I know. That's what you told me. It's also what made me think of Harlon Swain."

Sharon's lips tightened in interest. "You mean, he could be a suspect?"

"Well . . . you'd have to know David."

"I'm learning," Sharon said. "I'm learning that he wasn't exactly Mr. Popularity and that a lot of people could be suspects, and that's what we've got to emphasize. Did he have a tiff with this writer, too?"

"David's ego required all sorts of stroking. During the time he was committed to the part, he had the writer over, oh, four or five times. Trading input over the depth and purpose of the character, that sort of thing, but anyone who knew David understood that he was going to play the role his way whether the writer liked it or not. But having this poor miserable peasant of a writer fawn over him . . . David got off on leading people on. I mean, smokes, Sharon, when Curt Nussbaum optioned the book, the writer was living in a hovel out in West L.A. David used to send the limo over to pick Swain up, more to impress the guy than anything else.

"Then when David decided he'd rather do more dope and screw more young girls than really concentrate on playing a meaty role," Darla said, "he suddenly dropped the writer flat. In the weeks after David backed out on the deal, Harlon Swain must have left a hundred messages on the machine which David never returned. There at the end, some of those messages were pretty wild."

"Threatening messages?" Sharon laid her sandwich aside.

"Not per se, like, I'm going to kill you. But he did curse a lot. Called David a lying fuck in one. David just laughed at that. That writer was really green, and didn't understand that out here, no one's word means anything."

"Did you save any of the tapes?"

Darla slowly shook her head. "Recorded over."

"Seems I've heard there are ways to retrieve recorded-over messages," Sharon said. "I'll have to check on it. If I wanted to visit with Mr. Harlon Swain, how would I go about it?"

"I don't have a number for him. David may have had one, but he would've disposed of it once he was finished jerking the poor man around. I suppose I'd try Marissa Cudmore."

Sharon tilted her head, wondering where she'd heard the name. She remembered. "Oh, the—"

"Right," Darla said. "Mammoth Studios. She was the studio liaison for the entire project—the writer, the actors, a director if they'd gone far enough to hire one, everything coordinated through her. I'd soft-pedal it with Marissa, Sharon. I doubt if *Dead On* was a real highlight of her career."

"Not exactly a feather in her cap," Sharon said.

"To put it mildly. Once David showed an interest in the project, the novel became a heavy buzz for a couple of weeks or so. *Variety, The Hollywood Reporter,* the trades picked up on it, then really roasted Mammoth when the deal fell through. They were all pretty embarrassed, with Marissa shouldering the blame."

"I'll be in touch with Ms. Cudmore right away."

"You'll need direction there," Darla said. "These studio execs won't talk to just anyone. You'll get an assistant with whom you'll leave a message. If you're someone important, she'll return your call in a week or two; someone she never heard of, forget it. Someone hot at the moment, say Harrison Ford, they'll punch right through. Chevy Chase can wait until hell freezes over."

"How about at home, in the evening?"

Darla laughed without humor, a bitter, hollow sound. "It's easier to get the number for the hot line in the Oval Office. Marissa would probably talk to me, if I were to call in person." She looked ruefully at the barred window. "Though I'm sort of occupied at the moment."

Sharon dug into her purse and then held Cherry Vick's business card between a thumb and forefinger. "How about an agent?" Sharon said.

Darla's plucked eyebrows moved closer together. "Let me see that."

Sharon got up and carried the card over to where Darla sat. Darla looked at the logo and read the name. "Not that agent. That woman's bad news."

Sharon sighed. "I was afraid of that. Poor old Preston Trigg." She showed Darla a look of intense concentration. "We need desperately to find out if there's anything to this, sweetheart. I don't have two *days* to wait to see this woman, much less two weeks or the rest of my life. Think hard. Do you know anyone with the pull to get me together with her like, after court today?"

Darla looked thoughtful, crossing her legs and clasping her hands over her knee. She looked at the ceiling. "You're becoming sort of a celebrity yourself over all this. Are you willing to conduct a little subterfuge?"

Sharon turned her palms up. "At this point I'm willing to try anything."

Darla licked her lips. She folded her arms. "I know of one person, then," she finally said.

22

Aaron Levy had three phone lines in addition to his fax. The number listed in the Los Angeles directory under Levy Talent Agency fed directly to his computer so that would-be clients, out-of-work writers, and bit-part actors could leave voice-mail messages. These were the calls to which Levy responded at his leisure, or sometimes not at all.

His other telephones weren't listed. One of these numbers he gave out to his special clients: major or minor stars, writers whose work had recently made it to the screen, or character actors who were constantly in demand as straight men to comedians or serial killers, the talent which made up the bread and butter of Levy's agency.

Only studios and producers were privy to Levy's third and most secret line, the one over which he made ninety percent of his outgoing calls, most of which went to the same studios and producers to whom he provided the number. Often the movie makers were just as unavailable to Levy as Levy was to his minor or would-be clients. In the long run, who was most in need of whom determined the outcome of the game.

It was one-fifteen in the afternoon when his special-client incoming line buzzed. He had one foot out the door, headed for a late lunch with a producer in Tarzana, and retreated to his desk with his mouth puckered in irritation. Even with special clients Levy was abrupt and businesslike. He made it a point never to deal with anyone on a personal level, because today's special client was often tomorrow's minor client, and the day after that was no longer a client at all. He sat down and spun his chair around, gazing through venetian blinds at traffic going back and forth on Ventura Boulevard. Sunlight filtered through a curtain of smog, illuminating the forest-covered San Gabriel peaks to the north. "Levy," he said brusquely. He pulled a notepad over in front of him and picked up a pen.

A cultured female voice with a slight Texas drawl said over the line, "Sharon Hays, Mr. Levy. How are you?"

Levy said nothing. He drew a dollar sign on his pad.

"I'm calling from behind the courtroom," Sharon said. "Are you keeping up with Darla's trial?"

Levy had no time for chitchat. "You coming around? If you are, I got to establish parameters."

There was a pause. Sharon said, "I'm not sure I . . ."

"Chet Verdon's a good guy, but don't get no idea I'm joined at the hip. I do business with a lot of lawyers. So the tabloid deal is still laying there. The television movie people are still calling; so far I'm putting them on hold. The exposure you're getting helps, but don't get no idea you're going to retire on this. Personally I think here, right now, the book is the thing."

"Darla's fighting for her life, Mr. Levy. Even if there is a possibility of a book, now isn't the time."

"Darla Cowan is old news. You are new news, hot right now. You are one of the focal points in what can be the trial of the decade. The movie guys are in a cautious pattern, but the book people get caught up. In a month the next greasy mechanic that schlongs the Long Island Lolita, who knows? But at this instant here, no telling what they might piss off trying to sign you."

Sharon's tone was puzzled. "Piss off?"

"That's, ha-ha, a term I use. What I mean is, they are more attuned to the proper value of your signature on the line." Levy pictured Sharon Hays, a tall, photogenic brunette with a forceful, crackly-sexy courtroom voice, Christ, every woman's fantasy, the previously unknown Texas female thrust into the spotlight and fielding the pressure. Maybe a cover photo wearing jeans, a little cheesecake with a rack of lawbooks in the background. A western shirt tight enough to show her figure, some pocket fringe . . .

"I'd be lying if I said it wasn't fascinating, Mr. Levy," Sharon said. "Do you know a woman named Cherry Vick?"

"Jesus. She hanging around?"

"She has been."

"Well, listen," Levy said, "you do not talk to her. You converse on this matter with Aaron C. Levy, no one else. I don't get where I am, letting my people down."

"You're Darla's agent. You don't feel as if you're letting *her* down? She might be entitled to a visit from you."

"She's a nice little girl. They are all nice little girls, but I'm making a living here."

There were five seconds of silence, with a hubbub of voices in the background. Sharon said, "I'm going to be late returning to court. I do have a favor to ask."

"Name it. Hey, you need a little front money, I can—"

"Could you get me a conference with Marissa Cudmore?"

Levy groped for a tin of Altoids. "That would not be a prudent move."

"She's the one I have to see," Sharon said.

"Which is why you need an agent. I know these things. Marissa Cudmore is a theatrical movie person. She is in search of the next Steve McQueen, not the current Marcia Clark, which happens to be the category in which you fall. No way is that the route you should go."

"There are reasons I'll have to explain, Mr. Levy. I speak with Ms. Cudmore, or I speak to no one."

"She can't make no theatrical movie on this. Look . . . may I call you Sharon?"

"Why not?"

"Look, Sharon, keeping your interests in mind,

you'll be spinning your wheels. Best you'll get from her, she'll call in people from the television division. And TV isn't the route here. Think book. Book, with a capital B. A couple of feelers, the proper calls placed to the two-one-two area code—"

"I have to go, Mr. Levy. I'm due in court."

"You do not hang up, not without my cell phone number. Is there a number on that pay phone? Something comes up, I'll have to—"

"You can't call me in court, sir," Sharon said. "I've already experienced that. I have a pen here, give me your cell phone."

Levy dictated the number, twice, then said, "I carry it on my person. Any place, any time, you can interrupt, I got time for you."

"I have time for you," Sharon said, "as long as it involves a conference with Marissa Cudmore. Those are my terms."

Levy drew a vicious slash through the dollar sign on his notepad. "Suppose I could arrange this. You'd be wasting time when we could be talking New York, the real dollars."

Sharon gave a long sigh. "I can see we don't have any—"

"For you, however, I can do this. You can commit to me, I can commit to you. If you want to see Marissa Cudmore, done. I do not foresee anything workable there, but hey, she is a citizen and reads the newspaper along with the rest of the world. She could tell her watercooler cohorts you came to see her, and in her business, with whom you have conversed lately is a very big deal. For one of mine I will walk the extra mile."

"It'll have to be late afternoon. There are a couple of more witnesses, but I expect the judge to cut this off before we get into East Coast prime time. Listen, I really have to hang up."

"Consider it done. Call my cell phone the moment you're free."

"I will. Thanks, Mr. Levy." Sharon disconnected.

Levy hung up and drummed his fingers. Jesus Christ, another schizo female. There were times when Aaron Levy felt he should have stayed with his father, running the pawnbroker in Queens. Always problems in this business. Darla Cowan, Jesus, her fuck scenes had guys humping fireplugs, she wanted to star in *Little Women* or some shit. Now she was in jail for offing her boyfriend. No telling what that was going to cost Aaron C. Levy in commissions. Now this other woman, could collect three, four million dollars talking into a tape recorder while some ghost wrote the book for peanuts, she wanted to talk to movie people. Everybody wants in pictures, Levy thought.

He thumbed through his Rolodex, punched in a number, waited through a series of rings. Levy said, "Yeah, put Marissa on. This is Aaron . . . Hell, no, Aaron *Levy,* what fucking Aaron you think I'm talking . . . She'll speak to me. You want to be in a world of shit, you try taking my number. Yeah, okay, I'll hold." He scratched a front tooth with his thumbnail as he waited. Suddenly he straightened in his chair. "Yeah, love," Levy said. "How you doing? Listen, I'm giving you an exclusive. Nobody else but you, you're the first one I thought of. Think big, now. I will give you three guesses who I can set up for you to see this afternoon."

Sharon had made the call from Darla's cell phone, standing inside the holding cell as the deputies led Darla back into court. She was now alone in the divided room, the wastebasket outside the bars stuffed with cheeseburger wrappers, the cell door standing open, the wall clock showing, God, 1:35. She was already five minutes late. Sharon made tracks, juggling her purse and briefcase, the slip of paper containing Aaron Levy's car phone number clenched lightly between her teeth as she hustled into court through the rear entry, headed across the bullpen toward the defense table.

The judge stared at her. So did the gallery. The TV

cameramen aimed his lens in her direction. Well, look at me, I'm Sandra Dee, Sharon thought; Sharon Hays, Broadway dropout, now star of the freaking week, her purse and briefcase about to fall on the floor, a piece of paper dangling from her mouth. She stopped in her tracks, wrapped one hand around the handles of her purse and briefcase, and used her free hand to take the phone slip from between her teeth. She said breathlessly, "I apologize for my tardiness, Your Honor," and then headed for her place with her cheeks a bright shade of crimson. On the prosecution side, Milton Breyer grinned at her. Kathleen Fraterno had her head down, studying but looked up with a blink of acknowledgment as Sharon passed.

As she circled behind Preston Trigg, headed for her place, Judge Rudin boomed out, "So glad you could join us, Counsel."

Sharon ignored the jurist and sank into her chair. Preston Trigg leaned over and said, "The judge likes promptness."

"Thanks a load," Sharon hissed, then put her lips near Darla's ear. "I got it done," she whispered. "Might've fudged a little on the circumstances, but—"

"If you're ready, *Miss Hays,*" Rudin growled from the bench, "we will now proceed."

Sharon closed her mouth with an audible click of teeth.

Rudin addressed the courtroom at large. "We will now hear the state's rebuttal to the defense's motion to exclude." Not *the court* will hear, Sharon thought, but *we* will hear, Rudin including himself as one of the viewing audience. The judge nodded to Breyer.

Breyer stood and grandly extended a palm-up hand toward Fraterno. "If the court please," Breyer said, "I'm going to defer to my colleague. Allow me to introduce Miss Kathleen Fraterno, who came in last night from Dallas."

Rudin folded a hand over his knuckles. "Ah, more Texas flavor." He waited for a laugh, got none, then said, "Proceed, Miss Fraterno."

Kathleen rose and peered around as if to say, If anyone's expecting me to bow, they're wasting their time. She looked every bit as put off by the judge and all the TV bullshit as Sharon felt. Sharon was glad that Breyer hadn't referred to Kathleen as his "assistant," or more to the point, his flunky, and suspected that old Milt would have done so if he thought he could have gotten away with it. Fraterno took a final cursory look at her notes and approached the podium, carrying a copy of Sharon's exclusion motion. She stood in erect posture and addressed the bench in her pleasant, well-modulated courtroom voice. "First of all, Your Honor, we wish to defer our rebuttal until tomorrow morning. We request briefing time in order to address all pertinent issues."

A murmur of surprise went through the gallery. Preston Trigg's mouth opened like a fish's on dry land. "We'd object to any continuance, Judge. If they've got argument, let's hear it."

Trigg made his statement with out-thrust jaw, and Sharon was certain that the viewing audience was impressed, but her co-counsel's objection was a waste of time. Fraterno was entitled to research before responding in a *legitimate* court of law. And in this sideshow, if Drake Rudin saw an opportunity to spend one more day in front of the camera, Kathleen would win her request, hands down. The state's motion was a stall—Sharon hadn't read Kathleen's brief, but was certain that Fraterno wouldn't have found any points of law which Sharon herself had missed—but why on earth would they want a delay? Sharon popped her briefcase open and stared at the printout from Rob's bank as she waited for the judge to come to a decision.

Rudin spoke up in a hurry. "Overruled, Counsel," he said to Trigg, then looked to Fraterno. "How much time does the state of Texas need?" he asked.

"Overnight, Your Honor. And so this session won't be a complete waste of time, we have another witness to present."

Rudin pinched his lower lip. "Not having to do with the weapon?"

"Not the weapon per se, your honor, where it was found, but . . . Well, with the court's permission, I'd like to go ahead." Fraterno's tone was polite yet forceful; the court had no option other than to let her put her witness on, which Kathleen damned well knew.

Sharon looked to the back. She supposed that Stan Green was about to make a filibuster appearance, or perhaps another of Dallas County's forensics people. Not the gun per se, Fraterno had said, which meant that Texas was about to produce testimony about the .38 without addressing Sharon's motion to exclude. Fraterno was a whiz at this sort of thing. Once when Sharon was a prosecutor, she and Kathleen had tried a particularly sticky murder case. The police had burst into the suspect's apartment with insufficient probable cause—none, actually, just a patrol cop's off-the-wall statement that the suspect had acted suspiciously when carrying out his garbage—and taken a knife from the dishwasher which was flecked with the victim's blood. Sharon and Kathleen had agreed going in that the judge wouldn't admit the knife, no way, so Fraterno had devised a different plan of attack. She'd produced the suspect's sister—under the guise of testimony as to the suspect's activities prior to the crime—who'd told from the witness stand how the suspect had fixed her dinner the night before the murder. Kathleen's direct examination had brought out a description of the knife—which the suspect had used in carving a roast—down to its ivory handle, which had been sufficient, along with graphic forensic testimony regarding the vicious sawing wounds in the victim's torso, to plant the knife in the jury's mind without actually introducing the weapon into evidence. Something similar was coming with regard to the .38, Sharon knew, and she had to be on her toes. She sat slightly forward as Fraterno called her witness.

"State calls," Fraterno said, "Curtis Nussbaum."

Sharon recoiled as if slapped. She fought to recover,

and pulled out the bank printout along with the photo
of Nussbaum and his security man on the set of *Spring
of the Comanche,* as she waited for the witness to
come down the aisle.

Nussbaum made his entry with a minimum of
aplomb, man-behind-the-scenes fashion, his walk brisk
and businesslike, no sag, no swagger. His head was
recently shaved, and he wore a conservative blue suit
and navy tie. His shoes were dully polished, Mr.
Believable-in-the-flesh, here to do his civic duty. He
took the oath in a slightly gravelly voice and ascended
to the stand.

Fraterno regarded her witness like an old friend.
"State your full name, please."

"Curtis Laydon Nussbaum." The agent's expression
didn't change. His permanent smirk was gone, replaced with an honest, bland look, and Sharon decided
that Nussbaum might be a better actor than some of
his clients. Where had the state come up with this
guy? Agents normally kept hidden from the public eye
while their clients took center stage, and most agents
would flee the country rather than make a courtroom
appearance, so why was Nussbaum all of a sudden Mr.
Cooperative? If he's willing to talk, Sharon thought,
he's got a profit motive.

Fraterno leaned on the podium, bent one knee, and
rested one high-heeled shoe on its toe. "And what is
your occupation, sir?"

"Theatrical agent."

"More to the point, are you David Spencer's agent?"

Nussbaum's gaze flicked to Sharon in a manner
which made her uncomfortable, then went back to
Fraterno. "Was."

"Before he died, yes. But you have other clients,
don't you?"

"More than a hundred." Nussbaum's answer caused
Sharon to blink; most agents' client list was the dark-
est of secrets. *Famous* clients, sure, no one minded
being photographed at dinner with Tom Cruise, but
the ninety-nine percent of the actors whom the agent

sent to F.A.O. Schwarz as Playskool blocks, or who
dressed up in chicken suits and stood on the curb to
wave passersby into restaurants, those were assign-
ments the agent would leave swept under the rug. Out
of the hundred clients Nussbaum represented, Sharon
imagined that the viewing audience would recognize
four or five names, no more than that.

Fraterno flipped over a page in Sharon's motion to
exclude. "Mr. Nussbaum, generally, how would you
classify your relationship to your clients?"

"I take a personal interest in all my clients," Nussbaum said. He pronounced the adjective "poisonal,"
Brooklyn fashion, and shifted his weight in the chair.

"Do you perform more functions than just getting
your clients acting jobs?" Fraterno asked.

"Most certainly." Most soitanly.

"And could you describe a few of those?"

Nussbaum assumed a tone of pride. "I do everything for my people so that they can concentrate on
their careers and not worry about the details."

"So you pay their bills . . ."

"From a trust account, yes."

". . . provide financial advice . . ."

"When I'm requested to."

"So your relationship is much closer than, say, lawyer to client."

"I would hope so." Nussbaum favored the defense
table with a disdainful blink.

"More so with some than with others?" Fraterno
asked.

"I try not to play favorites. But it's natural that, in
dealing with large numbers, you're going to be closer
to some."

"Mr. Nussbaum, how would you describe your relationship with David Spencer?"

"More uncle to nephew. Even father to son. I got
that boy his very first acting job."

He got most of his clients their first job, Sharon
thought, but David Spencer was on Nussbaum's A-list
because he'd just happened to hit it big. She suspected

that if Spencer had been a flop on the screen, Nussbaum would have been less his surrogate dad and more his distant relative. She glanced at Darla. She was doing a good job, holding her head up and listening intently.

"Did you and Mr. Spencer see each other socially?" Fraterno said.

"Alla time." Nussbaum leaned on his elbow. "Alla time."

"Exchange gifts?" Fraterno's lashes lifted as she looked up at the witness.

"Uh-oh, Sharon thought, here comes the gun. She straightened, her attention firmly on the coming exchange of words.

"He'd give me things at Hanukkah, even though he was Protestant."

"And would you return the favor? At Christmastime, say?"

"I tried to make my presents to David more practical. He had so much already."

Sharon permitted herself a grim smile. The image of Curtis Nussbaum thoughtfully shopping for tokens of his esteem was a bit much.

"I see." There was the barest pause, a change in Fraterno's cadence which Sharon recognized. The subtle alteration in diction meant that Kathleen wanted everyone's undivided attention. The ploy was more effective than some lawyers' tricks such as slamming books down on tables or yelling at the tops of their lungs. "Mr. Nussbaum," Fraterno said, "did you ever give David Spencer a pistol?"

"Yes. For protection. A boy in his position, strangers coming up to him all the time . . ."

"He could have been in danger?"

"Happens every day in Hollywood. Stalkers, you know."

Sharon pictured Spencer, staggering around in front of Planet Hollywood drunk as a lord, and wondered what the safety factor would have been if the actor had been packing his gun. Question of who was protecting whom from what, Sharon thought. She picked up her pen and wrote: Find out if Nussbaum tipped the FBI as to the gun's hiding place in the house. If he did, and if Darla was telling the truth that she'd never seen the weapon before, it stood to reason that Nussbaum had planted the gun or had it down. Curtis Nussbaum was at the top of Sharon's list for alternate theory number one, and the more the agent talked, the more Sharon liked the idea.

"When did you give him this pistol?"

Nussbaum reflectively regarded the ceiling. "It was, let's see, about a year ago."

"Was this an expensive weapon?"

Nussbaum firmly shook his head. "I wanted something for him, practical. A lot of Hollywood weapons are popguns, twenty-twos, would stop nothing if the situation was critical."

"I see. Could you describe this weapon for us?"

"I had a client, used to be a cop. He gave me this gun. It was a revolver."

Fraterno shifted her weight and crossed her forearms on the podium. "Wasn't it what is commonly known as a police special?"

"That's what he called it," Nussbaum said. "Myself, I'm not into weapons."

"A thirty-eight-caliber?"

Sharon tensed her thighs, ready to stand.

"Yes," Nussbaum said.

Fraterno glanced toward the prosecution table, but as yet made no move to walk over and pick up the box containing the pistol. Sharon relaxed some, but not much.

"When did you last see David Spencer, Mr. Nussbaum?" Fraterno's tone was matter-of-fact, almost casual.

"Alive? I flew down to Dallas and identified his—"

"Alive, sir," Fraterno said, "before the . . . tragedy."

There was a sniffling sound from within the gallery, and the television camera swiveled in that direction. Sharon turned as a young woman in the second row blew her nose. Sharon counted three more females in tears, then faced the front once more. One gotcha for Kathleen, Sharon thought. She wondered how many of those women had personally known David Spencer. She'd bet that none of them had.

"I was at David's house," Nussbaum said, "the day he flew to Texas. Helped him pack and then drove him to the airport. Him and his lady." He glanced at Darla, then steadied his gaze on Fraterno.

"David's house being on the beach? Malibu?"

"Yes."

"Did he pack the .38 pistol you'd given him?"

"Yeah. I remember it was loaded. David didn't pay a lot of attention to details. I had him unload the pistol and put the bullets in another suitcase, which is the only way the airlines will let you check a weapon."

"Thank you. To be very clear, Mr. Nussbaum, immediately after David packed his gun, what did you then do?"

"Carried both pieces of luggage to my car and put them in the trunk." Nussbaum smiled sadly. "You're a person's agent, sometimes you're his valet." He chuckled, and there were a few small titters in the courtroom.

"Did you drive him to the airport immediately after that?"

"Hadda wait awhile. David finally brought Miss Cowan's things, and the two of us, the butler and I, loaded her stuff in beside David's."

"During the entire time, were you ever away from David's luggage?"

"Only when I was behind the wheel and the luggage was in the trunk," Nussbaum said. Sharon felt a surge of admiration; Fraterno was conducting one crackerjack of a direct examination. She'd subtly lapsed into calling the slain actor "David," omitting his last name, an age-old prosecutor's trick designed to humanize the victim in the jury's eyes. Or in this case the viewing audience's eyes, which for all practical purposes amounted to the same thing.

"Was the trunk locked?"

"Yes. It's automatic."

"So, without unlocking your trunk, is it fair to say that no one could have tampered with David's luggage?"

"More than fair."

"So, Mr. Nussbaum . . ." Fraterno looked as if she were deep in thought, stumped. Which was all an act; Kathleen had never examined a witness in her life when she didn't plan ten or fifteen questions ahead. When she had everyone's attention riveted on the witness, she finally asked, "When you arrived at the airport, did a skycap take the passenger's luggage? Miss Cowan's and David's?" With the same subtlety with which she humanized David Spencer, Fraterno distanced prospective jurors from Darla by calling her "Miss Cowan." Sharon made a note that during her cross, Darla would be Darla and David would be Mr. Spencer, anything which might turn the tables a bit.

"Rolled a cart right up to the curb," Nussbaum said.

"And carried the baggage directly to check-in," Fraterno finished. "Mr. Nussbaum, are you relatively certain that the pistol and bullets were in David Spencer's luggage when he left for Dallas?"

"Oh, they were in there." Nussbaum flashed a tiny grin. "Unless Houdini was inside one of those suitcases."

Kathleen smiled back at the witness as if the two of them shared a secret. She then tossed the spitter without missing a beat, without altering her tone so much as half an octave. "When did you next see the weapon, sir?"

Nussbaum opened his mouth to answer.

Sharon bounced to her feet. "Approach, Your Honor?" Kathleen had almost pulled it off, lulling the defense with the baggage routine. Sharon's voice trembled with anxiety. At the podium, Fraterno's shoulders slumped.

Rudin gave come-hither gestures. Sharon went quickly to the bench with Kathleen bringing up the rear. "She's sandbagging us, Judge," Sharon whispered.

"Oh?" Rudin raised his eyebrows. "How is that?"

"The witness is about to testify," Sharon said, "that he's seen the gun today, probably in this courtroom or just out in the hall. Miss Fraterno then plans to have him identify the weapon."

Caught, Fraterno tried to salvage what she could. "He did see the weapon, Your Honor, out in the witness's anteroom, and he identified it. What's so . . . ?" She was the picture of innocence. Rudin's forehead wrinkled in puzzlement.

"What's *so*, Your Honor," Sharon said, "is that Miss Fraterno is attempting to make an end run around our motion to suppress. If the witness identifies the gun, our motion becomes moot."

"I hadn't thought of that," Rudin said, scratching his eyebrow.

"How about," said Fraterno in her best helpful soprano, "if he merely says he's seen it without making a physical identification?"

"Oh, come on." Sharon threw a glare in Fraterno's direction, then appealed to the judge. "Mr. Nussbaum can take the pistol up to the point of embarkation for Texas, Your Honor, which he's already done. If he'd made the trip to Dallas himself, he could testify that he saw Spencer unpacking the gun at the hotel. But that's as far as it goes. He can't core the apple. We'll forcefully object to any identification of the weapon subsequent to the FBI search." She caught the look of hesitation on Rudin's face and narrowed her eyes. "Straight to the appellate court if necessary, sir, before this witness utters another word."

Rudin sputtered and spewed. "You'd appeal me?"

"Right on," Sharon said.

"I don't like threats, Counsel," Rudin snapped. He soft-pedaled his anger, however; not only was the nation watching, Sharon had him and he knew it; an irate lawyer stalking to the appeals court in the midst of a hearing, and then returning minutes later with a reversal, would tarnish Rudin's star for all the world to see. He said apologetically, "But don't have him identify the weapon, Miss Fraterno. Anything which occurred after the FBI search, I won't admit it until after you've presented your rebuttal in the morning."

Fraterno pouted in defeat. "Yes, Your Honor," she said.

"So your witness may have to return." Rudin glanced at the TV camera. He bent his hands at the wrists, palms down, and made a shooing motion. "So let's move along now," he said.

As the lawyers marched side by side away from the bench, Sharon hissed from the side of her mouth, "Nice try, Kathleen."

Fraterno cut her eyes in Sharon's direction. "You think so, huh?" she whispered with a smile.

Sharon flopped back into her chair as Fraterno moved in behind the podium. Darla flashed Sharon a curious glance. Sharon patted the actress's arm, and thought that Darla was responding as well as could be expected. The inclination to offer emotional support was something which Sharon had to ignore. She knew what was coming; her attempt to skirt the exclusionary motion defeated, Fraterno would close as quickly as possible. Sharon bent her head and thumbed through photos. Fraterno's expression was bland and effectively covered her defeat at the bench. She said to Nussbaum, "To capsule, sir."

Nussbaum rested his elbows on the armrests of his chair, and let his hands dangle loosely over his lap.

"You helped David pack for his flight."

"Yes."

"You carried his luggage to the airport, with the gun and the bullets in separate suitcases?"

"That's right."

"And the last you saw of the luggage was when the skycap loaded it onto his cart."

"And rolled it inside the terminal, yes."

"And during all this activity," Fraterno said, "no one had the opportunity to remove the gun from the luggage."

"Not so's I wouldn't have seen."

"Thank you." Fraterno offered a perfunctory glance toward Milton Breyer, then faced the judge. "I have no further questions of this witness now, Your Honor. But will respectfully notice the court, we intend to recall Mr. Nussbaum tomorrow morning. *Prior* to any ruling on the defense's motion to exclude."

Sharon nodded silently. Unable to come right out and have Nussbaum identify the pistol, Kathleen had done the next best thing by showing that her witness knew more and that the audience would hear from him again. Sharon laid the photos aside and folded her hands.

"All right," Rudin said. "The witness is excused until nine a.m."

Fraterno strolled toward the prosecution table as Nussbaum stepped down from the witness box. Sharon stood and said over the whispered hubbub from the gallery, "Your Honor, we have cross to offer."

Rudin looked mildly amused as Nussbaum halted in his tracks. Rudin said, "Isn't the proper time for cross after the prosecution has completed examination of the witness? I know things are different down in Texas, but . . ."

And things in California, Sharon thought, are straight from looney tunes. "In all due respect, Your Honor, no. Miss Fraterno has announced that she has no further questions. Any recalling of the witness amounts to fresh direct examination. This direct is finished, and I submit we're entitled to cross." She tried to look apologetic, but thought she failed in the attempt. "Just a few, Your Honor. Five minutes."

Rudin's look told her that she'd just qualified as Number One Pain. The judge said irritably, "Make it fast, Counsel. We should be winding this up."

Which made Sharon wonder if Rudin had an appointment with Cherry Vick, the literary agent. She flashed a grateful smile. "Thank you, Your Honor." Then, as the judge simmered in place, she approached the podium. She left Mrs. Welton's pictures at the defense table; she'd made a snap decision not to get into the mysterious stranger as yet, but had a couple of things she wanted to establish here and now.

"I'm Sharon Hays, Mr. Nussbaum," she began, "representing Darla Cowan. We've talked before."

Nussbaum was in the act of sitting down, having returned to the witness's chair. "Yeah, I remember."

"You remember the occasion of the call?"

"Yeah." Nussbaum's attitude was hostile, his eyes dead coals. "About your little girl."

"My daughter, yes. Do you recall the gist of our conversation?"

"You had a kid with Rob Stanley."

"Another of your clients?"

Milton Breyer was on his feet. "Objection. This isn't relevant."

"That's how I see it," Rudin growled. He pointed a finger. "We'll have no self-promotion in my court-room, Miss Hays."

Sharon was stunned. No self-promotion? In *Rudin's* court? And what, she thought, is self-promoting about admitting to being the unwed mother of Rob Stanley's child? She fought her anger. "If the court will bear with me," she said, "the relevance will show itself in just a couple of more questions."

Rudin leaned back and folded his arms. "See that it does, Counsel." There was an open threat both in his tone and his expression.

"Thank you." Sharon turned back to the witness. "Do you represent Rob Stanley, Mr. Nussbaum?"

"Yes." Nussbaum's answer sounded like an admission of guilt.

"And in your capacity as Rob Stanley's agent," Sharon said, "do you also handle his financial affairs? Pay his bills and whatnot?"

Nussbaum pinched the crease in his trousers. "Sometimes I forget."

"Forget whose bills you're paying?" Sharon sounded incredulous.

"Never that. Only, with so much going, occasionally

I might let one or two go unpaid awhile. Like in your case."

There was an audible gasp on Sharon's left, Kathleen Fraterno. In trying to pre-rationalize that he hadn't been paying Rob's child support, Nussbaum had opened the door a crack. Sharon placed her shoulder firmly against the wood and barged on in. "I didn't ask you, sir, what you forgot occasionally or what you did in my case. I asked you if, in addition to your agent's duties, you also rode herd on Rob Stanley's financial affairs."

Nussbaum was obviously flustered. "Yeah, I guess I do."

Sharon discontinued the line of questioning regarding Rob; she'd established what she'd wanted, that Nussbaum's signature appeared on bank accounts other than David Spencer's, and now laid the groundwork for her next ten questions or so. "How many of your clients have you as a signatory on their bank accounts, sir?"

"Well . . . off the top of my head . . ."

"The top of your head won't suffice, Mr. Nussbaum. Do you handle financial affairs for all one hundred of your clients?"

Nussbaum waved a hand as if batting a mosquito. "I wouldn't have time for all that."

"Fifty?"

Nussbaum squirmed in place. "I wouldn't—"

"Twenty?" Sharon tilted her head. "If it's less than twenty, sir, I'd think you'd be able to remember that many. Off the top of your head, the bottoms of your feet, off of anything."

"Objection." Fraterno was standing. Sharon was certain that Kathleen didn't know where this line of questioning was going, but sharp-as-a-tack Fraterno would hold down the damage any way she could.

"Sustained." Rudin scowled with his face angled toward the camera. "No more levity, Miss Hays."

"Yes, sir." Sharon gripped the edges of the podium.

"Mr. Nussbaum, let's go the other way. Do you handle financial affairs for as many as *five* of your clients?"

Nussbaum shrugged. "Four."

"Only four. Odd you wouldn't remember that figure. Are all four of these clients in David Spencer's category? I believe you said, he was like a son to you. So these other three, Rob Stanley included, do you feel parental instincts toward the other three as well?"

"That was a figure of speech."

"Oh? Well, David Spencer and Rob Stanley, we're all familiar with those names. Are these other two persons for whom you write checks, are they novices in the business?"

Nussbaum regarded her with dark liquid eyes.

"I'll rephrase," Sharon said. "Are they actors who, say, play the bellman who schleps the star's baggage up to his room?"

"No one like that," Nussbaum said.

"Well, then, are they perhaps what you would classify as stars?"

One corner of Nussbaum's mouth tugged to the side. "You might."

"Could we say, then, that your fatherly instincts intensify in direct proportion to the size of the client's bank account?"

"Objection." Fraterno shot up. "This is badgering, Your Honor."

"Sustained." Rudin seemed on the verge of apoplexy. "Miss Hays . . ."

"I'll withdraw it, Your Honor." Sharon glanced at her watch. "I have only one more question, perhaps two." She smiled at the witness. "These other surrogate children, Mr. Nussbaum. Have you given firearms to all of them?"

Nussbaum bristled. "I don't see what that—?"

"Your Honor." Sharon turned to the bench. "I'm simmering down here, but I think that's a legitimate question."

"You'll have to answer, Mr. Nussbaum." Rudin

spoke as if it was an effort to get the words out of his mouth.

"Is Mr. Spencer," Sharon said, "the only client to whom you gave a firearm? It's a fairly simple question, sir."

Nussbaum raised the white flag in surrender. "Just him," he finally said.

Sharon looked at Darla, who watched her with an expression near hero worship. I'm not deserving of any applause just yet, Sharon thought. A long way from it, in fact. She smiled once more at Curtis Nussbaum. "So, did you feel that Mr. Spencer was the only one of your clients who might've needed protection?"

"He went out in public more."

"Was he more in danger for that reason? Or were there other characteristics of Mr. Spencer's which could have put him in danger from others? His overall attitude perhaps?"

Nussbaum went on the defensive. "That boy had a tough upbringing."

"How unfortunate for him. Mr. Nussbaum, during your association with Mr. Spencer, how many times did you furnish bail for him?"

Nussbaum spread his hands as if in supplication. "Time or two."

"Time or two. Did that include last Friday night in Dallas?"

"He got misunderstood a lot."

"Seems he did," Sharon said. "One more thing, sir. Did you feel that arming Mr. Spencer with a weapon was in the best interests of the public in general?"

"I was looking out for him. Nobody else."

"Obviously." Sharon closed her legal pad. "And you watched over him so well that David Spencer is the only one of your clients who's dead at the moment. Isn't he? Maybe you should think of some different goodwill gifts for your clients in the future. I anticipate we'll be talking again before this hearing is over, sir." She turned to the bench. "No further questions, Judge. Just for today, I'm through with this guy."

Judge Rudin recessed the hearing until tomorrow, and Sharon noted the jurist in animated conversation with Curtis Nussbaum as Darla's guards came forward to take the actress to jail for the night. Yesterday, Rudin had inquired about an agent for his daughter, but Sharon now wondered if he was hustling Nussbaum in his own behalf. After all, every lawyer, witness, judge, and juror connected with the O.J. trial had secured a book deal, so why should Rudin be any different? And not only was the *judge* interviewing an agent right there in the courtroom, so was Preston Trigg. As soon as the judge had recessed the hearing, old Pres had lit out as if his pants were on fire, and now jabbered earnestly with Cherry Vick in behind the spectators section. Sharon held up a hand, palm out, in order to halt Darla's guards in their tracks, then leaned over and said softly to the actress, "You know I had to do that, don't you?"

"Attack Curt Nussbaum?" Darla seemed totally confused.

Sharon nodded. "We're seeing a lot of this guy, Darla, in more ways than one. He's just too damned interested in this case to be an innocent bystander, for one thing, and dollars will get you doughnuts that he, or someone he's hired, is the anonymous tipper who told the FBI where to look for the gun."

"You think Curt had something to do with David's murder?"

Sharon felt a surge of pity and gently touched Darla's arm. With all of her ability onstage and onscreen, all of her wealth and fame, Darla continued to be frightened and insecure. "First of all, right now," Sharon said. "Quit thinking of that guy as Good Old Curt Nussbaum. Think of him as an asshole, a rotten s.o.b., whatever, but dismiss any respect you've ever had for this man. The prosecutors never would have thought of going to him. He approached them, which means that for some reason he wants to help them convict you. He is not your friend any more than Milton Breyer is your friend.

"Now that that's off my chest," Sharon said, "I'll answer your question. As to whether he could be the killer, I don't think anything, but I intend to find out. If he knew where the pistol was hidden, he either put it there or had someone else do so. A lot of questions I have, they'll be answered between now and in the morning. So for now let's leave it that you don't love Nussbaum any longer, okay?" She motioned for the guards, who stepped forward. "I can promise nothing, Darla," Sharon said. "But know this. If you're still in jail tomorrow night and we haven't gotten your arrest warrant thrown out or the case dismissed entirely, it won't be because I haven't broken my neck trying. Sleep as well as you can tonight. Tomorrow is a big, big day."

Her eyes misted as the uniforms led Darla out the prisoner's exit, Darla casting a fearful look over her shoulder as she disappeared from view. Sharon firmed her mouth, walked quickly to the rear and out into the corridor. On the way she passed Cherry Vick and Preston Trigg without a word to either of them. In the hallway she stood near a bench and tugged up the antenna on Darla's cellular phone. She punched in Aaron Levy's number. As she waited for the connection, Preston Trigg came out of the court and walked up to her. Sharon flipped the hinge, disconnecting her call.

Trigg placed hands on hips. "How come you don't want to cooperate with this woman?" He thumbed over his shoulder.

Sharon looked past him and saw no one. She said, "You mean, Cherry Vick?"

"Yeah."

"I'll ask you, how's come you *do* want to cooperate with her?" Sharon said.

"She's talking serious dollars, for one thing."

Sharon sighed, folded her arms, and jutted one hip

outward. "Go for it, then. Just don't include me in any plans."

Trigg frowned. "She wants us both. Why'n hell not?"

"Don't think I'm playing goody two-shoes. We're all in it for the money in the long run, Pres. It's just, I don't think talking book deals before you've fulfilled your obligation to your client is the right thing to do. And even then, I'd have to think long and hard on it. I can't exactly explain why, but it's against my nature. I know something about that kind of deal. They'll want to hire a ghostwriter and then have you pretend you wrote the book yourself. I'd feel like the biggest fake in the world. But if you can live with it . . ."

"Is it your nature to blow the deal for me? She doesn't want to talk, just me, she wants us both."

Or me alone, Sharon thought, but didn't say so. She hesitated. She needed Preston Trigg, at least for the duration of the proceedings in California. To hell with it, she finally thought, I can find another lawyer on the same block where I found this one. She said, "I wouldn't want this to upset our cozy relationship, Pres, but hear me out. As lawyer to lawyer, I think it's a gray area as to ethics, so let your conscience be your guide. If you can make a book deal, more's the power. But as someone with a little experience on the show-biz side, I'll give you the benefit for what it's worth. If an agent's out chasing you, she's hard up. The ones who can do you the most good wait for you to call them. That's the way it works." She flipped open the cell phone. "Now if you'll excuse me, I've got a client to represent. If Ms. Vick puts any more pressure on you, just tell her that Sharon Hays had her own agent to call."

23

Sharon found a vacant office in the building, borrowed an unoccupied word processor, and prepared a couple of legal papers. She worked with one eye on the door, rehearsing her response should anyone come in and question what she was doing.

She finished her task in ten minutes, signed her applications, and then hustled back upstairs to Judge Rudin's court. Rudin had left, but his clerk was at her desk, working away. She was a woman in her forties who, considering the mountains of files stacked on all sides of her as her boss goofed off for the afternoon, exhibited a cheerful attitude which was nothing short of amazing. Sharon presented her applications. The clerk read the papers over, then looked up with one eyebrow raised inquisitively. "You'll have to get private service on these," she said. "It's too late in the day for our warrant officer to—"

"I plan to serve them myself," Sharon said, smiling in appreciation. "If you could just certify them for me."

The clerk nodded, placed a couple of official-looking stamps on the documents, and then added her initials with a pen. Sharon thanked the woman, then stuffed the papers into her briefcase. She hurried to the elevators, rode to the ground floor, and left the building. Aaron Levy was waiting for her.

She would say this for the agent, he gave the impression of a man on the move. Levy paced back and forth on the courthouse steps, checking his watch over and over, his pinched features set in impatience. He wore a checkered houndstooth coat and didn't bother with formalities. As Sharon walked up, he said, "I'm double-parked. I can get a ticket here." He pointed to where a white four-door Chrysler sat near the curb, motor running, then headed down the steps at a near jog.

Sharon stood dumbstruck and watched him go. Then she shrugged, hefted her satchel, hiked up her shoulder bag, murmured, "Hello, Mr. Levy. How are you?" and fell in rapid step behind him.

The drive out the Hollywood Freeway was the weirdest trip in Sharon's memory. She believed in business before pleasure, but Aaron Levy took the impersonal approach to levels which Sharon had never before imagined. My God, she thought, the man is Darla's agent. You'd think at least he'd ask about her.

Levy drove with both hands on the wheel in stop-and-go traffic, sending his passenger lurching forward every time he threw on the brakes. Sharon sat as up-right as possible, clutching her satchel to her chest and holding onto the door for dear life. As they passed the Normandie Avenue exit, Levy said, "If you're going to interest these people, you're going to have to play up the sexual angle."

Sharon listed to the left as Levy whipped around a vegetable truck, and laid on his horn with an ear-splitting blare. "I don't know that there is any sexual angle," she said.

"Well, there you may have to improvise." Levy waved one hand around, then wrapped his fingers around the steering wheel. "Works this way, for which you need some experience to understand. No way is anyone going to put a film in theaters rehashing what everybody in the country has already seen on televi-sion. You got to have a different angle. If you know, maybe, who David Spencer was shtupping which might have caused Darla Cowan to kill him, you got maybe a ghost of a chance. I think you're wasting time regardless of what angle you got. But if it takes this for you to see the light and talk literary contracts, it takes it. Some people, you have to let see for themselves."

Sharon carefully set her satchel on the floorboard. "I'm not presenting any angle, sexual or otherwise, to the effect that Darla committed the crime, Mr. Levy. Because she didn't."

"Yeah, well. I'm just what-iffing here."

"Someone's interested in something. At least Marissa Cudmore's agreed to talk to me."

"Ah. That means nothing in this business. That means that Marissa Cudmore can say at the cocktail party, she talked over a deal with Sharon Hays, Darla Cowan's lawyer, who everybody's seen on television. She can wave her drink around and say"—here Levy changed to a mimicking falsetto—"'I just couldn't get excited' or, 'It just wasn't for us,' which are both bullshit nebulous terms meaning she'd have her ass in a sling with the people upstairs if she tried to produce such a picture. The deals she turns down are as much to talk about as the ones she does. Either way gets her noticed. No way is this meeting going to amount to anything."

It's going to amount to more than you expect, Sharon thought. She measured her words carefully before saying, "You know Curtis Nussbaum was in court today, don't you?"

Levy took his gaze off the road and glared at her. "That kind of talk will get you nowhere with Aaron C. Levy. Nussbaum can do nothing I can't. You want to talk to him, feel free."

"Look out," Sharon said breathlessly. Then, as Levy jammed on the brakes and stopped no more than six inches from a Porsche's rear bumper, she said, "No, he was testifying. That's all I was saying. Other than cross-examining the man, I didn't say a word to him."

"Better for you you didn't." Levy's tone showed total lack of curiosity as to what Nussbaum might've said from the witness stand. "That's not a smart thing for an agent to do, testifying in court. Depending on which side you're taking, might get you in the middle between a studio and an actor. Lose your stroke in both places."

"What's your overall take on Curtis Nussbaum as an agent, Mr. Levy?"

Levy vigorously shook his head. "You don't get Aaron C. Levy to bad-mouth nobody in the business. Curtis Nussbaum has been around a lot of years."

"Which means you'd know a lot about him." Sharon gentled her tone. "A man who has his finger on the pulse as much as you."

Levy seemed to think that one over. He steered the Chrysler to the right, into the exit approach lane. "Curtis Nussbaum's got some good clients," Levy said. "Let's just say, he takes risks that the rest of us wouldn't talk about. Beyond those words, you're getting me to say nothing bad about the man."

Visiting a movie lot was one of Sharon's fantasies, another hangover from her actress days, so her interest perked up when Levy, talking business and filling her in, gave her the rundown on Mammoth Pictures as they neared the studio. Mammoth was one of the biggies, Levy said, with a reputation somewhere between Universal—which offered liberal benefits and vacation policies—and Disney, which was known in the biz as Moushwitz or Duckau, depending on who you talked to. Mammoth was easier on its actors and writers than Disney, but was a lot more conservative profit-wise, which meant, according to Levy, that they wouldn't be interested in a movie about a murder case which hadn't even been to trial. Dustin Hoffman, John Travolta, bankable stars, were all that Mammoth would talk about, betting on projects reasonably sure to score big, first box office weekend. Levy cruised up to the studio gate at five o'clock. As the guard used the phone to check Levy's entry credentials Sharon peered through the gate into the grounds. God, the Mammoth lot was a freaking beehive.

Low-slung buildings and house trailers stood on

both sides of a path as far as she could see, and barely visible in the distance were scaled-down replicas of the White House and Treasury Building exactly as they appeared in Washington. Abutting the White House was a big-city tenement neighborhood, and farther to the right towered a snow-capped peak. As Sharon watched, an Indian in full headdress talking on a cell phone wandered by, and a man tugged a wheeled cage along as a tiger snarled and paced inside. There were cops in uniform buddying around with muscular Tarzan types clad in loincloths. The guard hung up the phone, came to the window, and waved Levy's Chrysler through.

Levy drove past a row of one-story buildings, dressing rooms with glitzy stars on the doors, and parked in front of a trailer house. On the roof was a sign reading, CUDMORE PROD. He got out without a word, stepped up onto a porch, and went through a wooden door. Sharon waited a moment, unsure of herself, then lugged her satchel out of the car and followed the agent in.

She was in a low-ceilinged, paneled reception area which contained one wooden desk, a water cooler, and a table piled high with movie scripts. The scripts all looked identical, plain white typing paper with a single brad at the top to hold the pages together, and a pasteboard cover bearing an agent's name. Behind the desk sat a longish-haired, smooth-cheeked man in his twenties, reading a screenplay with his feet propped up. He wore jeans, an oversized tee, and sandals without socks. He tossed the script aside, mumbled, "Piece of shit," got up, and pulled another script off the pile. He paused between the table and his desk, and offered Levy a bored impersonal stare.

Levy said. "Yeah. Aaron Levy for Marissa. I got Sharon Hays with me."

The youngster looked Sharon over head to toe. His expression brightened in recognition. "Sure, Darla Cowan trial, right?" His manner and tone of voice were slightly effeminate.

Sharon shifted her weight and let her satchel dangle by her hip. "Hearing. It's a hearing."

"Whatever. Marissa's expecting you, but she's on the phone. Wait here, I'll signal her." He walked to the back, opened a door, and stuck his head in around the jamb.

Levy took a step closer to Sharon. He smelled of tangy aftershave. "We wanna get in and out as fast as we can," he said in a low tone. "This woman's a time waster. No way is she interested in this. You just listen to her bullshit and then we'll leave. East Coast is three hours ahead of us, I can still call New York and talk book deal today. You with me?"

"I'll keep it in mind," Sharon said.

The youngster returned and hooked a thumb over his shoulder. "Be a minute," he said. "She's still talking." Then he sat, picked up a script, and began to read.

Sharon glanced at the young man's desk; his phone had three line buttons, none of which were lit. Levy followed her gaze, folded his arms, and leaned against the desk. "They're always on the phone," he said, "even if they're not. They're going to tell you they're busy even if they're back there looking out the window. Part of it. Nobody's that busy." He jammed his hands into his pockets as a woman literally flew from the office into the reception area.

She came on like a miniature whirlwind, a trim brunette with sunglasses perched on top of her head, wearing molded jeans, six-inch platform shoes, and a filmy pink scarf around her neck. "Aaron! Is it you? Is it *really you?*" She took both of Levy's hands and touched her cheek against his, then turned wide-eyed to Sharon and looked her up and down. "You've brought her. You've really *brought her*. You're taller than you look on TV, dear."

Sharon allowed the woman to go through her cheeks-touching routine, smelling face makeup and noting up close that Marissa Cudmore was older than she would appear at a distance. A whole lot older, in fact; the woman's voice plus the lines around her eyes placed her around fifty, even though she was dressed like a college girl. Sharon said simply, "How are you, Ms. Cudmore? Darla sends her regards."

"She does? She *does*? That she'd think of me at a time like this . . ." She looked at Levy, at Sharon, and back at the agent again. "Shall we?" She extended a hand and ushered her visitors into an office half the size of the reception area. The room contained one junior executive desk, a bank of files, a pile of scripts on a table, a smaller stack than the one outside. Sharon supposed that the assistant weeded out the bad stuff, giving Marissa Cudmore only the surefire hits. All of Cudmore's scripts had notes stapled to the front. "Sit," Marissa Cudmore said. "Sit at once and give me the news."

Sharon didn't have any news and remained silent. Aaron Levy said nothing. After a ten-second pause, Sharon reached for her satchel and said, "Actually, I'm here to—"

"Don't speak." Marissa Cudmore held up a hand, palm out. "Don't . . . speak."

Sharon pulled out her legal papers and held them in her lap.

"Aaron, did you hear?" Cudmore said. "Steven and Jeffrey are talking about splitting the blankets. Those two wills, those egos."

Levy's eyebrows lifted. "You're kidding. Didn't take long."

"I got it from a casting director over there. They've had these screaming fights." Cudmore leaned forward and conspiratorially lowered her voice. "Word is, it's over a woman."

"Yeah?" Levy said. "Who?"

Cudmore scrunched her eyelids together. "I'm not at liberty." She grinned at Sharon. "Your timing is perfect."

Sharon waved the papers. "Listen, I've got a—"

"Never the more perfect moment," Cudmore said.

"Did Aaron tell you, your kind of thing, it's something we normally wouldn't consider?"

Sharon watched the woman in astonishment. "He mentioned it," she said.

"Until now. You're a wonder, Aaron. How did you know?"

Levy lifted his leg and rested his ankle on his knee. "I was telling Sharon on the drive over, knowing these things, it's an agent's job."

Sharon looked at Levy and wondered if she'd missed something he'd said on the drive out. Nope, she'd listened pretty carefully.

"It's true," Cudmore said, her chin moving up and down in a rapid nod. "She called. She actually *called*."

Sharon pinched her chin and didn't say anything, trying her best to appear really in and with-it.

"Aaron." Cudmore's tone was mockingly reproachful. "You didn't *tell her*?"

Levy expansively waved a hand. "I thought you'd want to."

"*Weh*-ell." Cudmore looked past Sharon. "Is the door closed?" she said.

Sharon twisted her head around. The door, obviously, was closed. She looked back at Marissa Cudmore.

Cudmore leaned over until her chin practically touched her desktop. Her eyes dancing, she said in a stage whisper, "Michelle."

Levy reached out to squeeze Sharon's upper arm. "See," the agent said. "What'd I tell you?"

You told me that these people wouldn't be interested, Sharon thought. No way, you said.

"Mi-*chelle*." Cudmore sounded like a woman in the throes of orgasm. "That she wants to play you. It's really"—she punched the air with her fist—"high concept. The highest."

Sharon looked back and forth between the agent and the producer, both of them really into it now, getting their cookies over Michelle having called. Michelle fucking who? Sharon thought. Pfeiffer? Lee? Hartman? Jesus, there were a thousand Michelles.

Sharon decided to break up the silliness before she got caught up in all the hoopla. She firmly gripped her legal papers. "I've got to tell the truth. I came here with something else in mind."

"I'm a step ahead of you," Cudmore said. "I know you've had acting. But playing one's self? It's been done before, but with *Michelle* waiting in the wings?"

Sharon expelled a sigh. "Look, my pretenses for being here are a bit false, that I'll confess. But there's something I have to ask you about."

Cudmore showed just the slightest hesitation. "Anything. But keeping Michelle waiting for an answer, that's not—"

"*Dead On*," Sharon said. "I want to ask you about *Dead On*."

It was as if a cloud had covered the sun. Cudmore's features rearranged like Play-Doh, dissolving from starry-eyed rapture to seething hatred in an instant. She glared at Levy. "Aaron. You *brought this woman here*?" The words came out in an eardrum-shattering wail. "To utter that name, to say those words? Those words are not to be spoken in my presence. And you know that. How *could you*?"

Levy said, "What's *Dead On*?"

Cudmore pressed her wrist against her forehead. "You did it. You said those words *again*."

God, Sharon thought, compared to this woman, Darla Cowan is Sane Jane from Saginaw. "Hey," she said, "I didn't want to upset you. But it's critical for Darla to—"

"Out." Cudmore pointed at the exit with a long red nail. "Out at once. I am accommodating Aaron by having you here, and you . . ."

"I toldja they wouldn't be interested," Levy said.

"Oh?" Sharon said. "What happened to Michelle calling?" She straightened her posture. "Interested or not, you're going to talk about it. The D-word and the O-word, as in *Dead On*. I have to know the whole story, from who did what to cancellation of the project. Why Darla was supposed to play the romantic interest, yet never got to read the book, down to what happened when David Spencer backed out on the picture."

"Oh. *That* deal." Levy put his elbow on his armrest and massaged his forehead. "Marissa don't like to talk about that deal."

Marissa Cudmore glared in hatred, and for just an instant Sharon thought the woman might hurl a paperweight. "Obviously," Sharon said.

Cudmore stood. She walked to the door. "Nice to see you, Aaron," she said stiffly.

So it's come to that, Sharon thought. She hefted the subpoena she'd prepared at the Criminal Courts Building and handed the paper to Cudmore without saying a word. Cudmore read slowly through dully glazed eyes.

"I hate to do this," Sharon said. "But I'd hate for Darla to go to prison over something she didn't do even more. It's official, Ms. Cudmore, it's a subpoena. If you're not in court in the morning, deputy sheriffs will come after you. They are one group that even the guards at your gate won't be able to stop."

Cudmore returned to her desk and flopped into her seat. Levy fished in his pocket for a toothpick, which he dangled from one corner of his mouth. He didn't look upset, more like a man resigned, watching dollar bills sprouting wings, flying away. . . .

Cudmore clenched her teeth. "That goddamned Harlon Swain."

"The very guy I'm going to ask you about on the witness stand," Sharon said. She pointed at the subpoena. "You can avoid this, Ms. Cudmore. Would you like to?"

Cudmore flashed a look of desperation. "How?"

Sharon crossed her legs. "By talking to me here, right now. I'm only looking for information. Informally, here in your office, that's more pleasant. Under subpoena and on the witness stand if I have to, but hey."

"Talk about what? What can the most fucked deal

in the history of motion pictures have to do with a murder trial?"

"Everything, or nothing. Depends on what I learn."

"That writer," Cudmore said. "His fault, all his. Nothing but a schmuck with a computer. Just like all writers . . ."

"But schmuckier than most?" Sharon asked. "Excuse me, but I know a little about this already, from Darla. I thought Curtis Nussbaum brought you the deal."

"God, you wouldn't . . . You'll never get me to say anything bad about Curt. Never. Never bad-mouth anyone in the business, that's tantamount to suicide."

"That's what Mr. Levy told me," Sharon said. "But, excuse me, didn't you just bad-mouth the writer? Writers in general?"

"Those schmucks are different."

"I . . . see," Sharon said. "We're not progressing very fast. Maybe we'd better stick to what happened."

"*Dead On.*" Cudmore seemed on the verge of hysterics. "Jesus H. Christ, *Dead* fucking *On.*"

Levy regarded the floor like a man at a wake.

"What Darla told me," Sharon said, "is that Curtis Nussbaum personally optioned the novel. Is that unusual for an agent to do?"

Cudmore and Levy exchanged a look. "Nussbaum takes some risks," Levy said. "Guy gambles high. Always has."

Cudmore switched into gossip mode. "His debt is astronomical, Vegas and points beyond. Foolish money management. Not that I'd ever . . ."

"Bad-mouth anyone in the business," Sharon finished. "Yes, you told me. Start from day one, when Nussbaum optioned the book."

"Before that writer fucked everything up?" Cudmore said.

"Yes, even before then." Sharon had her legal pad out, taking notes. "What was the option price? If you're privy to that."

"It was a whole lot more than an option," Cudmore

said, blinking. "It was an outright sale. Two million dollars. Poor Curtis . . ."

"I'm assuming on the logistics," Sharon said. "But I suppose he buys the book, and then turns around and sells it to the studio."

Cudmore opened a drawer and withdrew a prescription bottle, which she squeezed until her knuckles whitened. "Now, don't be blaming me. Everyone's blaming me, don't you start. *Anyone* would have bought that deal. David Spencer committed. *Darla Cowan* committed."

"Now, wait a minute," Levy butted in. "Spencer, yeah, he's Nussbaum's to commit. I never made no commitment for Darla."

Cudmore undid the cap, popped a pill into her mouth, and swallowed water from a glass near her elbow. "You would have, Aaron. You would have. Jesus Christ, with *David Spencer* involved? Talk about *high concept*. The highest of the high."

"*Dead On* must have been quite a story," Sharon said, "to interest all those people."

Cudmore looked puzzled. "It must have been. I didn't read the proposal." She looked at Levy. "Did you read the proposal, Aaron?"

The agent waved a hand as if battling mosquitoes. "Nah. David Spencer backed out before we talked real turkey to you people."

Cudmore's eyes were suddenly moist. "Poor David. He had *such* a schedule . . ."

"Before the writer screwed everything up?" Sharon asked.

"That *schmuck*," Cudmore said.

"Asshole," Levy said.

"Oh?" Sharon blinked in amazement. God, these two. She said, "How much did this writer get the studio to commit to this disaster?"

Cudmore looked off. "Preproduction budget, sixty million. That's before a director got involved."

"Let me get a feel for this, Ms. Cudmore. That isn't money you pay out immediately, is it?"

Cudmore showed a determined pout. "To a writer? We're not that crazy."

Sharon wasn't so sure about that. "How much *did* you pay Mr. Swain?"

"I'd have to check the record. Twenty thousand, I think. Through Curt, of course. We don't deal directly with these people."

"I see. And part payment to the actor as well, I suppose."

Cudmore exchanged a glance with Levy. "Well," Cudmore said, "David was an artist. Much in demand."

"You paid him more?" Sharon doodled a question mark on her pad.

"You don't get a David Spencer for nothing, Sharon. You up-front before he'll even discuss."

"And David Spencer's asking price was . . . ?"

"Six million. Not *all* up front. Only a portion."

"How much of a portion?"

Cudmore shrugged with her hands. "Only a third."

"Only . . . Let me be sure I'm following here. Curtis Nussbaum brought you a property, *Dead On*, an unfinished novel to which you didn't know the story. You advanced the writer twenty thousand dollars against two million, and advanced David Spencer two million against six. Without a manuscript to work with, without reading the author's proposal . . ."

Cudmore nodded. Her anger seemed to have subsided some, now a woman explaining her position. "Curt Nussbaum's word plus David Spencer's commitment was plenty for anyone in the business to set the gears in motion. Put the novel with our publishing arm in New York, commit a promotional budget for the book. Our publishing people hired a jacket-cover designer, made commitments to the major bookstores. On this end we commissioned a screenwriter to do a treatment. We're not talking minor expenditure here."

Sharon blinked in disbelief. "All of this without a finished book?"

"We put the writer with David," Cudmore said.

"I'm assuming," Sharon said, "that both the writer's

and the actor's money, all of that went initially to Curtis Nussbaum?"

Cudmore's lashes lowered in sympathy. "Poor Curt. So much to ride herd on."

Sharon made rapid notes. She was getting a grasp of what went on, her lawyer's instinct already translating the wheeling and dealing into terms understandable to a jury. It wouldn't be easy, making the twelve tried and true see the point. "I don't suppose you know," Sharon said, "what *poor Curt* did with all this money. While the actor and the writer were collaborating."

"Not ours to know. Not ours to know. And don't call that abortion a collaboration, Sharon. The schmuck wouldn't cooperate."

"The writer," Sharon said.

"What other schmuck is there?" Cudmore said.

Sharon looked at Aaron Levy, the agent stoic in his chair, acting as if this type of transaction went on every day. She said to Marissa Cudmore, "What is it that this writer wouldn't do?"

Cudmore rolled her eyes upward. "Anything. Everything. Poor David told me after a month, the schmuck refused to develop a character to whom David felt he could do justice."

"I did some acting," Sharon said. "I'd think, if the story, the book, was powerful enough, the actor could tailor the character to suit his persona once the project was in production."

Cudmore's expression went livid once more. "Now you're talking like the schmuck, the writer. That's what he thought, kept turning in a pile of drivel. Never did satisfy poor David, which finally killed the project." Visible beyond her through the window, a couple of actors wandered by dressed in what appeared to be spacesuits.

Sharon tapped her ballpoint against one front tooth. "Didn't you have a way to monitor the writer's progress?"

"Monitor? You bet your sweet ass, monitor. What,

you think we let these schmucks wander around with no direction? After three months with nothing concrete, I took charge personally. Called the schmuck, six in the morning, noon, again in the evening. Asked for pages to read, something to show he wasn't just sitting on his ass. Two months of solid bullshit, lies, promises . . ."

"Maybe he was busy with David Spencer, developing this character," Sharon said.

"He tried that lie," Cudmore said. "But I was in constant touch with David as well. David told me after a few months he just couldn't work with this schmuck any longer."

Sharon chewed her inner cheek. She allowed some sarcasm to creep into her tone. "You were calling him three times a day, and David Spencer didn't like the character he was creating. You'd think under the circumstances he would have whipped the book right out, wouldn't you?"

"Right." Cudmore nodded vigorously. "Right."

God, Sharon thought, this woman's too caught up to realize it when someone's pulling her chain. "So what happened?" Sharon asked. "I assume you can't let something like that go on and on."

"Eventually you can't. In this instance, with what we'd committed, we tried everything. I even tried buying Swain out, commissioning a ghost to finish the novel. The schmuck wouldn't even talk about it. Claimed it was his book. *His book,* with our money sitting in his pocket."

"The whole twenty thousand dollars," Sharon said.

"Right," Cudmore said.

"And two million dollars sitting in the actor's pocket. Or more to the point, his agent's pocket," Sharon said.

"David was an artist," Cudmore said. "You have to understand."

"I think I do," Sharon said, writing down, *Check Nussbaum's other bank accounts*. She crossed her forearms over her notepad. "How did you resolve the issue?" she asked.

"We had no choice. We had to cancel."

"You asked for your money back?"

Cudmore's tired gaze rested on her desktop. "Poor Curtis."

"He had difficulty anteing up?"

"Oh, no." Cudmore shook her head. "Curtis, God, no. Took a few days, but he came right in with a check. Poor David as well, it must have been a blow to him."

"The writer lost his advance, didn't he?" Sharon asked. "The twenty thousand dollars?"

Cudmore nodded furiously. "Just what the schmuck deserved."

"So you, meaning the studio, you're not out any of the money?"

Cudmore stared off in space. "The embarrassment . . ."

Poking out from Sharon's satchel was the printout of Rob Stanley's account, the one whose balance, on the day of Spencer's death, had amounted to fourteen bucks and change. "Let me ask you something," Sharon said. "Do you have any knowledge of where the money came from when Nussbaum refunded to you?"

Cudmore looked at Levy. "Not our problem," she said. "I assume from David and the writer, though it's been our experience that the writer never has anything left of the advance to refund. Always blows it all . . ."

"On rent and such?" Sharon said.

"Not our problem. God, these schmucks."

"The writers," Sharon said. "Not the actors."

"Right," Cudmore said.

Sharon batoned her pen between her fingers as she considered more questions. "I'll need Harlon Swain's address and phone number," Sharon said. "So you'll know, I'll be talking to him."

Cudmore went over to a file cabinet, tugged open a drawer, and thudded two inch-thick folders onto her desk. "Hope you have better luck than I." She showed an urgent look. "Sharon, I can't be testifying to any of this. I simply can't."

"With your full cooperation here and now," Sharon said, "I can't see that you'd have to." She tore a slip from a pad. "Write Mr. Swain's address and number on this, please."

Cudmore bent her head to write. "What do I tell Michelle?"

Sharon felt a pang of regret, which subsided in an instant. As an actress she'd always wanted to play a movie star's role. Having a movie star play *her* role, however, just wouldn't thrill the same. She said, "Afraid you'll have to put her on hold."

Cudmore slid the paper over, blinking in disbelief. "Put *Michelle* on hold?"

Sharon accepted the paper, read the writer's address and phone number, folded the paper, and slipped it inside her satchel. "For now."

Slowly, incredulously, Cudmore shook her head. "No one puts Michelle on hold. Not even Mike Ovitz."

"And he puts *everybody* on hold," Levy said from off to the side.

Sharon moved her gaze from Cudmore to Levy and back again. She smoothed her skirt. "Look, I know this is hard to believe, and I'm not sure I believe it myself. I got into this by agreeing to help a friend, Darla, wound up as her attorney, for which I'll collect a fee. My fee's all I'm entitled to ethically, no residuals, no other deals. Tough pill to swallow, huh?"

Cudmore rocked back in her chair. "Now, that I like. A woman of morals. Definitely a high concept. Highest of the high."

"And friends in low places," Sharon said wryly. "I'm sorry, Ms. Cudmore. Thanks, but no thanks." She gathered her gear. "Now I've got to . . . *oh*." She set her satchel on the floor, opened the snaps, and dug inside.

Cudmore gave Levy a knowing look. "I just knew

it. She has her own proposal. If it's something one can live with . . ."

"Could you look this over for me?" Sharon said, sliding the *Spring of the Comanche* photo over in front of Cudmore. "I'm interested in the guy far right. The rest of the people in the picture, we all know who they are."

Cudmore picked up the picture and studied. Levy got up, went behind Cudmore, and looked over her shoulder. Levy said, "Nussbaum's man."

"Security man," Sharon said. "That much we already know. I'm looking for a name."

Levy waved a hand. "Lots of these guys. Blend in with the furniture."

"So I'm told. If you could just search your—"

"Chuck Hager," Cudmore said.

Sharon stared at her.

Cudmore tossed the photo aside. "I knew him at Central Casting. He was an aspiring actor once. I heard he got into security. I've seen him around. Lousy actor, but as a gofer, a lot of credentials."

Levy poked his tongue into his cheek. "Lot of these guys hanging around."

Sharon ignored the agent and concentrated on Marissa Cudmore. "What credentials are those, Ms. Cudmore?"

"He could fly airplanes, for one thing."

Sharon felt a surge of excitement. "Jets?"

"If it has wings, that guy can fly it," Cudmore said. "Persian Gulf vet. We used him once here at the studio to take some actors and directors to a premiere in Kansas City. Kept them from having to ride with the flyovers."

Now Sharon was puzzled. "Flyovers?"

Cudmore nodded vacantly. "Flyover people, yeah. That's the people we generally fly over, going from L.A. to New York. Ride commercial with a plane load of them, they'll drive you crazy. Ask a lot of questions. Much easier to fly private, just with your peers."

Sharon quickly wrote *Chuck Hager* on her notepad.

"Do you know if Curtis Nussbaum has access to a private jet?"

"Curt, sure," Cudmore said. "If he doesn't own one, he has access."

"How about, a way to get in touch with Mr. Hager," Sharon said.

"Try Mathis Security. Last time I saw him . . ."

Sharon scribbled the name of the agency. Her adrenaline was pumping. She snatched up the photo, put it away, and gathered her things. "I can't tell you how much help you've been. We'll hold the subpoena in abeyance, Ms. Cudmore. Unless you hear differently from me, I won't be needing you in court." She stood. "I have my own transportation from here. Sorry to lead you on, Mr. Levy. But thanks for the ride." She hurried toward the door.

From behind her Levy said, "Hey."

Sharon turned. He stood stoically behind Cudmore, both the agent and the producer staring at Sharon as if they couldn't believe that such an airhead existed. Which they probably can't, Sharon thought, and I can't believe myself sometimes. "Yes, sir?" Sharon said.

Levy shifted his toothpick from one corner of his mouth to the other. "Look," he said, and then said, "Look," a second time. He glanced at Cudmore as if wondering if he should speak in front of her. Then he shrugged and zeroed in on Sharon once again. "This don't kill no book deal, does it?" Aaron Levy said.

Sharon hustled through the movie lot, high heels clicking, her satchel bumping her hip, and used the cell phone as she headed for the gate. Directly in front of her was a girl wearing a gorilla costume, the ape's head tucked underneath her arm, and a man with ears pointed like Spock's, who was also using a portable phone. There was a click in Sharon's ear, and Lyndon Gray answered. She said, "It's Miss Hays, Mr. Gray. Do you know where the front gate to Mammoth Studios is located?"

The Englishman chuckled. "Been there often, mum. Twenty minutes?"

"If you can't make it sooner. Any luck in locating our mystery man around the courts building?"

"Negative. Even had Benny Yadaka search a six-block area. Nothing. If you have better ideas . . ."

"Not only do I have better ideas," Sharon said, "I've got the guy's name. Chuck Hager. On the way here, Mr. Gray, I'd appreciate it if you'd find me the number for Mathis Security."

"I know the firm, Miss Hays. Not the whitest of reputations."

"Why am I not surprised at that?" Sharon said. "See you in a few minutes, unless . . ."

"Unless I can get there more quickly," Gray said cheerfully. "I have the pedal to the metal, as they say." He disconnected.

Sharon folded up the cell phone and stuffed it away as she reached the gate, stepped up onto the walk-through, and passed the guard's station. She fought the urge but couldn't resist, and threw a final wistful look behind her. The White House and Treasury Building loomed in the distance, with the ghetto neighborhood to the right and, farther still to the right, the snow-capped peak towering over Dreamworld U.S.A. What wouldn't I have given? Sharon thought. She did a determined eyes-front and paraded ahead, conscious of the guard watching her through the window. He was a man in his fifties, with pale blue eyes beneath the brim of his uniform hat.

Sharon continued on to stand on the curb, set her satchel on the ground, and watched the traffic roll by. She folded her arms and placed one foot in front of the other. She fidgeted in place, drumming her fingers on her upper arms, frowning impatiently, peering up the road in search of the limo.

A tenor male voice said from behind her, "The bastards. The rotten bastards."

Sharon turned.

It was the guard, who'd come out from his station

and followed her to the curb. He had a paunch which strained the buttons on his shirt. "The bastards," he said again.

Sharon blinked. "I beg your pardon?"

"See it every day, these poor little girls," he said. "Bastards didn't even offer you a ride." He had a kind face, which was wreathed in a smile of sympathy.

Sharon looked back toward the movie lot, then at the guard. She got it. She said, "Oh. I'm not—"

"Let them come in with their hopes, you think they give a damn?" The guard was practically in tears.

Sharon relaxed. "I suppose they don't."

"Hell, no, they don't," the guard said. "For what it's worth, I've seen 'em come and go. It's no life, hon. No life at all, even for the ones that make it big. You'll be better off, go back to your hometown, marry the local druggist, teacher. No life at all."

Sharon pictured Rob, playing the role even in public. And Darla, who, if she got out of jail, would live alone in her mansion by the sea. "I'm learning it isn't much of a life," she said.

The guard pulled out a handkerchief and blew his nose. He stuffed the hanky away, then jammed his hand into his pants pocket. "Listen, if you need cab fare," he said.

24

Sharon spent the next five minutes trying to convince the guard that she didn't want his money, then watched his jaw drop in surprise as the Lincoln stretch pulled to the curb and Lyndon Gray hopped out to open the door for her. Just before she entered the limo, she stopped and offered the guard a little curtsy. "See. I didn't need their old part anyway," she said.

She sat on cushioned leather and swung her legs inside as Gray slammed the door and moved up to sit behind the wheel. Her gaze shifted to the right, the empty front passenger seat. "You're missing a sidekick."

Gray's clear hazel eyes were visible in the rearview. "Benny won't be with us this evening, miss. He had an emergency, to see his sister in the Valley."

Sharon wondered suddenly about Melanie, how her day had gone. "We all need more time for family," she said. "Hopefully when this is over we can all take a month." She unfolded the slip of paper, squinting to read Marissa Cudmore's handwriting, and dictated Harlon Swain's address through the opening. "Take us there, please," she said.

The Englishman frowned at her through the open panel. "Where, miss?"

Sharon tucked the slip of paper away. "A writer's place. He wrote *Dead On*."

"What?" Gray seemed even more puzzled than before.

"A . . . novel. Just get us there, please. I'll fill you in later."

"Certainly, miss. But you should know, it isn't a nice neighborhood."

Sharon fastened her seat belt. "Why am I not surprised." She offered the Brit a devilish smile. "Wherever else would you expect a schmuck to live?" As Gray hummed the partition closed, he scratched his head.

As the limo rolled onto the Hollywood Freeway, Sharon got busy on the cell phone. Rob answered on the second ring. "Hi, it's Sharon," she said, making her tone friendly, but curling her lip in spite of herself.

"Couldn't we have dealt with this this afternoon?" Rob was testy, his words slightly slurred. God, he'd been drinking again.

Sharon's manner changed at once, icicles hanging from her every syllable. "I can't talk on the phone in the middle of a hearing. If you can't understand that, well, tough."

"This had better be important, Muffin. Do you know how many people you've made me keep waiting?"

"It should be important to you. Have you noticed much fluctuation in your bank balance lately?"

Rob assumed a petulant tone. "My bank balance is none of your business. If that's all you—"

"As of last Friday it was fourteen bucks," Sharon said.

There was sudden total silence, static on the line.

"They gave me some hassle, negotiating your check at the bank," Sharon said. "But finally it cleared."

"There must be some mistake." Rob's voice caught, the barest of tremors, almost unnoticeable.

"They say computers don't lie, though I've known people who would argue the point. Don't you reconcile your statements?"

"I . . . don't see my statements." Rob was obviously stunned, sobering as if doused in the face with cold water.

"Not surprising. They go to Curtis Nussbaum, right?"

"My agent. He . . ."

"Does all that," Sharon said. "I know, you told me at the restaurant the other night. I'd assume you'd know it if your bills weren't being paid."

"My bills go to Curt."

"So as long as your phone works and no one shuts off the electricity, you're completely in the dark as to your financial condition. Rob, do you have the vaguest idea how much money you have in the bank?"

"Must be a lot. I get fifty thousand a week from the show. Plus some endorsements, those Dodge commercials . . ."

"All of which goes to your agent." Sharon looked off to her left, at lights twinkling in the Hollywood Hills under a curtain of smog. The limo's radials *click-thud*-ed over freeway expansion joints. She inhaled and said, "I want you in court tomorrow."

"Now, hold on, Muffin. "I've already told you, I can't afford to get involved in Darla's criminal problems."

Sharon tried to calm herself as anger coursed through her. She lost it. "Goddammit, Rob, I refuse to believe that you've turned into such a horse's ass. Darla's responsible for your major break, don't you remember? And you distancing yourself from her at a time like this is the ultimate slap in the face."

There was a pause. Now Rob's voice was childlike, an apologetic whine. "Not my choice."

"Whose choice is it, then?" Sharon sagged in the seat as realization dawned. She held the phone at arm's length, then jammed the receiver against her ear. "Your agent's orders, right? Your fucking agent?"

There was a choking sound over the line. Rob said, "He told me it would be professional suicide."

Sharon wondered how much she could safely tell him. The limo cruised past Normandie Avenue, the downtown skyscrapers visible over Gray's broad shoulders in the front seat. Sharon said, "If one word of what I'm about to tell you gets out . . . Well, if you don't get my drift, you've gotten dumber as you've fallen more in love with yourself. I think your agent has been stealing you blind, and I also think he may have had David Spencer killed."

Rob uttered a sharp gasp. "David was his number one meal ticket. Compared to David's income, I'm just a minnow in the stream."

"Which means Nussbaum would have had his fanny in a pretty tight crack to jeopardize that relationship, right? I think that's just what happened, Rob. Prepare yourself for a string of rapid-fire questions. Have you ever heard of a book project called *Dead On*?"

A five-second pause. "Doesn't ring a bell," Rob said.

"I don't suppose that's surprising. Even the studio wants that one under wraps. How about a novelist, Harlon Swain?"

"No. What are you—?"

"Try Chuck Hager. That name do anything?"

"Sure. Curt's pilot and security man. He's been at my beck and call, mine and a few more of Curt's clients. We shot a mountain chase scene once, and Chuck took me on location in a helicopter."

"A real flyboy. Think back to last Friday. Did you talk to your agent on Friday?"

"I talk to him most days. I may have."

Sharon slowed down, thinking. "Try, Rob," she said. "Anything at all about last Friday which might've pinpointed this Hager's whereabouts."

"Well, there was . . ." Rob sounded sincere, completely sober now. "No," he said. "That was on Thursday."

Sharon sat up straight. "What was on Thursday?"

"Well, a friend and I had thought about going to Puerto Vallarta for the weekend. I'd called Monday to see if Chuck could ferry us down." There was a guilty pause. "I've got a confession to make, Muffin. It was a lady friend."

Sharon tightly closed her eyes. "If you think I give two shits what bimbo you were . . . never mind. Good old Chuck wasn't available, right?"

"Curt's assistant called on Thursday. Said Hager would be out of town. But if we wanted, Curt could arrange for a commercial flight. Muffin, these women don't mean a—"

"Thing to you. Jesus Christ. And for the thousandth time, it's Sharon. Be at the Criminal Courts Building at eleven in the morning."

"I don't know. Would I have to testify in front of the camera?"

"You'd have to testify in front of whatever I tell you to, including all these women you don't care about. I don't suppose you know what clients' bank accounts Nussbaum handles besides yours."

"Not a clue," Rob said.

"Of course you don't, Nussbaum wouldn't . . . Never mind, I can find out on my own. Eleven a.m., Rob. Stand me up, and some sheriffs will call on you. Right on the set, wouldn't it be loverly?"

Sharon disconnected, feeling her weight shift as the limo curved around the elevated portion of the freeway. Downtown buildings looked close enough for her to reach out and touch, lights glowing through windows as lawyers and accountants burned nighttime oil. She rapped on the glass. As the partition hummed open, she leaned forward and said, "Did you get that number I wanted, Mr. Gray? Mathis Security?"

The Brit reached inside his coat. "Right here, miss." He handed a folded slip of paper over the seat. The partition hummed closed.

Sharon flipped on the interior overhead and held the slip of paper at arm's length as she punched in the number. She put the phone to her ear in time to hear a click, followed by an electronic voice saying, "You have reached Mathis Security. Our office hours are from seven a.m. to six p.m. If you wish to leave a message, wait for the tone. If this is an emergency, please call 555-7878." There was another click, followed by a high-pitched beep.

Sharon disconnected and called the emergency number. This time the voice told her that if she'd leave

her number, someone would get back to her within
the half hour. She waited for the beep, then said,
"This message is for Chuck Hager. Please have him
call Sharon Hays at . . ." She left the cell phone number and disconnected once again. She didn't expect
Hager to call her back but suspected that the message
would cause an immediate conference with Curtis
Nussbaum. Which was exactly what she wanted to
happen.

She tossed the phone aside, crossed her legs, and
leaned her head against the cushions. Gray had negotiated the interchange and steered onto the Harbor
Freeway, headed south, and Sharon recognized the
outline of the Criminal Courts Building sandwiched in
between a couple of skyscrapers. She relaxed in
thought, her eyes misting slightly as she moved her
gaze to the county jail. She pictured Darla Cowan
beyond one of the lighted windows, alone and afraid,
sleeping restlessly inside her cell.

25

When he'd said that Harlon Swain didn't live in a nice neighborhood, Lyndon Gray was being kind. The row of shotgun wooden houses sat behind tiny yards infested with weeds. Weeds, that is, if there was any vegetation at all; a couple of the lawns were bare clay with rocks jutting above the surface. Apparently the L.A. Sanitation Department serviced the area on a catch-as-catch-can basis; there were overflowing garbage containers lining the sidewalks and crammed-full plastic bags sitting in the driveways. Sharon's eyes bulged in horror as they passed two rats fighting over a chicken bone, their tails lashing, their vicious bites punctuated with bloodthirsty squeals.

The writer's house was even more dilapidated than most of the hovels in the block, an ancient two-story whose roof had split in two, and whose foundation was lower at one end than at the other. Wild vines twisted around the railing of a rotted wooden porch. Gray parked the limo behind a fairly new four-door sedan. A single lamp glowed in one ground-floor window. As Sharon alighted to the curb, her scalp tingled. The air was cool, bordering on cold, and there was a dampness here that she hadn't felt in Malibu, downtown at the courts, or at the studio in Universal City. She pictured the house where the Munsters lived.

Gray escorted Sharon up the cracked and broken sidewalk. The Englishman's bulk offered some comfort, though not nearly enough. Boards creaked dangerously as they climbed the steps onto the porch. Gray looked around for a doorbell, found none, then rapped his knuckles on rotting wood. They stood back and waited. Sharon folded her hands in front and rose on tiptoes to tighten her calves. Thirty seconds passed. The Englishman knocked again.

Heavy footsteps sounded inside, then the door handle rattled and turned. There was a squeak of hinges, and light slanted from inside onto the porch. Sharon glanced at Gray, then stepped forward and said, "Hi, I'm Sharon . . ." She trailed off in mid-sentence and her muscles tensed. She was looking down the barrel of a gun.

Slowly, cautiously, Sharon backed away as a man came outside. His features weren't distinguishable in the dimness, but he wore a suit and was a couple of inches taller than she. He held the pistol at waist level, but didn't seem particularly menacing. He used his free hand to reach inside his coat and exhibited an open wallet. "Police," he said. "You have ID?"

Sharon breathed a sigh of relief. "In my . . ." She raised her handbag.

"Get it, please," the man said. As Sharon dug inside her purse, Gray reached carefully for his wallet. The cop held Sharon's driver's license and Gray's billfold in one hand, and backed into the light from inside to look them over. He holstered his weapon, said over his shoulder, "All right, David," then nodded to Sharon and said, "Could you explain what you're doing here?"

A second man came onto the porch lowering a shotgun. He wore a lighter-colored suit than the first guy, and stood idly by while cop number one returned Sharon's and Gray's identification.

Now that her fear had passed, Sharon was more than a little nettled. She said to the head policeman, "And you are . . . ?"

"Detective Leeds. L.A. Homicide." Leeds glanced down at the shotgun, which the other man held with its barrel pointed down. "Excuse the informalities," Leeds said, "but this is a murder scene."

Sharon looked out into the yard. "Shouldn't there be some yellow tape or something?"

"There was, on Saturday. We're doing a follow-up visit. I apologize again, ma'am, but when people come up on you in a place like this, you use caution." Leeds stood back and pinched his chin. "Once again, do you mind if I ask what you're doing here?"

Sharon tried to peer inside the house. Visible in the glow from the lamp was a threadbare rug and one end of a worn sofa. She said, "We're trying to find Harlon Swain."

The policeman looked down, then back up, his expression changing to one of sympathy. It was the standard bad-news-bearer's look. "I'm sorry," he said. "Are you related?"

"No, just business. I assume Mr. Swain is the deceased?"

Leeds nodded curtly, his look of sympathy gone. "At the morgue. Mind if I ask what you wanted with Mr. Swain?"

"I'm a lawyer. He could have been a potential witness in a case I'm defending."

Leeds brightened in recognition. "I thought I'd heard that name. Sharon Hays. Hey, David, this is the lady on television."

The shotgun toter seemed impressed, leaning his weapon against the wall and extending his hand. "Detective David White," he said.

Sharon shook the man's hand, then rose on tiptoes once again to peer inside the house. "Are your CSU's finished in there?"

"Several days ago," Leeds said. "Look, maybe we can help each other. This guy is somehow connected to David Spencer?"

Sharon glanced at Gray, who remained quietly in the shadows. She said to the cop, "He was a writer."

"And how." Leeds gestured to the interior of the house. "Manuscripts piled all over inside. Bet that's the only computer in the neighborhood."

"He wrote a book," Sharon said, "that was supposed to get made into a movie with Spencer as the star. It didn't pan out."

Leeds gazed out at the trash-strewn lawn. "I guess it didn't."

Sharon stepped over the threshold. "Do you mind?"

Leeds exchanged a look with his partner. "I don't suppose. The lab guys dusted and vacuumed. I wouldn't be touching things."

Sharon nodded in thanks, then led the way inside the house. She inhaled a noseful of dust and sneezed.

The place was a mess. A lone ancient floor lamp cast its glow over ragged chairs, a pile of manuscripts held together with rubber bands, an empty pizza carton on a folding table. As Sharon passed through the foyer, something scuttled and squeaked inside the wall. She stepped over a circular stain in the rug, probably blood.

A pristine work station sat against waterstained wallpaper, as out of place as a hooker in a nunnery. Atop the work station was a glistening Compaq with its monitor on. The screen saver was a garden scene, flowers waving in the computerized breeze and raindrops drifting lazily down and occasionally jellying the view. Sharon turned to Detective Leeds. "I'm curious," she said.

Leeds had puggish features, deep creases prominent in the glow from the computer screen. "Makes two of us. Guy on a one-way ticket to nowhere, somehow hooked up with David Spencer? Wow."

"All through an agent," Sharon said. "My question is . . . this murder was last Saturday?"

"Reported on Saturday, by a guy here to repo that entire rig." Leeds nodded toward the computer and work station. "Coroner places the time of death around four p.m. on Friday. Needless to say, the repo man's merchandise is going to sit awhile."

Sharon placed her feet side by side. "So why are you here? I'm somewhat familiar with investigation procedure, Detective. Normally after the initial walk-through, dusting and photographing and whatnot, the crime scene sits vacant until there's a suspect. Someone drops by every few days to pick up mail if there is any, but . . ."

Leeds and his partner exchanged frowns. Leeds said, "Don't know as I should answer that question."

Sharon smiled. "Oh? I thought you said we might help each other. I've answered all of yours so far."

Leeds was pensive. "*Touché.* We were following up on something."

Sharon stood her ground. "So am I. Want to trade?"

Leeds appeared thoughtful, then reached inside his coat and brought out a green pasteboard card. "A receipt for certified mail. Was in the victim's box this morning. Do you know a Curtis Nussbaum?"

God, Sharon thought, can we be this lucky? "You must not have watched *Court TV* today. He was the prosecution's star witness."

"Someone named A. Lanning receipted for the piece of mail. We assume that's someone in Mr. Nussbaum's office."

Sharon nodded. "Likely his secretary. He told me once that he was going to jump her."

Both cops stared at her.

"You'd have to be there," Sharon said. "Harlon Swain mailed something to Curtis Nussbaum?"

Leeds raised the card to eye level. "There's a notation at the bottom of this, like some people use to connect it to their file. It could be an expression. It could be the title to something he wrote."

"*Dead On?*" Sharon asked.

Leeds raised his eyes, surprised. "How did you know?"

"When did Nussbaum's office receipt for that?"

Leeds turned the card around. "Last Friday. Mr. Swain didn't live through the night."

Sharon gestured around the room. "I suppose you've looked through all these manuscripts."

Leeds nodded. "To no avail. Every other title you can imagine. But no *Dead On.*" He pointed at the

Compaq. "Unless it's stored in there. Can you operate one of those?"

One corner of Sharon's mouth bunched. "I'm a computer zero."

"Me, too," Leeds said. "We've called downtown for an egghead, but until he or she gets here . . ."

Lyndon Gray came from the entryway, passed the shotgun-toting policeman, and stood in the center of the room. "I can call it up, miss, if it's on there."

Sharon's forehead wrinkled. "You're a computer expert as well?"

"I'm not in Olivia's class." Gray looked around as if waiting for applause.

Leeds gave Sharon a questioning look.

"Olivia is one of Mr. Gray's associates," Sharon said. She gestured toward the computer, palm up. "Go to it. The file is *Dead On*. Maybe just novel-dot-wpt, some writers identify files that way."

"Might take awhile. If it's password-protected I'll have to hack a bit."

"We've got all night," Sharon said.

Gray hauled a dusty chair over, sat at the work station, and clicked the mouse. Sharon blinked as the screen saver vanished. The Englishman rattled the keyboard. A list of options appeared on the monitor. As Gray scratched one cheek, reading the options, a high-pitched ringing noise pierced the room.

Sharon grabbed for her cell phone as Detective Leeds dug in his inside breast pocket. "It's me," he said, swung open his receiver, and said, "Leeds," into the mouthpiece. Sharon relaxed as the detective said, "Yeah, okay, give me the number." He laid a pad on a table and scribbled with a pen. "I'll get on it," he said, disconnected, and looked at Sharon apologetically. "Another brick on my caseload. Excuse me while I return a call, okay?"

Sharon nodded and smiled and, as Leeds retreated to the corner, punching in a number, she leaned over Gray's broad back and watched the monitor. The Englishman had brought up a list of files entitled "work prog.wpt." Sharon scanned the list. *Dead On* wasn't among the titles. Gray hit the mouse, and another list appeared. Near Sharon's elbow, a second loud *brinng* shattered the silence.

She turned. Detective Leeds was still in the corner, hunched over his phone. This call had to be for her. She dug the phone from her purse, opened it up, and said breathlessly, "Yes?"

A male voice, oddly familiar, asked, "Sharon Hays?"

"Yes?" she said again.

"Did you leave a message with Mathis Security earlier, for a Charles Hager?"

"Chuck Hager, yes." Sharon turned her back on the computer and inclined her head, listening.

"Why did you want to speak with Mr. Hager?" the voice said.

"That depends," she said. "Who wants to know?"

"This is Detective Leeds with the . . ."

Sharon's eyes widened. She turned slowly, as if in a trance, as Leeds did a slo-mo turnaround as well. The two gaped at each other, both with their cell phones pressed to their ears.

Leeds dropped his receiver to his side and grinned sheepishly. "Sharon Hays. I thought that name was familiar."

Sharon lowered her phone as well. "And I thought the voice was familiar. You're returning calls for Chuck Hager?"

"After they're relayed," the cop said. "From his business phone, home phone, wherever."

"That's the other case you're working on?" Sharon asked.

Leeds tilted his chin, nodding.

"Jesus," Sharon said. "Meaning, Chuck Hager is another stiff at the morgue?"

Leeds spread his hands, palms up, and pressed his cell phone's antenna down. " 'Fraid he is," the detective said.

*   *   *

Harlon Swain had been a man in his fifties, a harmless-looking guy with a brush mustache and graying, unkempt eyebrows. Deep lines in his face reflected a lifetime of hunching over keyboards as he poured out his life's blood on paper, crafting page after page as he waited for his break to come along. Well, finally it had. The poor, poor little schmuck, Sharon thought.

She stood inside the icebox at the L.A. County Morgue, drawing Detective Leeds's overcoat closer around her shoulders. Harlon Swain's body was stretched out on a gurney with a sheet up to its waist, its legs beneath the fabric bent out at odd angles. A row of autopsy stitches ran up the center of the chest. They'd done the whole bit, peeling back the scalp, sawing through the skull, weighing the brain. The autopsy report stated that Swain had suffered from stomach cancer. There was a jagged hole in the left side of the chest, through to the sternum, obliterating the nipple. The first autopsy Sharon had observed, back when she was a prosecutor, had made her queasy. She looked away. "Did the lab people collect fragments?" she asked.

Standing behind her and to her left, Leeds inhaled through his nose. "Some pretty good ones, nearly intact. A shell casing as well. An amateur, this one." He was in his shirtsleeves, his breath fogging, seemingly oblivious to the cold.

"Panic hurries people. I think you'll find that this person had never shot anyone before." Sharon raised her lashes to look at the detective. "Please tell me it's a thirty-eight-caliber," she said.

Leeds offered a craggy smile. "You've been reading my mail."

She cast her gaze over a row of tables, bodies sprawled grotesquely, a black man with the back of his head blown away, a Hispanic woman with a garrotte still tightened around her neck. She showed a questioning look. "And the other guy . . . ?"

"Over here." Leeds led the way to the fourth gurney down. Sharon followed at a leisurely pace. She was tired, and her legs ached from spending the day in spiked heels. She suspected that by dawn's early light, she'd be at the point of exhaustion.

Chuck Hager had a sheet up around his neck. He wasn't as handsome in death as when she'd seen him in Dallas or on the L.A. Criminal Courts front steps, but he was still good-looking. A lock of hair hung over his forehead at a rakish angle. "Where was he?" she asked.

Leeds poked his hands into his pockets. Keys and chains jingled. "Alley off of Main Street just south of the Hollywood Freeway."

"Shot?"

Leeds shook his head. "Knife on this one. Opposed to the other one, professional. Up underneath the point of the breastbone. A little left-hand twist . . ."

Sharon reached out and bunched the sheet, and gave the detective a questioning look. He nodded. She pulled back the sheet. The wound was in the shape of a three-quarter pie. "No autopsy?" Sharon asked.

Leeds gestured around the room. "You see all these. M.E.'s work eight-hour shifts, around the clock. Still might take a day or so."

Sharon folded her arms and poked her hands inside the overcoat's sleeves. God, she was freezing. "Do you have influence, to push this one through?"

Leeds's mouth canted wryly. "They bitch about it. I'd have to justify, such as, I could put the case to bed if they'd hurry it up."

Sharon stepped back and stood with her head down, thinking. Lyndon Gray was still at the writer's shack, wrestling with the computer. Sharon had ridden downtown in the detective's car, and had used the cell phone to contact Mrs. Welton. The Englishwoman was now at the beachside mansion, making long-distance calls. Be a lot of weary folks tomorrow, Sharon thought.

She smiled at Detective Leeds. "Could you go the extra mile to please a lady? I can't swear it'll solve your case, Detective. But it damned well might."

Leeds stretched his neck, peering to the front. Visible through plate glass, a white-coated M.E. spoke into a recorder as he loaded squishy internal organs onto a scale. "Well," Leeds said, "I'm not popular in this department anyway, Miss Hays. I'm known as a pushy guy. To tell you the truth, the coroner stays constantly pissed at me."

26

Curtis Nussbaum parked his Land Rover in his exposed aggregate driveway, got out, and looked to the south. Christ, the beauty, stars twinkling bravely through the smog at the northern rim of the San Gabriels, the Ventura Freeway snaking its way toward the Valley, headlights brilliant pinpoints, passing each other going in opposite directions. Nussbaum squinted; he thought he could make out the Mullholland Drive exit from the freeway, the twisty road past hidden mansions and breathtaking lookouts, the route into Hollywood. He left the boxy four-wheel-drive vehicle and walked up on his wide front porch. His hands shook and his feet were numb.

He punched his code into the security panel, heard the click of tumblers, and pushed his way into his entry hall. He stood on marble tile, a six-foot grandfather clock on his left with the pendulum rocking back and forth. Photographs in expensive frames lined the walls: Nussbaum with Dave Selznick in the old days, their arms around Angie Dickinson's waist; another shot of Nussbaum along with Swifty Lazar—Christ, Nussbaum thought, the prick finally died and gave the rest of the world a chance—at Lazar's Oscars party, with Jimmy Stewart, Kirk and Michael Douglas in the background. Christ, the times back then.

He went through his den, past low-slung leather couches, glass cases filled with pewter cups, paper-thin China plates and saucers, crystal goblets which hit notes like xylophones when tapped with a spoon. In front of his bar lay a bearskin rug, the beast's mouth

open in a permanent expression of shock. The toe
of Nussbaum's shoe struck the bear's heavy skull; he
stumbled and nearly fell, clutched the edge of the
maple bar for support. He dug frantically underneath,
came up with a liter of Jack Daniel's, filled a tumbler
with shaking hands. He used tongs to drop three ice
shards into the whiskey, then turned up the tumbler
and glugged. The liquor burned going down. Nussbaum rolled the glass across his forehead. Christ, the
mistakes, piled one on top of the other, the pretty
female lawyer, her expression calm as she questioned
him on the witness stand . . .

Music drifted through the high-ceilinged den, coming from the back of the house. A Broadway show
tune, class which the movies would never see again,
Nancy Kwan, her strong voice belting the lyrics. *Grant
Avenue, San Francisco, California, You Ess Ayy,*
Christ, *Flower Drum Song,* when Broadway was great
and pictures were greater still.

Nussbaum moved toward the sound, the liquor
steadying his walk, calming his nerves. He moved
down a carpeted hallway, went through a door, and
stood in darkness. The *click-click-click* of a projector
was soothing to his ears. The room slanted downward
away from him, six rows of cushioned theater seats,
the projector beam expanding toward the silver
screen, dust motes drifting in the light like confetti.

Nancy Kwan had had the star power, Christ, the
dancing, perfectly muscled calves and thighs flashing
as she led a chorus-line troupe through Chinatown.
Visible over a front-row seat back, shadowy in the
light from the projector, was a massive wealth of hair,
long and fluffy, falling to slim, elegant shoulders. Nussbaum forgot the pressure, the testimony, for an instant
as he hurried down the aisle to sit beside the woman,
Christ, continuing to marvel over her, the legs in black
tights, the firm chin, the most beautiful Oriental features since Nancy Kwan. She didn't seem to notice
his presence, just watched the screen as if frozen as
Nussbaum pushed down the adjacent seat and sat be-

side her. He shifted his drink from one hand to the other and palmed her thigh. Still she didn't move.

He gestured with his glass toward the screen. "That will be you someday."

"Shh!" She placed a silencing finger to her lips. "The last time, I want to remember it all."

"You have the same moves," Nussbaum said. "The high kicks, I'll never forget them, the first time I saw you at Caesar's . . ."

"Shh!" she said again. "Right . . . here, it's what I want to remember." On-screen, Nancy Kwan held a perfect split, left leg outstretched with her toes pointed, balanced on a vegetable cart which rolled down the sidewalk of Grant Avenue. The woman seated beside Nussbaum sighed. "To be able to hold that pose, that long . . ."

"You can." Nussbaum's voice was a fierce whisper. "You will. Just a few more months, more auditions . . ."

She swiveled her head to look at him, perfect almond-shaped eyes, coal black corneas. "They don't make that kind of movie anymore, Curtis. You know it. I know it. Stop bullshitting me."

He fervently squeezed her leg. "You can be the revival." He followed the curve of her hip, sent his gaze on past her knee, her tensed calf, tiny foot in a spike-heeled pump perched on a . . . "What's that?" he said.

She scooted down in the seat. "What's what?" She looked at him, followed the line of his gaze down to her foot. "Oh," she said. "It's a suitcase."

Nussbaum swirled his whiskey around in irritation. "I know what it is. What's it for?"

"It's got my clothes inside. The ones I brought. The silk kimonos, all that Japanese crap, I left in the closet."

"Your legacy . . ."

"Your fantasy is what you mean. I'm going back to Vegas, Curt, while I'm still young enough to get a job." She stood and gripped her suitcase handle,

clicked the handle upward. "Been nice knowing you."
She bent to kiss the top of his bald round head.

Nussbaum stood, sneering. "How do you think
you'll survive?"

She glanced toward the back of the viewing room.
"I think that's a bigger problem for you than for me.
Surviving. Bye, now." She jiggled away, pulling her
luggage on wheels.

Nussbaum stood, furious. "You do not go. You
owe me."

She continued to strut, turning toward the exit,
bumping the suitcase up on the next-to-bottom step.
"And you owe him," she said.

He hurried after her, drink sloshing around and
spilling on the floor. "I do not owe a goddamn—"

The projector quit running, the film whirring to a
standstill, plunging the room into blackness. There was
a click, and the overheads came on, blinding the agent
for an instant. He closed, then opened his eyes. The
woman was halfway up the steps to the door. "You
owe him." She nodded toward the back of the room.

Nussbaum swiveled his head to look, fright clutching
at his windpipe. Just inside the viewing room stood
Benny Yadaka. He wore Docker pants and a light
cotton shirt. He came down the stairs two at a time,
pausing beside the woman for long enough to kiss her
cheek. "Hi, big brother," she said, then continued
along.

Yadaka went down two more steps, then stopped
and turned to her. "Won't be long, sis. Just wait in
the car. Your flight's at eleven, right?" She nodded
and he nodded. Then she left the room. Yadaka continued on down the aisle, whistling. He said, "Curtis,
you going to throw such bullshit around, try a woman
hasn't been the places my sister has. She knows
better."

Nussbaum was rooted in place. He looked wildly
behind him, Christ, but he'd designed the room with
only one way in or out, make it tougher for the starlets
to leave . . .

Yadaka walked up to Nussbaum, put a hand on his chest, and gave a little push. "Sit down, Curt. We're going to visit."

Nussbaum sank down, bourbon dribbling on his knee. Yadaka took the seat beside him. "Now, look," Nussbaum said.

"No, you look." Yadaka took the drink from Nussbaum and set the tumbler on the floor. "You got shaky nerves, Curtis, you're spilling that crap around."

Nussbaum leaned back and covered his eyes. "I'm expecting guests."

"You're not expecting shit, unless it's another day on the witness stand with the woman frying your ass. If I'd had her for a lawyer, I likely wouldn't have had no juvenile record." Yadaka sadly shook his head. "You people. You run around them movie studios thinking you're a tough negotiator. You think you're tough, Curtis? I should show you some things, standing on a street corner at twelve years old with them *tongs* flashing steel in your face. That's tough. You don't make a pimple on my baby sister's ass being tough, that's how hard you are. Now." Yadaka beckoned. "Tell me about my money."

Nussbaum raised his chin, a pleading look. "You know already, the insurance . . ."

"You told me, yeah, the insurance. But guess what? While I've been waiting to take my sister to the airport, after she ditched your gutless ass, guess what I've been doing. I've been at your desk upstairs, going over a couple of things."

Nussbaum tried to appear angry. "Those things are private."

"Damn right," Yadaka said. "Private between you and me. I tell you something, Curtis. I didn't come to you, you came to me. Had my baby sister look me up, you're wanting to off this actor, and you're looking for someone with the cods to pull it off. It wasn't me pissed off all that money in Vegas, got to pulling bread from bank accounts I didn't own to cover my ass. Everything here, Curtis, you brung it down on your head. So don't be telling me anything's private, not between you and me."

Nussbaum bent forward, hugging his belly. "I need some time."

"Which you have none of, you lying fuck. You tell me you buy this policy on the actor to safe your bet, you buying some book about which I know nothing, and you need this money to make things right with some movie studio, protect your reputation in the business. Don't ask me how you got any reputation to protect, because I don't know. I'm assuming in Hollywood there are a lot of bogus assholes like you running around talking about these reputations they got, I care?

"So you hook me up with your own security man, this Chuck Hager, who is as dumb as any post on the road. I formulate a plan a genius might not consider. I have you bring me this gun you have, haul the gun all the way to Texas to shoot the guy, bring it back here in this private airplane to plant in the actress's kitchen, I do all this shit perfectly even as far as tipping the FBI. And then what do I get for money? I get a story, that's what. A fucking story, Curt, which I do not need."

"It will come," Nussbaum said.

"You are right it will come. You collected the insurance already, Curtis. That's in your records up there, only instead of paying who you're supposed to pay, you ship two million dollars off to some movie studio and then load up all these bank accounts so these actors won't know you been stealing from them. Problem is, you're robbing Peter to pay Paul. Only this time Peter is not holding still for it. So tell me something, Curtis. How badly do you want to stay alive?" Yadaka produced a buck knife and cleaned the blade with a handkerchief.

Nussbaum watched the blade, a ray of light glinting from the handle of the knife. "Christ."

"Aside from you now paying me there are other little glitches here, Curtis. This should have worked perfectly. The actress and the actor got into it in Dallas, outside Planet Hollywood, the perfect setup, only your dumbass security man has to stand around posing and gets his picture took. Jesus Christ, where you come up with this guy?

"You meet me at LAX and bring me this gun at five in the afternoon. By ten p.m. I'm in a Dallas hotel waiting for the opportunity. So what happens? We wait, the actress comes and goes, the actor beats the shit out of her to make things even better for our side. Only your Einstein of a security man busts in and starts stabbing the fucking guy. Dribbles blood all over everywhere, which makes shooting the guy not look so routine to the police and everyone else. This is a major glich, but there are more. For example, how come you don't tell me this lawyer Sharon Hays is someone you've been stiffing for child support?"

"It was a coincidence," Nussbaum said.

"Which will also make it a coincidence when you are not walking around no more."

Nussbaum began a desperate whine. "I have a house in Mexico."

"Good idea." Yadaka finished cleaning the knife and leaned back. "Great idea, it will only take about fifteen minutes for someone to find you there. Disappearing before tomorrow is the worst thing you can do. *After* tomorrow you might disappear permanently, but not before. You have got to climb back up on that witness stand and continue to help the prosecutors by lying your ass off. Getting the actress convicted is the only way out for you. If you can do that, then the very next thing you will do is rob some more bank accounts and pay me, Benny Yadaka. After you do that, I don't give a shit what happens to you."

Nussbaum rolled his head back to stare at the ceiling. "Christ, that woman, the questions she asks."

"Sharon Hays?" Yadaka laughed. "Yeah, she is pretty smart and you are pretty stupid, which I confess puts you at a disadvantage. But dumb as you are, even you can stick to a story. You gave the actor the gun.

He hauled it to Texas. He turned up shot down there, all of which is enough to get the actress convicted, which gets you off the hook. So, what's so fucking hard?''

"I just don't know if I can face her," Nussbaum said.

"Well, you are going to try, Curtis. Look at it this way. If you pull it off, the testimony, that is a chance you have to keep walking around. The only chance you got, Curtis. Remember that. Without a sterling performance in court tomorrow, you have absolutely no chance at all."

27

Sharon's eyelids felt as if she might need a couple of toothpicks in order to prop them open. As she cracked the door an inch to peer from the witness room out into the corridor, she nearly went to sleep standing on her feet. As she watched in a daze, Milton Breyer and Kathleen Fraterno ushered Curtis Nussbaum down the hall and into the courtroom. The theatrical agent wore a blue suit. His head was freshly shaved, and his shoes were polished like mirrors. Following the trio were a pack of reporters along with several minicams. Sharon closed the door, turned her back, and sagged against the jamb. "They're inside," she announced wearily.

The witness room was wall to wall. Detective Leeds had showered and shaved and seemed none the worse for wear, though Sharon suspected that with his puffy, bent nose and thick lips, Leeds would appear exhausted no matter how much sleep he'd had. He was seated on a padded bench beside Vernon Tupelow, the Dallas County AME, and a man from the L.A. County Coroner's office whose name Sharon couldn't remember. Sharon had rousted Tupelow at his hotel at four in the morning, and wondered if the AME would ever forgive her. At the moment Tupelow had his head together with the coroner from L.A., and Tupelow's expression said that his skepticism was fading fast. Leeds caught Sharon's eye, nodded and winked. Sharon walked over, put a hand on the detective's broad shoulder, and leaned on him.

Leeds continued to grin. "You ready?"

"As I'll ever be," Sharon said. She pointed at the papers which lay in the L.A. coroner's lap as he and Tupelow looked them over and talked in whispers. "I'll need those now," she said. "They're about to crank up." She gestured in the direction of the courtroom.

Tupelow leaned back and removed his glasses. "I never would have believed this."

Sharon arched an eyebrow. "But you do now?"

Tupelow picked up the pages and straightened them on his knee. "This kind of evidence doesn't lie."

"You'd testify to it?"

Tupelow waved his glasses around, holding the frames by an earpiece. "Hell's bells, Miss Hays, I'm Milton Breyer's witness, not yours. But, yeah, put me under oath and I'll have to."

Sharon plucked the pages from Tupelow's hand and grinned at him. "I don't think it will come to that. If it does, don't worry about guff from the district attorney. I've got more than enough on old Milton to keep him in line."

Tupelow laughed. The rifts between Sharon and Milton Breyer during her last days as a prosecutor were legend, constant grist for the Dallas County gossip mill. "I've heard that you do," he said.

"You've heard correctly," Sharon said, then walked over to where Lyndon Gray and Mrs. Welton sat. Gray's cheeks were a bit puffy, and Mrs. Welton had dark circles under her eyes. Yadaka sat off by himself in the corner, his expression a mask. Sharon said to Lyndon Gray, "Wrote a doorstop, didn't he?"

Gray hefted a manuscript which was easily four inches thick. "Seven hundred and twenty-six pages. A bit prolific, wot?" The pages were held together with four thick rubber bands.

"And the contracts and letters?" Sharon asked.

Gray thumped the manuscript. "Top twelve sheets here, miss."

"Good. I hate to ask for one last favor, Mr. Gray, but I don't know if I could lug all that into court without falling on my tush. Would you mind terribly, taking those in and setting them on the defense table? It's where Darla will be sitting. She's officially in custody and not supposed to converse, but if you gave her an encouraging pat on the arm, I'm sure the guard wouldn't mind."

"My pleasure, miss." Gray stood, hefted his load, and left the room. Sharon noted that the Englishman's shoulders slumped a bit. Been a long night for everybody, she thought.

She turned to Mrs. Welton. "I hope all this hasn't left you too pooped to cavort with your grandkids," Sharon said.

"I may have to rest some first." Mrs. Welton showed a tired smile and handed over her own stack of papers. "The hotels, the amounts, the people I spoke with. They're all in there, mum."

Sharon added the papers to the stack in her hand. "I think these will be my first shot out of the barrel," she said. "You've done yeoman's service."

Mrs. Welton brushed her sleeve. "All part of it," she said.

Sharon nodded and moved on down the row. She yawned. God, if she could only stay awake for a few hours more . . .

If anything, Holtzen the banker looked even more conservative than when Sharon had stolen Rob's checking-account figures from his office computer. His glasses were perched just so on the bridge of his nose. His suit was blue. He wore a matching tie with tiny white check marks. His cuffs were white. He held a stack of shaded printouts clutched against his chest.

Sharon extended a hand, palm up. "In spite of your resistance I'll say thank you, Mr. Holtzen."

Holtzen's expression had been one of shock when Sharon served her subpoena at eight a.m., when the bank first opened its doors. At nine Holtzen had still been in conference with his lawyers. Reluctantly, he now handed over the printouts. "Everything your subpoena called for," he said. "Nothing more, nothing less."

Sharon didn't think she could learn to like this guy, never in a million years. She added the printouts to her stack. "All I'd expect from you," she said, nodding curtly. "Appreciate your business, sir."

She had now everything she needed. She took a deep breath and marched toward the exit. Yadaka stood and opened the door for her. As she stepped over the threshold, Detective Leeds stopped her.

Sharon sighed and smiled wearily. "Yes, officer?"

"None of my business, but a thought. Why wouldn't you save all that for trial? An acquittal's final. Even if you make your point in an extradition hearing, they could still indict your client later on."

Sharon liked the detective, even thought he was sexy in an offbeat way. As they'd worked together through the night, she'd caught him watching her. She hadn't minded at all. She leaned conspiratorially close. "Let you in on a secret, copper. Ninety-nine times out of a hundred you're right. But those"—she pointed at the minicams, two of which were aimed in her direction, grinding away—"change the rules. You had a small local case out here, O.J. He's acquitted, but how's his lifestyle?

"Darla's been accused in the media, and that's where she has to win acquittal, here and now. If she goes to trial and we vindicate her through suppression of evidence, smoke and mirrors and such, the rest of her life people are going to believe she committed murder. That's unacceptable, both from my standpoint and hers. With these"—she rattled the papers in her hand—"we're not going to leave a question in any-one's mind as to who did what. Darla deserves a hell of a lot more than reasonable doubt, Detective. She deserves to live." Sharon left Leeds standing in the doorway, took three firm strides in the direction of the courtroom, then stopped and turned. "I know it's bad law, Detective Leeds," she said, winking. "But what the hell, it's dandy p.r."

*   *   *

Sharon sat in between Darla and Preston Trigg at the defense table, and allowed Kathleen Fraterno to get away with murder for a good half hour or more. Whereas in yesterday's session she'd objected vehemently whenever Fraterno tried to bring up the pistol, now she acted as if Kathleen could ask any question her heart desired. On a couple of occasions Preston Trigg made as if to pop up from his seat, but each time he did, Sharon grabbed her co-counsel's sleeve and yanked him down. Even Fraterno was puzzled. Twice she paused in midquestion, casting sideways glances at the defense table as though certain an objection was coming. Each time she did, Sharon flashed Kathleen a happy smile.

Nearing the end of her direct, Fraterno leaned over the podium. "Are you certain, Mr. Nussbaum, that the pistol you just identified is the same pistol you watched David Spencer pack in preparation for his trip to Dallas?"

Nussbaum was emphatic. "Absolutely."

The gun lay on the court clerk's table, inside a plastic bag with an evidence sticker attached. Fifteen minutes earlier Judge Rudin had admitted the .38, and the defense hadn't uttered a peep in protest. Rudin, obviously expecting to strut and swagger as he ruled on Sharon's objection, had thrown an unguarded frown in her direction. Sharon had sat unmoving with folded hands. Preston Trigg had bowed his head and massaged his eyelids.

Now Fraterno continued her barrage. "The same gun which you gave David Spencer as a gift?"

Nussbaum's jaw thrust out. "I'd know it anywhere."

Fraterno thumbed through her notes, giving Sharon a long sideways look. Preston Trigg could stand it no longer. He leaned near Sharon and hissed, "What in hell are you doing? Any objection at all, Rudin wouldn't have admitted the damned thing. Are you out of your mind?"

Darla looked at Sharon as well, and for the first

time since the hearing had begun there was doubt in the actress's expression. It was, after all, Darla's ass on the line.

Sharon gave Darla's shoulder an encouraging squeeze. Then she looked Preston Trigg eye to eye. She smiled at him. "How's your book deal going, Pres?" she whispered.

Fraterno completed her direct examination and sat. She exchanged whispers with Milton Breyer. He shook his head in bewilderment. The pistol continued to rest on the counter, admitted once and for all into evidence.

Rudin said from the bench, "Cross?" His gaze was toward the gallery. Seated in the second row, Karen Warren, the *20/20* reporter, waggled her fingers at him. Rudin snapped his head toward the defense table and said more forcefully, "Cross, Counsel?"

Oh, you bet, Sharon thought. She stood, selected three pieces of paper from the stack on the table, and approached the podium, feeling Darla's doubtful gaze on her.

She took a second to scan Mrs. Welton's list, then lifted her chin and looked at the witness. Nussbaum sat relaxed, elbows on armrests. Sharon nodded. "Morning, sir. Do you gamble?"

There was a cacophony of whispers throughout the courtroom as Nussbaum's features sagged. He straightened and said in puzzlement, "Do I . . . ?"

"Gamble. Seven come eleven. Dance with Lady Luck."

Kathleen Fraterno started to rise, but Milton Breyer beat her to the punch. He said from his seat, "Your Honor," and then stood and said, "come *on*."

Sharon turned a deadpan gaze toward the prosecution side. "Is that an objection?"

Breyer sat down. "Of course it is."

"I wasn't sure," Sharon said. She looked at the bench. "Your Honor, this witness has testified that a firearm found in the defendant's home under a federal search warrant is the same gun which left California on an airplane with the defendant and the victim. The Dallas County medical examiner has testified that it's the same caliber weapon used in the crime. I suspect that the M.E. will return to testify that ballistics tests have found it to be the *same identical* .38 as the murder weapon. Under that set of circumstances, I'll respectfully direct the court to *Wainscott* v. *Massachussetts,* inform the witness that it's my intent to show that he hasn't been truthful in his prior statements, and ask for latitude here." She swallowed. "The court will soon see where I'm headed, and if I fail to comply with the spirit of the Wainscott decision, I'm sure the court will intervene."

Rudin pursed his lips. Out came the pocket watch. He wound the stem. Oh, boy, Sharon thought, is this ever up this joke of a judge's alley, cameras grinding and the viewing audience on the edges of their seats. She pictured Russell Black, back in Dallas watching in his office, and even considered winking at the camera and tugging on her ear like Carol Burnett signaling her mother. Conducting cross-examination using *Wainscott* v. *Massachusetts* was one of Russ's favorite ploys. Just as you taught me, old boss, Sharon thought.

Rudin stopped winding and dropped the watch into his pocket. "I'll allow it up to a point, Counsel."

Fraterno uttered an audible sigh. Her hands were now tied except for the standard badgering-the-witness and asked-and-answered objections. With the witness advised that his veracity was in question, Sharon was free to slash away until the judge called her off.

She returned her attention to Curtis Nussbaum. "I asked if you gambled, sir."

Nussbaum shifted his weight. "Oh, a little. Yeah, I have, some."

"Some?" Sharon raised her eyebrows. She referred to her list. "Are you acquainted with Mr. Ross Versace?"

Nussbaum's gaze went stone cold. He didn't answer.

"Leonard Prinz?" Sharon went on. "Douglas Barnett? Do you know these gentlemen?"

Nussbaum offered what Sharon assumed was his most disarming smile. "Yes. Seems I do."

"Are these men employees of Las Vegas casinos?"

"I believe they are." Nussbaum kept up the front, but there was resignation in his tone.

"Are they credit managers?"

"I think so. They work in the hotels."

"I see." Sharon went back to the list. "Mr. Versace with the Circus-Circus, Mr. Prinz with Caesar's Palace, and Mr. Barnett with the Golden Nugget?" She pretended to think. "The Golden Nugget is downtown, isn't it?"

"If you know that," Nussbaum said, "then you've been there more than I have. I don't keep up with these places."

"Oh? They keep up with you, sir."

Fraterno shot up. "Objection. Argumentative."

"Sustained," Rudin barked. "Latitude, Council, doesn't mean you can take off in any direction at all."

The objection was proper; so was the judge's ruling. Sharon accepted the hit, nodding, then asked, "Mr. Nussbaum, as of two weeks ago, what was your debt to those three casinos?"

Nussbaum played to the audience. "Not that much. I don't really keep up."

Sharon kept her voice low, her expression matter-of-fact. "Is four hundred thousand dollars your definition of 'not that much,' sir?"

Nussbaum feigned surprise. "Was it that high?"

Sharon didn't bat an eye. "Yes. Isn't it a fact that your debt to those casinos has reached that figure not once, but several times over the past three years?"

Nussbaum spread his hands. "It might have. What's—?"

"How much do you owe these casinos today, Mr. Nussbaum?"

"I'm not sure. I'd have to check."

"Have to check? Isn't your current balance zero,

sir, paid in full? I'd think you'd be proud of your credit rating."

Nussbaum waved a hand. "A man owes, a man pays," he said.

Sharon kept her gaze riveted on the witness. "I've heard that's the code." She retreated purposefully to stand in front of the defense table, leaned over and rummaged through the stack of papers. Darla's expression was one of pure terror. Sharon winked at her. She briefly wondered if Holtzen had clued Nussbaum in this morning, even as the banker ran printouts of the agent's trust accounts. She doubted it; Holtzen would have been in a hurry, and Nussbaum had likely breakfasted with the prosecutors. She hauled the pile of computer paper back to the podium. "Mr. Nussbaum," she said, "did you once represent Natalie Thom?"

Nussbaum froze in place, like a man about to take his first step onto the gallows.

"Come on, sir," Sharon said calmly. "Surely you've heard of her. *The Illusion? Step in Time?* She costarred with—"

"She used to be my client," Nussbaum choked out.

Sharon found the printout she was looking for, and held the pages at eye level. "Two years ago, did she make a change?"

Nussbaum assumed a look of innocence. "She thought she could do better elsewhere."

"Oh? Wasn't there some money missing from her bank account?" Sharon tilted her head. The nine a.m. hassle with Natalie Thom's lawyers over providing this information had been a nerve warper. "Ms. Thom was short over two hundred thousand dollars, wasn't she?"

Nussbaum grimaced. "I settled that out. Natalie wasn't supposed to . . ." He trailed off, looking as if he was surrounded by pygmies with blowguns.

"Yes, sir," Sharon said. "Part of your settlement agreement was, she wasn't to reveal the shortage. Under subpoena of her records, however, Ms. Thom has no choice but to do so." Sharon told a little white lie. Actually, she'd only threatened the subpoena, and the actress's attorneys had caved in. "But you did repay the money, didn't you?"

"Of course," Nussbaum rationalized. "Was nothing but a bookkeeping error."

Sharon whipped out another printout. "Oh? On September 12, 1994, you placed two hundred and eleven thousand dollars in Natalie Thom's account, didn't you? After which she closed the account and transferred her money to another bank?"

Nussbaum squeezed his knuckles. "Her new agent did business elsewhere."

"Yes. But her old agent continued to do business at the same location. Mr. Nussbaum, on the same date as the deposit to Natalie Thom's account, did you remove one hundred and eight thousand dollars from David Spencer's account, and one hundred and three thousand dollars from Taylor Noble's account, for a total of two hundred and eleven thousand dollars, the same amount as you deposited? Quite a coincidence, sir."

Nussbaum gaped like a fish out of water.

Sharon couldn't resist a little smirk. She watched Fraterno from the corner of her eye. Kathleen was as shocked as everyone else in the courtroom. So hell-bent for leather had Texas been in rushing to judgment against Darla Cowan, when Nussbaum had come forward they hadn't even investigated the guy. Sharon said to the witness, "Perhaps you're having trouble remembering Taylor Noble. Would it refresh your memory to go over Mr. Noble's screen credits, sir?"

Nussbaum lost it completely. He showed a look of pure hatred. "No, hell, I know who he is. I've represented that boy for years."

Sharon blinked. "That relationship could be in its waning stages." She paused. The question was pure badgery, giving Fraterno a legitimate cause to object, and Sharon damn well knew it. Kathleen didn't stir. Sharon went on. "Let's fast-forward a year." Back to the table she went, grinning openly at Darla, and hefted the book manuscript. God, the freaking thing weighed a ton. She carried the manuscript back to the podium and dropped it with a thump heard in living rooms throughout the country. The jury box cameraman fiddled with something on his minicam, and Sharon suspected that he was zooming in on the book. Sharon zeroed in on Curtis Nussbaum. "Let's talk about *Dead On,* sir."

Nussbaum stirred nervously, uncrossing and recrossing his legs.

Sharon feigned surprise, straight from acting class. "That was a big deal, Mr. Nussbaum. Surely you haven't forgotten."

Nussbaum wheezed out, "That writer . . ."

"Messed up everything, didn't he? Mr. Nussbaum, did you accept a two-million-dollar payment from Mammoth Pictures in David Spencer's behalf, as an advance for his agreeing to act in *Dead On*?" Sharon was conscious of a rustling noise, reporters snatching up notepads.

"They paid an advance," Nussbaum said. "Whatever it was, it came to me."

"Such an insignificant sum that you don't recall." Sharon rattled the printouts. "Could you tell me the date, possibly, when that advance went into David Spencer's account?"

Nussbaum sucked in air.

"There is one deposit here," Sharon said, brandishing the shaded pages, "in the amount of five hundred thousand dollars. Was that a part payment to David Spencer?"

Nussbaum touched his fingertips together. "My bookkeeper . . ."

"Had a hard time getting things straight, didn't she?" Sharon gave the witness a crooked grin, and couldn't resist saying, "Perhaps you should jump her, sir."

"Objection." Fraterno rose only halfway to her feet, and spoke in a less than forceful tone.

"I'll withdraw that," Sharon said before Rudin

could sustain. The judge looked miffed, as if she'd stolen his line in the climax scene. She reached underneath the stack of printouts and pulled out Mrs. Welton's survey of the casino people. "On the same date as Mr. Spencer's deposit, sir, did you make three four-hundred-thousand-dollar payments in Las Vegas?"

"I could have," Nussbaum snarled. "I'd have to check."

Sharon inhaled, pretending to gather herself as she glanced at her watch. Quarter to eleven. Rob should be dragging his fanny into the courthouse shortly. Having set Nussbaum up, establishing that he'd been playing fast and loose with his clients' money, she wanted to back off from the bank-account questions until she could get Rob's testimony on record. She needed a fifteen-minute filibuster. She'd planned her knockout punch for some time after Rob took the stand, but . . . She looked at the pistol, still in its baggie on the court clerk's counter. She looked at the bench. "Permission to approach the witness, Your Honor?"

Rudin looked from Nussbaum to the podium and back again. "Do you think that's safe, Counsel?" the judge said. Titters and guffaws erupted throughout the courtroom.

As the laughter subsided, Sharon gave Rudin a frozen smile. Anyone who'd thought they could keep this judge from Jay Leno-ing a bit was sadly mistaken. Finally there was silence. Sharon said again, "Approach the witness, Your Honor?"

"Permission granted, Counsel," Rudin said, grinning.

Making her walk brisk and professional, Sharon went to the clerk's station. She lifted the baggie by one corner. The pistol dangled heavily. She carried the gun up and laid it in front of the witness. "Mr. Nussbaum, you've previously testified that this is the pistol which you gave David Spencer, and which he carried with him to Dallas in his luggage, haven't you?"

Nussbaum seemed relieved to change the subject. "Yes."

"To be absolutely certain, sir, would you please identify the weapon one more time."

Nussbaum regarded the .38 as if it might suddenly explode.

One corner of Sharon's mouth curved upward. "This isn't a David Copperfield disappearing trick, sir. It's the same gun that's been laying there all along."

"Then it's the same gun I gave David, for protection."

"Good." Sharon left the weapon on the rail and went back to the defense table. The only remaining documents were L.A. County lab reports on Harlon Swain and Chuck Hager, their corpses at the morgue. She picked these up and returned to stand at the podium. "Once more for the record, Mr. Nussbaum. What time did David Spencer and Darla Cowan board this plane for Dallas?"

Nussbaum shrugged warily. "Not sure exactly. Midmorning sometime."

"Before noon?"

"Way before that. They had an appearance in Texas, at Planet Hollywood."

"Right." Sharon lifted the lab report on Harlon Swain. "Mr. Nussbaum, you are aware, aren't you, that ballistics reports show that's the weapon which killed David Spencer?"

"So I'm told."

"Would that indicate to you that someone in his hotel room took his own gun and killed him with it?"

"Wouldn't indicate anything to me. That's for the police."

"Right. But by, say, two in the afternoon, four Dallas time, that pistol would have had to have been in Texas, wouldn't it?"

Nussbaum showed faint bravado. "Beats me. Whenever the plane landed."

Her trap sprung, the mouse firmly inside, Sharon now slowly lifted the lab report to eye level. Keeping

her gaze firmly on the witness, dangling the report by
its corner, she said, "Well, can you explain, sir, how
the *same weapon* was used to shoot a man in East
Los Angeles at four o'clock on that same Friday afternoon? A Mr. Harlon Swain?"

There was a frozen-in-time moment as pin-drop silence reigned, Sharon at the podium, Nussbaum staring at the paper hanging from her fingers, all rustling
of pen and paper in the courtroom ceasing as if a
switch had been thrown, the minicam in the jury box
recording the scene for posterity.

"A writer, wasn't he?" Sharon said. "Harlon Swain?"

Nussbaum managed to say, "I . . ."

Sharon's gaze darted to the bench. "Conference,
Your Honor?"

Rudin gestured to both sides, obviously tickled to
death to get in on the act. Sharon went quickly up to
the bench. Fraterno held back for an instant, then Milton Breyer joined her as both prosecutors approached.
Harold Cuellar made it a foursome, the L.A. assistant
district attorney evidently unable to keep his curiosity
in check. Conscious of Nussbaum seated only feet
away in the witness box, Sharon lowered her voice to
a whisper.

"I want to keep this guy, Judge," Sharon said. "But
I have another witness to present." She checked her
watch. Five to. If Rob was late, she was going to wring
his neck. "What I propose is a ten-minute recess, with
Mr. Nussbaum held for recall after the interim witness
testifies. I think I'll be wound up before lunch, Your
Honor." She jerked her head toward the witness box.
"Or he will be."

Rudin slowly massaged his forehead. "Interesting
development."

Milton Breyer stuck his head in between Sharon
and Fraterno. "What's going on here, Sharon? Are
you somehow pointing fingers at our witness?"

Sharon favored Breyer with a long sideways look.
"Fingers and toes," she said.

Breyer turned to Fraterno. "What is this, Kathleen?

Have we somehow charged the wrong party?" His eyes were innocently wide.

Sharon snorted through her nose. She looked at the defense table, where Darla sat alongside Preston Trigg with an empty seat in between. She turned back to Milton Breyer. "You've made a career out of that sort of thing, Milt," Sharon said. "Haven't you, now?"

Rudin called the break, and told Nussbaum sternly not to leave the building. As the hubbub built to a crescendo, spectators rising, stretching, talking back and forth, Nussbaum climbed down from the witness stand. He was practically staggering. He said something to Kathleen Fraterno. She ignored him. Nussbaum went through the gate and up the aisle, turning away from hostile looks aimed at him from all sides.

Sharon turned in her chair, took both of Darla's hands in hers, and squeezed. "He set you up, babe, from the beginning."

Darla's look was anguished. "When can I go home, Sharon?"

Sharon stood, still holding Darla's hands as the guards approached to take the actress to the holding cell. Sharon beamed at Darla. "How does tonight sound?" Sharon said.

The guards took Darla away, and Sharon made a beeline for the corridor. Damn Rob all to hell, if he wasn't . . . She dodged spectators right and left on her way up the aisle. She hustled out into the jam-packed hallway, ignored a minicam as its operator swiveled the lens in her direction, and looked around for Rob. He was nowhere in sight, which didn't particularly surprise her. Rob had likely sent advance scouts to survey the lay of the courtroom floor, and would plan his arrival accordingly. When the hallway was the most crowded he would saunter casually from the elevator, feigning surprise at the recognition he'd receive. If he received none, Sharon thought, he might fall down kicking and screaming like a two-year-old. She pictured his grand entry at the restaurant in Malibu, wherein he'd shot her with an imaginary bullet as he'd strolled across the floor. She hoped, God, that she could get through his stint on the witness stand without barfing in front of the judge and national viewing audience.

Sharon's forehead tightened as she spotted Curtis Nussbaum, the agent moving jerkily along toward the men's room across the corridor. Nussbaum's expression was drawn, panic piled on fear. She placed her hand over her mouth to hide a grim smile. Grillings on the witness stand affected the guilty in odd ways; she recalled one Dallas criminal suspect who, out on bail in the middle of his trial, had plunged to his death from a third-floor railing in the Crowley Building. As Sharon watched, Nussbaum neared the entry to the men's. He paused in mid-stride, did a sudden column-right, and walked in the direction of the elevators. He passed a knot of reporters, none of whom paid him any heed. His pace quickened.

Sharon's throat tightened. Nussbaum had seen the writing on the wall and had made up his mind. No way was he going to hang around for more exposure on the stand to this tenacious female lawyer. The s.o.b. was making a run for it.

She looked quickly up and down the hall. Strung out on a corridor bench were Gray and Yadaka along with Detectives Leeds and White of the L.A.P.D. The four men sat in relaxed postures, likely swapping lies. Sharon's heels clicked on tile as she hurried over and tapped Leeds firmly on the shoulder. Leeds regarded her with quizzically lifted brows.

Sharon pointed after the fleeing agent. Nussbaum had it in gear now, practically trotting as he neared the corner leading to the elevators. He rounded the corner and vanished from view. Sharon said, "This is only intuition, and there's no warrant for the guy. But Mr. Nussbaum is leaving us. If you don't want to have to organize a manhunt, I'd think up a line of questioning for him pronto."

Leeds followed her direction as Gray climbed to his feet. Leeds muttered, "Jesus, David, go after the guy."

Detective White showed reluctance. "What's my probable cause?"

Leeds shook his head. "Probable cause, hell. We just want to question him." He took off at a gallop, dodging men and women as they snapped their heads around and gaped at him, his feet thudding heavily on corridor tile. He disappeared around the same corner where Nussbaum had gone just seconds ago.

White followed suit, charging in pursuit of his partner, as Sharon walked quickly after the young detective. Gray and Yadaka fell in step on either side of her. The trio rounded the corner. The bank of elevators came into view. There was quite a crowd in the foyer, including a baseball star and an actress who'd been in court every day, and who now were holding hands. Sharon was barely conscious of the minicam operator who trailed a couple of paces to the rear.

Detective Leeds had Nussbaum by the arm in front of the nearest of the three cars. The cop had his nose just a few inches from the agent's face, the policeman's jaw working, his features set in the cop's standard just-a-few-questions-to-clear-this-up, we're-here-to-help expression. Sharon advised all her criminal clients to avoid such confrontations like the plague, but now hoped that Nussbaum fell for the ploy. She desperately needed for the agent to remain in the courthouse. As Leeds spoke in a soothing tone, Detective White stood off to the side with his arms folded. Nussbaum shook his head and tried to pull away from the policeman's grasp; Leeds tightened his grip on the agent's arm.

Nussbaum spotted Sharon, locked gazes with her across the foyer. His lips peeled back from his teeth. He yanked his arm away from Leeds, and backed up against the wall between the elevators. Terror in his look, his voice quaking, Nussbaum screamed at the top of his lungs, "Not me. Not fucking me, you hear? It was *him*." As heads turned toward him from all directions, the agent extended his arm and pointed across the hall.

Sharon felt total confusion, and at first thought Nussbaum was pointing at her. And indeed the agent's finger was extended loosely in her direction. She looked to Lyndon Gray. "What in hell is he . . . ?" Sharon said, then was conscious of movement on her right as Benny Yadaka reached inside his coat.

Sharon's head turned slowly. Yadaka's hand cleared his lapel with a pistol in its grasp, a small automatic of blued steel. The Oriental's expression was calm, like a postman's delivering the mail. He slowly shook his head as if in regret and muttered softly, "That dumb son of a bitch." Then, taking his time, he extended the gun in both hands in classic shooter's pose and, from twenty steps away, shot Curtis Nussbaum in the forehead.

The sound was a soft *pop,* like someone breaking a paper bag blown up with air. There was a tiny whistling noise as the bullet flew across the corridor, and the instant stench of burnt gunpowder filled the air. A round hole appeared in Nussbaum's forehead as if by magic. Blood spattered the masonry behind the agent's head. Nussbaum slumped against the wall, grinned foolishly as if he'd forgotten something, then crumpled to the floor.

For a long instant, no one moved.

A woman screamed, her cries echoing down the corridor. Sharon glanced toward the sound and realized that the actress had pulled free of the baseball player and covered her mouth with both hands. Sharon looked once again at Yadaka, who stood poised with the gun extended, and had an odd thought. *How in God's name had Yadaka gotten that pistol through the courtroom metal detectors?* A second thought came fleetingly: *Hey, this guy is supposed to be on our side, isn't he?* Then a third idea died inside her consciousness as the Oriental stepped calmly behind her, put his arm around her throat, and placed the pistol's barrel firmly against her temple. Yadaka raised his voice. "Nobody moves, or she's dead."

Lyndon Gray backed up with his palms out. "What is this, Benny?"

Detective Leeds moved forward, Curtis Nussbaum's grinning corpse visible in the background. "Don't do nothing foolish, friend."

Yadaka ignored both men. He adjusted his forearm downward until it was draped across Sharon's breastbone with his hand cradling the point of her shoulder. "Keep back," he said. Slowly, a foot at a time, he steered his hostage in the direction of the elevator.

Later Sharon would be limp with fear, but at the moment she was oddly calm. It was as if she were having an out-of-body experience, Sharon Hays's mind observing from some other viewpoint as the Oriental held a gun to her head and moved her across the corridor. The crowd parted like the Red Sea, men and women backtracking fast, their eyes riveted on Yadaka and his captive.

They reached the bank of elevators. Yadaka backed up to the sliding doors, keeping Sharon out in front. "To your left," he said softly into her ear. "Press the Down button."

Sharon nodded. Visible in the corner of her eye, Curtis Nussbaum twitched and tremored. She extended her left hand, felt first one button, then the other above it, and got ready to push the Down arrow. As she did, the overhead light dinged on and the doors slid open. Yadaka moved in obvious surprise, pulling Sharon along with him, captor and captive now flattened against the right-hand side of the car entry.

Rob Stanley strolled forward, accompanied by his bodyguard. The bodyguard exited first in a wary crouch, ready to fend off any overzealous fans, as Rob carefully adjusted his sunglasses on his nose. He wore chinos and a polo knit, and polished brown shoes with rounded toes. An actor's smile was plastered on his face, bridgework gleaming. He moved in a casual swagger until he was half in, half out of the car, and surveyed the corridor. Sharon was abreast of Rob, his profile even with her as his head turned slowly in her direction, his smile fading a bit as he zeroed in on her. His lips parted. "What's going on?" he said.

Sharon gave her former lover a tight grin. "Hi, Rob," she said. The pressure of Yadaka's arm around her shoulders intensified.

Quicker than thought, Yadaka released his grip on Sharon and pushed her roughly into the elevator. Backward she went, her spike heels slipping on carpet, the small of her back hitting the rear elevator wall. Down she tumbled, her skirt riding up to her crotch, her legs akimbo. She gasped.

Yadaka moved up and jammed his gun against Rob's head, the actor's smile still frozen in place, and quickly herded the TV star onto the car along with him. "You just stand there," Yadaka said. He pressed a button. The bell dinged, the doors slid closed, and the car began its descent.

Rob's grin dissolved as if by magic. He cringed against the wall and threw his arms up to shield his face. "Please don't shoot me," he begged.

Sharon had come up on one knee, feeling her panty hose rip, and now lifted her head. The Oriental stood side-angle to her with his pistol aimed at Rob, the TV idol cowering and babbling. In spite of her fear she nearly giggled. God, if Rob's fans could only see him now. Yadaka seemed to have totally forgotten her. In the breadth of a half second, she made up her mind.

She came up into a crouch, lowered her head, and charged, one step, two steps, the top of her head slamming into the Oriental's midsection, the downward trajectory of the elevator throwing him off balance just enough. He stumbled and went back toward the button panel, ran into the wall with a soft *oof,* his gun hand raising instinctively. Sharon didn't hesitate. She grabbed the hand holding the gun and sank her teeth into Yadaka's wrist as hard as she could. Flesh tore in her mouth.

The Oriental yelled in pain. The gun flew from his

grasp and clattered across the elevator. Sharon released her tooth-hold and dove after the pistol as Yadaka instinctively grabbed his wrist. He grimaced, took a long stride after Sharon, too late. She was facing him from the floor with a gun aimed at his nose.

Yadaka backed away, hands outstretched. "Be careful with that," he said.

Sharon came up on her feet. "I'll be careful not to shoot myself. Shooting you is another story, Mr. Yadaka. Seems we've misjudged you."

She glanced fleetingly at Rob, down on his knees now, eyes tightly closed, his arms up to shield his face. He whimpered, "Jesus Christ, I'll pay anything, just don't . . ." His body shook with terrified sobs. The elevator continued down, the light flashing across the overhead panel as they passed the sixth floor, then the fifth.

Sharon reached with her free hand to pull a shred of skin from between her teeth. There was a salt taste in her mouth. Carefully, keeping her gaze riveted on the Oriental, she stepped sideways and bumped Rob with her hip. "It's over, Rob-oh," she said. "You can get up now."

"Jesus," Rob pleaded. "Anything, Christ, I'll . . ." His hands came down. He looked slowly up.

"Dammit, Rob," Sharon said. "On your feet. In about three seconds that door's going to open. You want to greet your public in *that* freaking pose?"

Rob looked from Sharon to Yadaka and back again. Yadaka stood unmoving, backed up to the button panel. The car stopped its descent. Sudden gravity sank Sharon's feet deeper into the carpet.

Rob sprang to his feet. He adjusted his sunglasses, then held out his hand in Sharon's direction. "Give me the gun, Muffin."

Sharon expelled air. "Be my guest," she said.

Rob took the pistol, aimed the barrel at the Oriental, and held the grip in both hands in a shooter's pose. He showed Yadaka a stone-cold smile. "Make my afternoon, punk," Rob said.

Yadaka gaped in disbelief. Sharon took a step back and folded her arms as the elevator doors opened. "Not very original, but a definite improvement," Sharon said. "Smile as you exit, Rob. Your daughter may be watching at home."

28

There was a picture for the ages sprawled across the *L.A. Times*'s front page the following morning, Benny Yadaka exiting the Criminal Courts Building elevator with his hands up, Rob Stanley following with a pistol trained on Yadaka's back, Sharon Hays bringing up the rear with her head down. A Pulitzer winner if ever there was one. The five-point headline below the picture read TV COP TURNS REAL-LIFE HERO, with the following caption underneath: "*Minions of Justice* star says he was protecting the mother of his child."

Sharon saw the photo and read the accompanying story as she sat in the backseat of the limo on her way to LAX, with Darla beside her thumbing through a script which Aaron Levy had sent over. The panel between the front and back seats was open, Lyndon Gray driving. Sharon said to Darla, "Two mistakes, babe, is all that kept them from getting away with it. I won't swear we couldn't have gotten you acquitted, but finding the real killer would have been something else again."

Darla looked up, her expression mildly curious. Though she'd been brimming with gratitude upon her release from jail, her demeanor had changed drastically over the past eighteen hours. She was still in partial shock, retreating within herself. It might take weeks for her to regain her composure. The script in Darla's lap was called "Passionate Temptress," a softcore which, only a week ago, Darla wouldn't have even read. Anything to keep her mind off the awful week she's endured, Sharon thought. She offered

Darla an encouraging smile. Darla's lashes lowered as she returned her attention to the page.

"The first mistake wasn't really that," Sharon went on, "only a coincidence, David and Rob having the same agent. If I'd never tried to negotiate Rob's check, I never would have uncovered the discrepancies in those bank accounts. The other mistake, well, it's not in the paper. Detective Leeds called me last night. Mr. Yadaka is talking a mile a minute, trying to make a deal to escape the death penalty." Sharon didn't mention the fact that Detective Leeds had talked pretty fast as well, trying to arrange a date with her. Sharon would have accepted if—dammit!—she hadn't been leaving town.

Lyndon Gray turned his head slightly to the side and cocked an ear. "I feel responsible," he said. "Benny's credentials weren't sterling, but in the future we'll keep a more watchful eye."

"Don't beat yourself up over that," Sharon said. "His only criminal record was as a juvenile, and as such was sealed. Nussbaum's most colossal foul-up had to do with the writer, Harlon Swain. On the day of the murder, David's murder, Nussbaum was supposed to meet Yadaka at LAX and give him the .38 to transport to Dallas. The same day Nussbaum received Mr. Swain's completed book in the mail. His problem was, his contract with the writer didn't contain the same cancellation clause as Nussbaum's contract with the studio. Mr. Nussbaum was both overextended and overgreedy, it turns out. The studio had offered two million for the book, but Nussbaum had only offered the writer eight hundred thousand. In his haste to get the sucker's name on the dotted line, Nussbaum didn't mind his p's and q's on the contract clauses. So not only had the studio demanded its money back from Nussbaum—which he couldn't pay without collecting on the life insurance policy he'd bought on David— now the writer had finished the book and was expecting the balance of *his* money. Which was quite a bit, since Nussbaum had not only lied to Harlon Swain about the purchase price, he'd also fibbed about the amount of the advance. The studio initially advanced twenty thousand dollars for the writer. Nussbaum told Harlon Swain that the advance was *ten* thousand dollars and pocketed the other ten. Lovely man." She gazed thoughtfully to the west, at whitecaps rolling under a sky of crystal blue, the limo rolling south on Highway One.

Sharon looked to her left. Darla had returned to her reading, obviously trying to concentrate, though her gaze wandered occasionally out the window. Sharon leaned forward and spoke to Lyndon Gray through the partition. "Nussbaum made an appointment with Swain, and went to Swain's house on his way to meet Mr. Yadaka at the airport. Or maybe I should call him Benny, you think? One thing led to another, an argument broke out, and Nussbaum killed the writer with the same gun Yadaka planned to use on David and then plant at Darla's. Nussbaum didn't tell Benny about killing Harlon Swain, partly because he didn't trust Yadaka and partly because he was just plain scared. If he had, Benny likely would have changed weapons.

"Yadaka flew commercially to Dallas," Sharon said, "met Nussbaum's security man, Chuck Hager, at the Mansion Hotel, and then the two of them murdered David after he'd beaten Darla up and she'd gone to California. Made a bloody mess of it, with the stabbing, which Yadaka claims was Hager's doing. He's probably telling the truth. Apparently Mr. Hager wasn't the coolest of heads.

"Benny killed Hager," Sharon said, "because he kept hanging around where he wasn't supposed to. Another man wanting his money. Nussbaum spent his life juggling money around, which worked all right with movie stars who wouldn't miss an extra half million or so. With Chuck Hager and Harlon Swain he was dealing with two desperate men. Guys in their financial condition are harder to jerk around."

Sharon leaned back, slightly out of breath, and

turned a page in the newspaper. On page two was a story to the effect that Harlon Swain's niece and only living heir, a topless dancer in Burbank, was taking bids from publishers for the rights to *Dead On*. The niece's agent, Cherry Vick, expected the book auction to set records. Sharon scanned the piece, then turned her attention to another story. This was an article about a California senator under federal investigation for taking bribes. The politico was negotiating with several lawyers to defend him, one being Darla Cowan's famous attorney Preston Trigg. Trigg's picture was beneath the article. Sharon thought that Pres had better seek new office space. She grinned and tossed the paper away. "I still don't know how Yadaka got that pistol into the courthouse through the metal detectors. Something Detective Leeds would like to know as well."

Darla closed the script, folded her arms, and stared vacantly at the back of the front seat. Sharon reached out and gently touched the actress's arm. Darla smiled fleetingly, then looked away.

"I can supply the answer to that dilemma," Gray said, "assuming the answer stays between us."

Sharon leaned forward, all ears. "Assuming it's not a capital crime," she said.

"Only a minor felony, miss." The Englishman kept both hands on the wheel. "Every security person in L.A. knows the trick, at least those who do work for celebrities. You must be armed at all times, even in a courthouse situation. It's a sad fact, but movie stars are subject to physical attack anywhere. If the authorities learn our little tricks of the trade, the tricks won't work any longer. I had my own pistol with me in the courtroom yesterday, Miss Hays." He turned for long enough to smile at her, then returned his attention to the road. "If you'd moved in the slightest so that I had an open shot, Benny never would have made it onto the elevator."

Sharon watched the broad back, the slightly graying head of hair. Having Lyndon Gray covering one's backside on a regular basis would be comforting. "My lips are sealed, sir," Sharon said.

"It's pretty simple, really," Gray said. "You disarm your weapon, open the cylinder on a revolver or remove the clip on an automatic, and place the gun inside a sealed evidence bag with a sticker attached. Your ammunition goes into a second evidence bag. When you pass through the metal detectors you place the weapon and bullets in plain sight on the table along with your keys and other metal objects. So many weapons come into court as evidence, the guards pay you no heed."

"That simple, huh?" Sharon felt a little chill. "Not particularly reassuring, knowing it's that easy."

"It's unfortunate that the protection business can also become the killing business," Gray said, "but it happens. Occasionally a Benny Yadaka . . ." Gray trailed off thoughtfully, then continued in a firmer voice. "One of the tricks of the trade, Miss Hays. One of the tricks of the trade."

The paparazzi were out in force, having trailed the limo from the beach house to the airport, and cameras flashed all around as Sharon and Darla exited onto the curb at the entrance to the American terminal. Reporters stood back, notebooks in hand, and fired questions which the women ignored as, heads down and sunglasses in place, they ducked into the building. Sharon noted with amusement that the photographers were just going through the motions, as if their hearts weren't in their work. The abrupt closing to *Texas* v. *Darla Cowan* had brought the media circus to a screeching halt; anticipating another O.J. with all the bells and whistles, the networks had beefed up their coverage staffs for nought. A week of excitement, suddenly over and done, on to the next grisly murder story. Aaron Levy had left a message for Sharon at the beach house that morning, to the effect that the best he could hope for now was a paperback deal. Sharon hadn't returned his call.

Lyndon Gray handled Sharon's luggage, then ushered the women out the walkway to the gate and into American's VIP lounge. Sharon's flight wouldn't take off for three-quarters of an hour. She followed Darla down a plush-carpeted aisle, headed for a back booth. The bar was in front of a picture window, bottles in a row with gleaming chrome spouts extending from their necks. The bartender was a bearded youngster wearing a black vest and tie. Visible beyond him through the window, a 747 revved its engines on the runway. Halfway to the booth, Sharon stopped in her tracks as Darla moved on ahead.

Rob was seated at the bar along with his bodyguard. He spun around on a stool and showed her an anxious look. He was dressed in new jeans and a soft cotton pullover. His actor's grin was hesitant and uncertain. Sharon gave Darla a just-a-minute wave and went over to the bar. "Good afternoon, hero," she said.

Rob looked guardedly toward his escort, then leaned near Sharon and lowered his voice. "I'm relieved I caught you. I need a minute, Muffin."

Sharon supposed that, God, Rob would use the sickening nickname until one of them went to their grave. She didn't bother correcting him. "It so happens I have a minute." Sharon perched on an adjacent stool, leaned on the padded bar, and crossed her legs.

"There's a problem." Rob continued to look surreptitiously around him.

"If there wasn't, you wouldn't be here," Sharon said. "What is it?"

"The goddamn bank has frozen my account. Say they're doing an audit, that the insurance company has stopped payment on a check Curtis Nussbaum deposited."

Sharon thought that over, then nodded. "Sounds pretty s.o.p. Insurance companies have clauses that if the beneficiary murders the insured there isn't any payoff. Eventually they'll have to pay the money into David Spencer's estate, but they'll string it out as long as they can. A lot of interest at stake on two million dollars."

Rob's expression was desperate. "They've fucking paralyzed me."

Sharon stifled a grin and refrained from laughing out loud. "How about your fifty thousand a week from the show?"

"I don't get paid until next week. Until then . . . Christ." Rob's voice took on a pleading whine. "Look, Muffin, that check I gave you. Could you . . . ?"

"I've already negotiated it, Rob. It's in my account back in Dallas."

"I know that. Could you give me a check and return the money? Just for a week or so."

Sharon stared at him. She couldn't believe the guy. Finally she smiled. "So join the crowd, Rob-oh. Payday to payday, that's the way I've been doing it for thirteen years or so." She balanced her purse on her thigh and snapped it open. "Tell you what, though. I could loan you a couple of hundred bucks for a week, if it would help." She frowned at him. "I'd have to have it back on payday, Rob. No way could I grant any extensions, you know?"

Melanie said excitedly over the phone, "You're big news, Mom, you and my dad. Everybody thinks it's really romantic, that he saved you."

Sharon paused, selecting her words carefully. "He was really . . . something to see," she finally said. She stood at the front of the VIP lounge, using the pay phone. Visible down the way, Rob hunkered over his drink as if contemplating suicide. Over on the right Darla sat alone in a booth, staring vacantly out at the runway. Sharon checked her watch. Twenty minutes until takeoff. She said, "I have to get a move on, Melanie. Just tell Mrs. Winston my flight lands at six-oh-four. If my daughter's not waiting at the gate to hug my neck, I may break down in tears."

"We'll be there, Mom." There was hesitancy in Melanie's tone, indicating that she was about to explore territory which she wasn't certain she should get into. "Mom?" she said.

Sharon blinked patiently. "Yes?"

"The paper says you might have some acting offers. Would we be moving to California if you did? It's cool if you want to, but . . ."

Sharon caught Melanie's concern. Next year she'd be in high school, and moving away from her friends would be a heartbreaker. What acting offers? Sharon thought. News to me. She took a long look at Rob, about to shed tears on the bar, and at Darla, her vacant expression as she sat in the booth all alone. She switched the phone from one ear to the other. "We're not moving anywhere, Melanie," Sharon said. "Never in a million, sweetheart. Mark it down. Never in a million years."